Praise for Jonathan W...

SHADOW-MAZE

'Exceptionally goo...
rounded characters ...
is often adroit and ...
intriguing and colourful fantasy setting a bit different
from most'
Stan Nicholls, *The Dark Side*

DREAM-WEAVER

'This is a marvellously realized tale of intrigue and
growth into adulthood. The plot is easy to follow yet
excitingly woven. Nothing is predictable; everything is
riveting. The best book I've read this year'
Graham Ing, *Auguries*

'All accolades should go to *Dream-Weaver* which starts
with a world-making bang and continues without
unnecessary diversion along a path of high originality
. . . It is engrossing, marvellously written and most
surely one of the best of its type. Applause all round'
John Gilbert, *Fear*

'A strong new fantasy . . . makes the most innovative
use of salt since Lot's wife'
Carolyn Cushman, *Locus*

'The whole book may be classed as a good read . . . it
leaves a satisfying aftertaste'
Pauline Morgan, *Critical Wave*

The SERVANTS OF ARK trilogy

'Unlike most trilogies, these books can be read separ-
ately; each focuses on a different character and a
separate crisis . . . Kings, queens, princes and wizards
all live like regular folks, loving and quarrelling and
raising their children as best they can in the face of a
magical war . . . *Servants of Ark* is enjoyable fantasy

reading, with plentiful light touches that bring a gentle humour to the books'
Carolyn Cushman, *Locus*

'The range of setting, character and emotion has grown more complex with each volume . . . This is effective, memorable heroic fantasy'
Ian Covell, *British Fantasy Society Magazine*

THE UNBALANCED EARTH trilogy
'A distinctly different sort of fantasy . . . *The Unbalanced Earth* gets many points for originality, and not just for the unusual magic system. The floating city, with its eccentric wizards and a cat that talks in echoing riddles, is notably charming and strange'
Carolyn Cushman, *Locus*

Also by Jonathan Wylie

SERVANTS OF ARK
Book One: THE FIRST NAMED
Book Two: THE CENTRE OF THE CIRCLE
Book Three: THE MAGE-BORN CHILD

THE UNBALANCED EARTH
Book One: DREAMS OF STONE
Book Two: THE LIGHTLESS KINGDOM
Book Three: THE AGE OF CHAOS

DREAM-WEAVER
SHADOW-MAZE

ISLAND AND EMPIRE
Book One: DARK FIRE

and published by Corgi Books

Island and Empire
Book Two

ECHOES OF FLAME

Jonathan Wylie

CORGI BOOKS

ISLAND AND EMPIRE BOOK TWO:
ECHOES OF FLAME
A CORGI BOOK : 0 552 13979 3

First publication in Great Britain

PRINTING HISTORY
Corgi edition published 1994

Set in 10/11pt Linotype Times by
County Typesetters, Margate, Kent.

Corgi Books are published by Transworld Publishers Ltd,
61–63 Uxbridge Road, Ealing, London W5 5SA,
in Australia by Transworld Publishers (Australia) Pty Ltd,
15–25 Helles Avenue, Moorebank, NSW 2170,
and in New Zealand by Transworld Publishers (NZ) Ltd,
3 William Pickering Drive, Albany, Auckland.

Printed and bound in Great Britain by
Cox & Wyman Ltd, Reading, Berks.

PROLOGUE

Admiral Iayn Barvick woke up on the last day of his life and wondered what he had let himself in for. Surely now, at fifty years of age, he was beyond pride. What did he have left to prove? Why then had he left his comfortable home in Brighthaven to take personal command of this mission?

Memories assailed him, and though he berated himself for giving in to nostalgia, Barvick could not escape their lure. As a young sailor, he had travelled halfway across the world and back; a life full of adventure and opportunity. He had visited the island of Zalys many times, but the place and its people had made little impression on him. It was just one more outpost of the vast Xantic Empire, though its strategic importance was known to every schoolboy. The island's remote location, near the centre of the Larenian Sea, made it a crossroads for many vital trade routes between the Empire and the western lands, and it was therefore also of great military significance. But the main reason for the island's importance was the fact that it was the Empire's only reliable source of amberine crystals. These mysterious stones were the means by which the Empire's telepathic Far-speakers were able to relay messages instantly, sometimes over great distances. No one knew for certain how the stones worked, but they were an accepted and essential facet of imperial life.

There were three Far-speakers with Barvick's fleet — one on the flagship, the *Southern Flame*, and the other two on separate vessels captained by the two squadron commanders. The Far-speakers would be used to relay any further news from the mainland, and to report the success of Barvick's mission once that had been accomplished.

Demand for these telepathic abilities had grown even greater of late, and new crystals were thus needed constantly as many more embryonic talents were pressed into service. Without its vast network of communications, Xantium would be in a sorry state. Barvick, like most intelligent men who were aware of some of the facts, knew that the Empire was under severe pressure, maintaining its far-flung influence only by ever growing vigilance and the exercise of its financial and military might. The Empire could not function properly without the Far-speakers, and so the news that the people of Zalys had risen in revolt against their imperial overlords was serious indeed. This had been emphasized by the instructions which had been sent to the Admiral by Chancellor Verkho himself. Part of the message had read, 'The population of Zalys is to be punished severely. All leaders and all those active in the revolt are to be executed.'

There was no telling whether the rebellion had succeeded – no further contact with Zalys had been possible – but Barvick had been forced to assume the worst. He had set sail with two full squadrons of the Southern Fleet, fifty ships in all, many of them heavily laden with troops. There were several thousand men under his command, more than enough to retake the island, if indeed it had fallen into enemy hands – and to administer the necessary retribution.

However, Verkho had said nothing about who should take charge of the fleet. That had been Barvick's own decision – and one he was now regretting. With favourable winds the voyage from Brighthaven to Zalys could be accomplished in seven or eight days but, as was common at this time of year – just past the height of summer – the wind blew gently but steadily from the west. The fleet was thus having to tack into a headwind, and now, five days out of port, they had not even covered half the

6

necessary distance. The Admiral was growing restless and although he retained the balance of an experienced seaman, moving easily over the swaying decks, his legs grew weary and he slept badly. Each day he rose at dawn and was on deck before sunrise, unable to bear the unaccustomed confinement of his cabin.

Why had he come? This action was important – but in the past he had sent others to take charge of equally vital missions. Many of his younger officers were fully capable of carrying out this task successfully.

Could it be that – for some unknown reason – he was trying to please Verkho? The Chancellor was the most powerful man in the Empire, more feared than even Emperor Southan himself, but Barvick felt no special awe for the man who never left the capital city. The Admiral was a veteran of countless battles and, even though his rise to his present rank made it inevitable that he had some knowledge of the murky world of politics, he had little time for plotting now. His ambitions had all been fulfilled.

The last four decades of his life had been spent in the service of the imperial navy. He had started as a lowly cabin boy, and by a combination of endeavour, intelligence and luck he had risen through the ranks quickly until, five years earlier, he had been given command of one of the three great imperial fleets. He had settled in Brighthaven, a port in the western province of Nadal, a country which bordered the Xantic homeland to the southwest. The town was a drab place, belying its name, but Barvick had chosen a fine house with large grounds, taking leave of the sea for good – or so he had thought.

Since then he had been fighting battles of a different kind – for men, money and resources – in order to keep the Southern Fleet in a constant state of readiness. In his younger years, the Empire had still been vigorous, even expanding in some regions, and the navy was in the forefront of many campaigns, proving itself a formidable force of war. Today, though, Xantium was struggling to maintain its existing borders, and was threatened on many sides by barbarian peoples who were envious of the Empire's land and wealth. And, even worse in Barvick's eyes, the Southern Fleet was slowly, inexorably, falling into decline.

Perhaps that's it, he wondered thoughtfully. *I want to see them in action once more, while there is still something to be proud of.*

The Admiral looked around his ship, and knew that there was still glory to be found in the speed and effectiveness with which his men could strike, even if on this occasion they would be facing ill-trained peasants. This mission would be his final gesture, the epitome of military precision.

Barvick had the heart of a warrior and now, as he stood on the foredeck of his flagship, it began to beat a little faster. *There will be blood on my sword once more before I die*, he vowed silently.

In that at least, he was right.

The first portent of what was to come was a deep, cavernous rumbling which seemed to rise from the depths of the sea itself. None of those aboard had ever heard anything like it before, and when it faded away, the remaining quiet seemed doubly ominous. While the splash and thump of the waves and the creak of timber and canvas went unheard, every man fell silent, waiting.

The noonday sun still shone from a calm blue sky and the motion of the sea had not altered, but the whole atmosphere had somehow changed. The day felt colder. The officers who stood on the command deck of the *Southern Flame* exchanged glances, but no one spoke. Even Barvick was unable to find the confident words he knew were needed to reassure his lieutenants. Before long, however, a shout from below decks indicated that a message was being received by the Far-speaker, and the Admiral ordered the telepath to be brought on deck.

The Far-speaker, a young woman known as Sunflower, had to be helped from below by a junior officer because she, like many of her kind, had been weakened by addiction to nectar, a drug which enhanced their natural talents. Sunflower had been Barvick's personal assistant for the past three years but had never been to sea before, and the unaccustomed motion was adding to her miseries. Even so, the Admiral was shocked to see how ill she looked. Her forehead was swathed in a white cloth band, which had an amberine crystal sewn within its folds, but her face seemed even paler than the fabric, and her eyes were full of inarticulate fear.

'Well?' Barvick demanded.

'It's from the *Wavecutter*, sir,' the junior officer replied, naming the squadron leadship which was positioned at the front of the armada. 'But Sunflower's not making much sense.'

'Repeat the message, Sunflower,' Barvick said kindly but firmly.

The Far-speaker's lips parted, displaying her discoloured tongue, but she uttered no sound. The Admiral began to feel impatient, but was distracted by an urgent call from the ship's lookout, high above in the crow's-nest. It took a few moments for the import of what he said to sink in, but when it did every face registered shock, every eye turned forward to see the truth for themselves.

The *Wavecutter* had capsized.

Barvick turned back to Sunflower.

'Contact the *Wavecutter*,' he barked. 'Find out what's going on.'

The Far-speaker's large brown eyes reflected helpless terror and she screamed, covering her ears and shaking as though in the grip of a fever. By now, Barvick was thoroughly alarmed. He had never seen her react like this before, but knew that it would be useless to try to force her. He turned to look forward again. What could possibly make a good ship keel over in a calm sea? It made no sense, and a tangible feeling of horror began to fill the air. But that was only the beginning.

As they watched, three more of the leading vessels capsized in quick succession, two falling to port and the other to starboard. Yet the sky remained clear and the wave patterns were normal. There was no sign of a sudden water-spout or whirlpool to explain the catastrophe.

It was then that one of the sharper-eyed officers saw – or thought he saw – something else moving round the distant stricken vessels. He drew in his breath sharply but did not speak at first, reluctant to voice such absurd notions. And yet the images persisted.

'What is it, man?' Barvick growled eventually.

'It looks . . .' the officer began, 'it looks as if they're being attacked by giant birds!'

Once again, the Admiral found himself at a loss for words.

After that, events moved at terrifying speed. First came the lookout's report that ships on the outer edges of the fleet were in trouble. Within moments, more than a dozen had crashed broadside into the sea and the sounds of destruction – splintering wood and the screams of men – carried over the waves to the *Southern Flame*. Then the sailor in the crow's-nest yelled, sounding out of his wits with fear, and pointed to the spot where the *Wavecutter* was now sinking.

They all saw them then, grey shapes above the water, small at first in the distance but growing larger at an astonishing rate.

'What are they?' someone breathed.

Whatever they were, they were heading directly towards the flagship.

'Battle positions!' Barvick roared, drawing his own sword. 'Prepare to defend the ship. Get the archers ready. Now!'

His crew had soon taken up their preassigned stations. Barvick turned to the helmsman.

10

'Turn us to head directly at them,' he ordered. 'I don't want them to come at us broadside.'

'Aye aye, sir.'

As the *Southern Flame* heeled over gently, most eyes were fixed on the approaching creatures. Closer now, their strong, slow wingbeats could be seen as they flew, skimming over the waves. At the same time, a thin, angry screaming filled the air, rising in pitch and volume with every moment.

'They're not birds, sir,' the keen-eyed officer reported in disbelief. 'They look like . . .' His mouth hung open.

'What, man?' Barvick snapped.

'Rays, sir. Giant manta rays.'

'Impossible!' But even the Admiral could see the resemblance now.

Then, suddenly, there was no more time for speculation. To the port side of the *Southern Flame*, only about two hundred paces away, the surface of the sea began to boil. Three enormous rays erupted from the water, one after the other, in sun-glittering explosions of spray. The roar of their emergence was overlaid by a fierce, high screeching sound as, instead of falling back into the sea, the creatures flew on. Massive triangular wings undulated fluidly, double horns protruding from either side of their mouths, and long, thin tails lashed back and forth like whips.

They flew directly at the flagship, moving at unbelievable speed.

'Come about!' Barvick yelled, while all about him was reduced to terror-stricken chaos.

But he was too late. The helmsman hardly had time to react before the monsters were upon them. The wingspan of the largest of the three was as wide as the ship; by rights, a creature that size should have weighed as much as thirty men – and yet it flew!

Even beyond their fearful size and the terrifying screaming, the rays possessed a cold, blind malevolence which left most men paralysed. The creatures moved

11

purposefully, as though their malice was being directed by some higher instinct, and before anyone realized what was happening, the three monsters crashed into the ship's masts. The *Southern Flame* heeled over violently but recovered – just – and righted herself. Even so, she was crippled now. The two smaller masts had been smashed to matchwood, beams and rigging cascading down on to those members of the crew who had not already been thrown overboard. All thoughts of defending themselves had long gone; all they could hope for now was survival.

Barvick had been thrown down heavily, but he had had something to cling to and now recovered his sword, intent on one last act of defiance. He struggled to his feet, and found that he was standing over the inert form of Sunflower. The ship shuddered beneath him as two of the monstrous attackers thrashed in the shattered rigging fore and aft; a sudden impulse made him look upwards.

Above him, descending with the force and inevitability of an avalanche, the largest ray blotted out the sky. Barvick raised his sword against the grey, screaming harbinger of death. For the briefest moment he felt the blade strike home, vile liquid spurting over him, but then the full force of the ray's descent crushed him, shattered the deck beneath his feet and drove deep into the bowels of the ruined ship.

The Admiral died instantly, and so did not witness the carnage as dozens more of the impossible beasts emerged. Every single vessel was attacked by the ravening creatures, and all but a few were sunk. Those left afloat were useless hulks, with their surviving crews already half mad, cowering within the broken shells, and with no hope of ever seeing land again. Anyone left on deck was exposed to the insane onslaught of the remaining screamers, who swooped down, seemingly intent on leaving no man alive. Powerful wings crushed their prey or hurled them into the sea; horns and unnatural fangs tore into soft flesh and the scything tails flayed their victims. Even in the water, the men were not safe from the ferocious assaults as they struggled hopelessly to keep from drowning.

The rays suffered too, many of their number impaled upon or torn to shreds by the wreckage of the ships – apparently quite willing to kill themselves in order to destroy their prey. But many of them survived and eventually, their blood lust sated, they returned to their natural element. With flat-winged dives which sent peals of thunder rolling over the waves, they crashed into the sea and swam away into the unseen depths.

From far below, as if in response to their return, there came another drawn out, low-pitched rumble, which made the ocean tremble for leagues around and seemed to mark the end of the one-sided battle.

CHAPTER ONE

*From far above, I roll the dice of augury. Yet the hands
are not mine. They are young and innocent, untroubled
by the weight of destiny.*

*Seven dice; four red, three white. The whites settle first.
All skulls – for death and danger. Of the reds, one is
the star of love which can also predict the unknown, one
is the 'emperor', the crown of mortal power, and two
show the scythe for the passing of time. Symbols etched in
blood, as the seasons pass and fade from memory. And
the dream ends.*

*Awake, the dice are lost in a burning maze. My hands
are like smoke.*

Another howl of anguish echoed from the locked cell.
Inside, Iceman capered and grimaced, then turned to
glare through the bars of the door. The observers
flinched at the obsessive hatred in his cold burning eyes.
To meet the gaze of the former Far-speaker was to invite
madness.

'There must be *something* we can do for him,' Fen
Amari whispered. Even though Iceman had been a
servant of their bitter enemies, Fen could not help but
feel compassion for the young man's plight.

'He's paying the price for working for Farrag,' Dsordas Nyun replied unsympathetically. 'If he survives, then
he might be of use to us. If not . . .' He shrugged.

Dsordas and Fen were husband and wife in all but
name. In appearance they were opposites – Dsordas
was dark-complexioned with black hair, while Fen was

15

blonde, with pale skin and startlingly bright green eyes. In Nkosa, the couple were known as Light and Dark. In temperament too they were very different. Fen was passionate and impulsive while Dsordas was calm and almost always obsessively rational. Somehow they complemented each other perfectly, both physically and emotionally, and they were inseparable.

'Nectar!' Iceman yelled suddenly, making them both jump. Then the prisoner's anger turned in an instant to pathetic grovelling. 'Let me have some,' he whined. 'I need it. I *need* it. I'll do anything.'

'Gods!' Dsordas breathed in disgust. 'I almost wish Natali hadn't woken him up.'

Six days had passed since the revolt which – at least temporarily – had freed the island of Zalys from the tyranny of the Xantic Empire. Much had happened in that time, but the reawakening of Iceman had been one of the more remarkable events.

In planning the revolution, the island's underground organization – known as the Children of Zalys – had made the death or capture of the imperial garrison's Far-speakers their first objective. They had almost succeeded in this, but one – Iceman – had escaped, and Xantium had thus been warned of the uprising. As leader of the Children, Dsordas had been greatly troubled by this failure and even now lookouts were on constant watch, scouring the eastern horizon for the first signs of the imperial fleet. Few had any doubts that it would be on its way by now, intent on exacting revenge.

When the Far-speaker complex within the garrison headquarters had been stormed, the telepaths were found either dead or deeply unconscious. Some time later, Iceman was discovered in the personal quarters of Marshal Farrag, the hateful sorcerer whose evil machinations had provided the final impetus for the revolt. Iceman too was in a coma.

After the Children had gained control of Nkosa, the island's capital, and subsequently the rest of Zalys, there had been several unsuccessful attempts to rouse the inert Far-speakers. However, as the days passed, the tele-paths all grew weaker and closer to death. The island's physicians and herbalists were bemused and, in any case, had little time to spare during the cruel aftermath of battle. Even Dsordas, who reluctantly admitted to some undefined and instinctive healing skills, could find no response in the unmoving bodies, knowing only that they were doomed to a gradual slide into oblivion.

The breakthrough came in a most unexpected fashion. Three-year-old Natali, the youngest of the six Amari children, became so insistent that he go to see the friend 'who didn't talk any more' that Etha, his mother, and Fen, the oldest child, let him have his own way. The boy led them first to Fournoi Square, the central plaza of the town, and thence to the cell where Iceman lay. The guard posted there was at first reluctant to let them in, but was eventually persuaded by Fen. Natali went straight to the Far-speaker's side, prodded his arm gently, then with more force – but to no avail.

'Wake up!' he said indignantly.

'He can't, little one,' his mother told him. Etha was uncharacteristically nervous. She had suffered the loss of her husband, Antorkas, who had been killed in the fighting, and was exhausted by all that had happened recently. There was much that she did not understand. All she wanted was a return to her quiet, ordered life – but knew that was impossible. A woman of less inner strength might have collapsed under such a strain, but Etha was resilient – a characteristic which showed in the firm gaze of her green eyes, a legacy of her northern heritage, and one which she had passed on to some of her children. Even so, she was worried about her family and about Natali in particular. He had played an important part in the mysterious events of the last few days – but he was still just a little boy.

'He wants to,' Natali persisted, poking the Far-speaker again.

'We've been trying to help him, Natali,' Fen began. 'No one . . .'

'Roll three skulls, Iceman,' her brother intoned unexpectedly – and under the astonished gaze of the watching adults, the Far-speaker's eyelids had fluttered, then opened. The young man sat up, slowly and painfully. Hunger burned in his eyes as he glanced about the cell, as if searching for something.

'Nectar,' he croaked.

Etha pulled Natali away and Fen went to find Dsordas, filled with a mixture of excitement and unease.

Since that time – only a few hours ago – they had learnt nothing. Natali had no idea where the code-words had come from, but Fen suggested that he had somehow overheard them when Farrag had used Natali, among other island children, as unwitting telepathic spies. The same phrase had no effect on any of the other five Far-speakers, and two of them had since died. The others would soon follow, as neither Natali nor anyone else could suggest a means of rousing them.

Iceman himself had done nothing except confirm his own name and, with increasing vehemence and desperation, demand or plead for 'nectar'. This, the islanders realized, was the drug made from the poisonous excretions of giant toads, which augmented the Far-speakers' natural telepathic powers. Some of these repulsive creatures had been found in a small, enclosed garden within Farrag's quarters. It was a rancid place; the odours of decay and the whine of insects filled the fetid air behind the double doors. Farrag himself had apparently used the drug to enhance his own sorcerous powers – the reason for his repulsively black-stained tongue. In the end, however, he had been overcome, his own dark fire snuffed out by a greater magic. And then Dsordas' sword had stilled his vile heart for good.

Iceman's tongue was also discoloured, but not to the same extent, and the speculation was that he needed the poison as well as his amberine crystal – which had been taken away – to operate effectively as a Far-speaker. Even so, Dsordas flatly refused to give him any of the drug, his whole being recoiling instinctively from such abuse of a human being. Now, watching the pitiful ravings of the young man, Fen wondered whether it would have been better to leave him to die.

'But he's the only chance we have of using a Far-speaker of our own,' she said, half to herself. 'You know how valuable that would be.'

'Perhaps.' Dsordas did not sound wholly convinced. 'But how could we trust him?'

Inside the cell, Iceman wailed incoherently, his whole body trembling. Footsteps sounded along the corridor, and Fen and Dsordas turned. The newcomer was Foran Guist, a physician and an old friend of the family. He looked tired and old beyond his years, testament to his ceaseless exertions over recent days. He greeted them with a wan smile and a slight wave of the hand.

'You wanted to talk about him?' Dsordas said, without preamble.

'Yes. He's getting worse, you know that.'

Dsordas nodded.

'The addiction to nectar is playing havoc with his body processes,' Foran went on. 'Stopping altogether like this might mean that he never recovers. Have you thought of giving him just a little, and gradually reducing the dose?'

Iceman's voice responded instantly from inside the cell.

'Yes, yes. I must have some!' he said in an intense whisper. 'I want it . . .'

'No,' Dsordas replied resolutely. 'It would only prolong the sickness. That stuff is unimaginably vile. I saw what it did to Fen, remember?'

Fen had been forced to drink some of the poison when she had been captured by Farrag just before the revolt. She had been close to death, sinking into the void that was her only escape from the unbearable pain, when Dsordas had found her. For the first time in his life, he

19

had found the resolve to use his innate healing skills, and had saved her. It was an experience which had shaken the very foundations of his life.

'Fen wasn't accustomed to the effects of nectar,' Foran persisted. 'Iceman is. His body is obviously immune to some degree, but he can't control the craving.'

'No,' Dsordas repeated with finality.

A wail of bitter anguish came from within the cell, and the sound of weeping, but Dsordas remained unmoved.

'All right,' Foran conceded. 'In that case, Habella has a possible alternative.'

'How is she?' Fen asked quickly.

'Her face is still very painful and will be for some time,' the physician answered gravely. 'And there'll be some scarring. But that's not stopping her – she's been working as hard as any of us.'

At this Dsordas looked away, obviously uncomfortable, but Foran made no further comment. Fen understood her lover's embarrassment and did her best to let the moment pass.

'I'm glad Habella's on the mend,' she said.

Habella Merini, a respected herbalist, had been struck a vicious blow in the face by an imperial soldier shortly before the uprising. Her only crime had been that she had tried to help the crippled Nias Santarsieri, Zalys' Patriarch, who had been whipped at Farrag's whim – and who had died two days ago.

'What's the alternative?' Dsordas asked now, his face set.

'She wants to examine Iceman,' Foran replied. 'She has a theory that the drug is like a forced allergic reaction. If she can discover a natural counterpart among her potions, she might be able to calm him down and eventually wean him off the stuff altogether.'

Although Foran had been speaking quietly, Iceman had evidently been eavesdropping. His hearing was as keen as ever.

'Nothing else. Nothing else! No!' he cried. 'I must

have nectar. *Give it to me!*' His voice rose into a hysterical scream, and the others moved away.

'Tell her to come,' Dsordas decided. 'It's worth a try.'

'You can't let her go in there alone,' Fen objected.

'Of course not. I'll arrange for a couple of men to keep him under control. Has she any idea how long this will take?'

'Several days at least,' Foran replied.

Dsordas shrugged.

'In that case it may not matter much,' he remarked. 'Thanks to him we'll probably be under attack by then.'

CHAPTER TWO

There are layers of meaning within the dark labyrinth of the human mind. Fire brings danger to one, comfort to another. Risk is balanced against reward. Yet who knows when the gambler hazards more than his outward stake?

There are many turnings within the maze. And many dead-ends. All life is a gamble. But who fixes the odds?

Ever since their hard-won victory over the imperial forces that had oppressed them for so long, the people of Zalys, and of Nkosa in particular, had been in two races against time. The first and most immediate of these was the need to care for the wounded, rehouse the homeless and comfort the bereaved. The final battle of the island's revolution had been timed to coincide with a particularly high tide. Pushed on by the unexpected ferocity of an easterly storm, this had inundated the vulnerable, canal-crossed town and caused extensive damage. Nkosa had been increasingly prone to flooding in recent years, but no one had ever seen anything as bad as this. Even so, it was possible that without the storm their position might have been even worse, because the islanders had used the surge to channel a man-made tidal wave from the fast-rising lagoon directly towards the garrison barracks. The tactic had been devastatingly successful, but its unforeseen ferocity had claimed some friends as well as countless foes.

This, combined with the wounds of battle, meant that anyone with healing skills was fully occupied. Many people were beyond help, and almost every family was in mourning for one or more of their members. This, as much as anything, put all the survivors on an equal footing. But their sorrow was mixed with hope for the dawning of a new era. Freedom – even if it proved to be short-lived – galvanized the islanders' efforts, and made sharing the available food and shelter not merely a duty but a joy. Whatever their differences before the revolt, the people of Zalys were united now – and most looked to Dsordas for guidance, now that his hitherto secret role as leader of the Children of Zalys had been revealed. He in turn vowed publicly to do whatever Zalys required of him but, at the moment, the needs of his family were paramount, and he left the direction of the salvage operations to his deputies. Dsordas spent the first day of the new age with Fen, grieving with her over the loss of her father and sharing her joy at the reuniting of the rest of her remarkable family.

After that, Dsordas was prevailed upon – by Fen among others – to put his new-found healing talents to use. He was reluctant at first, but so many forces beyond his understanding had come into play on Zalys recently that he eventually agreed. At first he scored some minor successes – his touch eased the pain of many sufferers, without his understanding what he was doing – and his status as a folk-hero grew.

However, Dsordas himself was distracted. He knew that he was producing only superficial, if welcome, results, and he kept expecting the ghost of his mother to appear – as she had done when he brought Fen back from the brink of death. He believed that without her his efforts would achieve no lasting benefits. More experienced physicians, such as Foran, kept encouraging him, and so Dsordas persevered. But then he came to treat an old man, whose wounds were slight but which had become infected after he had fallen into one of the swirling canals. Dsordas took the gnarled hands in his own, surprised to find them cold and clammy despite the fever in the old man's watery eyes. He tried to relax, shutting his eyes and letting his consciousness spread instinctively, tendrils of awareness growing, seeking out ill. At first, as he had done with Fen, he felt his hands grow hot, felt the old man's pain as his own and moved to counteract its sullen advance. But then something happened and Dsordas reeled in the grip of sudden vertigo. It was as though a dark whirlpool had opened up beneath him, threatening to suck him in. A cold dread assailed him but he fought on, not understanding. *Help me, mother!* he pleaded silently, but there was no response, and Dsordas was pulled deeper into the whirling abyss. He no longer controlled his progress; he was helpless, losing all sense of his own existence.

Leave me. The cracked old voice was full of pain. *I want to go.*

'No!' Dsordas cried, but he could stand the pressure no more.

Somewhere, in another world, someone uncurled his clenched hands, shook him gently by the shoulders and whispered in his ear. When he opened his eyes, he saw, through the blurring of his tears, Habella's battered face, her kind eyes full of concern.

'He's gone, Dsordas,' she told him gently. 'He's dead. There's nothing you can do for him now.'

Dsordas looked at the old man, now quite still. At peace. *I want to go.*

'I can't do this any more,' he said flatly. 'It's not natural.'

Without another word, he left and went home. After that no one, not even Fen, could convince him to try again. The experience had clearly had a traumatic effect on him, but the hurt went deeper than that of losing a patient, and it was only after considerable coaxing that he eventually tried to explain himself to Fen.

'He didn't want me there. He told me so. All I did was hold him back, prolong his agony.'

'You were only trying to help,' she pointed out.

'I know, but it was wrong,' he said with conviction.

'Only in this case,' Fen began. 'Others . . .'

'No. I won't do it.'

'You did for me.'

'That was different,' he objected, meeting her eyes for the first time. 'I would have *died* for you. And my mother was there to help me. She knew it was right. I can only help those I'm willing to die for.' He had become agitated as he spoke.

'Then all you have to do is let the others go,' Fen suggested calmly. 'When there's nothing else you can do.'

'It's not as simple as that,' he replied with a shudder. 'He almost took me with him!'

'You mean . . . ?' Fen was unable to keep the shock from her voice.

'Yes,' he told her fervently. 'I only just drew back in time – or I would have died when he did.'

After that Fen did not press him any further, even though she did not see how he could be so sure of his facts. However, she found the other after-effects of the encounter baffling and eventually intolerable. It had left Dsordas unsure of himself, deeply depressed and unwilling to venture out for whatever reason, in spite of the pleas from his deputies in the Children. Fen's heart grieved for him – and for the change in the man she loved so fiercely – but she could not understand his lethargy. In the end she gave up and took matters into her own hands.

Zalys' second race against time was, of course, the preparation of defences before the expected arrival of the Xantic fleet. Because the plan to capture all the enemy Far-speakers and thus prevent the news being sent to Xantium had failed, there was little time to spare. If the imperial forces had set sail immediately, it was possible that they would arrive within eight days or so. The islanders hoped that it would take the Empire longer to gather the necessary ships and troops, but they had to be ready for the worst.

25

In Dsordas' absence, leadership of the Children had devolved to his three surviving lieutenants, each of whom had his own area of expertise and commanded respect from most of the population of Nkosa, but none of them shared Dsordas' organizational ability. There was so much to be done that the task sometimes appeared hopeless, and the lack of strategic vision led to duplication of effort and waste of resources. So when Fen requested a meeting with all three men, they agreed gladly, thinking that she would be bringing their leader with her. However, Fen arrived alone, her beautiful pale face set in a determined expression.

'Dsordas isn't coming,' she announced before she was asked. Her tone implied that she had lost patience with him. 'You'll have to make do with me. If we can't get him to take decisions, I'll have to make them for him.'

'You?' Yeori Alektora was obviously surprised. He was a small man, immensely strong, and an expert in all forms of combat. His specially trained fighters had been in the forefront of the recent battle.

'Why not?' Fen's challenge flashed in the golden flecks in her eyes. 'I know Nkosa and its people – and the dangers we're facing – as well as he does. My sword arm may not be as strong as his – but that's not what we need now. Right?'

The three men stared at her. They had never seen Fen like this before. She was quaking inside, but she had never felt more determined in her life, and found herself smiling at the thought that she must have sounded just like her mother. If Etha had managed to cope with a loving but occasionally foolhardy husband and six impetuous children for all those years, taking everything in her stride, then surely Fen must have inherited some of her talents. *There's much of the northern lands in you, Fen*, her mother had told her. Although she had been born on Zalys, Fen sometimes thought that she did share some of the resilience and independence of the people of

Etha's distant homeland. But it had taken this desperate situation to bring her abilities to the fore.

She took a deep breath.

'Our starting point is that we've got no vessels capable of matching them at sea,' Fen began. 'So we'll be fighting on *our* territory, on the island. We've got to make the most of that. We need a regular system of lookouts all along the coastline, with beacons to pass on any sightings. We can't be sure which direction they'll be coming from.'

The men exchanged glances.

'Due east, surely?' Yeori said. 'The Southern Fleet's based in Nadal.'

'Not necessarily,' Skoulli Visakia countered. 'Fen's right. They could circle round to catch us off guard.' Skoulli was one of the most perceptive members of the group, and his skills with words and people made him the best qualified to coordinate communications. 'Beacons are a good idea too – we should place them anywhere there are possible landing sites.'

'Fine. Can you arrange it?' Fen was feeling much better now.

Skoulli nodded.

'Nkosa's still the prime target though,' Yeori put in sceptically.

'Of course,' Fen agreed. 'But they can't come at us directly. I'm assuming no imperial commander would be foolish enough to try to sail his fleet right into the lagoon. If he did we'd have a few surprises for them, eh, Mouse?'

Yani Paphos, who was known universally as Mouse, grinned and nodded.

'That'd be easy,' he said confidently. 'The two entrances aren't wide enough for more than two ships at a time, and we could attack them from either side. Once they're inside, they'd be at the mercy of fire arrows. And half of them would probably run aground, the way the channels silt up and move.' Mouse was a builder by trade

27

and immensely practical. He had been responsible for channelling the tidal wave and unleashing it upon the imperial barracks. 'They won't come that way,' he concluded, 'unless they're unbelievably stupid.'

'So where are the most likely landing places and how can we protect them?' Fen asked. She was beginning to enjoy herself.

The next few days passed in a blur. Fen worked ceaselessly, always on the move within Nkosa or further afield. She witnessed the building of fortifications, and saw them being modified on the sandbanks which surrounded the lagoon, on the town docks and alongside the river. She saw defensive positions prepared near beaches and other sheltered inlets where the imperial troops might come ashore. She watched with Skoulli as the system of beacons encircling the entire island was tested. Everywhere she went, she talked, listened and encouraged, and everywhere she went – even if people sometimes assumed that she was there as Dsordas' representative – she was appreciated. All Zalys knew of the part her family had played in the revolution and of their various sufferings, and Fen's uncommon good sense and evident determination within such a pale, slender frame made a considerable impression. Before long, even Yeori, initially the most sceptical of the three deputies, was coming to her for advice without a second thought.

One such discussion concerned the imminent arrival of a large trading vessel, the *Frozen Star*, some three days after the uprising. Skoulli had discovered, from documents found in Farrag's quarters, that the captain of the ship was a friend of the late Marshal and had often carried special cargoes for him. Therefore, although the *Frozen Star* was not an imperial vessel and on her own presented little threat, they had to be prepared for possible hostilities. Fen suggested that Yeori prepare his men to take the ship by force if necessary, but to offer to trade amicably if possible. Whatever cargo she was carrying, it was almost certain that Zalys would have a use for it. As it happened, however, the matter was decided by the ship's crew – much to Fen's relief.

As they were docking in Nkosa, the Captain quickly became aware of the new circumstances, and tried to set sail again immediately. This engendered an instant mutiny from the already disgruntled crew, and the Captain was killed. Even if the new authorities in Nkosa had been inclined to punish the murderer, they would have had difficulty identifying him; he was protected by a conspiracy of silence among his fellows. In turn, Yeori befriended the first mate, a man called Bark Madden, who was more than willing to trade. Yeori had the sense to realize that the time might come when Zalys would have need of a good ship and in spite of the unstable situation, it took little persuasion to ensure that the *Frozen Star* remained in dock while the crew enjoyed a rare period of shore leave.

It was also Yeori who brought Fen a much less pleasant piece of news. Nias Santarsieri, the island's Patriarch, died the day after the *Frozen Star* came into port. He was a very old man and had been seriously ill since Farrag had had him beaten, so the tidings came as little surprise, but it still saddened her. Nias had been a venerable figure, much loved and widely respected, although he had been virtually powerless under imperial rule, and he would be hard to replace. At least he had died having realized one lifelong ambition. He had seen Zalys free after many decades of tyranny. The island would need a new spiritual leader now – but that would have to wait. There was so much else to attend to.

Fen derived great satisfaction from her work, but nonetheless a dark cloud hung over her. At night she would return to the family home and to Dsordas, who was still sunk in deepening gloom. Although Fen told him everything that was happening, he seemed to take little interest in her achievements, and his continuing listlessness made her anxious and afraid. His prolonged absence was making his fellow Children wonder – although they never voiced their fears to Fen – whether Dsordas was more ill than she would admit. Indeed, he complained constantly of headaches and fatigue, though Fen was too exhausted herself most of the time to do more than comfort him. She still loved him as fiercely as ever, and defended him vehemently if anyone suggested that he should be doing more, but Dsordas was no longer the same man. And she wondered whether the real Dsordas would ever come back to her.

CHAPTER THREE

I cannot remember my life as a child. Could it be that I was born old? Hurled into existence fully formed? Did my fire ever burn as brightly as her distant flame?

Who could refuse her beckoning? Yet I fly on ancient wings and I grow tired. So tired.

While Fen threw herself into her work and Dsordas hid himself away, rarely even leaving his room, the Amari household continued as best it could. They were still adjusting to the death of Antorkas, and no one felt his absence more keenly than his widow Etha. After more than twenty years of marriage she had had no illusions about her husband. He had been a handsome and imposing figure, but for all his undoubted flair and love of life, he could also be vain, pompous and impetuous. It had been Etha who supplied practicality and discernment both to their home lives and to the jewellery business from which Antorkas had made his living. Yet she missed him terribly, and there was an awful, aching void in her heart. Characteristically, she reacted by driving herself almost to the point of exhaustion, caring not just for her own family but also helping many of those in need throughout Nkosa.

Her children did what they could to comfort her, each in their own way. Antorkas junior, who was known to everyone as Anto and who at the age of seventeen was the eldest of her three sons, had inherited much of his father's character and dark good looks, but there was a touch of his mother in his green eyes and in the solemn way he tried to take on the mantle of man of the house. In calmer times – if such ever returned – it would be Anto who would take over the family business. He was overly aware of his position, especially as Dsordas remained in self-imposed isolation, and his sometimes self-conscious efforts would have been funny had they not been so sad.

Anto still felt guilty about his father's death. He had been with Antorkas in the battle, but had been left behind in the chaos of Fournoi Square. Even though intellectually he knew he was not to blame, emotionally he could not convince himself of this. Even so, the serious manner in which he approached his new responsibilities was a comfort to Etha – even if she, like the others, found him rather overbearing at times.

Of the younger children, Tarin, a serious minded ten-year-old, who had also inherited his father's dark colouring, and Ia, at seven the youngest of the girls and the only one with dark brown hair, were in constant emotional turmoil. They veered between guilty, hysterical laughter and tearful misery, and took refuge in fantasy worlds. Tarin's imaginings were full of battles, heroes and vengeful deeds, while Ia's encompassed magic, ghosts and legends. Like all the rest they were pressed into helping Etha and the others – and did so willingly, but escaped whenever they could.

Much to everyone's relief, Natali, whose fourth name-day was now only a month away, remained his own sweet self. Neither his father's absence nor his own extra-ordinary part in events during the revolt seemed to unnerve him. When, in answer to an innocent question, he was told that his father was in a different place now and could not return, Natali's response was typically idiosyncratic.

'He'll come back on my name-day,' the little boy had decided. 'Then he'll know we're all right.'

Natali was the only one to remain dry-eyed at his father's burial and, even though the family's tragedy was only one among hundreds, most of the onlookers were moved to tears when Natali smiled at his father's coffin and waved a small hand in farewell as he left the graveside.

To many people it seemed odd that Natali remained happy, taking his usual delight in so many things, and most put it down to his lack of understanding of the situation. But Gaye, the second daughter, who had shared some of her young brother's recent adventures and had a unique insight into the child's mind, had another theory. She believed that Natali understood what was going on far better than anyone, and she was comforted by his cheerful company.

Gaye had more reason than most to be miserable, but she shared some of Etha's strength of character and refused to be downhearted. For that reason she was perhaps more distressed than anyone but Fen by Dsordas' withdrawal, and after several days' indecision, she made up her mind to talk to him while Fen was out.

There was no response to her knock on the bedroom door, but she went in anyway.

'Dsordas? Are you there?'

He did not reply, but Gaye could hear the sound of his breathing. She walked carefully over to the bed and sat down at the foot, feeling the mattress move as Dsordas shifted away from her.

'You've been feeling sorry for yourself for too long,' she told him bluntly. 'You promised to help Zalys.'

She paused, waiting for a response.

'Go away,' he whispered eventually.

'I won't,' she said firmly. 'Not until you see sense. Don't you know that Fen, Mother, Anto – even Tarin – are all out there playing their parts. I would be too if I weren't blind.'

Gaye had lost her sight when Farrag had struck her down with a bolt of sorcerous power on the day she was to marry her childhood sweetheart, Bowen Folegandros. That same attack had turned her blonde hair pure white.

The wedding had not taken place; Bowen had been exiled, chosen by Farrag as a hostage to Xantium to replace his brother, who had apparently escaped. Sagar Folegandros had been taken nine years earlier, when he had been no more than a child. It was common practice within the Xantic Empire to ensure the obedience of conquered nations by abducting the children of important families.

'What's your excuse?' Gaye went on. '*You're* the reason Zalys is free. You, of all people, should be preparing to keep it so! Ever since I've known you, you've been obsessed with the idea of releasing us from the Empire. Why abandon it now?' She paused and took a deep breath. 'We need you.'

'I'm useless,' he whispered softly, miserably. 'I've done my part.'

'But you've only just begun!' Gaye exclaimed. 'Why should you give up your whole life's work because of one small failure?'

'You don't know what it's like,' he told her resentfully.

'Don't I?' she exploded. '*Don't* I? You think you're the only one who's been through things they don't understand? I've been given incomprehensible advice by *ghosts*, for pity's sake. I've flown with bats and ended up in the Arena.'

Gaye had been transported from her home to the place that was Zalys' spiritual focus by something she could only call magic. Natali had experienced the same thing, but unlike his older sister, he had taken it in his small stride.

'I've conjured a storm out of nowhere just by telling a story!' Both storm and bats had played a vital part in the success of the revolt. 'And I've talked to people who aren't there and seen another world beyond our imagining,' she concluded. 'Do you think what you went through could be any worse than that?'

'But I could have been killed,' he protested feebly.

'Just like my mother.' She had been a healer and had died while trying to save another, when Dsordas was still an adolescent.

'Are you so afraid of dying that you'll spend the rest of your life in bed?' Gaye snapped contemptuously. 'I thought you had more guts. You were right at the front of the fighting.'

'That's different.'

'Why?' she demanded.

'That was confronting an enemy,' he told her hotly. 'It was a clean fight. But I've seen what my meddling can do, the pain and misery it causes – to my own people!'

'But you brought health and happiness too!' Gaye countered. 'Look at Fen!'

'That wasn't me,' he muttered. 'That was my mother.'

'Ghosts can't *do* that!' she told him. 'I've talked to them, remember?'

'Go away!' Dsordas shouted, his sudden blaze of anger making her flinch as she felt him move.

'What will you do if I don't?' she needled him. 'Would you hit a blind girl?'

Dsordas was silent and still.

'I know you better than that,' she said gently. 'You're the only one who doesn't recognize your worth. And no one can work out why.' There was sadness in her voice now.

'I'm useless,' he repeated. He sounded exhausted. 'I can't do anything. Leave me alone.'

'Give me your hand,' she instructed.

'Why?'

'I want to show you something.' Gaye did her best to sound confident. This was a gamble, and one she could not be sure of winning. She held out one hand and felt Dsordas take it, sensed his suspicion. Her other hand was in her pocket, clasped about an amberine crystal. *Alasia*, she begged silently. *Help me.*

'Close your eyes,' she told him.

The world became an infinite, chaotic latticework of

35

glowing lines, shifting and weaving, a strange kaleido-scope of life – and death. She heard Dsordas gasp and knew that he shared the vision.

'This is how the world looks to me now,' she told him quietly. 'Here we are not limited by distance or time. Everything is here; good and evil, warmth and cold, love and hate. It is real, and no more to be feared than the world you see. The old man who died is here.' A spectral face glimmered briefly in the endless network. 'And there are guides to help us.'

The pale face of Alasia, the woman who had guided Gaye's first tentative steps in this nether realm, appeared. She looked weary, but her smile was radiant, lit from within.

It does not pay to argue with a beacon, healer. Her eyes held the light and colour of a clear winter sky, and her gaze was fixed upon Dsordas as she spoke. *Heed her words. Your fire cannot remain hidden in darkness for ever.*

That evening, when Fen returned home, she was overjoyed to find Dsordas up and dressed and eager for news. They spent hours talking and then, in the darkest time of the night, they made love for the first time since the uprising.

The next morning, the couple went out together to inspect the progress that had been made. Dsordas' deputies welcomed him back joyfully, and before long it was as if he had never been away. Fen deliberately stepped back and watched her lover taking over the reins with an odd mixture of emotions. She was glad that he seemed back to normal, but deep down – although she tried to deny it – she was resentful. For the first time in her life she had been fulfilling her potential, using all her resources. But now . . .

However much Dsordas praised her efforts and emphasized his gratitude, she could not escape the feeling that for him the last few days had not really existed; that everything she had achieved in that time had somehow happened by itself. Yet she hid her feelings well and rejoiced with the others at Dsordas' return to the helm. The next few days would be a critical period in the history of Zalys – a point emphasized the following day by Natali's unexpected reawakening of Iceman.

But that day was also marked by another inexplicable and far more ominous event. Shortly after noon, anyone who was within a few hundred paces of the eastern coast heard a deep, cavernous rumbling which seemed to rise from the sea itself. It faded into silence eventually – only to be repeated a short time later, causing many anxious glances to be cast over the water. It was the latest in a long sequence of peculiar occurrences in the sea – occurrences which had led many of the islanders to distrust the ocean on which they all relied.

CHAPTER FOUR

My heart beats with butterfly wings.

There are tapers burning in the land of tunnels, fireflies within the earthworm's realm. That much I foresaw in a dream, when I could still fly. But I am heavy now.

My heart beats like a mountain.

The Swordsman allowed himself a last glance at the burning outline. Its giant shape was unmistakable, wreathed in flame, bright against the night sky. He had positioned it well, on one of the uppermost turrets of The Spires, and it had become a beacon that could be seen from almost everywhere within the walls of Xantium.

The sight gave him some satisfaction. It was a gesture, no more, but it might provide a useful distraction. Right now, he had real work to do.

Sagar Folegandros shivered, feeling the chill of the dark cell sink deeper into his flesh. He was dizzy and nauseous, and the stale air rasped in his throat. For three days now he had seen no one, neither man nor ghost, and in that time he had eaten nothing at all. His meagre water ration had run out long ago. His sleep had become even more fitful and he was no longer sure which was more real, the fevered snatches of dream or the windowless stone room in which he lay.

By his own uncertain reckoning, Sagar had been incarcerated for at least ten days, though he had been given no indication of his crime. And now, it seemed, he had been forgotten and left to die.

He was overwhelmed by self-pity. His life had always seemed an exercise in futility, but not even Sagar could have predicted that it would end in such an inexplicable and unjust manner. Nine years ago, at the vulnerable age of thirteen, he had been taken from his home in Zalys as a hostage to the Xantic Empire. Since then he had lived a circumscribed but not uncomfortable life in the closely guarded enclave housed within the imperial city. Sagar never lost his longing for his home or for freedom, but he had grown to accept his lot and even to appreciate certain aspects of his fate. He had matured into a self-contained, well-built man who, even among his fellow hostages, bestowed his friendship sparingly and his trust not at all. He gave his captors no excuse to punish him – or his family on faraway Zalys. He was a model prisoner, his only rebellion locked away in his heart; his current situation was therefore all the more baffling and distressing.

What have I done to deserve this?

Day and night meant nothing in his underground cell. For Sagar, daylight was an illusion, a half-remembered mirage. The only way for him to calculate the passage of time had been the visits of the gaoler with his meagre daily meal, and the unreliable signals of his own body. His tongueless keeper had not been back since he had been frightened away by Sagar's most recent visitor, a tiny woman who was so pale that at first he had taken her for a ghost. By his own estimate, that had been three nights ago. He felt terribly sleepy now, despite the protestations of his empty stomach. Yet he fought to stay awake, fearing that he might miss his last opportunity to save himself. And he knew that if he slept now, he might never wake up again. Even so, he could not help his eyelids flickering shut every once in a while.

After nodding off on one occasion, he jerked awake, suddenly aware that the meagre lamplight filtering through the bars of the doorslit had changed. He glanced up to see a face outside, piercing black eyes staring in at him. It was a few moments before he realized that he was hearing the sounds of bolts being drawn back, a key turning in the lock. Sagar tried to jump to his feet but staggered, his head whirling, heart pounding recklessly. His tongue would not work.

The door swung open and the man beckoned.

'Don't speak. Come quickly.' The whispered words were partially muffled by a cloth tied over his lower face.

Sagar stared, swaying.

'Can you walk?' the man asked anxiously. 'There's not much time.'

From somewhere, Sagar found reserves of strength as his befuddled mind finally recognized that he was being given a chance to escape from the nightmare. He needed no second invitation, and lurched towards the door.

'This way,' the stranger urged, taking Sagar's arm and propelling him deeper into the dungeons. He glanced over his shoulder towards the distant lamp which gave the only light in the corridor.

'In here.' Sagar was pushed into another cell and surrendered to a momentary panic, but the man quickly followed him inside and pulled the door to. Sagar waited in the pitch black, and heard the sound of a metal blade scraping along the stone wall.

There was a clink as the knife found the cleft it was seeking, and then a creaking noise. Slivers of light crept into the darkness as a section of the stone wall grated open like a door. Sagar followed the other man through, wondering if this was a dream, if he had finally gone insane. Behind him the massive door closed again with a heavy crunch.

'It can't be opened from this side,' the stranger told him. 'Come on.'

They hurried down a narrow corridor which was lit by an unnatural luminescence. In places the walls and the uneven, low ceiling were covered with green slime. Water dripped. The sound of flapping wings came from a side tunnel, as if they had disturbed the roosting place of underground birds. After turning several corners, the two men came to a flight of steps leading upwards.

'Wait here,' Sagar's rescuer instructed, then bounded lightly up the stairs, making hardly a sound. Moments later, he called down. 'Come on. It's clear.'

Sagar climbed as fast as he could, his legs stronger now. He still could not quite believe his good fortune. At the top a trapdoor stood open. The man was already above and offered his hand to pull Sagar through. The prisoner found himself in a dusty room full of broken furniture, a dark, forgotten storeroom.

'Who *are* you?' he croaked.

'Not yet,' the other told him. 'Explanations can wait until we're outside The Circle.'

Sagar was not sure what that meant, but did not feel inclined to argue. He followed obediently as his saviour led him through another door, down some rickety wooden steps and into a cluttered alleyway. Above him, unimaginably remote, the stars shone, casting a spectral radiance over the scene, and Sagar noticed, for the first time, that the blade his companion carried was stained with fresh blood.

'Watch your step,' the man advised. 'Even in The Circle the street cleaners don't bother with these back alleys too often.' He had drawn down his mask, revealing a square jaw and a wide mouth turned up in a grin.

'I'm outside the enclave?' Sagar grated, then immediately felt foolish. There was nowhere like this within the enclave.

'A long way outside,' his companion laughed. 'And you'll be further still very soon. Come on. Not too far now and you'll be able to rest.'

'And drink?' Sagar asked desperately.

'Of course.'

The alleyways the stranger led him through were mostly deserted. A few late-night wanderers were abroad, but they were intent on business of their own and paid

41

the two men no attention. At one point, however, the dark-eyed man ducked into a shadowy doorway and pulled Sagar in with him, where they waited until a patrol had passed by. Sagar had not seen or heard the soldiers coming and knew he would have been helpless on his own. As they marched past, the soldiers looked tired and bored.

At last they came to a larger thoroughfare, lit at intervals by flares and oil lamps. A short way downhill, the roadway passed under a stone arch in which wooden gates stood open. Sentries were on duty on either side.

'No one's searching for you yet. We just walk through, all right? Try to look as though you know where you're going.'

Sagar almost laughed. He had never been more frightened.

'The guards are there to watch for undesirable elements coming *in*,' his tutor explained. 'They're not going to bother about us going out. All right?'

Sagar nodded, because it was obviously expected of him, and smiled inwardly as he thought that the most likely thing to betray them would be his bursting into hysterical laughter. He swallowed hard, trying to compose himself, then followed his rescuer out into the open, tagging on to a group of men – merchants by the look of them – who were strolling towards the gate, arguing good-naturedly. The soldiers took no notice of any of the men as they passed, and after a few score paces, his companion drew Sagar into yet another alley and thence, via several more streets, to a small square.

'Welcome to The Levels,' the man exclaimed, breaking a long silence. 'Realm of the unwashed masses, province of the rabble, the riffraff and scum of Xantium. The underworld dunghill of imperial existence . . . Your new home!'

Sagar didn't know whether to laugh or cry. *Sooner or later,* he told himself, *it'll start to make sense. Just keep going.*

'It's been so long . . .' he whispered, looking about in disbelief, drinking in all the mundane yet suddenly magical details. Dirty, dusty streets; shuttered houses; a guttering lamp; smoke from a distant fire, pungent in his nostrils. The sound of conversation; people walking freely, alone or in groups; a drunken voice raised in tuneless song. Cats prowling; the distant barking of a tethered dog.

'Is it real?'

'It's all *too* real,' his companion replied, watching the former hostage with some amusement. 'Xantium in all its squalid glory. Come. A friend of mine runs an . . . establishment, over there. We can get you a drink.'

He led the way to an unmarked door and knocked. An eye-hole slid open with a bang.

'The girls are all busy. Come back . . .' The gruff voice faltered. 'Oh, it's you.'

They heard the sound of bolts being drawn back, an eerie echo of Sagar's imprisonment, and then the door opened.

'My young friend here needs drink, food and a quiet place to rest. In that order.'

The grizzled doorman glanced at Sagar incuriously.

'Come in and welcome,' he said, standing aside.

A short while later, Sagar was gently sipping a second tankard of watered ale, having downed the first so quickly that it made his head spin. He was ravenous, and devoured a plate of overcooked vegetables and gravy – which nonetheless tasted like an epicurean feast. Their host had brought the provisions and then left them alone in the snug room.

'Take it easy. You'll make yourself sick.'

Sagar paused for a moment, sensing the well-being that coursed through his body, and looked at his saviour. Calm blue eyes blazed back, so dark that they were almost black. Something about them seemed oddly familiar.

'Who are you?' he repeated.

'Most people call me Martyn.'

Curiosity made Sagar temporarily forget his hunger.

'Why . . . ?' he began, then found himself lost for words.

'Why did I get you out?'

Sagar nodded.

'I've been interested in you for a while,' Martyn went on. 'When you disappeared from the enclave, I thought it was time to move.'

'But . . . how did you know where I was?' There were so many questions, Sagar didn't know where to begin.

'Alasia told me.'

Sagar looked blank.

'A very remarkable lady,' Martyn added. 'Small and pale. Looks as though a puff of wind would blow her away.'

'Her!'

'You've met?'

'I thought she was mad!'

Martyn laughed.

'So do most people,' he said.

A new thought struck Sagar.

'You,' he breathed, staring. 'You're . . .'

'Not now,' his rescuer said sharply, raising a finger to his lips as the door opened and their host came in. He glanced at the half-full plate.

'Not finished then,' he muttered. 'Kitchen boy wants to go home.'

'I'll take care of the dishes, Trestman,' Martyn said. 'Let him go.'

The doorman nodded but made no move to leave. The real reason for his coming in was soon obvious.

'Heard the news then?' he asked.

'What news?' Martyn asked calmly as Sagar looked up in alarm.

'They say the court's in an uproar,' Trestman told them. 'Did you see the giant sword burning in The Spires?'

'I saw it,' Martyn said evenly.

'The Swordsman's up to his tricks again,' the older man went on eagerly. 'And Verkho's spitting blood. Someone'll pay for that sign, you mark my words. Can't help but laugh, though. What a cheek! Where everyone can see it!'

'Yes, but what does it achieve?' Martyn asked dourly.

Trestman shrugged, disappointed that his guests did not share his amusement. Martyn seemed bored and the newcomer just stared stupidly, his spoon halfway to his mouth.

'Have to keep an eye on the girls,' Trestman said glumly and left again, closing the door behind him.

'He's a terrible old gossip, but his heart's in the right place,' Martyn commented.

'You're the Swordsman, aren't you?' It was an accusation rather than a question.

'Yes,' Martyn admitted easily. 'But I'd rather not have everyone knowing it.'

'Why tell me then?' Sagar asked, becoming more bewildered by the moment.

'I've a hunch you won't be in a hurry to denounce me to the authorities,' the dark-eyed man answered. 'I don't know what you did to get thrown into gaol, but I'd be prepared to wager that you'd rather not go back. Verkho takes a dim view of those who escape his clutches. Besides, since you've guessed it already, I've nothing to lose. I've a feeling I can trust you.'

'It's still a risk,' Sagar pointed out, his natural caution re-emerging.

'All life's a gamble,' Martyn quoted. 'I've helped you. I'm hoping you'll help me in return.'

'How?'

'We'll have time for that later. Eat!'

Reflexively, Sagar ladled another spoonful into his mouth, then swallowed rapidly as another thought occurred to him.

'Alasia told me to wait for you,' he said. 'I thought it was a joke.'

'What Alasia says may *sound* funny,' Martyn told him, 'but I don't think she ever jokes.'

'I thought you were the reason I was in there in the first place,' Sagar blurted out. 'That note you sent me . . .'

The Swordsman nodded, his expression rueful.

'Yes. In retrospect, that was a mistake,' he conceded. 'But I was frustrated by my lack of progress and wanted to try something more direct. What else did Alasia say?'

'She told me I was free!'

'I'm not sure she lives in the same world as the rest of us,' Martyn said thoughtfully. 'Time may be different for her. Perhaps she meant that you *would* be free. Or she may have been talking about something else entirely. Philosophy, for all I know. I've given up trying to understand Alasia,' he concluded. 'I just accept her help. She's a very special person.'

'She also told me,' Sagar went on, as his thoughts slowly cleared, 'that my brother was coming here.'

Martyn showed surprise for the first time.

'Go on,' he prompted.

'I asked which one – I have two, Bowen and Nason – and she said "the beacon".'

'Do you know what that means?'

Sagar shook his head.

'She also said that he was carrying two burdens,' he added. 'But that made no more sense than the rest.'

'It'll be clear eventually,' Martyn said. 'Did she say when he'd arrive?'

'No. Do you think it's true?'

'Yes,' the Swordsman replied, considering. 'Come to think of it, that might be why you were locked up. Perhaps Verkho needed an excuse to get your brother here, and if he removed you, he could pretend that you'd escaped – giving him the perfect excuse to send for another hostage from Zalys.'

'But why would he want my brother?'

Martyn shrugged.

'With Verkho, who can tell?'

Sagar did not think to wonder how Martyn knew where he was from, and now a new fear assailed him.

'Once they learn of my escape, won't they take reprisals on the island?'

'If you'd still been in the enclave, yes,' the Swordsman replied. 'But now, I don't know. If we're right, you've probably already served your purpose.'

Sagar shivered to hear his companion speak so dispassionately.

'It seemed as though they'd forgotten I existed,' he said hopefully.

'They'll remember,' Martyn responded grimly. 'I had to kill three guards to get you out. They'll want to know why it happened.' He stood up abruptly and stretched. 'Finish your meal, then get some sleep. You can stay in here – it's quite safe. We'll talk more in the morning.'

'Don't leave me!' Sagar was gripped by a sudden fear.

'I won't be far away,' Martyn reassured him. 'Stay in this room until I get back. You can call Trestman if you need anything.' At the door he paused, grinning. 'I think we might have some adventures, you and I. Sleep well, Sagar.'

And with that he was gone. Resisting the impulse to follow his protector, Sagar ate the remaining food, even though his stomach now felt bloated, then arranged cushions on the floor and lay down. He did not expect to sleep, but it seemed that in the next instant, sunlight was filtering through cracks in the shutters and he was remembering fleeting glimpses of a dream in which he had been a newborn baby again. Everything in the world had looked big and frightening, and he felt so cold. He wanted to climb back into the warmth of his mother's body, but she wasn't there any more. Then he had heard Alasia's voice telling him that he was free – and that was all he could recall.

Sagar looked around the drab room, listening to the small sounds of the building and trying to think. Was his

47

freedom illusory? Exactly who was the Swordsman, and why had he rescued him? Was his brother really being brought to Xantium? And would he ever be able to return to Zalys? The questions were endless. And for the first time in his adult life, he was outside the protective womb of the enclave.

Freedom felt cold.

CHAPTER FIVE

Untombed bones danced within the flames, skulls laughed at the chaos of the living. Blood, now smoke, drifted above the improvident pyre, the air a funeral haze.

It was an omen even then – for those who could read the symbols. Am I the only one versed in such lore? Does the bitter taste mean poison?

Sagar's dream still echoed in his head, and he hardly had time to compose himself when the door was kicked open with a bang. He leapt to his feet, ready to die rather than return to the horror of that dark cell. But it was Martyn who entered, balancing a tray on each hand.

'Sorry to startle you,' he said, noticing the other's fearful expression. 'Had my hands full with breakfast. Hungry?'

Sagar nodded, realizing that he was famished. As his racing heart calmed, he fell upon the food while the Swordsman sat back and watched, chewing thoughtfully on a slab of bread.

Eventually, his initial hunger sated, Sagar looked up.

'Why are you doing this for me?'

'I recognized a kindred spirit.'

'Me?' The idea seemed implausible at best.

'You've a cool head. You rely on no one but yourself – and you've every reason to hate the way the Empire is being run,' Martyn explained.

Sagar was silent for a few moments, but remained far from convinced.

'I've kept myself to myself,' he agreed, 'but I've *done* nothing.' Unlike you, his tone implied.

'Out of fear for what might happen on Zalys?'

The cloud that always hung over Sagar descended. He nodded dumbly, imagining the terrors that might be visited on his long lost home.

'Well, you've no choice now.' The Swordsman's eyes were as hard as stone. 'You can't go back to the enclave, so Zalys will just have to look out for itself.'

'How can you be so callous?' Sagar found the Swordsman's logic hard to take.

'It's something we all have to live with,' Martyn replied.

'We?'

'I used to be a hostage too.'

As Sagar stared into those deep blue eyes, which once again seemed strangely familiar, memories fell into place.

'Your name's not Martyn,' he exclaimed. 'It's Guyland. Guyland Brak. But . . .'

'But I'm dead,' the Swordsman completed for him.

Sagar remembered the night of the fire. He had not been in any direct danger, but several hostages had been temporarily relocated until the blaze in one section of the enclave was brought under control. By then three hostages and at least two soldiers had burnt to death. One of the victims had been Guyland Brak, a dark-eyed madman from the northern lands whom Sagar had always done his best to avoid. The man was a trouble-maker, who had tried to coerce others into provoking the guards, always vociferously protesting against his imprisonment.

'The nice thing about a fire is that, if it's done properly, one skeleton looks much like another,' the northerner said with a grin. 'So I was free to begin a new life as Martyn Waysinger.'

Sagar was suddenly sure that he did not want to know all the details of that fateful night, some three summers earlier. It was abundantly clear that, whatever his motives, the Swordsman could be utterly ruthless.

'Of course I looked a bit different then,' Martyn went on. 'Hair down past my shoulders, the beard of course – and refusing to change my clothes meant that I was dressed in rags.' He smiled. 'My appearance was a political statement then. Now I'm a bit more practical.'

Sagar could not tell how serious his rescuer was being, but nonetheless he glanced at the short cropped dark hair and neat, unremarkable tunic. It was quite a transformation.

'You must have a good eye for detail to be able to recognize me at all,' Martyn added appraisingly.

'Your eyes . . .' Sagar was having difficulty in getting his tongue to work.

'Ah! The Swordsman's eyes!' Martyn's voice became an awe-struck whisper. 'They hypnotize you while his blade strikes for your heart.' He laughed. 'It's a good job I don't believe everything people say about me.'

'If you escaped three years ago,' Sagar asked, still struggling to make sense of this new information, 'why are you still here? Why didn't you go home?'

'Because there's nothing to go home for,' Martyn replied simply. 'And because Verkho's here.'

'The Chancellor?'

'That's one of the names he's known by. It's not one that I'd choose.'

'You don't like him?'

The Swordsman laughed at Sagar's understatement, but the humour never touched his eyes.

'Let's just say that I hope one of the legends about him is true,' he said. 'That he *did* exchange his soul for other powers. That way, when I kill him, he won't be able to infect any other worlds with his evil. I'd prefer to see him in eternal torment – if it could be guaranteed – but I'll settle for his obliteration, even though that seems too good for him.'

The words were lightly said, but the undercurrent of

hatred made Sagar's blood run cold. This was a new form of madness. He said nothing, but Martyn read the questions in his eyes.

'There's more, of course,' he went on. 'The Empire's become his creature, as corrupt as he is, and Southan hangs on his every word. When Verkho dies, I want to make sure that the Empire dies too, that no one takes his place. For that I need all the help I can get.' He paused, watching the islander closely. 'What do you say, my friend? Shall our names go down in history as two of the men who caused a mighty empire to crumble into dust?'

Inside, Sagar was a mixture of crazy excitement and bewildered fear. Could he really believe in the vision of this apparent lunatic? But then, he reminded himself, this lunatic was the one who had saved him from helplessness and possibly an agonizing death. He no longer knew what was real. His life had been too strange; his childhood abruptly cut off, the years as a powerless hostage. And now this. He thought of Zalys, of her seemingly endless subjugation, and of his own small suffering multiplied by hundreds. Suddenly the demise of Xantium seemed the most desirable thing in the world.

'I'd like nothing better,' he said quietly.

'Good!' Martyn spat on his right palm, leant over the table and offered his hand.

Sagar followed his example and the two men clasped hands.

'Brothers in arms, then,' Martyn said jovially. 'Sealed in spit. Not as painful and less messy than blood – but just as binding.'

This statement was made in the same light tone, but Sagar was aware that their two futures were now inextricably linked. The Swordsman was not a man with whom to even contemplate betrayal. He thought of the skeletons within the ashes of the fire, and of the blood glinting on a metal blade.

'Brothers in arms,' he echoed solemnly, wondering how he might be of use in their undertaking.

'We have a lot to talk about,' Martyn began.

'There's so much!' Sagar exclaimed. 'I've been in there for nine years, only ever hearing what *they* wanted. Some news got in, of course, but we had no way of knowing what was true.' His ignorance suddenly seemed overwhelming. Where was he to begin?

'Did many rumours reach you?' Martyn asked unexpectedly. 'The city's full of them just now.'

'Some, I suppose,' Sagar replied uncertainly, 'but I never paid them much heed.'

'How did you spend your time?'

For a moment, Sagar was at a loss. How had he filled those nine years? What had he achieved? The sheer waste of it all made him want to weep, but he pushed his emotions aside.

'I read a lot,' he offered, feeling ridiculously inadequate. 'Learnt as much as I could. Languages, logic . . . anything really. History . . .'

'The approved versions, no doubt,' Martyn put in. 'Indoctrination can be a wonderful thing.'

Sagar was once more thrown by his companion's flippant tone, and hesitated.

'What about poetry?'

'Some,' the islander admitted, self-conscious again.

'Me too,' Martyn said, then went on to declaim a verse from a dramatic epic in his own, guttural northern tongue. Until then, without thinking, both had been using the universal trading language.

'*The Pengarron's March*,' Sagar responded, smiling.

'You know it!' Martyn exclaimed with delight. 'A man after my own heart. Best not to recall it in public though. The story's not too popular in Xantium. Smacks of disobedience to the Empire. Might give people ideas!'

Sagar found himself thinking that if he had not seen Martyn's earlier flashes of hatred, he might be tempted to believe that the Swordsman was never serious about anything.

'I studied law as well,' Sagar added, for the want of anything better to say.

'Imperial law! The base stone upon which civilization is founded,' his companion responded with heavy sarcasm. 'What a shame it's so far removed from justice. If you've enough power or money you can make the law stand on its head. If you're weak or poor, the lawyers will use it to nail you to the floor.' He grinned crookedly, and waited for Sagar to continue.

'That's about it, really,' he said, appalled at his own words.

'No girls?'

Sagar found himself blushing, and shook his head. He had not allowed romance to enter his life.

'Wise man,' Martyn said. 'They're always trouble – although the women here could teach you a thing or two.' He grinned, then added, 'So you found other ways to keep yourself in shape then. You look fit enough to me.'

'I exercised every day for the last few years,' Sagar answered. *Until I was thrown in gaol.*

'And you spent some time in quiet contemplation.'

'When I could,' the islander agreed, surprised once more. How did he know such things? 'It helped to keep me sane.' Abruptly, Sagar's mind rebelled. What was he thinking of? He didn't want to waste time talking about himself! But he had not even formed his first question when there was a knock at the door.

'Come,' Martyn called.

The door opened and Trestman entered.

'Come to collect the trays,' he mumbled, shuffling across the room. 'Do you want anything else?'

Martyn glanced at Sagar for confirmation before answering no. Trestman took an age rearranging the plates, then looked at the islander.

'Sleep well?'

'Yes,' Sagar replied, wishing the man would go.

'Don't let us keep you from your work,' Martyn added.

'Will you be staying tonight?' their host enquired.

Sagar did not answer, and glanced at his companion.

'My friend has more sense than that,' Martyn said.

'The beds upstairs are comfortable,' Trestman persisted doggedly.

'No doubt,' Martyn said patiently. 'But we'll be moving on.'

The older man still seemed reluctant to leave.

'There's a rumour going round about an uprising on some island or other,' he remarked. 'Verkho's sent the fleet to put it down. Empire's crumbling at the edges, if you ask me.'

'Do you know which island?' Martyn asked as if it were a matter of no importance.

'Zalyn or Zalyk or some such.'

'Zalys?'

Sagar had done his best not to react but he knew that his face must have betrayed him. Even so, Trestman went on unperturbed.

'That's the one,' he said, nodding. 'Don't know why there's all the bother. Seems to me we've troubles enough closer to home.'

'True enough,' Martyn agreed calmly. 'Trestman, we have business to discuss. In private.'

This time the bringer of gossip reluctantly took the hint and left. By now the questions in Sagar's head had multiplied beyond reasoning; this latest piece of news had thrown him completely.

'Seems as though we got you out just in time,' the Swordsman commented. 'This sort of thing won't go down too well with Verkho.'

'The other hostages!' Sagar gasped in horror. 'We have to get them out.' There were several more prisoners from Zalys in the enclave, some of them no more than children. The thought of the Chancellor's possible revenge upon them was appalling.

'Let's be realistic, shall we?' Martyn replied sharply. 'It's probably already too late. And with all this going on, there'll be no chance of a mass escape. Just be thankful *you're* out of harm's way.' Sagar said nothing. 'And think on this,' the Swordsman went on, deadly serious now. 'If the report is true, Zalys might be free. Your family, your people. If a few have to suffer so that many can rejoice, isn't it worth it?'

Sagar could still find no words. It was all too confusing.

'It's another sign,' Martyn continued. 'The Empire is crumbling – even an old fool like Trestman can see that. And *we* can speed up the process. Verkho's the only one holding the whole rotten edifice together, him and his cursed Information Ministry, his Far-speakers and spies. If we disrupt that, Zalys won't be the only place that's free – and then you can go home. We all can.'

Home. Sagar found it hard to believe that such a place actually existed – and harder still to hope that he might ever see it again. Yet the fervour of his companion's words had struck a chord.

'I can't go home yet anyway,' he said quietly. 'One of my brothers is on his way.'

'Don't worry about him,' Martyn responded eagerly. 'I'll talk to Alasia, try to find out what she meant. You may yet be fighting side to side when the time comes.'

Sagar realized that he was being forced into constant reevaluation of the man who called himself the Swordsman. How much of what he said was true, and how much was idle dreaming? It was ridiculous to even think of toppling the Xantic Empire. And fighting? Sagar had never even held a sword – except a wooden plaything in an earlier life in Nkosa.

'I'll do whatever I can,' he vowed, still not sure what he was committing himself to.

'Good,' Martyn responded. 'Your formal education was thorough enough. Now let's teach you something about real life.'

Sagar felt singularly ill-equipped to cope with real life, but he had no choice now but to try.

CHAPTER SIX

There is a temple, far away from here, perched upon a pinnacle of rock. It is built of memories, not stone; its truths are woven into the very fabric of the place, not wished upon it by the remote pantheon.

History will judge, they say. But who is to blame – the torturer or his overlord? Who is guilty – the commander who orders an atrocity from afar, or the soldier who obeys?

And who will suffer the ultimate revenge?

As the morning wore on, Martyn did his best to fill in the vast gaps in Sagar's knowledge. He described the Empire's recent history, and explained how it had now stopped expanding, thus coming under pressure on almost all its borders. He told him how Verkho, the former starets, or self-proclaimed holy man, had come to power and how he had maintained his position through his genius for communications, intrigue and the use of military power. Sagar listened avidly and was surprised by how much – even in slanted form – had filtered through to the closed world of the hostage enclave. However, he was, quite naturally, completely ignorant of the events of the last few days and the rumours now circulating in the city, and he hung on his tutor's every word.

'It's been a difficult time for our beloved Empress Ifryn,' Martyn remarked sarcastically. 'She gave birth to a long-awaited son – Southan Azari – eleven days ago. The new imperial heir. Surely you heard about that?'

'I knew the baby was due,' Sagar replied. 'But it was around then I was shut away.'

'Her father died a couple of days later,' Martyn went on without a trace of sympathy in his voice. 'But no doubt Verkho has organized a suitable successor in Idiron by now. Then, of course, we come to the occasion of the tenth imperial wedding anniversary and the joyous celebrations that went with it. You won't have seen much of them, either.'

'No.' Sagar swallowed hard. 'I knew they were coming up, but . . .'

'So you won't know that, at the banquet that night, there was an unsuccessful attempt to poison Azari, or Ifryn, or both – depending on which version of the story you believe. Something happened, that's common knowledge now, and so is the fact that I am supposed to be behind it!'

'But you weren't?' Sagar asked uncertainly.

'Please. I have more self-respect than that.' The Swordsman seemed genuinely hurt by the suggestion, and abandoned his habitually cynical tone. 'Poisons are more Verkho's kind of weapon than mine,' he said earnestly, 'especially as he himself is immune to them.'

'Is that true?' Sagar had heard the claims made on the Chancellor's behalf, but had not known whether to believe them.

'Apparently so,' Martyn admitted grudgingly. 'One day we'll see whether he's immune to a sword in the throat.' His face twisted at the thought. 'Besides, what would be gained by killing Ifryn or Azari?' he went on. 'She's always been ineffectual, not interested in power. She's done her duty at last and produced a son after two useless daughters, so now she'll probably retreat even deeper into the court shadows. And the boy's only a few days old.'

'So who *is* responsible then?'

'Who knows?' Martyn laughed. 'Perhaps a jealous lady of the court who feels she'd make a better empress.

Perhaps Verkho, for devious reasons of his own. Perhaps no one?'

'No one?'

'The whole thing could have been an elaborate hoax, set up to make me look bad,' Martyn explained.

The suggestion seemed to be made in all seriousness, and Sagar was not sure what to make of it. Could it be true? Or was self-aggrandizement part of the Swordsman's complicated make-up? He found it impossible to judge.

'Anyway,' Martyn went on, 'the whole episode led to the inevitable rumours about Ifryn and the baby's health, especially as they hid from view for a few days. But most of those fears were allayed by their noticeably public appearances two days ago,' he added sardonically. 'In the meantime, the mystery grew even more complicated when General Kerrell disappeared. No one's seen hide nor hair of him for three days now.'

'Kerrell?' Sagar put in. 'The commander of the imperial army?' He knew of the man by reputation. That he should simply vanish seemed improbable to say the least.

'The very same,' Martyn confirmed, apparently relishing his tale of intrigue. 'There's all *sorts* of gossip about him. Some people think he's dead, that he had a disagreement with Verkho or got in his way. They may well be right. Other rumours link him with the assassination attempt – which is utter nonsense – and still others reckon he's in league with me!' Anticipating his companion's question, he added, 'No such luck.' There was an expression of regret on his broad face.

'You admire him?' Sagar asked tentatively.

'He's a soldier, the best,' Martyn replied promptly. 'I can admire that, even in an enemy. The Empire would be very different if he was Southan's closest adviser rather than Verkho.'

'Mightn't he have gone into hiding for his own reasons?' the islander suggested.

59

The Swordsman smiled.

'Your training in logic obviously wasn't wasted,' he commented. 'The same thing has occurred to some people, but the only reason they could come up with is the idea that he's Ifryn's lover. Absolutely ridiculous! It just shows the state that Xantium is in if people actually believe such garbage.' He shook his head in disbelief.

'How can you be so sure it's garbage?' Sagar asked innocently.

'The same reason I know he's not the would-be assassin,' Martyn replied. 'Kerrell Adjeman is the latest in a long family line of sworn servants to the Emperor. You must have read about them in your history books. Loyalty to the throne is in his blood, going back through a dozen generations. Treason like that would be unthinkable.'

'But he's only human,' Sagar pointed out. 'And Ifryn is reputedly an attractive woman. Kerrell might have abused his position of trust.'

'No.' Martyn was vehement. 'He at least is a man of honour. Unlike most. It wouldn't surprise me if this was all part of some devious plan of Verkho's to make himself Emperor – and that's just too appalling to even think about! He'd probably grant himself the status of a god, like the emperors of old. He's bad enough now, but there'd be no limit to his evil then.' He shuddered.

'If you could prove that,' Sagar suggested, 'then maybe Kerrell might join us as an ally – if he's still alive.'

'Indeed he might,' the Swordsman replied, then paused, obviously deep in thought. Sagar waited, wondering what ideas were being considered behind those uncanny eyes – and wondering what small part he might be asked to play in the unfolding drama. But when Martyn spoke again it was to raise a quite different subject.

'And through all this,' he said, 'the city's been swarming with ghosts. They're everywhere. No one can understand why there are so many more than usual. It makes my flesh creep.'

Sagar did not share the northerner's instinctive reaction to phantoms. He knew that the living had nothing to fear from the dead, and had become used to their benign, unobtrusive presence as a child on Zalys. He had seen few ghosts during his years in Xantium, but news of the spectral infestation brought back memories from his recent incarceration.

'A ghost visited me in my cell,' he offered. 'He seemed to be trying to tell me something. And later I saw him with Alasia.'

'She's acquainted with many.' Martyn smiled. He was obviously fond of this eccentric woman.

'She *talks* to them?' Sagar asked incredulously. Communication between worlds was supposed to be impossible.

'So I gather,' his companion replied. 'Perhaps that's how she knew where you were. In any case, I'll wager Verkho's behind it. It's well known that he's been meddling with the arcane.'

Sagar refrained from mentioning his own reading on occult subjects, wanting – for reasons he couldn't quite fathom – to retain a few secrets of his own.

'He was up to something at the old temple a few days ago,' Martyn said. 'That was when the ghosts first started appearing.'

'The temple?' Sagar queried.

'The ruin on the small hill in the south Levels,' Martyn explained, but Sagar was still mystified. 'I forgot how little hostages know of Xantium,' his tutor continued. 'If you're going to move among us and be of any use, you'll need to know your way around. It'd take you years to know the place properly, but you can learn the basics quickly enough, and it just so happens . . .' With the air of a conjuror, he produced a folded parchment from inside his tunic and laid it out on the table. '. . . that I have here a map of the city. It's out of date now, but the main features haven't changed.'

The battered chart showed the imperfect circle of the

city walls, built within a long loop of the aptly named Brown River, which ran parallel to all but the southern quarter of Xantium's perimeter. Sagar had only seen these walls once, after a nightmare journey across the dusty, barren tract known as the Deadlands, which surrounded the city for leagues on all sides. Although that had been at the end of his enforced voyage from Zalys, and he had been young and frightened, his memories were clear. The city walls, which were built of a pale grey stone that glittered in sunlight, had appeared almost unbelievably tall. With their towers and battlements, they formed a stunning testament to the labour of the men who had built them centuries earlier. They were a statement of man's determination to dominate his environment.

Sagar's convoy had approached from the southwest, and so had not needed to cross either of the two massive bridges which spanned the river to the northwest and east of the imperial capital respectively. Each of these led directly to one of the city's Great Gates. Instead, the new hostage had entered by the nearest gate, which faced them directly. The fourth gate faced due south, a short distance away.

Once inside the walls, the young Sagar had lost all sense of direction amid the maze of streets, and was only vaguely aware that his journey continued generally uphill. The hostages had been deliberately kept ignorant of the lay-out of Xantium beyond the high-walled enclave, so Sagar studied the map eagerly. At first it appeared to be an incomprehensible, complex jumble, but then Martyn began to put it into context and the city took shape before his eyes. His tutor explained that Xantium was built upon a conical hill, whose slopes grew steeper as they neared the centre, and that, generally speaking, the higher up the hill you went, the more affluent the neighbourhood became. It culminated in a series of large ring-shaped terraces, each with its own outer wall.

'All this,' Martyn began, pointing to the outermost region, which accounted for the vast majority of the area, 'is known as The Levels. That's where we are now.' A forefinger tapped the northeastern section of the city. He went on to point out other significant places within The Levels; the temple, the Stadium, the Great Dice Hall, and the vast cisterns which drained water from the river.

'Most people in Xantium live in The Levels,' he went on, 'but if you've got money – or the right sort of lineage – you might be lucky enough to get a house in The Circle.' He indicated the first inner ring. 'Merchants, minor nobles, that sort.' He sounded contemptuous. 'Inside that is The Domain. Most of the city's garrison is in there, as well as all the pen-pushers – the ones who keep the whole gargantuan apparatus of the Xantic Empire grinding forward. The hostage enclave is inside The Domain, here.'

Sagar looked at the small space that had been his whole world for nine years. It was high on the eastern side of the hill, its upper edge abutting the outer wall of the next ring.

'Little did you know it,' Martyn continued, 'but just above you was the imperial court itself. That's where Southan, Ifryn, their advisers and the top-ranking nobles live in luxurious splendour.'

'And this?' Sagar asked, pointing to the small circle which marked the summit of the hill. This section was filled with a spiderwork maze of alleyways and buildings.

'That's The Spires,' Martyn told him. 'You needn't worry about that. Only bats live there. It's a mad place, full of weird shapes and sculptures. It was built by some lunatic Emperor long ago, and no one's ever thought it was worth the effort to tear it down, so it's been left to crumble slowly.'

'That's where you put the burning sword.'

'Yes.' The Swordsman grinned.

'Why did you do that?'

63

'I like to keep them on their toes,' Martyn replied. 'Show them I'm still around.'

'That's a dangerous game.'

'At least I play by my own rules.'

'How did you get in there?' Sagar asked, intrigued.

'There are ways,' the northerner replied. 'The hill is practically honeycombed with tunnels. You've seen some of them yourself. Emperors are a suspicious breed, always looking for bolt-holes. I probably know as many of them as any man except Verkho. His quarters are here, by the way.' Martyn outlined a wedge-shaped section which cut across both the court and The Domain, and also bordered the hostage enclave at its northern end. 'Best not to have you wandering in there.'

'I'll try not to!' Sagar promised. 'Was that where . . . ?'

'Yes. The dungeons are under the Ministry of Information offices.'

Talking about the Chancellor again reminded Sagar of an earlier part of the conversation, and of something that Martyn had not explained.

'Why did you have nothing to go home to?' he asked quietly.

The Swordsman did not answer for a while.

'It just so happened,' he said eventually, 'that my country being swallowed by the Empire coincided with Verkho becoming Chancellor – and he obviously felt that he had to give his newest territory a taste of his power.' Martyn's tone was determinedly light, but his dark eyes were haunted now. 'He made us an example. I was taken hostage; others weren't so lucky.' There was another pause. 'Let's leave it at that, shall we.'

Sagar stared fixedly at the map, wishing he had never raised the subject. Martyn's pain was still vivid. No wonder he had been a trouble-maker in the enclave. He had been half-mad with grief then – and might still be now.

With a resolute effort, the northerner pushed his memories aside.

'No more study!' he exclaimed heartily. 'You've had more than enough of that for a lifetime. It's time for you to see the real world.'

'Won't I be recognized?' Sagar was suddenly fearful. Was it safe to go outside?

'You think you're so remarkable?' Martyn grinned. 'Hostages don't know anything about life outside the enclave, and by the same token, very few people outside have ever seen the hostages. Certainly no one round here. Xantium is always full of strangers, and even if the soldiers *are* looking for you, they'd take months to cover even a quarter of The Levels.'

Despite these reassurances, Sagar still felt apprehensive – but his companion left him no choice, hustling him from the room.

Stepping out of the front door, Sagar felt the warmth of sunlight on his skin for the first time in twelve days.

'So life begins again,' Martyn commented, echoing the islander's thoughts.

CHAPTER SEVEN

*Time plays tricks on those who do not see it for what it is.
Lives are trapped, thoughts ensnared, and fate becomes
an inescapable circle. But love is not so constrained.
    Rebellion begins in the heart.*

It had been a bad night for Chancellor Verkho Yulsare.
The flagrant challenge of the burning sword, closely
followed by the news of the revolt on Zalys, had sent him
into a towering rage; now, in the cold light of morning,
he was able to plan his responses with his usual scheming
intensity. Perhaps it might be turned to his advantage
after all.

His initial reaction to the message from the island –
and one he saw no reason to change – had been to
instruct Admiral Barvick to despatch a fleet to recapture
and punish Zalys. That in itself was a simple enough
exercise, but one that was wholly necessary. What
concerned Verkho more was the fact that the uprising
was symptomatic of a greater problem, namely that the
Empire's power was stretched beyond its genuine
strength. Naval resources in the south would be spread
thin for the next month or so – and if that information
reached other outlying territories, they too might be
tempted to rebel. Therefore some diversions were
necessary.

The Chancellor's grey eyes, so bright that they seemed
almost silver, glittered as he began to plot intrigues in
remote areas. An assassination here; an unexplained
crop failure there; bloody raids by mysterious bandits on

both sides of a crucial border; the sudden decline into senile madness of a country's nominal ruler. Verkho smiled at his own inventiveness and, from time to time, called in the Focus to issue another set of secret instructions. His assistant was a telepath of great talent who acted as the Chancellor's main link with the many active Far-speakers in Xantium, and thus with all the Empire. Her own name long forgotten, the Focus was a plain girl, unquestioningly obedient, supremely efficient but without any will or personality of her own. Like all of her kind, she wore an amberine crystal sewn into her headband, and her tongue was stained an unpleasant blue-black.

Once he was satisfied with these arrangements, Verkho's mind returned to the affair on Zalys. There might be more to this than met the eye. With luck, some remnant of the imperial garrison there would have survived and might eventually provide further information – although no Far-speaker relays had been received since Marshal Farrag's infuriating plea last night. If Farrag himself was still alive – and Verkho sincerely hoped that he was – he would have many questions to answer. The Chancellor looked forward to conducting that interrogation himself.

For all his bungling, Farrag had apparently been on the verge of an interesting and potentially important breakthrough in the use of telepaths. His exact words had been, 'Recent discoveries in the manipulation of excess Far-speaker power will be of great value to the Empire'. The man's arrogance was intolerable, but what gave credence to his claims was an independent report that Far-speakers in Xantium had become unusually drained by recent contacts with the island. In the Empire's current hazardous state, power was the ultimate prize – whatever the source – and so the Marshal's claim could not be ignored.

Verkho's own researches into the realm of occult power had been extensive, especially of late, utilizing the vast numbers of talents and investigators employed in the so-called Ministry of Information. This experimentation was progressing well, although never fast enough for the Chancellor's liking. However, one recent attempt at turning theory into practice had proved a spectacular success. And there was the possibility of another, even more potent triumph when a certain talisman arrived in the city in a few days' time. That this item had been brought ashore on Zalys and was being transported with a party which included a promising talent from the island – one Bowen Folegandros – was the sort of irony that Verkho greatly appreciated.

The Chancellor had long been aware that certain objects stored memories of the past, and in some cases held a power of their own. If sufficient talent and will were there, both could be drawn upon. He himself had summoned the ghosts of the dead using artefacts from their lives in this world. Translating this knowledge into real, usable power was much more difficult, but Verkho had great hopes for the potential of the talisman. However, his researches were continuing in many areas. No avenue would be left unexplored.

In the meantime, the Chancellor had the intriguing problem of what to do with the Zalysian hostages. Several enticing alternatives had occurred to him. Public torture and execution was the obvious option, and allowing the hostages from other lands to send descriptions of this to their former homes would have a satisfyingly salutary effect. On the other hand, their simple disappearance – and the subsequent uncertainty and rumours – might prove even more effective. Another consideration was that some of the island's hostages were minor talents – having been chosen partly for this reason – and might be exploited interestingly now that they were expendable.

Verkho had just decided that this pleasant problem deserved further thought and that, for the time being, all he need do was place the hostages in the dungeons, when he recalled that one of them was already there. Sagar Folegandros need not be hidden away now. In fact, his plight could be used to ensure the cooperation of his more talented brother. Verkho had come to consider Sagar as insufferably dull, with little spark and no esoteric potential whatsoever, but now he might produce a little more entertainment. Several days in a dark and lonely cell might have shaken him up a little. Verkho decided to speak to the prisoner at once, and sent a servant to bring him to the Chancellor's austere study.

However, when the man returned, his nervous look told Verkho that something was wrong. He stood and faced the messenger squarely. Tall and broad-shouldered, with a glistening black beard and long hair, the Chancellor was an imposing figure, and he knew it. His mesmeric eyes and unmistakable aura of power ensured that everyone who met him understood just why he was the most feared and influential man in all the Empire.

'Well?' he demanded shortly.

'He's gone, my lord,' the servant replied, knowing that dissembling was pointless. 'Escaped.'

Verkho fought to control his temper. The one thing he could not tolerate above all others was incompetence among his subordinates.

'Why was I not told of this earlier?' he asked coldly.

'The bodies of the night guards were only discovered a short time ago,' the man replied, not meeting his master's gaze. 'When they changed the watch. They're all dead. Then the cells had to be searched before it was certain that the prisoner was missing.' Everything about the way he spoke and held himself was crying out, *It's not my fault!*

'Send the captain of the dungeon guards to me,' Verkho said, his voice flat. 'Immediately.'

The messenger departed hurriedly, relieved that someone else would be bearing the brunt of his master's terrifying displeasure. The Chancellor, however, found that he had remained remarkably calm. There was work to be done. He was in no doubt as to who was responsible for Sagar's escape, and he vowed to do everything in his power to ensure that the culprit paid dearly for it. In many ways Verkho had always enjoyed their game, but this time the Swordsman had gone too far.

Empress Ifryn looked up, hope flickering briefly, as the door to her private chamber opened. Her husband entered and came to embrace her, his expression solemn and concerned. Yet even in his arms, Ifryn felt remote, unable to respond.

'There's still no news of Kerrell, my love,' Southan said softly, releasing her.

Ifryn nodded. She had expected nothing else, and her last hopes were fading. It had been three days now, and the burden of her suppressed emotions was becoming harder to bear. Southan was aware of her unhappiness but, as always, he was not sure how to console her. The Emperor's imposing appearance masked a compassionate but emotionally inarticulate character. He had grown to love his wife and children dearly but never really understood them, and this lack of self-assurance had always carried over into his public life. More and more, without his really being aware of it, he had fallen under the influence of Verkho, who far outstripped the Emperor in intellect and cunning.

For her part, Ifryn appreciated her husband's qualities but was increasingly aware of his faults. Ever since her arrival in Xantium ten years ago, as a bewildered, eighteen-year-old bride-to-be, she had relied increasingly upon Kerrell, who was nearer to her own age and so much easier to talk to than the father of her children.

During that journey to the Empire's capital, Kerrell, then a young captain but already clearly destined for high office, had told her, 'My friendship is something you can count on for as long as I draw breath.' He had been true to his word, and although Ifryn deliberately took a background role in court politics, knowing that she was out of her depth, it was Kerrell who had always guided her through any difficulties. But in spite of their close friendship, their relationship had been defined by a strict sense of propriety, something emphasized by Southan's absolute trust of them both. It had taken this crisis for the Empress to admit – even to herself – her real feelings towards Kerrell. She loved him with an explosive passion that frightened her – but now it seemed as though more than a sense of decorum would prevent her love from ever being granted release. Ifryn believed – hoped – that Kerrell would have told her if he were going into hiding of his own accord. Therefore she believed that he must have been kidnapped – or killed. And she had to keep the true extent of her misery to herself.

Southan looked sadly at his wife's beautiful face and saw the hurt in her gentle brown eyes, yet could do nothing to heal the pain.

'This business with the Swordsman has started up all the rumours again,' he said awkwardly, 'but they'll die down soon enough. The best thing we can do is to go on as though nothing has happened. They'll soon see it's all nonsense.'

Ifryn could hardly believe her ears. *As though nothing had happened?* Something of her thoughts must have shown on her face, because Southan found that he could not meet her gaze.

'This time will pass, my love,' he offered. 'You and Azari are all right – that's the main thing. And Verkho has taken control of the army.'

Is that supposed to make me feel better? Ifryn wondered incredulously. With Kerrell, she shared a deep mistrust of the charismatic Chancellor, and had only recently realized just how dependent on him her husband was. Southan, she recognized, had always been ineffectual, and his main concern now seemed to be to

71

keep up appearances. Ifryn wanted to shake him, to make him see how desperately she needed him to be strong – but he appeared even more withdrawn than ever, and she drew back in turn. But deep inside her heart, she felt the first stirrings of rebellion. *If I can't get him to help me, I'll have to do it myself.* The beginnings of a timid resolve were forming.

'I know nothing can bring your father back, my dear,' Southan went on, still trying in vain to comfort her, 'but Idiron is in safe hands now, and your mother will be here before too long.'

King Fyle's ghost had appeared briefly to his daughter on the night of his death. He had come to say farewell, but Ifryn had been too stunned to respond, and her lack of a proper leave-taking added to her misery. She had seen her parents infrequently since her marriage, and had never returned to Idiron. Now she found herself longing for the comfort of her mother's presence – until she realized that the Queen was in mourning too, and would need comforting herself. Was there no consolation to be found anywhere? Sternly she pushed self-pity aside and looked up into her husband's anxious face, forcing herself to smile. Southan's relief was palpable.

'And we always have each other,' he said.

Over the years, Ifryn's feelings towards the Emperor had changed from fear to acceptance, then from tolerance to a quiet, undemanding form of love. So she was able to nod in agreement and spend the best part of the next hour talking about inconsequential topics, and pretending to share Southan's genuine delight at the tiny antics of their baby son. She played the dutiful wife, but all the time she was silently railing against fate.

Eventually Southan had to leave, and it was a relief to be able to behave naturally. Taking Azari back to his cot, she laid him down tenderly.

'If only you knew,' she told the infant quietly, filled with a sudden fierce surge of protectiveness. Nothing must be allowed to harm her children. But how was she to ensure that? Vrila and Delmege, her daughters, were mere imperial chattels and had never been threatened, but Azari was the new heir, a potent symbol of power – and therefore much more vulnerable. Ever since the banquet and the frightening implications of the events of that night, Ifryn had sometimes been afraid to feed the baby, unable to trust her own body. Even though no poison had entered her, she felt tainted and in need of healing. Although she knew that this feeling was irrational and ridiculous, she still could not shake the notion. Alasia had assured her that the boy was well – and Ifryn had good reason to trust her eccentric friend in such matters – but even that was not enough. She was living on an emotional knife edge.

Going over to the open window, Ifryn looked out over the city and the Deadlands beyond. Her apartments were high on the western side of the court, abutting The Spires. The only view was thus to the west, a fact which had always seemed significant to the Empress, as this was directly away from her old homeland. It seemed to symbolize her permanent separation from her old life. Idiron was worlds away now, both in distance and time. Ifryn would never be able to recapture the innocent simplicity of her life as a young princess there, a life shattered by an arranged marriage necessitated by political expediency. For a few moments she tried to picture what she would be doing now if she had never come to Xantium. Her imagination failed hopelessly.

The Empress' daydreaming was interrupted by Doneta, the maid who had accompanied her from Idiron and stayed with her ever since. She was only a few days younger than Ifryn, and had matured into an attractive, dark-haired woman, but she had resisted all romantic advances, showing a loyalty which her mistress would have insisted was unnecessary, but for which she was nonetheless very grateful.

'Do you want something to eat, my lady?'

'No, thank you, Doneta. I'm not hungry.'

'It's after midday,' the maid protested mildly. 'You should be keeping up your strength for him too, not just yourself.' She nodded towards the cot. 'And you ate nothing this morning.'

'Oh, all right,' Ifryn conceded. 'You're worse than my mother used to be. Goodness knows how I'll survive when she's here to nag me too.'

The two women grinned at each other and Doneta went to bring in the meal, then left her mistress alone again. Ifryn picked at the food for some time, then gave up, her thoughts returning inevitably to Kerrell. Even now she had no idea whether he reciprocated her feelings. Their friendship was unquestioned, but could it ever have been more than that? Surely it could – if the circumstances had been different. Ifryn cursed the iron grip of convention which had ensured that they hold their emotions and their words in check. In all the years they had known each other, Kerrell had never even used her own name, always referring to her as 'my lady'. It made the hideous rumours about the reason for the General's disappearance unbearably ironic. Unless, of course, the mere suggestion of an improper relationship, coupled with Kerrell's love for her, were enough to make such an honourable man hide himself away. That thought was almost too painful to contemplate.

And now, was it too late? It was quite possible that she would never see him again, even that he was dead. For a fleeting moment Ifryn wondered whether, if Kerrell were dead, his ghost would visit her as her father had done – and wished even for that ephemeral contact. Then she caught herself up, aghast at such an idea, and took a deep breath.

'I'll find him,' she said aloud. 'I will.'

As yet she had no idea how to go about such a task, but that did not shake her resolve. She had already asked for Alasia's help – her pale friend often knew things

without having any discernible source of information –
but with no results so far. Who else was there? Ifryn
thought for a while, then raised her voice.

'Doneta!' she called. 'Come in here a moment.'

CHAPTER EIGHT

Far away, in a snow-blighted land which I have never seen, a raven flies in the shadow of the past. In its beak the bird of omen carries three dice, and within the forest the oracle waits, listening to the song of the leaves.

The raven glides past on silent wings, and the dice fall to settle on the frozen earth. A skull for death and danger, a star which stands for love or the unknown, and . . .

The last die does not come to rest, but spins for ever in the shadows. The moving shadows of trees.

Opening his eyes was the hardest thing Kerrell had ever done, and he managed it only after a terrible struggle. His dreams were reluctant to let him go, and they called him back to sleep, to the painless darkness. But he persisted, and at last was able to look around.

In the bright sunlight, his bedchamber looked unreal. The shelves of books glowed, the polished wooden furniture shone and the canopy above his bed glistened with a rich pattern of colour. Everything was radiant, perfect – as if newly made.

How long have I been asleep?

The open shutters revealed the clear blue sky of midday. On the table stood a half empty flagon of wine and a curiously shaped glass. Yet Kerrell did not recall drinking before he retired. Pushing himself up on his elbows, he shook his head as if to clear it, but the scene before him did not change.

Abruptly the General threw off the bedcovers, and put his legs over the side – only to freeze where he sat.

His skin was suddenly clammy, his heart pounding. The sheets had not rustled. The mattress did not creak. No sound came through the open window; birds, the city, even the wind – all were quiet. He was encased in absolute silence.

'What is this?' Kerrell muttered.

His tongue moved, his vocal chords vibrated – but there was no sound. None at all.

Kerrell bellowed. And the void swallowed his scream.

He glanced down at his feet, and the world tilted. The floor beneath the bed had gone. Instead there was only a depthless chasm. The room began to waver and dissolve about him. Reality crumbled with his belief. *None of this is here.*

The distorted glass was one he had broken months before. The table was brand new, with no sign of the scratches caused by long hours of work. The whole room was a patchwork made up of pieces of his memory, a vision his own mind had imposed upon him because to see reality was to invite madness. But the cracks had appeared now, and nothing could stop the disintegration.

Soon it was all gone, vanished into a white, neutral nothingness, a blank winding sheet like an infinite cloud. Kerrell was weightless, only able to move in relation to himself. His own hands felt real enough but there was nothing for him to grasp, nothing to hold on to. He was adrift in an impossible, silent realm where only he existed.

Kerrell knew now why waking up had been so hard. He wished he had listened to his dreams.

Martyn rolled the last two dice, producing a skull and a star. Together with the three crescent moons and two skulls he already held, they were enough to beat his opponent's three stars and three lanterns.

'Wish I hadn't raised you now,' the man said resignedly, and pushed over his pile of small coins.

'The odds were in your favour – just,' Martyn commented. Like his opponent, he had known that one of the last pair of dice did not have a moon side. Each of the seven dice used by the players had one of the seven symbols missing.

'Never seems to matter against you,' the other man said without rancour. 'That's enough for me.'

As his beaten adversary left, Martyn turned to Sagar and smiled complacently.

'Well, we can afford to eat for another day,' he remarked.

The two men had spent all evening in the tavern which, like most public places in Xantium, had facilities for a wide range of games of chance. Gambling was the universal addiction in the city, something Sagar had been aware of but of course had never seen at first hand. Martyn had spent most of the evening playing one or other of the many variations of a complicated dice game known as emperors. He seemed to lose as many rounds as he won, but the shrewdness of his wagering meant that his stack of coins continued to grow, while his opponents' dwindled. As an onlooker, Sagar had been ignored by most players, and he was happy to remain quiet and just watch.

Two days of freedom had left him feeling almost giddy. Xantium was bewildering enough to any novice, but especially so to one who had led such a constricted life. Sagar was grateful that Martyn had rarely left his side. His tutor had guided him through the intricacies of street protocol, the ways and means of procuring food, shelter and money.

Martyn appeared to know a great many people, and introduced most of them to Sagar, who had been given the name Folly – a choice which Martyn found amusing. Few paid the quiet foreigner much attention, accepting him as one of the endless stream of newcomers to their quarter of the city, and Sagar was content to remain as unobtrusive as possible. He still found it hard to accept that he could live openly. Just walking down a street in daylight seemed an act of brazen provocation. It was true that there had been an increase in the number of guards patrolling the area, and that The Levels were thick with rumours about Verkho's spies, but Martyn avoided the soldiers with almost contemptuous ease, and ridiculed the stories about a network of informers.

'It's not like the court out here,' he had said. 'You couldn't trust anyone there, but Xantium is just too big. Even Verkho couldn't separate fact from fiction. Sure, there are some people who'd sell their own children for a few coins,' he admitted, 'but they're just as likely to tell plausible lies for gain as to reveal something useful – even if they *knew* anything.'

'How many people know who you really are?' Sagar had asked.

'A dozen.' Martyn shrugged. 'No more.'

'Do you trust them?'

'Most of them are like you,' the Swordsman had replied confidently. 'They've good reasons for not betraying me.'

As time went by, Sagar grew to share a tiny fraction of Martyn's conviction – no one had enquired after an escaped hostage after all – but there was still much that confused him. If the Swordsman was genuine, a man who wanted the Empire to crumble, then he had a strange way of going about it. And Sagar still had no idea why he had been singled out for rescue or what part he was expected to play. He was thoroughly bemused, and had formed the opinion that Martyn was not an entirely stable character. His moods changed rapidly, though he rarely remained serious for long, and everything he did seemed to be on a whim. It was quite possible that Sagar's release had been one such escapade – and that the Swordsman himself was not sure why he had done it or what Sagar was to do now. Even so, Sagar was in no hurry to be put to the test. Everything was too new – and, he had to admit, enjoyable. All he could do was tag along with his guide, try to find his feet and learn as much as possible. The future would take care of itself.

One thing that did worry him was the possibility that one of his brothers was coming to Xantium. The idea that Bowen or Nason might already be in the city made him nervous and unhappy, and the hope of hearing any possible news of them – or of Zalys – was one of the reasons he listened so avidly to all the gossip in the streets of The Levels. Just now he was alone with his guide, Martyn having run out of prospective gamblers to challenge, and their conversation turned to more mundane matters.

'Do you want a drink?'

'No thanks.' Sagar had never drunk much and had no head for alcohol. He wanted to keep his wits about him.

'Food then,' Martyn decided. 'But not here. The meat in this place is tougher than my boots. We'll go to Myla's.'

Just at that moment the outer door opened, and an extraordinary figure entered. The man was almost as broad as he was tall, and filled the lower half of the doorway. His limbs were short and thick, and a bushy thatch of matted brown hair covered his head and most of his face, so that his mouth and ears were practically invisible. Deepset eyes peered into the lamplit gloom from either side of an oversized, flat nose. A long knife hung from his solid leather belt, which appeared to be the only thing keeping his soiled and threadbare tunic together.

The newcomer's gaze fell upon Martyn and he immediately strode towards their table. Sagar glanced at his companion, and was relieved to see him smiling.

'Well met, Martyn,' the man growled. 'Will you buy a fellow sufferer a mug of the piss-water that passes for ale round here?'

'I've won enough, sure,' Martyn replied, waving the other into a chair. 'Folly, this is Grongar. Another displaced northerner. Don't be put off by his disgusting appearance – underneath all that grime, he has the soul of a poet.'

Grongar grunted as Martyn stood and went to fetch the beer. Sagar and the newcomer eyed each other cautiously.

'You play?' Grongar asked, pointing a gnarled finger at the dice.

Sagar shook his head.

'No. I leave that to Martyn.'

'Labyrinth's my game,' Grongar said. 'Too much luck in emperors for my liking. Still, now that I'm here . . .' He picked up one set of dice and weighed them experimentally.

Martyn returned with the tankards.

'Don't even think of playing this man for money at *anything*,' he advised Sagar with a grin. 'Even I'm not that foolish.'

Grongar gave his fellow northerner a dark-browed look, then picked up his ale and swallowed half the draught in one noisy gulp. Flecks of foam adorned his moustache as he set the mug down.

'Stuff me, I needed that!' he sighed. 'Doesn't summer ever end in this stuffing town?'

'Pining for the snow-covered hills, are you?' Martyn enquired.

'It's been so long I've forgotten what home's like.' Grongar's tone was so doleful that Martyn laughed.

'Listen to the man!' he exclaimed. 'Here he is sitting pretty, but . . .' He turned to Sagar. 'Believe it or not, my friend here has his own quarters in The Domain, no less. And he's master of the imperial dogs, so he's paid a small fortune for doing nothing.'

'Hounds!' Grongar corrected him. 'They're hounds, you ignorant dungheap.'

'Oh yes,' Martyn responded sarcastically. 'And a lot of hunting you do on The Deadlands!'

'That makes no difference.' Grongar sounded aggrieved.

'Either way,' his tormentor went on, still grinning, 'Grongar here's the only one who can get near some of the beasts. And most of the time he's the only one who wants to.'

'I didn't come here to listen to you insulting my friends,' the hound-master said grumpily, but made no move to leave. He stuck a crooked finger into one hidden ear and twisted it violently.

'No,' Martyn agreed. 'You came here to drink free beer.'

'Can you think of a better reason?' Grongar asked, his eyes glinting.

Throughout this exchange, Sagar had been trying to shrink back into the shadows. Grongar was an imperial servant, and lived in The Domain! The former hostage did not remember ever coming into contact with the hirsute northerner, and indeed there was no reason for him to have ever been in the enclave. But Sagar was still nervous, although Martyn seemed quite at ease.

'Don't let Grongar fool you,' Martyn told him now. 'He claims to be a barbarian who came here to seek his fortune, but I reckon he came here to escape some jealous husband. He may be ugly, but he's still a lecher . . .'

'And a very successful one!' Grongar claimed improbably. 'Any woman of spirit is interested in more of a man than you can see on the surface.' Warming to his subject, he added, 'Did I ever tell you about the time . . .'

'Not now,' Martyn interrupted, laughing. 'Do you want to corrupt my innocent young friend here?'

'A friend of *yours*, innocent?' the self-styled barbarian said disbelievingly.

More than you know, Sagar thought, hoping the tavern gloom would hide his discomfort.

'What's the latest news, then?' Martyn asked casually. 'Any sign of our esteemed General?'

Grongar drained his tankard and belched with gusto.

'No one's so much as smelled him,' he said. 'Or at

least no one will admit to it. His disappearance is still a mystery, though, and the latest rumours are getting wilder by the moment.'

'Such as?' Martyn prompted eagerly.

'Some genius has decided that Azari is actually Kerrell's son, not Southan's,' Grongar replied, needing little encouragement to spread the gossip he professed to despise. 'So Kerrell's been disposed of to make sure that he never reveals the truth. Southan's not going to give up an heir after all this time – no matter how it was come by. Stuffing garbage, of course, but you know how people like a good scandal.'

'If that's true, how are they supposed to make sure that Ifryn keeps quiet?' Martyn asked. 'It's just possible she might have some idea who the father is.'

Grongar chuckled.

'You can't simply slit an Empress' throat,' he told them sagely. 'That's not the correct etiquette. In fact – so opinion has it – they can't do anything to her or it'll give the game away. Her reputation has to be preserved, at least for a while. And even then, if anything *does* happen to her, it'd have to look like an accident. Illness or something.'

'Poison?' Martyn suggested mildly.

All the humour drained out of Grongar's hairy face in an instant. Both men knew of Verkho's reputation as an expert in all types of venom.

'Only if it looks natural,' Grongar stated. Then he added with forced flippancy, 'Even Southan might suspect something if she suddenly turns purple and drops dead clutching her throat.'

'What about the rumour that the wine at the banquet wasn't actually poisoned?' Martyn persisted. 'What does your friend Corton have to say about that?'

A momentary hesitation gave away Grongar's increasing unease. Corton was the wine-master at the imperial court, and Grongar's closest friend. The northerner had already said too much on this subject on an earlier occasion, and was not about to repeat his mistake.

'He's no idea,' he said, trying to sound casual. 'He never got the chance to test it.'

In fact, Corton had confided in his friend that the wine had indeed been untainted – contradicting Verkho's claim – and was worried that he might be implicated in whatever was going on. Even Sagar could see that Grongar was not telling the whole truth, and was surprised when Martyn did not pursue the subject.

'So where do *you* think Kerrell is?'

'Dead,' Grongar answered promptly, glad to be on less dangerous ground. 'He must be. But the gods know why.'

'Have they appointed a replacement?'

'No. Verkho's got the senior officers reporting directly to him.'

'What a surprise!'

'Why, Martyn,' Grongar exclaimed in mock amazement. 'I get the impression that you don't hold our great Chancellor in the proper esteem.'

'It all points to him, doesn't it?' Martyn said with a shrug. 'Who else stands to gain from Kerrell's removal?'

'Gain what?' the barbarian countered. 'Surely he's already got all the power he wants?'

'No,' Martyn replied dourly. 'He'll never have enough.'

'I'd agree that you can't trust Verkho,' Grongar went on, 'but why should he deprive himself of a capable ally dedicated to the Empire? It's more likely to have been foreign agents – Xantium has enemies enough, the gods know. Or what about the Swordsman?'

'That charlatan,' Martyn replied with believable disdain. 'All he's good for is pretty fires and nuisance value.'

'Livens things up though, doesn't he?' Grongar said appreciatively.

'Sometimes,' Martyn admitted.

CHAPTER NINE

A stone cat prowls the skyline here. He is alive both with the spirit of the man who carved his shape and that of the creature who inspired such artistry. Many times I have stroked his granite fur and released him from an age of silence. His call echoes through the starlit halls, a warning and a claim. Who would invade this territory – unless invited by his purr?

'Why are you so sad, Mummy?'

Delmege's huge brown eyes looked up at her mother with the innocent determination of a seven-year-old.

'I'm not, sweetheart,' Ifryn replied.

'Yes you are,' her daughter insisted. 'You never laugh any more.'

Gods, am I so transparent, the Empress thought despairingly, *that I can't even hide my feelings from children?*

'And you're not eating enough,' Vrila chimed in. 'Doneta said so.' She was striving to sound like an adult, even though she was only a year and a half older than her sister.

'Did she now?' Ifryn could not help but smile at her maid's roundabout cunning. 'I eat all I want,' she told her daughters. 'You don't want me to get fat, do you?'

'You're not answering my question,' Delmege persisted indignantly.

Ifryn gave in.

'I'm sad because Kerrell has gone away and no one knows where he is,' she admitted. 'I'm sure he'll be back soon, though.' If only she could believe that!

'Why doesn't Daddy find him?' Vrila wanted to know. 'Emperors can do anything.'

'Not everything, my sweet,' Ifryn told her. 'Your father's trying to help, but he's a very busy man.'

'You love Kerrell, don't you?' Delmege asked solemnly.

Ifryn swallowed hard, and fought to keep her smile in place and her voice light.

'Yes. He's a very dear friend,' she said carefully. 'Like the brother I never had.'

'Like us and Azari!' Vrila exclaimed, pleased at the thought.

'He's not a real brother yet,' Delmege pronounced. 'He's too small.'

'Oh yes he is,' her sister challenged, turning her blue eyes – the same colour as her father's – towards Ifryn for confirmation.

'He's your brother no matter what size he is,' the Empress told them. 'He's tiny now, but one day he might be bigger than both of you.'

The two girls considered this statement with varying degrees of disbelief, but before they could respond, there was a knock at the door and Doneta's head peered round.

'The gentleman you wanted to see is here, my lady,' the maid announced. 'Shall I ask him to wait in the outer chamber?'

'Yes, please,' Ifryn replied. 'Then come and take these two off to bed.' Overriding their dismayed complaints, she added, 'It's getting late, and if you're good, Doneta will tell you a story. Off you go!'

The girls went, mollified by the promise. As she kissed her mother goodnight, Delmege whispered in her ear, 'I bet Alasia could find him.'

Alasia was a great favourite with the girls, because she was always able to produce the unexpected – and Ifryn was reminded of the time when her healing skills had saved Vrila.

'That's a good idea, little one,' she responded. 'I'll ask her.' Ifryn was touched by Delmege's obvious concern, but she had in fact already enlisted Alasia's help – to no avail. She was now having to explore other avenues.

The Empress turned towards the outer room as Doneta came to follow the girls.

'Have you set some wine out?' Ifryn asked in passing.

'On the table,' her maid replied, then added meaningfully, 'Some food too, in case you feel hungry.'

'Thank you. I'm sure my guest will appreciate the thought.'

Doneta shot Ifryn a look, then went on her way.

The visitor rose as the Empress came in, and bowed, but waited for her to speak first.

'I'm glad you could come, Baylin.'

'I am honoured to be at your service, your majesty.' His voice was full of charm, but he sounded sincere.

'Please, I have always hated that title,' she said. 'Call me Ifryn. If you can't get your tongue round that, my lady will do.'

'As you wish, my lady.' Like Kerrell, he would not presume to use her own name.

Ifryn waved him into a chair, sat down on the opposite side of the low table and poured some wine.

'I've been told much about you,' she said as she handed him a goblet, thinking that this man would repay study. His face seemed familiar, yet she could not say when or where – or even if – she had seen him before. He was well dressed without being in any way ostentatious, and appeared wholly unremarkable. Yet she knew that in this case appearances were deceptive. She remembered Kerrell saying that Baylin was a master of disguise, able to fit his bland features to any outward role.

'That being so,' he replied, 'I'm surprised you still wanted to see me.' He smiled easily. There was warmth in his brown eyes, and he watched her with unashamed interest. Ifryn remembered another of Kerrell's descriptions; that Baylin was the only man who could look into Verkho's eyes and lie with a straight face. It seemed that nothing could unnerve him.

'You do yourself an injustice, sir,' she replied.

'Hardly. I am a traveller who can be useful now and then. Nothing more.' Despite his words, there was a confidence about him that indicated a man who knew his own worth. Some people could have taken this for arrogance, but Ifryn found herself drawn to him.

'General Kerrell thought more highly of you than that,' she said.

'He and I have been friends for many years, my lady. His loyalty undoubtedly exaggerated my qualities – such as they are.' Baylin sounded a little stiff now, and his eyes had clouded, the first signs of any lack of composure.

Ifryn took a deep breath.

'Do you have any idea where he is?' she asked. 'What might have happened to him?'

'No, my lady. I wish I did.' He was in earnest now. 'I have been searching ever since I heard the news, but without success.'

'Tell me what you have done,' she said.

Baylin described his endless round, visiting all the haunts that Kerrell had been known to frequent, including some that the two men had visited incognito, places that only he was aware of. At each location he had questioned everyone who might know anything, but had drawn a complete blank.

'I've just about exhausted all the possibilities,' he admitted finally. 'I don't know what else I can do. There are others searching who have far greater resources than I, and they've had no luck either.'

'Assuming they really want to find him,' Ifryn said quietly.

Baylin stared at her in silence, not sure how to react. She had surprised him for the first time, and Ifryn was

88

aware of it. She could not blame him for being cautious. They were treading on dangerous ground, after all. But having started . . .

'May I speak frankly?' she asked.

'I would never betray your confidence, my lady,' he answered quickly. 'On my honour . . .'

Instinctively, Ifryn trusted him. Kerrell had said that Baylin was the best of men – and she had need of a reliable friend now.

'You must be aware,' she began, 'of some of the rumours linking Kerrell and myself. You must also know—'

'That they are false!' he cut in vehemently. 'Only a fool would believe otherwise.'

The Empress bowed her head in acknowledgement, though she knew that Baylin's certainty was based more upon his familiarity with Kerrell than on his opinion of her. It pleased her, nonetheless.

'Never doubt my friendship with Kerrell,' she went on. 'But our conduct has at all times been governed by propriety.'

'Of course.' Baylin appeared mystified. 'But what has this . . . ?'

'Why have such rumours started now?' Ifryn asked. 'Were they the cause of his disappearance, or the result?'

'The cause?' The idea had evidently not occurred to him, and was dismissed with disgust. 'Never! He would not flee from such obvious falsehood.'

'I agree with you,' she said. *At least I hope I do.* 'Then what is the cause?' she continued. 'Could it be connected to the birth of my son? Might it be that Kerrell discovered who tried to poison the imperial heir? And that they have taken measures to escape punishment?'

'As a theory, it's as plausible as any I've heard,' Baylin answered, after a moment's consideration. 'But who would have the ability to make the General vanish so completely?'

'The same person who has the power to make sure

that the official search does not find him,' she suggested, returning to her earlier point.

'The Chancellor?' Baylin was clearly uneasy at the turn the conversation had taken. They were both deeply committed now. There could be no turning back.

'I'm sure Kerrell kept it no secret from you that he disliked Verkho,' Ifryn went on. 'That he admired his expertise but distrusted his motives. I share some of his misgivings. Kerrell was too discreet to say so, but I suspect you feel the same way.'

Baylin bowed his head in mute acceptance.

'What if Verkho was not satisfied with his power as Chancellor but wanted to rule the army too – as he is apparently doing now?' Ifryn continued, feeling almost light-headed as the conspiratorial words flowed, giving her a sense of release that she had not known for days.

'Such accusations would require solid proof, my lady,' the traveller told her soberly. 'Do you have any?'

'Nothing but my fear,' she replied. 'But if it *were* true, there would be only one thing left for Verkho to achieve.'

They sat in silence for a time. Both knew what that step would be. It would be treachery on an unprecedented scale – but as yet it was only a theory.

'What do you want me to do?' Baylin asked eventually. 'I am hardly qualified—'

'If we can't find Kerrell,' Ifryn interrupted, 'perhaps you can find someone else who *can* help us.'

'Who?'

'The Swordsman.'

'But he's the one most people assume tried to kill you!' Once again Ifryn had succeeded in surprising him.

'Exactly,' she responded. 'If he is indeed my enemy, then finding him will be a great service to the Empire – and to me. If he is not, then it seems probable that Verkho is.'

'And the Swordsman is the sworn enemy of the Chancellor,' Baylin added, realization dawning.

Ifryn nodded.

'He might prove to be an ingenious ally,' she remarked.

Baylin stood up, preparing to leave.

'He'll not be easy to find, my lady,' he said. 'But I'll die trying if needs be.'

'I trust that won't be necessary,' she said with a grateful smile.

'I'll send word through your maid,' the traveller concluded. 'I saw the sword burning in The Spires. Perhaps it was a sign that now he *wants* to be found.'

Darkness turned The Spires into a landscape of nightmare. Moonlight animated the gargoyles and other statuary, and made stone curves appear more sinuous, almost alive. Sawtooth-edged pinnacles, battlemented towers and outlandish turrets competed with each other to reach for the distant stars, while lower down, the contorted maze of pathways, tunnels and bridges lay sunk in darkness, far from the reflected glimmer of the city which outlined the fantastic skyline. Within this anarchic stone labyrinth there were unguarded cliffs, precipitous bridges spanning man-made chasms, and nonsensical twists, turns and dead ends to confuse even the most observant explorer. And, in places, much of the masonry had been eroded by time and weather and was crumbling dangerously. Yet the Swordsman felt as much at home here as anywhere.

Here he found refuge from the noise and bustle of the city, and his cat-like senses led him past the pitfalls. The space here was shared only with roosting birds and the ever-present flickerings of the colony of bats, who found a thousand caverns and crevices in which to await the passing of the sun. Here too was where he met Alasia. Some sixth sense called him when the time was right, and directed him to her – or her to him, he could never work out which. He rarely missed an opportunity to talk to the only person who frequented the long-abandoned Spires.

91

It was Alasia, unknown to all but a very few, who rang the ancient bells in one of the towers to mark special events. Many legends had grown up concerning these uncanny peals, but Alasia was not concerned with their effect. She knew that she was simply performing a sacred duty.

Most people considered Alasia to be mad and shunned her, unnerved by her strange appearance and eccentric manner. A few knew better and benefited from her natural warmth, her love and her knowledge. Her speech was sometimes archaic, often nonsensical on the surface, but full of unexpected wisdom – to those who were prepared to listen. Physically she appeared drained of all colour, her smooth skin almost translucent, her wispy hair white-blonde and her eyes the palest shade of blue. She was also tiny and painfully thin, like an ill-fed child. People thought she looked like a ghost.

When the Swordsman found her she was, as usual, seated on the edge of one of her spire-top eyries, her stick-like legs dangling over the precipice. Alasia had no fear of heights. Below her the lights of the city spread out like a giant, star-filled canopy, and the air was filled with the darker shadows of the myriad bats as they flitted by. Moonlight made her seem even more insubstantial, as if she could float away, borne on the wind like a swirl of mist.

Alasia smiled as she listened to the stranger's careful approach. She had recognized his footsteps; besides, no one else came here now. She held up her hand, which he took and kissed gently. Few things in Alasia's life pleased her as much as the stranger's courtesy. She folded her hands neatly in her lap again and waited for his questions.

'Are you well?' the Swordsman asked.

'The night is kind to me,' she replied. 'My friends are near. Are your eyes clear?'

'As clear as they can be,' he answered. 'May I ask for your help once again?'

Alasia nodded, still smiling, her eyes faraway.

'Do you remember Sagar Folegandros? You told me where he was.'

'General Adjeman saw him first,' she said.

The Swordsman was momentarily nonplussed. This was indeed a revelation.

'Kerrell was in the dungeons?'

'No. His father,' Alasia corrected him reprovingly.

So that's who the ghost was, he thought. Coulson Adjeman had died many years ago, while his son was still only a boy. Sagar's description made sense now.

'Do you know where Kerrell is?'

'No.'

It was unusual for Alasia to give such an unequivocal answer to such a question. The Swordsman waited for her to qualify her response and eventually she did – in a way.

'There are holes in time,' she said earnestly. 'Even my friends can't see into them. There is no sound.'

'Is he alive?' Martyn asked, hoping for some clarification.

'Which faces do the dice show?' Alasia asked in return. 'The uppermost, or the ones hidden by the table?'

Martyn could make neither head nor tail of what she was saying, and knew better than to pursue the subject. Instead he returned to his original enquiry.

'Sagar is free now,' he told her.

'He always was,' she answered serenely.

'You told him that his brother was coming.'

'The beacon. Yes.'

'What do you mean by the beacon?'

'A fire that shines,' Alasia replied kindly, as though she were talking to a slow child who had just asked a very obvious question.

The Swordsman bit down on his frustration.

'Is that all?' he ventured.

'Is it not enough?' Alasia now sounded incredulous. 'To shine from beneath such a shadow?'

'Does he have a name?'

'There were two of them at first,' she remarked, ignoring his question, 'but they have been separated. They are learning to fly.' Her pale eyes flickered back and forth as she watched the passage of the bats.

Martyn tried a different tack. He already knew that Sagar had two brothers – if indeed that was what Alasia meant.

'When will he arrive?'

'Before the moon turns.'

The Swordsman glanced up at the sky. The moon would be full in four or five days' time. He had some solid information at last!

'You said he was carrying two burdens,' he prompted.

'His loss, and the shadow,' Alasia responded as if this were self-evident.

'What are they?' Martyn persisted without much hope.

'One is a teardrop of power.' Alasia paused, considering her words. 'The other contains the fate of all the world.'

CHAPTER TEN

Wine is curious.

How can it seem so much more than it is? How can it taste of the sun, of the perfume of a summer's day, of the light in lovers' eyes? How can it make lords of lowly men and turn nobles into swine, bring truth to liars' lips and transform honest vows to utter falsehood?

Such alchemy is beyond mere magic. It is as real as blood.

A deep rumble, like distant thunder, echoed around the main chamber of Corton Magna's apartments.

'Sorry,' Grongar muttered, patting his stomach. 'I haven't eaten all day.'

Corton looked at his guest with a pained expression, but said nothing. Everything in the room was a reflection of the wine-master's fastidious personality. The decor was tasteful, the furniture of the best quality without being grandiose, and the elegant crockery and cutlery laid out upon the table were precisely placed. The man himself was thin, with close-cropped grey hair, and was impeccably but soberly dressed. A life-long citizen of Xantium, he was unmarried and indeed seemed to have no interest in romance. His work was his passion, and he considered little else to be of much consequence. The art of wordsmiths, painters and musicians pleased him in a peripheral way, and he appreciated good food because it gave him the pleasure of matching it to his wines.

Corton and Grongar were opposites, both aesthetically and temperamentally, and it was a constant source of wonder to their acquaintances – and perhaps to the two men themselves – that they remained such firm friends, apparently united only by a shared enthusiasm for the board game known as labyrinth. Yet even in that the pair were quite different. Corton analysed each position in the complex battle for some time, and made only slow, considered choices. Grongar, on the other hand, played impulsively, relying on instinct and natural aggression. Corton could never understand why his opponent won as many games as he did.

The barbarian was ill at ease in his friend's home. He had rarely been invited there – their endless series of games were usually played in an out-of-the-way store-room – and he always felt constrained, as if he would break something just by breathing. Grongar's very presence seemed to strike an alien note of untidiness in those elegant surroundings. He was only there now because Corton, against his better judgement, had never quite given up hope that he might introduce the northerner to a few of civilization's finer points.

'Dinner will be ready very soon,' he told Grongar now, and went out to his tiny kitchen.

He had been collecting the ingredients for this meal for some time, and wanted to take his time preparing a dinner that would match the fine wines he had picked. Considerable ingenuity was required to produce food of such quality, because most of the supplies in Xantium had to be imported from some distance and fresh produce was therefore at a premium – but Corton was certain that he had succeeded. On occasions like this he sometimes wished for other, more refined company, but his high-handed reputation and sharp tongue meant that he had few close friends. A vague, wishful sadness washed over him when he considered this, but he had made his life what it was, as he reminded himself, and he was determined to enjoy this occasion to the full.

Pride of place on the table was given to the two wines chosen for this special evening. One, a deep rich red, had been lovingly decanted into a glass jug which sat at the centre of the table, winking seductively in the lamplight. The other was a clear golden colour, still in the bottle which he had removed only recently from the cool, dark cellars, placing it in an earthenware pot to keep it as cold as possible. Grongar had agreed, albeit with evident reluctance, to forgo his usual ale in order to share the wine with his host, and even though Corton knew his companion was unlikely to appreciate its finer qualities, he was glad not to be drinking alone.

Corton returned carrying two plates of meat in a rich savoury sauce, with delicately flavoured rice and other accompaniments. He placed one in front of his guest and then sat down in his own place and reached for the jug. He poured out the wine with great reverence, being careful not to spill a single drop. Pushing a goblet across to Grongar, he picked up his own and raised it to sniff the glorious aroma, his eyes closing in anticipatory pleasure as he ignored the various snuffling noises from the other side of the table. He took a sip, swirled it round his mouth, then swallowed, relishing each sensation – the taste and smell of liquid perfection.

Opening his eyes to see whether Grongar was enjoying the meal, he was flabbergasted to see his friend's plate empty. The barbarian's stomach growled again and he belched, although he tried to stifle it, covering his mouth with one thick-knuckled hand. Dark globules of sauce glistened in his beard. He was just reaching for his goblet when he became aware of Corton staring at him, and hesitated.

'Very good . . .' he declared guiltily. 'Delicious . . . just what I needed.'

'You can't even have tasted it!' Corton declared caustically. 'It could hardly have touched the sides on the way down!'

'I was hungry,' Grongar mumbled defensively.

'Evidently.' The wine-master's first reaction had been an involuntary spasm of anger, but this was rapidly quelled. Expecting the barbarian to change his ways was hoping for too much. Corton smiled; he knew that *he* was going to enjoy this meal! 'I'm glad you liked it,' he said indulgently.

Grongar relaxed.

'Any more?' he asked hopefully.

'No.' It was all Corton could do to keep from laughing now. 'I trust you won't mind waiting for the next course while *I* eat?'

Grongar nodded, encouraged by the prospect of more food.

'Try the wine,' his host suggested. 'But please, not in one gulp. It should be sipped and savoured.'

The northerner did his best to do as he was told, although his 'sip' emptied a third of the goblet. A few moments later, he grinned.

'Not bad,' he pronounced. 'Better than the usual stuff. Got a bit of body, this.'

Corton was delighted. This was a breakthrough!

'There's hope for you yet,' he said. 'I'm glad, because today is special . . .'

But his friend's evident pleasure had inspired Grongar. He swirled the wine beneath his slab of a nose, inhaling deeply as he had seen Corton do, then sipped again.

'Ah!' he intoned gushingly. 'Body without flab, cloaked in dark veils of spice, damsons and brambles perhaps.' He paused theatrically. 'A very well dressed wine, in fact. Fully clothed. Yes.' He drank again.

'Don't push your luck,' Corton advised him, laughing. '"I like it" would have been quite sufficient.' He would not have tolerated such sacrilegious mimicry from anyone else.

'I like it,' Grongar said, solemnly obedient.

Corton poured out more, feeling cheerful and mellow.

Some time later, the meal over and most of the wine gone, the two men lounged contentedly in well-padded chairs. The white wine had proved less to Grongar's liking than the red – though he had drunk a little to please his friend – and he now had a tankard of beer in front of him. Corton poured the last of the wine into his own goblet and looked regretfully at the empty bottle. He had drunk more this night than he had for some time, and he was feeling warm, light-headed and comfortably full.

'Today . . .' he began.

'. . . is special,' Grongar completed for him. 'Why?'

'Today is special,' Corton repeated, having to concentrate on his words, 'because today is my fortieth name-day.'

The barbarian's hairy face split into a wide grin.

'I salute your forty years!' he cried, raising his mug. 'Here's to the next forty!' He drank deeply and noisily before adding, 'I never realized I was taking advantage of a man old enough to be my father.'

'Lying toad!' Corton exclaimed. Grongar's age was a mystery – even to the man himself – but Corton doubted if his friend was much younger than himself. 'How is it you're such a very *gnarled* youngster?'

'We barbarians grow up fast,' his guest replied sententiously. 'We have to. Wait!' He pushed himself to his feet and set off unsteadily towards the door.

'Where are you going?'

'Back soon,' Grongar mumbled, and was gone.

He returned a short time later carrying an object wrapped in a piece of cloth.

'It's for you,' he said, handing it over.

'A gift?'

'Yes. Happy name-day.'

Corton was rendered temporarily speechless.

'I've been meaning to give it to you for some time,' Grongar added, 'but I was obviously waiting for today.'

Corton unwrapped the cloth carefully. Inside was a wooden carving of a length of vine. The exquisite detail of the leaves and grapes made the piece seem almost lifelike, and the pale, even-grained wood felt smooth and cool to the wine-master's long fingers. He was enchanted.

'Thank you,' he said, his voice filled with emotion. 'It's beautiful. Where did you get it?'

'I made it,' Grongar replied.

'You carved this yourself?'

'Yes.'

Corton looked at his friend with new eyes. So there *was* a soul under that brutish exterior. The carving had been done with skill and an eye for detail, but also with an ill-defined quality that he could only call love. The wine-master was almost moved to tears but blinked them away, feeling foolish.

'I shall treasure it always,' he said.

Grongar sank back into his chair, looking pleased.

They talked long into the night, and inevitably – although they managed to avoid the subject for some time – they discussed the affairs of Xantium. Eight days had passed since the alleged poisoning attempt at the imperial banquet, and still no one had thought to question Corton about the supposedly tainted wine. He was beginning to agree with Grongar that, with so much else going on – plots and counter-plots, rumours within rumours – no one was going to bother with him. Kerrell's disappearance was only one of several peculiar occurrences in a pattern of intrigue. In their drunken state, the latest gossip seemed fascinating to the two friends – even if they found much of it laughable.

'Ridiculous,' Corton exclaimed at one point, reacting to a more than usually absurd piece of speculation. 'Why do people invent such nonsense?'

Grongar belched solemnly.

'Wouldn't be like this if Xantium was in th'north,' he stated. 'Too cold up there t'produce all this fevered imagination.'

'Pining for the simple life among the swineherds?' Corton teased.

Something about the question reminded Grongar of

an earlier conversation, but in his slightly befuddled state, he could not remember exactly what.

'I'll wager th'Swordsman's a northerner,' he claimed.

'What makes you think that?'

'A certain style, a flair,' the barbarian replied. 'None of your lot have it.'

'Only flare he has is the one he lit in The Spires,' Corton said, then laughed immoderately at his own feeble joke.

'Ah, but that was only a ruse,' Grongar said triumphantly. 'To disguise his real intent.'

'Which was what?'

'Haven't you heard? Three dungeon guards were killed that night. The official story is that they quarrelled among themselves, but who's going t'believe that?' Grongar's derisive tone fell away as he leaned forward and whispered confidentially, 'I hear Verkho had one of the hostages shut up in there, and someone helped him escape. Who else would have done it but the Swordsman?'

'That man is dangerous,' Corton decided. 'It's madness to provoke Verkho.'

Grongar nodded wisely, then grew suddenly still.

'Folly!' he exclaimed, then laughed.

'What?' Corton was puzzled by his friend's apparent lack of sense.

Grongar's mind had made one of those inexplicable, intuitive leaps which served him so well on the labyrinth board. He smiled, remembering the chance meeting of the previous evening.

'I know who the Swordsman is,' he said.

CHAPTER ELEVEN

The mind can be fooled into seeing movement where none exists. Fate does not have the finite odds of dice or cards. Who can weigh augury on the scales of men? Or measure the future with an iron rod? Only gods or fools gamble with prophecy.

I feel the whole world folding in upon itself, but I see no movement.

'Have you lost your nerve, brother?'

Clavia Bhazak had gained access to Verkho's study and was intent upon a confrontation. He had been ignoring her of late – and the Chancellor's half-sister demanded better than that.

'What happened to your schemes to poison Azari?' she went on acidly. 'To take the imperial throne for yourself? All forgotten? Well, you'd better think again, brother *dear*, because my ambitions are not satisfied, even if yours are!'

The Chancellor looked up from his desk.

'All things are still possible,' he said mildly. 'I have had other things on my mind, but rest assured, our plans are not forgotten.'

'Other things?' she exclaimed in angry disbelief. 'What other things?'

'Just the small matter of an empire to run,' he replied calmly.

'So you can't manage without Kerrell?' Clavia said spitefully. 'Perhaps I should release him then, perhaps you *do* need him.'

'I wouldn't advise it,' Verkho said coldly.

'Then give me what I want!' she shot back. 'What was the point of making him disappear if you're not going to *do* anything?' Her green eyes flashed as she tossed her faded mane of red hair. Clavia had been truly beautiful once, but long years of scheming and discontent had lined her face, and her willowy figure no longer held all men in thrall. 'I won't wait much longer,' she snapped.

'Do you think to threaten me?' Verkho asked quietly, becoming very still.

Clavia did not heed the warning signs. Her relationship with her half-brother had always been tempestuous. Although she had, on occasion, been of considerable use to Verkho during his various political manoeuvrings, he had always held the upper hand in their partnership of intrigue – whether Clavia knew it or not.

'Southan would not take kindly to the fact that his Chancellor has abducted his senior general,' she pointed out. 'You forget that I know where Kerrell is.' She had in fact been the lure that had led Kerrell into Verkho's trap.

Her half-brother smiled contemptuously.

'I don't think you do,' he told her. 'In a sense even *I* do not know where he is, for he is nowhere – in this world at least. It's been one of the more obvious successes of my research programme, one even you can appreciate. I tell you this in all honesty, sister. You would be risking your own life even in trying to find him now, let alone releasing him. And Southan is unlikely to believe your deranged story without proof.' Verkho's smile never faltered as he spoke, but his glittering eyes were venomously cold. He was thinking that, for all the undoubted use she had been in the past, Clavia was so bitter now that her usefulness must be coming to an end. 'As for your ambitions,' he went on patronizingly, 'have patience. I am on the brink of discovering so much – discovering things that will help us. Would you rule an empire in ruins? What are a few more days to us?'

Clavia did her best to look disgusted and unconvinced, but her resentment had run its course for the moment – and she had recognized Verkho's mood.

'Aren't you putting too much store in this talisman?' she asked, subdued now.

'That is only one string to my bow,' he replied evenly. 'But even if it were the only one, haven't you understood *anything* I've told you? You yourself have seen me summon spirits of the dead using objects they owned in this life. Well, the talisman was once the treasure of a god. A god! One of the old pantheon. Does this mean nothing to you?'

'How do you know the pantheon still exists?' Clavia tried to sound dismissive, but she had been shaken by the conviction in her brother's voice. 'I haven't seen them around much lately.'

'Gods, by their very nature, are immortal,' he answered. 'You won't be so flippant in two or three days' time.'

'So soon?' The whole enterprise made Clavia very nervous. Ghosts were one thing, gods were another – and in her opinion, Verkho's obsession had made his judgement unreliable. 'If such power exists, how do you know that you can control it?'

'Oh, it exists all right,' he replied confidently. 'Control, as you so rightly point out, will be the key. I am aware that I will have to proceed carefully, but I have no doubt that I shall succeed. My experience in such matters is already greater than that of any man who has ever lived.' There was fire in his eyes now. The degree of madness that lay just beneath the surface had always been an important part of Verkho's overpowering character, and his obvious excitement was now edged with fanatic intensity. 'Here in Xantium we already have the greatest gathering of talents the world has ever known,' he went on fervently. 'Telepaths, those who "see" other worlds and who may eventually be able to talk freely with ghosts. We have other conduits of

104

power, able to project images of the past through the resonant memories of objects. Healers and their counterparts, who can maim or kill by mere touch; men and women who can smash things from the other side of a room or make kindling burst into flame with a single glance. The list is endless, and we are learning more every day. When such realms of knowledge are fully understood, there can be no limitations set to our achievements. With such power I can ensure that the Empire lasts for ever.'

'For ever?' Despite herself, Clavia had been swayed by Verkho's passion.

'For ever,' he repeated, calm again now, smiling as he saw his half-sister adjusting to these new ideas. 'And if we have the resources of a god,' he added, 'who's to say we may not live to see it all?'

'Immortality?' Clavia whispered, her eyes wide.

'The ultimate prize,' Verkho said, nodding. 'Isn't that worth gambling for?'

Captain Ofiah ordered his men to dismount, then watched as they dragged their unresisting prisoner, Bowen Folegandros, from his horse. They had reached the way-station at the southern edge of the Deadlands by mid-afternoon, but knew better than to start across immediately. The barren landscape ahead held nothing but dry, red earth and the seemingly endless heat and dust of summer. Nothing grew in this man-made desert; there were no habitations, the last homes having long since fallen into ruin, bleached skeletons of wood and stone in the vast desolation. With luck, if they set out at first light the next morning, they would only have to spend one night camped out in the parched and deadly wilderness – and that was something Ofiah and his soldiers would accept gladly, knowing that the comforts of Xantium were now so close at hand. It also meant they would all be able to rest and eat well before the last stage of their journey.

They had ridden hard since leaving Brighthaven, where the prisoner had come ashore eight days ago. With Chancellor Verkho's personal warrant ensuring fresh horses and speedy service at all imperial way-stations along the road, they had made excellent time. Their lunatic prisoner had – to their surprise – hardly slowed them down at all, proving to be an excellent if eccentric horseman. However, his occasional fits of madness had unnerved them, and even Ofiah, who was more tolerant than most of his men, would be glad to be relieved of his charge. He would also be glad to get rid of his other cargo, a sealed casket big enough to contain a man's head, which was destined for Verkho himself. The importance of both prisoner and casket had been stressed to Ofiah in no uncertain terms, and the dual responsibility weighed heavily. He carried a key to the box, but had kept his natural curiosity on a short rein. There was no way he could open it without the broken seal betraying his actions, and the Captain was certainly not foolish enough to give Verkho any reason for displeasure. Whatever the casket contained, Ofiah was happy for it to remain the Chancellor's secret.

Bowen accepted the unusually early end to the day's travel with uncaring quietness, his eyes dull and listless as he allowed himself to be led to a secure cell for the night. His mind, as always, was elsewhere.

When Farrag had disrupted his long anticipated marriage to Gaye, something had snapped inside Bowen. Since that Midsummer's Day he had lived in a nightmare world of guilt, rage and misery. His memory showed him endless pictures of his love falling, over and over again, as he was dragged away, protesting help-lessly. These visions were the closest thing Bowen had to sanity. At other times he retreated from the world entirely, but when the violent emotions took hold, he screamed and shouted and had to be physically re-strained. He lost consciousness on many occasions. His erratic mixture of mute subservience and incoherent raving had unnerved first the sailors and now the soldiers who formed his escorts from Zalys. Only Ofiah felt the slightest pity towards the young man, and even that was tempered by his necessary professional distance.

Once the prisoner was installed in his locked cell, the Captain came to check on him, carrying the heavy casket – which he never let out of his sight – in a bag slung over one shoulder. Peering through the bars in the door, he saw Bowen curled up, unmoving, in one corner of the bare chamber. Ofiah was about to leave when the islander glanced up, and his usual impassive expression was replaced by a terrible, manic alertness – as if he saw every detail of the world about him with absolute clarity. It was at moments like this that Bowen was at his most dangerous – not least to himself – but there was nothing in the cell which could be used as a weapon.

'You're wrapped in a shroud, did you know that?' the prisoner said, unexpectedly coherent.

'What do you mean?'

'A winding sheet. Grey. Can't you feel it?' Bowen's gaze seemed to rest on the bag, which was made of soft brown leather. 'Why aren't you frightened?'

'Frightened of what?' the Captain asked.

'The greyness.'

Ofiah was about to turn away, deciding that the captive's mind was wandering again, when Bowen spoke again.

'I dreamt of Gaye,' he said, his fear replaced by sorrow. 'I was flying with her and the sentinels. But I'm still here. Is that fair?'

'Nothing much in this life is fair,' the Captain remarked.

'Why can't you take me back to her?' There was childlike innocence and hurt in Bowen's eyes now.

Ofiah laughed uneasily.

'Because I have to take you, and this . . .' He shrugged the shoulder under the bag. '. . . to Xantium. It'd be more than my life's worth to disobey.'

Bowen moved then, faster than Ofiah would have believed possible. He sprang to his feet and hurled himself at the door, one arm thrusting through the bars as his body smashed into the wood and iron. The Captain staggered back just in time to avoid his grasp. As it was he almost dropped the casket, and had to steady himself on the far wall of the corridor.

'We'll all die if you take the shroud to Xantium,' Bowen hissed, withdrawing his arm, ignoring the blood running from cuts on his forehead and elbow. Then he screamed and clamped both hands to his ears, his eyes screwed shut in a grimace of pain. 'We'll all die!'

Ofiah retreated, shaken, and more relieved than ever that this ordeal would soon be over. As he went, he could not help wondering exactly what it was in the casket that was frightening Bowen so.

For his part, the islander returned to the corner of his cell and curled up as small as possible, whimpering quietly. The terrible looming presence that haunted even his waking hours receded a little, but it was still there, a pall upon the world.

'For the gravestones in the sky,' he whispered. Then his mind returned to the endless memory of Gaye falling, falling, falling . . .

Verkho was in a state of agitation for a long time after Clavia's visit. He paced his study restlessly, pulling books down from the shelves then replacing them unread, his mind in a ferment. He had been aware of the legends about the talisman, an ancient relic from a more elemental age, for many years, and he could hardly believe that it would soon be in his hands. Its reputed potential was unlimited. When the news of his investigations had finally borne fruit, and the discovery of a strange object had been reported, all of his instincts had told him that this was indeed what he had been searching for. Verkho had then taken steps to ensure that it came to Xantium.

The merchant who had made the mistake of trying to sell it to the highest bidder had served his purpose, and was now dead. So was the naval Information Officer who had identified the talisman on Zalys and brought it to the mainland. Verkho had had them both killed; he wanted this treasure all to himself.

Why then had he confided in Clavia? She could be trusted – self-interest if nothing else would see to that – but it had been an unnecessary risk. Her current dissatisfaction might make her a little less reliable, but she would still have her uses. Perhaps he should make contingency plans for her. None of which answered his original question. Perhaps he had told her because his own excitement was too great to contain, the secret too big. Verkho rarely felt the need to boast – his power and achievements spoke for themselves – but when he had first shown Clavia how he could summon ghosts at will, the temptation to reveal his next great project had been irresistible. It may have been a mistake, but it was one he could not regret. The look on her face had been priceless, and the Chancellor laughed at the memory. Then he grew quiet, and went to sit at his desk again, his face serious. Clavia had been right about one thing; there was plenty of work to do before the talisman arrived. He rang a bell to summon one of his servants.

'Bring Harios Kedhara here,' he instructed. 'Now.'

As the man hurried away to do his bidding, Verkho considered his last meeting with Harios. Intelligent and ambitious, the ministry official was in charge of the section dealing with ghosts and possible communication with them. Many people considered these efforts pointless, but the Chancellor disagreed. On that previous occasion, Harios had been anxious about two problems – the tenfold increase in the number of ghosts appearing in the city, and the disquieting and even violent dreams that were afflicting his talents. Verkho was eager to see how matters had developed over the last few days.

Harios came in, as usual carrying a sheaf of notes and reports. He was nothing if not thorough.

'What progress?' the Chancellor asked without preamble.

'The level of spectral appearances has stabilized,' the official reported, 'but it's still very high, and there's no indication as to what has caused the increase. I'm continuing to monitor, of course.'

'Did you test any of the talents to the point of possible overload?' Verkho had asked for this to be done at their last meeting.

'Of course, Chancellor,' Harios answered. 'It was as I feared. Prolonged exposure does have harmful effects, but we're learning all the time. Here's my report.' He placed a folder on the desk.

'Briefly?' Verkho prompted.

'I chose four talents of varying abilities,' the other replied, 'and forced them into almost continuous contact. The results were remarkable. The level of communication was higher than anything achieved before, in both directions, but little of it made any sense. Transcriptions are in my report.'

'I'll study them later,' the Chancellor said. 'What are the side effects?'

'One of the talents is dead,' Harios reported unemotionally. 'Sudden massive internal bleeding in his head. Messy business.' His expression displayed obvious distaste as he remembered the blood running from the talent's ears and nostrils. 'The physicians couldn't save him, but they're investigating the cause of death now. He was the most sensitive of the four, so perhaps he could have been expected to react most violently. However, another – the least talented – is now in a deep coma. None of the healers seem able to help her, and I believe she'll die soon. I was wondering if you'd look at her – if you have the time . . .'

'Perhaps,' Verkho said noncommittally. 'The other two?'

'They're showing signs of considerable stress, both mental and physical,' Harios told him, 'but they're continuing to work. They're highly strung at the best of times, but all the talents have been disturbed recently, as you know.'

'The nightmares are continuing?'

'Yes. If anything they're growing even worse. And it's affecting all of them, not just those in my section. I've collated the findings from all departments as you requested,' Harios went on, placing another report on the desk, 'though I'm afraid we're still no nearer finding the cause.'

'But the common factor remains the same?'

'Yes. There are a variety of descriptions, some of them particularly vivid.'

'Such as?'

'A vast grey blanket,' Harios quoted. 'A sea of smoke; a leaden cloud that fills the sky; a gigantic shroud; a thundercloud with wings . . .'

'Almost poetic,' Verkho mused. 'Is it still getting closer?'

'That's the general impression, yes,' the official replied. 'And they're still very afraid of it.'

Verkho nodded. Only he was in a position to connect this phenomenon with the approach of the talisman, and – if indeed that was the cause – it confirmed the vast power of the artefact. The only mystery was that *he* could not feel it coming nearer. The Chancellor had talents of his own, after all. Then he realized that perhaps he did feel it. Excitement and impulsiveness were as much an emotional reaction as fear – the only difference was knowledge.

'As usual, Harios, you've been more than thorough,' Verkho said. 'Do not doubt that such service will be rewarded.'

The official smiled in satisfaction, inclining his head in acceptance of his master's praise.

'May I ask when the new talent from Zalys is

expected?' he asked. 'I am anxious to include him in my investigations.'

'Three days, maybe less,' the Chancellor replied. 'I will inform you as soon as he arrives. Ask the Focus to come in as you leave.'

'Of course, Chancellor.'

Verkho watched the man go, then glanced through the closely written reports. He would scrutinize them later. The Focus came in and waited silently for instructions, her face expressionless.

'What's the latest from Zalys?'

'Still no contact, Chancellor,' she reported. 'At least one Far-speaker there is still alive – we sensed him only in the last hour or so. But he is not responding to us. In fact, we're not even sure that he is consciously receiving any of our messages.'

Verkho thought about this. Did it mean that part of the imperial garrison was still holding out? Or had the last Far-speaker – assuming the rest to be dead – been captured by the rebels? Why was he not responding? And was Farrag still alive? There was no way of knowing. He would have to wait for Barvick's report.

'Keep trying,' he ordered. 'Let me know of any progress.' As the Focus nodded, he went on, 'What's the latest position of the fleet?'

'Sunflower reports that all is well, but the weather is unfavourable for good progress. They estimate landfall on Zalys in about four days.'

'You may go.'

Alone once more, Verkho turned to other matters. It had been some time since he had thought of the Swordsman. After his initial spasms of anger at the burning sword and at Sagar's escape, the Chancellor had taken steps to intensify the hunt for his old adversary. Since then, however, he had virtually forgotten him. In Verkho's mind, the Swordsman had always been an agitator, a trouble-maker who provided entertainment and useful exercise for the Chancellor's intelligence

112

gathering network. That he had evaded them for so long added spice to the game, but compared to other developments he was no more than an annoying but elusive insect, buzzing round the city. In due course, Verkho would swat him out of existence. He made a mental note to quiz his senior officers about the progress of the search, then turned to more interesting matters.

From a drawer in his desk, he took out a box containing a dusty and fragile piece of embroidered cloth. It was a badge of office from an imperial military uniform, the red and gold threads of a general still clearly visible.

'Well now,' Verkho said aloud, eyeing this recently acquired relic. 'As Kerrell is temporarily unavailable, perhaps I should see what his father has to say.'

CHAPTER TWELVE

Dark fire, white fire.
  Either flame can scorch a butterfly's wings.

Ifryn had not heard from Baylin in two days. She was no
nearer finding Kerrell and her hopes were fading, so
when Alasia came to visit, in the middle of another warm
and sultry evening, the Empress was more than usually
glad to see her. The tiny woman arrived in the bedchamber silently and unannounced as usual. She was the
only one who seemed able to escape Doneta's vigilance.

Alasia curtseyed to the Empress – a habit Ifryn had
been unable to break her of – and they exchanged
greetings. Ifryn smiled, enjoying the warmth her pale
friend brought with her, and unhappily aware that she
had smiled very little over the last few days. She
enquired about Kerrell without much hope, but Alasia
could tell her nothing and so the Empress tried a
different approach.

'Do you know where the Swordsman is?' she asked.

'He visits me,' Alasia replied. 'He's very polite,' she
added approvingly.

Ifryn's hopes leapt.

'You know him? What's his real name?'

'Real?' Alasia seemed to consider this, as if the term
meant nothing. 'In another life he was known as
Guyland Brak.'

Ifryn did not recognize the name but she stored it
away in her memory, elated by this small, unexpected
success.

'Where can I find him?' she asked quickly.

'He is a butterfly,' her friend replied. 'Who can tell where he flies?'

'But where does he live?'

'In the air,' Alasia stated firmly.

'But he comes to visit you?' Ifryn tried desperately.

'Yes.'

'Where?'

'Where I sit in the wind above.'

'In The Spires?' the Empress guessed.

Alasia said nothing, her pale eyes darting about the room.

'Could I come with you when he next visits?' Ifryn asked. 'I'd like to meet him.'

She began to have qualms as soon as the words were spoken. Did she dare follow Alasia into The Spires? If the Swordsman really was her enemy, what better place was there for murder? But surely Alasia would not be friends with her enemy? She decided to talk to Baylin about it, then realized that he would want to take her place, and that would be a breach of her trust with Alasia. Also, it might be wiser not to risk a confrontation between the two men in such a strange and isolated place. No, she would have to do it herself.

'My friends will watch for him,' her visitor agreed. Ifryn knew that this was as much of a guarantee as she was going to get.

At least now I know his name, she thought, glad to have solid information to pass on to Baylin.

'He will be afraid of you,' Alasia added unexpectedly. 'And I do not know when he will come.'

Afraid of me? It seemed that it ought to be the other way round, but Ifryn supposed that Alasia meant he would be afraid of what she represented, afraid of being exposed to imperial eyes. She was about to ask more when something happened to distract her.

A faint flickering of light formed and grew in a corner of the room. A ghost took shape but seemed to waver, like a reflection in water. Ifryn felt her heart stop beating at the sight of Kerrell's spectral face. *Gods!* she wailed silently. *He's dead.* But then she saw the agony on his face, his lips moving as if he were gasping out secrets, and her distress redoubled. It was too much for her to bear, and she was on the point of fainting when she found her hand enclosed by Alasia's slim fingers, and felt strands of reassurance grow within her. She glanced at her companion but Alasia was staring at the ghost, her small face set in a determined expression.

'This will not be,' she said, apparently addressing the phantom. 'Not all fire is dark, Coulson.'

Coulson? Ifryn's eyes turned back to the ghost. *Coulson?* That had been the name of Kerrell's father, who had also once been commander of the imperial army, a man who had died even before she came to Xantium. Studying the spectre's contorted face once more, she saw the undoubted family resemblance – but saw the tell-tale differences too. He had a scar on his face that Kerrell did not bear. The hair was wrong, not tied back like Kerrell's, and the uniform looked old-fashioned. Ifryn's heart started beating again.

'What's happening?' It was clear, even in her relief that it was not Kerrell, that something was very wrong. Alasia had become rigid, her hand gripping Ifryn's tightly. She did not reply, and beads of perspiration began to form on her neck and cheekbones. Her concentration seemed fierce and the Empress did not like to speak again.

The ghost vanished suddenly, reappeared in the next instant, then vanished again. This went on for some time, the image flickering in and out of existence so fast that Ifryn began to feel dizzy. In all that time, Coulson seemed to be in the grip of some fearful agony, as if a battle was being fought within his being.

A tug of war, Ifryn realized. *Who's at the other end?*

At last, after what seemed like an age, the ghost remained in her room. The battle was over and he could now been seen more clearly than ever before, as though his image had just come into focus. He smiled, and his lips formed silent words even Ifryn could understand. *Thank you.* Then he turned and very deliberately walked through the wall of the chamber, vanishing from sight.

Ifryn was stunned, unable to comprehend what she had just witnessed. Alasia's hand had slipped from her own. She had fainted clean away, her frail body covered with a thin veil of sweat.

'Doneta!' the Empress called. 'Come quickly!'

There was no response, and Ifryn was in desperate need of help. Making Alasia as comfortable as she could, she ran into the outer chamber, but a hasty search revealed no sign of the maid. *Where is she?*

Ifryn ran back to the bedchamber. Alasia was nowhere to be seen.

Verkho stared at the last of the flames which were even now scarring the wood of his desktop. He felt a mixture of consternation, anger and a tiny sliver of fear. What had gone wrong? He had felt resistance right from the start. Coulson's ensnarement had been easy enough, inevitably drawn by his old badge of office. Yet his spirit had been able to draw on unknown strengths, forces Verkho had not encountered before, and the struggle had developed into a battle of wills. The ghost had flickered in and out of the study, as the Chancellor grew hot with exertion. At the last, Verkho had felt a burning sensation in the hand that held the embroidered cloth, and he had instinctively thrown the badge down on to the desk. A moment later, it had burst into flame with an audible thump, and now all that remained were a few glowing embers among unrecognizable ashes. The ghost had vanished.

The Chancellor glowered at the remains of the badge, his mind already turning to thoughts of revenge. Coulson, he knew, had had an ally. And Verkho had seen her face.

CHAPTER THIRTEEN

What malice can have bred such fury?
   These omens are plain, written in blood. I see them with blind eyes; I hear them in the silence of my dreams. There is no escape. Their screaming echoes still.

A day and a half had passed since Alasia had vanished, and in that time no one – to the best of Ifryn's knowledge – had seen her friend. There was still no news of Kerrell, and this latest disappearance only added to her despair. And so, when Doneta told her that Baylin had called to see her, the Empress could not help but hope for some good news. But when she joined the traveller in the outer chamber, his expression told its own story, dashing her hopes.

'I'm sorry, my lady,' he said. 'It's a dead end. Guyland Brak was a hostage here, but he died three years ago. If Alasia's right, then the Swordsman is a ghost.'

Chancellor Verkho had had no sleep for the last two nights. The failure of his hurriedly instigated but discreet search for Alasia had caused him bitter annoyance, but as he told himself, he was bound to find her sooner or later. She had proved herself to be far more than an insignificant madwoman. Verkho had underestimated her, and was looking forward to their next meeting.

In the meantime, the noonday heat was making the room seem airless. Verkho's patience was wearing thin. When the Focus came in he looked up expectantly, but his assistant was expressionless, giving no hint of whether she brought the only news he was interested in hearing now.

'Well?' he demanded.

'There have been messages from Admiral Barvick's second in command, Chancellor,' the Far-speaker reported. 'It appears that the entire fleet has been destroyed.'

'What!' Verkho sprang to his feet in an instant rage, but the Focus went on calmly.

'The first message passed on a report from the lead vessel, the *Wavecutter*, saying that it was under attack. The second came only moments later, and stated that half the fleet had already capsized and that the *Southern Flame*, the admiral's flagship, was crippled and sinking. It grew incoherent after that, but the essence was that they were being attacked by huge flying fish. Monsters, he called them. It seems that every vessel was smashed or overturned. The last message ended abruptly, and since then we've not been able to contact any of the three Far-speakers with the fleet. We think they're dead.'

Verkho had listened with growing disbelief, and for a few moments was too stunned to react. *Monsters? Flying fish?* This was insane. Yet what reason could the Far-speakers have for making up something like that? They were, by their very nature, incapable of lying, unless compelled to do so by their controller. But Barvick was no hysterical idiot. It made no sense. *The whole fleet destroyed?*

Eventually his fevered brain grew calm, and he dismissed the Focus with instructions to monitor the situation. The scale of the disaster was only just beginning to sink in. Not only did this mean that Zalys would have to go unpunished for the time being – there weren't enough resources in the south to outfit another force – but it would leave the whole of the southern Empire dangerously under strength. Zalys could be recaptured eventually – indeed it would have to be! – but

119

that must wait. It would take all his skill just to direct matters for the next few months and try to avoid a full-scale war.

In the meantime, all he could do was to order a single ship to head for the island, with one trusted man aboard to act as a spy, and a telepath to relay his findings. Perhaps on the way they might even discover some clue to the catastrophe that had befallen Barvick's fleet. It was to Verkho's chagrin that he could do no more than that at present, and he worked busily all afternoon to salvage what he could from the mess. He vowed to himself that his revenge upon Zalys, when it came, would be savage indeed.

And then, as day turned to night, he received news that drove everything else from his mind.

'There's a Captain Ofiah here, Chancellor,' one of his servants reported. 'He insists on seeing you in person, says he has a delivery which must be handed over directly. He won't tell me—'

'Yes. Yes. Send him in!' Verkho interrupted. He rose to his feet, controlling his eagerness with difficulty.

The talisman had arrived.

CHAPTER FOURTEEN

Sweet petals float on sunlit water, white above, pink below. Secrets pass from sky to prism, preserved within the glass. For other mysteries the blossom boils, its essence bursting in the swirling pot. From flame to steam, condensed within the vat.

I could wish the deepest hurts would yield to such remedies. But when a world bleeds, what is there to stop the flow?

'I can tell you secrets,' Iceman whispered, with a sidelong glance at Habella.

'What secrets?' the healer asked calmly. She was intent on her task, smearing tiny drops of various solutions on to the skin of the Far-speaker's arm, and observing the reactions. Iceman was bound to the armrests of his chair and a burly guard stood behind him, watching for any untoward move.

'They've been talking to me,' Iceman confided knowingly.

'Who?' Habella still did not take her eyes from her work, but knew that Dsordas would want her to learn all she could.

'From Xantium!' he replied triumphantly, and waited for her reaction.

'What did they say?' she asked indifferently.

'I won't tell you!' Iceman shouted, his conspiratorial mood turning abruptly to anger. 'Bring the dark one.' He meant Dsordas. 'Make him give me nectar. Then I'll tell!' In his sudden agitation, he struggled against his bonds, but subsided when the guard laid a warning hand on his shoulder.

Habella brushed away the latest droplets and inspected the results. Two small red marks showed on the Far-speaker's pale skin.

'I'm going to give you something else,' she told him. 'Something much better.'

With another instant change of mood, the Far-speaker began to whine piteously.

'Nothing else. Only nectar. Nothing else. I'll die without it!' Then with a look of mad cunning in his eyes, he added, 'I'll die, and then you'll *never* know my secrets.'

Habella almost smiled, thinking that he sounded just like a child. But she kept her face still. The ugly cuts that marred her face were healing well but they were painful, and she would be scarred for life. Even so, she did not regret her actions.

'You won't die,' she told him firmly. 'Dsordas won't let you have nectar, you know that. So why don't you tell me your secrets now?' She did not really believe that he had anything important to say. It was merely his latest tactic, aimed at satisfying his terrible craving. But she could not be sure.

'I hate him!' Iceman hissed. 'When my friends come, they'll kill him.'

'What friends?' Habella kept her voice level, despite her rising interest. If Iceman really knew something about the force coming from Xantium . . .

'Soldiers!' he blurted out, then shut his mouth with a snap. 'I'm not telling,' he added softly.

'Will they be here soon?' she asked casually, rummaging through her supplies of herbs, plants and cordials.

Iceman remained quiet, a small, satisfied smile upon his face. Habella glanced up at the guard to see if he had any advice for her, but he just shrugged. The islanders all knew that Xantium had been alerted to the revolt, and everyone assumed that a vengeful army was now on its way. It was possible that Iceman knew no more than they did – it was believed that he could not function as a telepath without his amberine crystal and the nectar.

The herbalist selected three tiny vials from her casket.

'We'll try these first,' she said, almost to herself, then thrust one under Iceman's nose. 'Smell this,' she instructed.

The Far-speaker, resolutely disobedient, held his breath. Habella merely waited as he turned red and twisted around, trying to get away. Eventually the guard grabbed both his ears and held him still. Iceman howled, exhaling explosively, then gulping air. It was difficult to judge amid the histrionics, but Habella could detect no special reaction to the fumes. She tried another potion. This time he was more cooperative – his ears were still held fast – but again there was no effect. The third, however, produced an instant response. As the scent filled his nostrils, Iceman jerked away instinctively, painfully wrenching his ears free, his face contorting into a grimace of revulsion.

'Mmm. How interesting,' Habella murmured with satisfaction. 'In that case, we can try a whole new sequence, but we'll start with this.'

There was fear in Iceman's expression now.

'I'll die,' he threatened. 'I'll die and then you'll be sorry.'

'No one will waste their time feeling sorry for you,' said a voice from the doorway.

The prisoner scowled and spat feebly as Dsordas came in. Habella wondered how long he had been outside the cell, listening to their exchange.

'Any progress?' he asked.

'Some,' she replied. 'A start, at least. I'm going to try an infusion of rock rose and sweet chestnut.'

'That?' Dsordas held out his hand and she gave him the vial. He was still for a few moments, appearing to weigh it in his palm, then sniffed it cautiously. 'It's not right,' he concluded eventually. 'But it's close.'

Habella regarded him thoughtfully. She was well aware of Dsordas' innate healing talent, but also of the torment it caused him, so she chose her words carefully.

'This whole process would be a lot faster if we worked together.'

Dsordas shook his head.

'I don't know the names of anything,' he said. 'It's only when I touch them that I get a sense of them. Besides, I haven't got the time.' It was a feeble excuse and he knew it.

'You've no idea what might help him then?' the herbalist persisted hopefully.

'No. That stuff might stave off the effects for a few hours, but then he'll be back where he was. You need something that'll have a lasting effect.'

Habella nodded.

'But this is close?'

'Yes.'

'Then you've helped already.' She turned back to her casket in search of new ideas.

'Can I have a few words outside?' Dsordas said. They went into the corridor, and when they were out of earshot, he turned to her. 'I heard the last part of your conversation with that disgusting little . . .' He bit down on his loathing. 'Do you think he really knows anything?'

'Probably not,' Habella replied, 'but who can be sure what goes on inside that mind?' She went on to detail Iceman's claims.

'Is he dangerous?' Dsordas asked abruptly.

'We've been able to control him easily enough,' she answered, 'but he's becoming more desperate. Why?'

'Natali keeps asking to see him. The two of them had some sort of telepathic link when Farrag was controlling them, and I wondered if he might be able to tell us something.' The doubt was clear in his voice.

'It's worth a try,' Habella decided. 'Natali's been through so much recently, but he's come out unscathed. I don't see how this could hurt.'

'And Iceman might be more open with him,' Dsordas added, sounding as though he were trying to convince himself. 'It was Natali who woke him up, after all.'

'Perhaps.' Habella paused, looking into his worried eyes. 'What about Gaye? She seems to have talent in that direction too.'

'She doesn't even want to see him.' Dsordas had already tried that approach. 'She's seen into some of the ugliness nectar causes, and I wouldn't want to force that on anyone.' The depth of his feelings was clear.

Ever since she had taken Natali to see Iceman, Etha had been unable to put the sight of the reawakened Far-speaker from her mind. She had responsibilities enough, the gods knew, but she could not escape the feeling that she should be helping the pale young man somehow. While she was painfully aware of the events of the past, Etha only saw the suffering in his eyes, and decided – if the opportunity ever presented itself – to try and comfort him.

Her instincts were reaffirmed by her youngest son. Natali spoke of Iceman often, referring to him as a friend, and obviously saw nothing evil about him. That might only be childlike innocence – after all, Natali was not yet four – but it seemed significant to Etha. She found herself wondering about the young man's history, his lost family. Where had he come from? How old had he been when the Empire enslaved him? Against all the odds and her better judgement, her maternal instincts had been aroused by the drug-addicted boy.

So when Dsordas and Fen returned home that evening and asked if she would be willing to let Natali visit Iceman, she agreed, on condition that she accompanied her son.

'Does he still have the amberine pendant?' Dsordas asked.

'I have it,' Etha said. The thought of Natali wearing it again made her nervous, but she realized that this would be necessary. 'He still likes to play with it, but he's not possessive about it like he was before.'

'That compulsion died when Farrag did,' Fen said. 'It's just a crystal now.' She was nervous too, but could see that Iceman would be valuable if he could be reliably converted to their side.

'What does Gaye have to say about all this?' Etha asked. 'She'd know if it was safe for Natali.'

'I haven't asked her,' Dsordas admitted. 'I don't think she has a very high opinion of me at the moment,' he added ruefully.

'Nonsense,' Etha said briskly. 'Go and talk to her.'

'I'll go,' Fen volunteered. 'We've not had the chance to speak for a while.' She was glad to be able to take a break from the constant toil, and knew that her sister appreciated being kept up to date with the island's affairs. She left her mother and Dsordas discussing Habella's treatment of Iceman, and climbed the stairs wearily.

'You're tired,' Gaye commented as Fen entered her room. 'You've been working too hard.'

'There's a lot to do.' Fen was constantly amazed by how much her sister could deduce just from the sound of someone's approach. So much suffering would have crushed a lesser spirit, but Gaye had adapted to her new loneliness with a steadfast determination that Fen could only admire. She sat down on the edge of the bed next to her sister's chair, and took Gaye's hand in her own. 'There's so much going on, I've no time to be tired,' she lied, smiling.

'Tell me,' Gaye said eagerly.

Fen obliged, giving her the latest news of the defence preparations and of all she and Dsordas had been doing.

'No sign of the fleet, then?' Gaye asked.

'No. Thank the gods. But we're ready for them now if they come.'

'If?'

'When, I mean.' She, like all the others, had to school

herself to avoid undue optimism. 'There's a lot we don't know about the workings of the Empire, but I can't believe that they'd let us get away with it. What we really need to know is when, where and how many are coming.'

They sat in silence for a few moments. Fen watched her sister's serene face, her blind eyes motionless, her thoughts obviously far away. She had hoped to lead the conversation round to Iceman, but Gaye's mind was elsewhere.

'I wonder where he is now?' she said softly. Since Midsummer's Day she had seen Bowen only in her dreams, and the pain of their separation was deep and fierce.

'He'll be back one day,' Fen replied, more in encouragement and hope than belief.

'He's a hostage for an island no longer in their control,' Gaye went on. 'That makes him very vulnerable.'

Fen could think of no reply. Her sister was right, of course. Bowen and all the earlier hostages were in dire peril, something which had given many on Zalys serious doubts about the uprising.

'But he's still alive,' Gaye added with certainty. 'I'd know if he'd been killed.'

'Have you dreamt of him again?'

'No. I just know. Even now, when he's far away.'

'Like a Far-speaker?' Fen probed delicately.

'Not like that,' Gaye replied with a shudder. 'They're vile.'

'Surely that's because of the nectar, not the Far-speakers themselves?' Fen added gently.

'With the Empire, the two things are indistinguishable.'

'Habella's trying to treat Iceman,' Fen told her. 'Wean him away from his addiction.'

'He'll die first,' Gaye responded fervently.

'Habella doesn't think so,' her sister countered. 'And

127

if he *does* have telepathic abilities that don't depend on venom, just think how valuable he could be to us! He might even be able to get news of Bowen.' Fen felt cruel to raise her sister's hopes, even with this wild surmise, but she had to try.

Gaye was quiet, taken aback.

'Natali's going to see him tomorrow,' Fen persisted. 'To see if he can tell what's happening in Iceman's mind.'

'No!' Gaye's face registered shock and outrage. 'Hasn't Natali been through enough? How can you be so cruel?'

'Natali says that Iceman is his friend.' Fen was hurt by her sister's words, but remained resolute. 'And we'll make sure no harm comes to him.'

'How?' her sister demanded angrily. 'Can you see what's going on in his mind?'

'Can you?' Fen asked softly.

Gaye's face went rigid, then she turned sightless eyes upon her sister accusingly.

'You're doing this on purpose, aren't you?' She sounded bitter. 'Did Dsordas tell you to?'

'No!' Fen exclaimed, but in her heart she knew what her intention had been all along. Perhaps some of Dsordas's ruthlessness had rubbed off on her. It was not a comfortable thought, and she was momentarily glad that her sister could not see her face. 'I'm sorry,' she began hesitantly. 'I only meant . . . And it was my idea, not his.'

Gaye heard the sorrow in Fen's voice, and her anger melted.

'You're only doing what you believe is right,' she said gently. After a pause, she added, 'Will Natali be wearing an amberine pendant?'

'Yes.'

'Then so will I,' Gaye declared. 'Natali and I worked as a team before. We can again.'

128

CHAPTER FIFTEEN

*One dark blaze burns less coldly now. I see streaks of
yellow within the void; the diseased flames of ice crack,
releasing the heat within.*

*They still shout, hurting my ears, but he will soon be
deaf to them. To hear, you must want to listen. Unless,
like me, you have no choice. Will I ever know silence?*

Gaye made her way downstairs to the kitchen the next
morning, refusing all offers of help. The voices of her
family greeted her arrival, and someone pulled back an
empty chair on the stone floor so that she would be
guided to it by the noise. She sat, feeling tension in the
air.

'You don't have to do this, Gaye.' It was Anto who
spoke. He was only seventeen but sounded very grown
up, obviously conscious of his nominal position as head
of the household.

'I know,' she replied. 'But I've made up my mind. It's
something I have to face up to sooner or later.'

'Guess what!' Natali piped up, his bright tone contrasting with the sombre atmosphere.

'What, little one?' Gaye asked, knowing that he was
looking at her.

'I've got my pretty stone back,' he told her proudly.

'That's nice.'

'And then, guess what? We're going to see my friend.
The one I woke up.'

'I know,' Gaye said, smiling at his cheerful enthusiasm. 'I'm coming with you.'

'Do you want any breakfast?' Etha asked her.

'No. I'm not hungry.'

'We're ready then,' her mother said. 'As soon as Natali finishes.'

The little boy had proved to be the only one with any appetite that morning. Gaye began to feel a little more confident and wondered briefly if this was due to her young brother, who was already wearing his pendant. Could his mood be transferring itself to her?

'Where's the other stone?' she asked.

'I have it,' Fen answered. 'Let me know when you want it.'

They left a short time later, Gaye with her arm through Fen's, Natali riding gleefully on Dsordas' shoulders and Etha following, carrying a basket containing her own preparations for the encounter. Anto remained at home, somewhat resentfully taking charge of the other two children.

They took the family's largest boat and rowed to the landing stages by Fournoi Square. From there they crossed the open space to the weatherbeaten building which had once been the headquarters of the imperial garrison and which now housed many new work-places for those who had taken on the task of the island's administration. Here too were the cells where the Far-speakers had been kept. Foran and Habella, their faces solemn, were there to greet Etha and her family with the news that the last three Far-speakers had all died during the night, almost it seemed by mutual agreement. Iceman was now their last hope.

'Do you want to go in with Natali?' Fen asked.

'No,' Gaye replied quietly. 'I'll stay in the corridor. I don't want him to see me.'

'How's the treatment going, Habella?' Dsordas asked.

The herbalist shrugged.

'It's too early to tell,' she said. 'We had a lot of trouble getting him to swallow anything last night, but we managed eventually. He's very quiet this morning.'

'What did you give him?'

'This.' Habella placed a small bottle in his hand and looked at him expectantly. 'Well?'

'I'm not sure,' he muttered. 'What is it?'

'Aspen and yellowbane.'

'But that's poison, isn't it?' Etha exclaimed.

'Not in the right form and the right quantity,' Habella reassured her. 'And it may allow his body to adjust to the lack of nectar.'

By now they were nearing the cell.

'It's probably best if just Natali and I go in at first,' Foran said. 'Too many of us might interfere—'

'I'm coming too!' Etha interrupted firmly. No one argued with her.

'He's awake!' Natali exclaimed suddenly and ran forward. Etha and Foran hurried after him, but they need not have worried. The cell door was securely locked and a guard stood outside.

'What's that mean?' Natali cried, coming to an abrupt halt and looking puzzled.

'What does what mean, sweetheart?' Etha asked quickly.

'Someone else is talking. She's angry.'

'What's she saying, Natali?' Dsordas said urgently, catching them up.

'I don't like it,' the boy wailed miserably. The others exchanged glances.

'Give me the crystal. Quick!' Gaye whispered to Fen.

'You're sure?'

'Yes!' Fen passed it over, and Gaye shivered involuntarily as her fingers closed around the cool, smooth stone.

'What's she saying, Natali?' Dsordas repeated.

The child screwed his eyes shut, then spoke in a voice that was hardly recognizable.

'Zalys garrison, respond. Urgent. Respond.'

'I hear it too,' Gaye breathed. 'She's far away.' There was pain in her voice and Fen held her tightly, aware of her sister's revulsion.

131

'I don't like it!' Natali cried.

Etha had had enough, and firmly removed the pendant from her son's neck. He made an ineffectual attempt to snatch it back, then subsided and became his normal, cheerful self once more. The transformation was so sudden and so complete that it took everyone by surprise.

'Can we go in now?' Natali asked.

The entire group was still outside in the corridor. There was a moment of hesitation, with no one knowing quite what to do, but then all their attention was drawn to Gaye as she screamed, her face contorted. Fen tried to take the amberine from her, but her fist was clenched tight, the muscles convulsed.

'They're dead!' Gaye gasped. 'All dead.' Her eyes were staring at dreadful scenes only she could see. 'Sunflower?'

With that inexplicable utterance she fainted and, as the others supported her, Habella gratefully plucked the crystal from her palm.

From inside the cell came the sound of Iceman cackling with laughter.

'Tell me what happened,' Dsordas insisted gently. 'I have to be sure.'

Since Gaye had come round, she had uttered only a few garbled sentences, but they had been enough to reveal the importance of what she had experienced. She was back in her own bed now, feeling ill and very tired, but her story was too incredible to let her rest just yet.

'The things Natali heard,' she began wearily. 'The angry sounding woman was one of a huge number of Far-speakers. All sick, all poisoned. You've no idea . . .' Words failed her, but the repugnance she felt was clear in her face. 'They were a long way away, but I sensed them clearly.'

'Xantium?' Dsordas prompted.

'I don't know.'

132

'Where else could it have been?' Fen asked, glancing at her lover.

'Go on,' Dsordas said, with a slight shrug.

Gaye swallowed hard, steeling herself to continue.

'They were getting more and more insistent, but were apparently getting no reply.'

'So Iceman's so-called "secrets" might have been the questions they've been asking him,' Dsordas suggested. 'But he couldn't answer?'

'Perhaps,' Gaye said. 'Whoever it was, they were desperate to know what the situation here was, and kept asking the same things over and over again. Then they seemed to give up. There was silence for a few moments, then she said, "Is Zalys responsible for the destruction of the fleet?" And then, after another pause, "Perhaps this will refresh your memory".' Gaye trembled again as she remembered what had happened next.

'Easy,' Fen comforted her. 'Take your time.'

'Suddenly, I was seeing the world through someone else's eyes,' Gaye went on when she had composed herself. 'She was on a ship, but everything was chaotic and I couldn't make much sense of it all. But I could feel her overwhelming fear. That's when I screamed, I think. There were huge crashing sounds, then no more.'

'She was the one called Sunflower?'

'Yes. She was a Far-speaker – I could feel the sickness all through her. And she knew she was going to die, that they were *all* going to die. She reported as much to the others.' Gaye hesitated, then went on determinedly. 'But this was like a memory, like something from the past. They're all dead now.'

'How far in the past?' Dsordas asked.

'I don't know,' Gaye replied tearfully.

'And you're sure this was the fleet that was heading here?'

'I think so. It was all so confused.'

'What destroyed the fleet?' he persisted, ignoring a warning look from Fen.

133

'Sunflower didn't know,' Gaye answered reluctantly. 'But she heard someone else say . . .' Her voice trailed away.

'What?'

'Monsters.'

That evening, drawn by an instinct she did not understand, Etha returned alone to Iceman's cell. As she arrived, Habella and the guard were just coming out, having administered the latest potion to her captive patient.

'What are you doing here?' the herbalist asked in surprise.

Etha's answer was uncharacteristically uncertain.

'I . . . I've done all I can for my family. Gaye's asleep and Natali's fine,' she said. 'I thought I'd come and see him.' As Habella raised her eyebrows, Etha added, 'I've brought some decent food. The gods know what he's been eating recently.'

'That's a kind thought.'

'He's ill,' Etha said, a little defensively. 'He has to eat properly if he's ever going to get well.'

'True enough,' Habella agreed. 'He's hardly more than a boy, and he's been treated terribly. Perhaps life owes him a few kindnesses.'

'Can I go in?'

The healer nodded.

'I'll come with you,' she said, then turned to the waiting sentry. 'Come with us, Lesec. Just in case he gets any ideas.'

The guard unlocked the door again, after checking on the prisoner through the grille, and then led the two women in. Iceman sprawled on his pallet, his eyes dull; his body looked as though all his muscles had atrophied and all his bones turned to jelly.

'I've brought you some food,' Etha told him.

Iceman did not react but when she began taking items out of her basket and the aromas of fresh bread, soup

134

and cheese began to fill the cell, he looked round warily. His gaze settled on the food in disbelief, and he slowly sat up, stretching out a tentative hand to remove the lid from the earthenware pot.

'For me?' he asked in wonder.

'Yes,' Etha told him. 'I cooked it myself.'

Iceman still hesitated, then picked up the loaf. Carefully, he broke a piece off and dipped it into the steaming broth. He put it in his stained mouth, watching the women all the time as if expecting to be punished. As soon as the tastes hit his tongue, his pale young face dissolved into ecstasy and he was soon ploughing his way through every morsel.

Etha watched, satisfaction warming her, while Habella was amazed. For a few moments, Iceman became a human being again, barely more than a child. Had her treatment begun to take effect, or was Etha's simple generosity the sole reason?

As the last crumb disappeared, Iceman looked up. He said nothing, but gratitude showed clearly in his once mad eyes.

'Just like mother used to make, eh?' Etha commented, smiling. 'Do you remember your own mother?'

Iceman stared at his benefactor.

'She had hair like yours,' he said, then burst into an uncontrollable flood of tears.

CHAPTER SIXTEEN

*Even the ravings of madmen can hold the bravest truths.
But most talk is cowardly, the resonance of nothing,
echoes of the void.*
The world is full of words.

The first island council for decades threatened to be chaotic right from the beginning. Its nominal purpose was to elect a new Patriarch, the spiritual leader of Zalys, to replace Nias Santarsieri, but such was the nature of the times that everyone knew it would concern much more than that. Village elders and many others had travelled to Nkosa from all over the island, swelling the crowd, so that even the wide expanse of Fournoi Square was full to overflowing by the appointed time.

The level of noise rose ever higher as the numbers grew and conversation and gossip became more animated. For obvious reasons, the main subject of speculation was the prospect of war. In the past two days, news of Gaye's vision had spread like wildfire, bringing hope and scepticism in equal measure. The blind girl had already been the centre of much conjecture because of the part she had played in the revolt itself, and opinions varied on how much of her story was the literal truth. But her latest revelation provoked even greater passions, and there were several instances, as the morning wore on, when talk turned to outright argument. Violence threatened as tempers frayed, and soon all manner of wild rumours and old grievances filled the air.

The men who had formed the Children of Zalys were the nearest thing the island had to a voice of authority now and, at Dsordas' instructions, they moved among the throng, trying to restore peace and bring a sense of order to the proceedings. Dsordas and his deputies had spent a long time discussing how to approach the council. Officially they had no standing within the community other than that of ordinary citizens, but they were realistic enough to know that they were the best hope of unifying the various factions on the island. In the end, although he hated having to do it, Dsordas decided to speak to the people in the square from the balcony beneath the ancient sundial in what had been the imperial headquarters. He was worried that this would evoke vile memories of their former overlords, and might be interpreted as an act of arrogance, but he saw no realistic alternative. However, he was determined to give as many other people as possible the opportunity of speaking, and to this end he had arranged to have four wooden platforms erected inside the square, giving them a place from which to be seen and heard. He had no great hope that this would satisfy everyone, or even that it would achieve the purpose of giving the council some structure – but it was better than nothing.

Dsordas had agreed with his deputies that he would appear on the balcony alone, leaving them to speak as and when they saw fit from the square itself. He wanted to keep his words to a minimum, and fretted for hours over what to say – and what to leave unsaid. But only Fen knew the extent of his nervousness and no amount of rational argument or heartfelt reassurance could convince him that all would turn out well. In the end, she was as nervous as he was. Now that his lifelong ambition had been achieved, the man whose iron will and sense of purpose had enabled him to secretly plan and execute the long awaited rebellion was suddenly uncertain of his own ability. It had been easier for Dsordas to face the imperial army than his own people.

Fen understood the confusion he felt about his healing talent and the guilt he still felt about his temporary withdrawal. Both had undermined some part of his self-confidence, but she was certain that he would soon win it back. She had no doubt that the citizens of Zalys respected Dsordas and would remember their debt to her lover. But she would still be glad when this day was over.

Fen kissed him soundly, then left him to make his way up to the balcony and went to join the rest of her family amid the crowd in the square.

When Dsordas emerged it took some time for quiet to fall, and as he waited, schooling himself to patience, he looked around, seeing the familiar place as if for the first time. The pink and yellow of the sun-bleached stone which paved the square was almost invisible beneath the tide of humanity, but the tall buildings on either side were plain to see in all their faded glory, their own balconies and open-shuttered windows filled with eager spectators. Taverns and merchants' shops lined the square. At the far end were the steps which led up and over the barrier wall that protected the square from the tidal surge of the Nkosa Canal beyond. Every mooring post was full, and the murky water was crowded with boats unable to make the shore.

Finally, all eyes were upon Dsordas, and the sound level dropped considerably. He took a deep breath, and raised his voice so that his words carried to all those gathered in the square.

'My friends, I stand here by no special dispensation. I speak only as a citizen of Zalys, one among many.'

The crowd rustled with whispers, approval of his modesty or expressions of disbelief, but Dsordas overrode them.

'You know me,' he cried, 'and such service as I have done. If you judge me worthy, I will do more, all that is within my capabilities, as every man and woman here will do also.'

The tide of murmurs rose again.

'Together we won a victory,' he went on, 'but many more battles remain to be fought. That means . . .'

But here he faltered. Some unheard comment from below had met with approval from those nearest, and the swell of sound grew, urging the speaker to send the message to a wider audience. Dsordas watched, caught between hope and dread, as an old, black-hooded woman was helped up on to one of the wooden platforms, amid cries of encouragement. She tottered up the last steps, her back bent, but when she reached the top, she straightened and looked up at the balcony with steadfast dark eyes. The gathering became silent and waited for her to speak. When she did, in a high pitched voice that wavered at the end of her sentences, almost all heard her – and those who did not were soon informed by passed-on whispers.

'I knew you when you were a boy, Dsordas Nyun,' she declared belligerently, provoking some muffled laughter. 'You were always one to undervalue your own worth. Everyone here knows your part in setting us free. Until a better man steps forward – and that I should like to see,' she added, looking round sceptically before returning her gaze to the balcony, '– you are the leader of Zalys, whether you like it or not!'

Cries of laughter and agreement filled the air, rising quickly to a roar of approval. Fen heard it with relief and joy, and looked up at Dsordas, smiling. He stood, apparently bewildered by this unexpected turn of events, his arms raised in a mute appeal for quiet. Finally he got his wish and called out once more.

'You forget, we meet here in council to elect a new Patriarch. He, and no other, can truly be the leader of Zalys – and I am unsuited by my years and my . . . character, for such a position.'

He got no further.

'Then leave the wellbeing of our spirits to him!' someone yelled lustily. 'But let you work alongside, as our civic leader.' There was another chorus of support.

'Is this what you all wish?' Dsordas asked eventually.

This time the tidal wave of acclamation was enough to sweep away even Dsordas' deep-seated doubts. He glanced down and saw Fen smiling up at him.

'I told you so,' she mouthed, and he could not help but smile back.

'So be it!' he yelled when the tumult had died down, his voice full of emotion. From then on he spoke as one inspired, his words carrying easily to everyone there. Even so, he was aware, as others were, that his newly confirmed authority would not solve all the problems facing them. The day was far from over yet. But an auspicious start had been made, and now he had a base on which to build.

The first matter to be determined was Nias' successor, but even that was destined to be the subject of heated debate and controversy – not so much about possible candidates, but about the means of his election. Before any names could even be put forward, an elderly and well-respected fisherman named Latchi Irini climbed on to one of the stands.

'We should be meeting in the Arena, not here!' he cried. 'That is where the Patriarchs have always been approved – by the old gods as well as the people.'

'But there's nothing there any more,' someone else shouted.

'Because we neglect the place!' the old man retorted righteously. 'The Arena is still the heart and soul of Zalys. We should be there!'

The noise level rose again in waves. Both sides of the argument had many supporters. Even Fen had mixed feelings on the subject. She remembered Latchi as the man who had started the inconclusive debate at the last meeting in the Arena, a few days before the revolt, and the man whose son had subsequently been executed by Farrag. She and Gaye had gone to the small, boulder-strewn valley to the south of the town, hoping in vain for some sign of the magic which Dsordas had decried as a false hope, a delusion which detracted from their more practical efforts. Since then he – and others – had experienced several strange happenings which had opened his mind to arcane possibilities, but his primary concern was still the natural, rational world. Fen looked up at him as he tried again to make his voice heard. Eventually he succeeded.

'I do not decry the old ways,' he explained, 'but Fournoi Square was chosen simply because it was more practical. Many people would not have been able to reach the Arena, while Nkosa is the natural centre of travel on Zalys. No doubt,' he continued appeasingly, 'once we have chosen the new Patriarch, he will wish to visit the Arena, with all who want to go, to have his new office witnessed and approved. But we are in need of haste, above all. There is still much work to do. We are here now – let us not waste this gathering.'

His appeal seemed to settle the arguments. The shouts of agreement and opposition subsided to muttering as everyone reached the inevitable conclusion. Somewhere, a wit saw the funny side of the situation and voiced his opinion. Laughter spread through one section of the crowd. Dsordas drew comfort from that, and inhaled deeply once more.

'Nias died without naming a preferred successor,' he began. 'We are thus left to make our own choice from among many worthy men. I have one such in mind, but is there any who seems to you an obvious choice?'

The square filled with whispers, but no one spoke up. Many names had been put forward in the town, some in all seriousness, some in jest, but there was no clear favourite. And besides, everyone wanted to hear Dsordas' recommendation first.

'Then I nominate Costa Folegandros,' he stated.

This provoked another storm of noise, composed partly of calls for and against but mainly of expressions of surprise. Costa was the head of one of the most

141

influential families on the island, a rich and respected merchant, and despite his worldly acumen, a man of strong personal beliefs. Thus, on the surface, he would have made an ideal Patriarch, but Dsordas' advocacy was surprising to many because Costa had also been noticeably lukewarm in his support for the uprising – until its outcome was beyond all doubt. He, unlike many, had much to lose by invoking Xantium's displeasure.

The buzz of speculation continued until the merchant himself emerged from the anonymity of the throng and climbed slowly on to one of the stands. He appeared solemn and dignified, aware of his own importance and now, albeit reluctantly, the centre of attention. He raised his hands for silence, and was obeyed almost immediately.

'I am honoured that my name has been put forward,' he began in his deep, resonant voice. 'But I regret that I must decline.' He waited for the subsequent chatter to die away before continuing. 'As you know, two of my three sons – Sagar and Bowen – are hostages in Xantium. Now that Zalys is free, for which I rejoice with you all, their lives are forfeit. Indeed, they may already be dead, unless Sagar truly *has* escaped. This weighs heavily on my mind, and until the matter is resolved I do not feel able to serve Zalys in the wholehearted manner you deserve.' There were tears in his eyes now. 'Forgive me.'

With that, he bowed to Dsordas and stepped down to rejoin his wife and youngest son, Nason. The crowd murmured in sympathy, even those who thought little of the man, recognizing his honesty and his plight. Fen had been as surprised as any at Dsordas' choice, and wondered briefly about his motives, especially because it had been Costa who had directed the imperial soldiers to the Amari household. All the families whose children were held hostage in the imperial capital were, quite naturally, terribly worried about their kin. She knew that some resented the way Dsordas and the Children had disregarded their predicament in staging the revolt. Perhaps this had been a peace offering. The hostages had been taken from the wealthiest and most powerful families, and Dsordas would need them as allies in the future, whatever the fate of their absent members.

In the lull that followed, Skoulli Visakia stepped on to the platform. After Dsordas, Skoulli was the best known and well regarded of the leaders of the Children. Everyone knew he was always worth listening to, both for his good sense and his eloquence. On this occasion he spoke briefly but persuasively, first commiserating with Costa and his family, then proposing another candidate. His choice was one Nikolas Vavara, an elderly wanderer who was well known all over the island. As soon as Nikolas' name was mentioned, he seemed an excellent selection, both for his gentle philosophy and his charitable nature. Nevertheless, the debate went on for some time, with several other possible leaders put forward for consideration. But this was more in the way of a good-natured game, and when Nikolas was eventually persuaded to climb one of the rostrums and declare, somewhat bashfully, that he was willing, the decision of the people of Zalys was quite clear. The old man with the long white beard accepted his confirmation as Patriarch with quiet humility, standing quite still in his threadbare dark robes, but his eyes were bright.

Dsordas returned his voice to the debate then, welcoming the choice and pledging himself to work with Nikolas for the good of all. Then, as everyone knew he must, he turned to other matters.

'Most of you know of the recent events which have given us hope that Zalys might escape retribution for a while longer,' he began. Having now gained the crowd's full attention, he went on to describe Gaye's revelation, hoping to put paid to the more exaggerated rumours concerning the incident. Gaye herself, seated in the midst of her family below the balcony, listened in silence, her face still. She had been the subject of many curious glances and not a little awe, but had not spoken to anyone except Etha and Fen.

Before Dsordas could go on, however, a voice was raised from the crowd.

'How do we know we can trust this vision? If the Far-speaker was involved, might it not be a trick to lull us into a state of unreadiness?'

'But the fleet should surely have been here by now!' another man objected.

'Not if they were delayed in port. Who knows what the situation is in Nadal?'

'And the weather's been against them,' someone else added. Since the storm on the night of the battle had abated, the wind had blown steadily but gently from the west.

Dsordas spoke up forcefully.

'No one can say what the full truth of such things are,' he declared, 'but we can hope that this was indeed a true vision, that it *was* the fleet bound for Zalys and that it *was* utterly destroyed. But even if that is the case, who is to say Xantium will not send another? My point is this; we must remain on our guard. We have made our defences ready, but they can still be improved. The watch must be maintained. This will mean sacrifices from every one of us, but all Zalys is at stake!'

A rumble of agreement filled the square. The islanders would not be tempted into complacency now. One day they would be able to discover their place in the world again, but until then their vigilance was assured.

It was at this point that a rough-hewn villager from the southern end of the island mounted one of the platforms. Few people in the square recognized him, but he gained their full attention with his first words.

'My friends, I am Elias Frankista, a fisherman from Eouli. I have no second sight, but I find it easy to believe in the destruction of our enemy's ships. For I have seen monsters with my own eyes.'

CHAPTER SEVENTEEN

A blight upon the sun will be the sign that the long dream is over. Thus it was prophesied long ago, in blood and smoke, in this realm and the others. What will such a waking bring?

A green sky fills my eyes. I am blind once more.

At the fisherman's words, a breathless hush fell on Fournoi Square and Fen sensed Gaye grow unnaturally still beside her.

'My fear is that these creatures may be even more of a threat than the hateful armies of Xantium,' Elias went on. 'For, though they look like fish, they are huge beyond nightmare, and they fly upon the air.' Although there were many sharply indrawn breaths, his evident sincerity was such that no one mocked his apparently ludicrous words. 'I myself – and others – have seen them flying over the sea, with great slow wingbeats, like sea-bats gone mad. And the air full of their screaming, so sharp as to pierce your ears.'

Gaye gasped involuntarily and her guardians moved to comfort her, seeing the renewed horror on her pale face.

'Sea-bats!' she whispered. Her blind eyes were prey to visions once more.

'It's all right,' Fen tried to reassure her. 'You're safe here.' But she was recalling, with mounting terror, her own sight of a captive manta ray – or sea-bat as the islanders called them – slaying one of the divers in the shark pools only a few days earlier. The horrible violence had been so alien to the creature's normal inquisitive friendliness that it had shocked her greatly. Now the incident seemed doubly ominous.

'Two of our fishing boats have disappeared without trace,' Elias continued, 'and many are afraid to go out any more, fearing that they too might fall victim to these unnatural monsters.' His revelation loosed a torrent of other tales of woe.

'I also come from the south of Zalys!' another man cried, clambering up on to a different stage. 'But from the hills, not the coast. I came here to tell of a terrible murder and to ask for justice, but now perhaps I can see the cause. Three days ago, some in my village were woken during the night by a terrible screaming. Dark shadows, like giant birds, blotted out the stars and we were sore afraid. But worse came. In the morning, we discovered a goatherd who had spent the night in the open and all his flock dead. The man's face was smashed and bloated with poison; all the animals had been flayed and left as bloody carrion. No meat had been taken. This killing was done from pure malice.'

After that, as the atmosphere of dread thickened, more voices added to the catalogue of horrors. No one else had actually seen or heard the screamers, but many had witnessed strange events. From the inland villages came reports that the great bat colonies, which lived within the mountain caves, were behaving oddly, flying even during daylight, making incredible noises and terrorizing every other living creature. But the majority of the tales concerned the sea, and came from the boatmen of Nkosa as well as those of other smaller ports. The sea was warmer now than it had ever been in living memory, and seaweed and other growths were clogging the water in places; great patches of luminescence moved within the depths, and the water was full of unexplained sounds and unpredictable currents.

And, in some respects most worrying of all, each high tide brought with it new perils. For years now, Nkosa and other coastal areas had been in increasing danger of flooding as the island slowly sank into the ocean. Great efforts had been made to minimize the damage, but the war of attrition was slowly being lost. Some people had put their faith in the ancient legend that said that Zalys was doomed to slide beneath the waves unless it freed itself from oppression, and had expected things to improve after the revolt. But since the time of its last monthly zenith, the tide level had not even fallen as far as it normally would.

'We're free, but the sea is getting worse!'

'If anything Zalys is sinking even faster.'

'So much for the old stories!'

This derisive shout was answered as others sprang to the defence of the old ways. It was an old argument, but one which had come to the fore again during the recent upheavals. One faction declared that the island's plight could only be solved by their own efforts, by practical means. Until recently, Dsordas had been one of the most vocal proponents of this view. Others said that only the ancient gods could save them, and insisted on reinstating the old rituals of prayer and reverence. Latchi Irini, among others, spoke up again.

'We can learn much from the old tales!' he cried. 'You do ill to mock. There was magic used in freeing us from the imperial garrison.' The story of how Gaye and others had prompted the storm and the arrival of the bats in Nkosa was known to all, and believed by many. 'Where else does magic come from but the gods?'

'It can only mean that we're not truly free,' another like-minded citizen chimed in. 'The threat of the Empire is still there.'

'Then we'll fight the Empire with swords and arrows,' one of their opponents declared. 'Not with superstitious nonsense.'

'Ask the ghosts.' Another voice rose above the melée. 'There are more of them than ever.'

Most eyes swivelled towards the balcony on the eastern side of the square. Here, as always on special occasions, the space was occupied not by the living but by the spectres of the dead. They were usually regarded as harmlessly irrelevant; they appeared to talk amongst themselves – although no sound reached living ears – and watch events with interest. On this occasion, the balcony was certainly more crowded than usual and even more phantoms could be glimpsed in the room beyond.

'And it's not just here,' another villager announced. 'They're all over the island. Their coming must mean something!'

The argument frayed into a thousand separate strands, with people crowding on to the platforms now and shouting at each other. Dsordas stood helpless, not knowing how to respond. Below him Gaye trembled, held tight by her mother and Fen.

'I have to go,' Gaye whispered. 'Get me away from here.'

They were only too happy to oblige.

Dsordas returned home much later, looking weary and depressed. Fen hugged him, then led him to the kitchen table where he sat down and mutely accepted a mug of herb tea.

'What happened?'

'It just got worse,' he said resignedly. 'With so many people . . . it was hopeless. In the end, Nikolas promised to visit the Arena and call on the old gods. That placated most, but I doubt it'll do much good.'

'You don't know that,' she told him. 'And Nikolas will make a good Patriarch.'

'He will,' Dsordas agreed. 'I was heartily grateful for his help.'

'And they made it plain they wanted you to lead Zalys.'

He nodded, his expression neutral.

'Then the day wasn't a total loss.' Fen smiled encouragingly.

'No. But now we have even more to worry about. All

eyes are on the sea, watching for monsters as well as the fleet.'

'You believe the stories?'

Dsordas shook his head in bewilderment.

'I don't know,' he sighed. 'There's too much that's odd about the sea to discount it all but . . . Zalys *depends* on the sea. Without fishing, half our food supply disappears, and sooner or later we're going to need to trade with the outside world. If there are monsters, we'll have to face them – one way or another.'

The next few days were a nervous time for the island. A faithful watch was kept, but much to everyone's relief, there was still no sign of the Xantic ships. The hope continued to grow that they were indeed not coming – whether the fleet had been destroyed or had never actually set out. There were no further reports of flying sea-bats, and with each passing day, that idea seemed increasingly ridiculous. Many began to say that the screamers were figments of unreliable imaginations.

Nikolas Vavara solemnly made good his promise. He and all those who still relied to some extent on the old beliefs met at the Arena. Fen and Gaye went, feeling it their duty to do so, with Dsordas' approval, although he did not join them himself. Many people glanced at the two sisters, who were made conspicuous by their pale hair, as they sat within the natural amphitheatre. But Nikolas' prayers evoked no discernible response, and Gaye felt nothing. The spirit of the place, the soul of Zalys as some called it, was dormant once more, and the ghosts who had visited Gaye on the fateful evening of the storm stayed away. When the gathering dispersed, the people were disappointed but most refused to believe that the magic of the place was dead. Gaye, who had called it into life once, agreed, but she had no more idea than anyone else how to do it again – or to what purpose. Whatever stories lay within the stones, whatever memories they kept, were buried deep and cold.

The Stone Eye, the curiously shaped rock which guarded the valley rim, was blind once more.

However, one fact proved incontrovertible. With the inexplicable exception of the Arena, there *were* more ghosts on Zalys than ever before. The silent images appeared everywhere; in Nkosa, in the villages, in the farmers' fields and even on board the few boats that ventured out on the unpredictable sea. Gaye especially was troubled by this phenomenon. She sensed their presence, though none spoke to her as they had done before, but she could no more explain their sudden increase than anyone else – until one evening four days after the council. She was in her bedroom at the time, talking with her mother, who was describing her recent visits to Iceman.

'He's just a boy,' Etha said. 'If Habella's potions succeed, he'll be able to live without the need of poison, and perhaps his memory will come back.' There was an almost maternal zeal in her voice as she recalled the occasional flashes of Iceman's early life that had returned to him.

Gaye smiled at her mother's seemingly boundless capacity for caring. There was an indomitable goodness about Etha which had made her recent sufferings even harder to witness.

'Natali seems to like him too,' Gaye remarked.

'Yes. He's not afraid of him at all.'

'But you be careful,' Gaye said, suddenly anxious. 'Iceman was Farrag's creature for a long time, and the evil may not be gone yet.'

'I'm careful,' her mother assured her. 'We're never alone with him.' She paused, her face growing stern. 'But when I think what Farrag put him through, my blood boils. Surely he deserves a little kindness?'

'I wonder if he'll ever remember his own name.'

'That'll be the day I know he's cured,' Etha began. 'I . . . Oh!'

'What is it?' Gaye was alarmed, feeling a sudden

unease, although she was almost certain she knew what had happened. 'What's wrong?' she asked.

'He's back,' her mother breathed. 'The ghost.'

'The swordsman?'

The spectral visitor, who wore old fashioned clothes with a sword in his belt, had spoken to Gaye before the revolution. His warning that Zalys was in great danger and that the Stone Eye must be reawoken had made no sense at the time, but later all had become clear when she and Natali had been magically transported to the Arena.

Do you hear me still? The silent words sounded only in Gaye's head.

'Yes. Why are you here?'

I have a message for you.

'Is Bowen alive?' she asked quickly, unable to restrain her longing.

He is still of your world. The ghost sounded taken aback, as if this was of no consequence.

Gaye sighed deeply. She knew from past experience that this was the only information she would get about her lover. It was not enough, not nearly enough, but it would have to do for now.

We are troubled, her visitor went on. *That is why so many of us have been called to visit your realm. A great power is reemerging from an age-long dream, and to oppose it it will take a circle of all the world. But the circle begins and ends on Zalys. Remember this well.*

'What power?' Gaye asked quickly – but at that moment, the door of the chamber burst open and Nason Folegandros, Bowen's younger brother, exclaimed breathlessly, 'Is he here? I came as quickly as I . . . Oh!'

'Get out!' Gaye screamed hysterically.

It was too late. The ghost had gone, vanishing as quickly as he had arrived, leaving her none the wiser.

'I'm sorry,' Nason said miserably. 'He came to our house like before, but . . .'

Etha had her arms round the distraught Gaye.

151

'Go down to the kitchen, Nason,' she told him firmly but kindly.

'I tried . . .'

'Just go!'

Gaye was crying quietly, her whole body trembling. After a time, the tears stopped and she whispered, 'It's not fair. He can't do this to me again. What am I supposed to *do*?'

'Tell me,' Etha said gently.

Gaye told her mother what the ghost had said but, although Etha was sympathetic, she could not enlighten the distressed girl.

'I'm so tired,' Gaye mumbled. 'Why does it make me so tired?'

Etha had no answer to that either as she guided her daughter to her bed. Once she was settled in, Etha's thoughts became melancholy.

'With all these ghosts about,' she said, speaking half to herself, 'it's a wonder Antorkas hasn't been back to see me.'

'They don't have the choice,' Gaye answered drowsily. 'They're called here.'

'Who does the calling?' Etha wondered aloud, but she got no answer. Gaye was fast asleep.

After his abrupt banishment, Nason had gone down to the kitchen where he found Fen and Dsordas, who had been roused from their own preoccupations by his noisy arrival.

'What's going on?' Dsordas asked.

Nason explained that the ghost had appeared at his home in much the same agitated state as before.

'I tried to tell him where Gaye was, but wasn't sure whether he understood. Then he disappeared, and I ran here as fast as I could. I didn't mean to scare him away.'

'Is Gaye all right?' Fen asked.

'I think so. Your mother's with her.'

He sounded so dejected that she took pity on him,

ushering him into a chair and bringing out a jar of biscuits.

'Etha will be down soon,' she said. 'She can tell us about it then. How are your family?'

Nason shrugged.

'The same as always,' he replied, then looked at Dsordas. 'Why did you ask my father to be Patriarch?'

'He's a good man, and capable.'

'He'd have been useless,' Nason said disgustedly. 'He never *does* anything. He didn't even fight.'

'Your father was in a difficult position,' Dsordas reminded him. 'He's no worse a man for loving his sons.'

'I wish Farrag had taken me instead of Bowen!' the youngest brother said fervently. 'At least then Gaye would be happy.'

'We can't always choose our own destinies,' Fen commented, with a meaningful glance at her lover.

'Well, I'm going to try!' Nason stated with all the pent-up determination of a sixteen-year-old.

'I'm sure you will,' Dsordas responded, smiling. 'But it's always right to consider others.'

'Is that why you lied to me?' the boy asked unexpectedly.

For a few moments they were not sure what he meant, but then the memories returned.

'We lied about our involvement in the Children because it was dangerous to do otherwise,' Dsordas said earnestly. 'You understand that, don't you?'

'Yes,' Nason answered grudgingly. 'I knew really, but I can keep my mouth shut.'

His boast was interrupted by Etha's arrival, her expression concerned.

'Is Gaye all right?' Fen asked.

'Yes. She's asleep now.' She went on to tell them all that had happened.

'I didn't mean to scare him away,' Nason repeated.

'I don't suppose you did,' Etha replied ruefully. 'I

153

can't see anything in you a ghost need be afraid of. Gaye was just upset, that's all.'

'A circle that begins and ends on Zalys,' Fen wondered aloud. 'What's that supposed to mean?' *And what*, she found herself thinking, *is at the centre of this circle?*

The next day began ominously, for in mid-morning the sun grew fleetingly dark. There were those on the island who studied the heavens, and knew that the eclipse was caused by the unseen passage of the moon, but many regarded the unnatural gloom with superstition and foreboding. Although the summer's peak was a month past now, the heat of the season lingered still. Yet for a few moments, while the ring of fire painted the black sky with rainbow hues, Zalys was cool. Even so, people shivered not from cold but from fear.

An even greater alarm, around noon, was caused by the sighting of a sail to the east. However, it soon became clear that it was a lone vessel, and dismay turned to excitement. Such a ship might bring with it news of the outside world. When it was closer still, it became obvious that it was a merchantman and, moreover, one flying the flags of the far southern lands beyond the borders of the Xantic Empire. Such traders came to Zalys only rarely, and so her arrival was awaited by doubly eager islanders.

Yeori Alektora stood at the head of the crowd which lined the quays as the vessel docked and it was he, in Dsordas' stead, who greeted the captain, a huge figure whose glistening black skin marked him as a man of the south. News was soon being exchanged and trade beginning, in a babble of several languages.

Almost unnoticed amid the bustle, a passenger came ashore, accompanied by his slack-eyed servant. The pair took no part in the hectic interchange between islanders and crew, but walked unhurriedly into Nkosa town. The traveller's keen eyes watched all that was going on around him, noting several conversations in passing, and eventually he installed himself and his attendant in a room in a back street tavern. Once there, in private, he took a strip of cloth from his personal luggage. Checking first to see that the amberine crystal was still secure within its folds, he tied the band around his companion's head.

'The sky turns green, Hunter.'

At his master's words, the Far-speaker known as Hunter became suddenly alert, his grey eyes shining.

'I have a message for Xantium,' the newcomer said calmly.

'I am ready,' Hunter replied.

An hour later, the screamers came.

CHAPTER EIGHTEEN

In the teeming labyrinths below, a single nightmare overshadows a thousand dreams – a demented possession so deep that not even sound can escape its chasm, not even the strongest beacon can shine.

In the realms of stone above, a new innocence is alone – alone but for those she cannot see nor hear.

I walk with demons too.

'Well, was it him or not?' Martyn was understandably exasperated.

'I'm not sure,' Sagar answered. 'I've told you, Bowen was only eleven when I was taken!'

'This is hopeless,' the northerner concluded wearily.

Above them the early morning sky was streaked with orange and grey, but Sagar was still preoccupied with the events of the previous evening. Ever since Alasia had told Martyn that the islander's brother would arrive 'before the moon turns', they had arranged for a watch to be kept on incoming convoys on the Deadlands. There were many places on the dust-smeared grey walls where it was possible to gain access to the battlements without the need to inconvenience – or be inconvenienced by – the soldiers who patrolled the ramparts or kept a lookout from the towers.

For the last two days, as the deadline approached, Sagar and Martyn had kept watch from near the southwest gate, which was the most likely point of entry for anyone travelling from Zalys. Sagar had been astounded by the massive walls, and had suffered from attacks of vertigo as well as a natural anxiety at being in so conspicuous a place. It was the first time he had seen the Deadlands since his arrival years earlier, and he was depressed by the endless desolation. To escape from Xantium meant having to cross that inhospitable tract, a task which would have seemed impossible if it were not for the obvious passages of numerous convoys.

They had had no reports of anyone remotely like either of his brothers until dusk of the previous day. Then they spotted a group of horsemen to the southwest, moving much faster than most travellers, a long cloud of red dust marking their trail. As they drew nearer, Sagar strained his eyes and realized that one of the riders was a prisoner while the rest were imperial soldiers. Martyn had noticed too, and glanced at his companion.

'Come on,' the northerner said, when he saw that Sagar was too tense to speak. 'Let's go down to the gate and get a closer look.'

They got there just before the horsemen arrived. However, the soldiers did not stop at the gate, but just slowed their mounts to a walk while the sentry waved them through. The party was obviously expected.

Sagar gazed at the prisoner in their midst, seeing a solidly built young man with dark brown hair and brown eyes. But there was a horrible slackness about his face, as if he were not really alive, that made Sagar feel sick.

'Well?' Martyn whispered.

Sagar said nothing, staring into the evening gloom as the shadows deepened beneath the bridge. Was this Bowen? He was the right age and had the right colouring, and his face seemed vaguely familiar, but . . . It certainly was not Nason. As he passed by, the prisoner turned to face Sagar, and for a fleeting moment their eyes met. In his own mind then, Sagar decided that yes, this must be Bowen, but the feeling did not last long. The man's expression did not change. There was absolutely no spark of recognition in his eyes. Then the group clattered past, and Martyn had to tug at Sagar's sleeve to get him to follow.

They had trouble keeping up on foot; the Captain was evidently in a hurry, but the troop's progress was impeded by a throng of the children who followed anyone who looked rich enough to spare a few coins – hoping that nuisance value would make their begging more effective. However, the Captain only shouted angrily and brushed them aside. He pressed on, as directly as the maze of streets allowed, towards the inner city. When he entered The Circle, Sagar and Martyn were some way behind; in any case, they could no longer follow openly.

'Is it your brother?'

'I don't know.'

Then Martyn simply left, disappearing without warning or explanation as Sagar continued to stare at the empty inner gateway through which the horsemen had vanished. When he realized that he was alone, he was almost paralysed with panic and only managed with great effort to find his way back to more familiar territory. As he walked, every shadow held nightmares, every stranger was an enemy.

After an almost sleepless night, Martyn had returned with the news that the prisoner had been considered important enough to be taken all the way to the Imperial Court, and was now – presumably – in Verkho's hands. And Sagar still could not make up his mind. Was it possible for two brothers to grow so far apart in nine years? Surely there should have been some vestigial trace of filial understanding. The newcomer had evidently felt none – and Sagar was hopelessly confused.

'We'll keep watching,' Martyn said resignedly. 'In the meantime, all we can do is try to find that Captain. He'll surely know who his prisoner was.'

Sagar could only nod. He had never felt more alone.

'This is outrageous!' Harios Kedhara was nearly apoplectic with indignation and exhaustion.

'I'm sorry. The Chancellor's orders were quite specific.' Verkho's steward did not sound apologetic at all, and eyed the angry official coldly. 'No one, absolutely *no one*, is to disturb him until he is ready. His study doors are locked from within. I would advise you not to knock.'

'What prompted this?' Harios had recently begun to feel that he was one of Verkho's most favoured deputies, and now, after the most appalling night of his life, he felt frustrated and betrayed. But no amount of pleading – which strained his sense of dignity – could sway the Chancellor's sworn protectors. The vital importance of the news Harios brought was irrelevant to them. He was in despair.

'The Chancellor received a delivery from Zalys last night,' the servant replied. 'Whatever it is commands his whole attention.' If he was curious, the steward knew better than to show it. He was not looking forward to this day. Harios was only the first of the petitioners with whom he would have to deal. By comparison with some, this self-important little scribe, with all his reports and tabulations, was easy to face.

'Zalys?' the ministry official asked with quickening interest. 'Did the same party bring a prisoner?'

'Yes. A madman named Bowen Folegandros,' the servant replied impassively.

'Is he with the Chancellor too?'

'No. Verkho's not interested in him. He's locked up in the holding cell, down there.'

'Then I will take charge of him,' Harios decided, seizing the opportunity to reemphasize his authority. 'I shall require two guards to escort him to my section.' At least a new project would provide some recompense for the disastrous night.

'As you wish,' the steward said, with every appearance of apathy. In fact, he would be glad to be rid of Bowen. No one had known what to do with the prisoner once Ofiah had left and Verkho had made his indifference plain. 'The two guards at the door will accompany you.'

'Good. Please inform me immediately the Chancellor becomes available.'

'Of course.' The servant's unchanging expression hid his contempt.

As Harios strode towards the cell, anticipation almost made him forget the dreadful scenes which had begun the previous evening and continued through the night. Dozens of talents had broken down within a few hours, apparently losing all grip on sanity, and in many cases having to be physically restrained. Three had actually died from these fits, and several more were close to it. The chaos had continued throughout the hours of darkness, with those talents who were able to sleep wracked by overpowering dreams, a danger to themselves and others as they thrashed about. Harios had done what he could to monitor the situation – although his resources had been hopelessly stretched – but by morning he had reached the end of his tether, and his normal methodical calm deserted him when he tried to compile his report for Verkho. In the end, he had decided to go and see the Chancellor in person – only to be turned away. It was intolerable. His only consolation was that daylight had brought some degree of respite. Whether this was because the sun drove away the dreams or their cause, or whether the talents were simply exhausted, Harios did not know. Only time would tell. And in the meantime, there was Bowen Folegandros.

Although the holding cell was sparsely furnished, it was vastly more comfortable than the dungeons below – and yet in some ways it was even worse. The room was suffused with the echoes of fear. Few of those who had been held there, awaiting the Chancellor's pleasure, had enjoyed the experience – and even Harios could sense the atmosphere. Bowen seemed impervious, however, lying on his back on the floor, eyes staring unseeing at the ceiling. All sorts of peculiar sensations and ideas were circulating in the outer reaches of his mind, but he had shut them out completely. He had retreated further than ever before, to the core of his being – a dark, soulless void that was his only sanctuary.

Harios paused at the door.

'Has he been any trouble?'

'None,' the guard replied sleepily, stifling a yawn.

'No disturbances, no dreams in the night?'

'No.'

'Interesting,' Harios whispered curiously. 'Unlock the door and bring him with me.'

Bowen did not stir at the sound of the key being turned, and only moved when the two soldiers lifted his unresisting body from the floor.

Ifryn gave Doneta a wan smile as she left the nursery. The maid was sitting cross-legged on the floor, playing an involved game with the two little girls, while Azari slept peacefully in his cot. Ifryn had already reduced her daughters to tears that morning by snapping at them for some trivial offence, and she had had to spend a considerable time trying to comfort them. The crying had stopped at last, but Delmege in particular was still nursing a grievance and pointedly addressed all her remarks to Doneta.

Outside, Ifryn sighed deeply, hating herself for taking even a tiny part of her frustration out on innocent children, but unable to rid herself of the rage she felt against recent turns of fate. First Kerrell, then Alasia, her greatest allies, had vanished, taking with them a large part of her strength and love. And the searches for both were proving equally fruitless. Even her pact with Baylin had produced nothing so far – except a new friendship which went a small way to filling the gulf of misery inside her.

What now? she wondered. Even the continuing hunt for the elusive Swordsman seemed doomed. Baylin had been certain that Guyland Brak was dead, but the

161

Swordsman could not possibly be a ghost. Ghosts could not erect burning signs in The Spires, nor could they do any of the other things credited to the outlaw. Yet Alasia had said, 'In another life he was known as Guyland Brak,' which seemed to indicate that he was dead. And that was impossible. Ifryn knew that Alasia would never lie to her, but could she have been mistaken? Or was Baylin's information wrong? Could the hostage have escaped both fire and enclave? It seemed unlikely.

The Empress wanted to scream.

Instead, taking advantage of Doneta's occupation with the children, she made one of her increasingly rare forays beyond the confines of her own apartments. She knew, from discreet enquiries, where she could gain access to The Spires. Most entrances had been walled up, preventing overly adventurous children from coming to harm among the crumbling, dangerous ruins, but a few secret ways still remained.

Making sure that she was unobserved, Ifryn did her own disappearing act. As she emerged from the hidden tunnel, she looked around in awe. Seen from outside, The Spires appeared eccentric and senseless; from within, the place was threatening and oppressive. No aspect was straightforward, and the Empress began to doubt her own sense of perspective. But – cautiously – she went on.

An hour later, she had only succeeded in frightening herself silly. She had felt lost several times, and at others cringed away from a suddenly leering gargoyle or an unexpected pitfall. Even in broad daylight the place was full of perils and monstrosities; at night it must be a nest of horrors. Ifryn shuddered at the thought, listening to the rustling of bats she had unwittingly disturbed in one dark crevice. Why had she come here? Even if Alasia *was* here, she would never find her – unless her friend wanted to be found. And if that was the case, there would have been no need for this search.

The Empress escaped from the stone nightmare and

returned, chastened, to her own chambers. How was she to endure it? *I'm going to do something very stupid soon.* Then another thought struck, even more disquieting than the last. *Perhaps that's what Verkho's waiting for.*

CHAPTER NINETEEN

*Long ago, when gods still chose to walk among their
subjects, the temples burned with grace. Those seeking
good fortune came to cast cherry stones upon the pitted
altar of Zidon, and her priests, who slept at night in
wooden coffins, would read the patterns of augury, then
choose the seeds to grow to maturity. The rest would be
taken away to be consumed by Elcar's sudden fire, the
fire of rebirth.*

*And there were three others, the pantheon's lesser kin,
who had their devotees too.*

*But other, braver folk prayed to the twin gods, torn
apart at the moment of their creation so that each looked
upon the world with only one eye. Meyu of the sun cast no
shadow, while Gar, the guardian of all living creatures,
breathed out the wind and rain. Those who found favour
with these two were doubly blessed – but the fate of those
found wanting was dread annihilation, beyond the reach
of even Elcar's power. So it was for many ages of man.*

Then came the rift.

Emperor Southan III came out of the hastily arranged
council meeting feeling, if anything, even worse than
when he had gone in. The situation was insane. Kerrell
had gone missing, and now Verkho had locked himself
away for three whole days! All of a sudden, the many
troubles of the Empire rested squarely on the Emperor's
own shoulders, and he had been forced into an awareness of just how out of touch he was. Even a casual
investigation revealed that Xantium was in more trouble

than he could have imagined. There was unrest and violence in many outlying territories, much of it for reasons Southan did not understand or could not discover. Reports came in from the Far-speakers every hour detailing new developments which required immediate action. It was true that the Chancellor's deputies were dealing with the more obvious needs, but there was much that was going unattended simply because – in Verkho's absence – no one was willing to take the ultimate responsibility for a decision. Hence the council.

Yet even there the shadow of the Chancellor lay upon them all. Southan had looked round the large table at the gathering of men – some of whom he hardly knew – and wondered where their loyalties really lay. These senior officials, advisers and army officers all shared a marked reluctance to reveal what they knew while Verkho was not present – even at the Emperor's command. They disguised their hesitation in formal, appeasing words which Southan did not have the wit to deflect, but which he knew were smoke-screens. The much needed council had been so much hot air.

How am I supposed to cope? Southan wondered impotently. Without Kerrell, he had no one to turn to. *What is Verkho doing? What is he waiting for?*

Alasia moved unnoticed among a multitude of ghosts. She heard their clamouring, their endless questions, but there were too many, their needs too confused, for her even to try and answer. Even so, their collective anxiety gnawed at her endlessly, and she wished her friends were there. But she knew that the bats would not fly during the day unless forced to by the direst need, and several hours remained before sunset. She had not been back to The Spires in six days – ever since her battle with Verkho over Coulson – and she felt out of place.

The ancient ruined temple was crowded with the shades of the dead, drawn here by old loyalties and echoes of past devotions. The silent pantheon looked on with cracked stone eyes, impervious to the suffering of the inhabitants of either realm. The living shunned the temple now, and so Alasia knew it was the safest place for her to be, but she felt her abandonment of Ifryn keenly.

After the conflict of wills, her only choice had been to fly away, in spite of her weariness, and even now – especially now! – she could not return to the upper part of the city. In the last few days, the whole spiritual fabric of the place had been ripped to shreds and rewoven in patterns Alasia no longer understood. For the first time in her life she knew what it was to be truly afraid. The clear sky above mocked reality; Alasia knew that Xantium was lying under a vast, grey shroud.

When the messenger first found Corton, in the massive, cool haven of the imperial cellars, the wine-master had been instantly nervous. Had the intrigues of Xantium finally reached out to ensnare him? So he was relieved to discover that the summons was from Ifryn. The Empress kept her own private supply of wines for guests in her own quarters and, quite naturally, relied upon Corton to assist her in her choice. Every few months he would visit her apartments with lists and a few carefully selected samples. The wine-master always enjoyed these occasions, approving of Ifryn's personal interest and excellent taste as well as admiring her elegance and imperial dignity. While he would never, even for a moment, presume that their acquaintance was anything other than that of servant and mistress, she made him feel truly appreciated. Therefore he arrived at the appointed hour in a cheerful frame of mind, accompanied by two fully laden assistants.

Doneta showed him in, the samples were set out, and then Corton was left alone to wait for the Empress. She came in moments later and greeted the wine-master warmly, although for an instant he thought he detected a haunted, sorrowful look in her gentle brown eyes. That in itself was hardly surprising given the disturbing events and malicious rumours that had marred the last month. However, such considerations were soon forgotten in their deliberations over Corton's pride and joy.

As the discussion came to an end, both felt a reluctance to move on, and Ifryn did not dismiss him immediately. The room was now infused with a rich, wonderful mix of heady aromas, and Corton's palate still tingled at the memory of the delicate tastes. He felt contented and relaxed – so the turn the conversation took then was all the more shocking.

'There is something I've been meaning to ask you for some time, Corton.'

'Yes, my lady?'

'That bottle of Embarragio, the one the Swordsman tried to poison me with,' she began. 'Did you examine it?'

Corton had never been good at hiding his emotions, and his dismay was mirrored in his face. So the tentacles were reaching out after all. This was the moment he'd been dreading – but he was surprised by the source of the enquiry.

'I did not have the chance to test it, my lady,' he said, after his initial hesitation. 'Chancellor Verkho removed it after the banquet.'

'But did you not oversee the decanting?' The haunted look had returned, but there was determination in her soft spoken words.

'Yes,' Corton admitted. 'I saw nothing suspicious then.'

'You did not taste it?'

'No,' he lied, his face a mask of unease, not least because of the self-imposed slur on his professional integrity.

'And no one else has thought to ask you these questions?' Ifryn sounded mildly surprised.

'No, my lady.'

'Not even the Chancellor?'

'No, my lady.'

The Empress said nothing for a few moments, but her expression seemed to ask, *Don't you find that odd?*

'I . . . I supposed,' Corton stammered eventually, 'that he, the Chancellor . . . already knew all he needed . . . His expertise in the ways of poison is well known.'

'Indeed,' Ifryn remarked coolly.

'It is a matter of profound regret . . .' Corton began agonizingly, his eyes downcast. 'My failure—'

'No blame is attached to you,' the Empress cut in. 'There is much evil in this world but none, I know, in you.'

'Thank you, my lady,' he breathed gratefully, looking up again.

'What do you know of the Swordsman?' she asked unexpectedly.

Caught off-guard again, the wine-master rejected several responses before he answered.

'Only the common gossip,' he said at last.

'It would mean a great deal to me if he were found,' she added carefully.

Corton did not know how to respond so said nothing, but his brain was seething with possibilities. Did Ifryn know that the wine had not been tainted? Was Chancellor Verkho himself suspected of treason? Could the Empress have motives for wanting the Swordsman found – other than the safety of her son? *Found*, Corton noted, not *caught*. Was her choice of words significant? And why was she asking *him*? Did she somehow know of Grongar's intuition? Surely the idiot barbarian had not been gossiping already! Corton felt the tentacles wind round him, squeezing the breath from his lungs.

Ifryn smiled suddenly, and stood to indicate that the audience was over. Corton scrambled to his feet, almost unable to believe that his ordeal was at an end.

'Thank you, Corton.'

'It was a pleasure, my lady,' he responded, bowing.

'My assistants will return to remove the samples, and your wine will be delivered this afternoon.'

With that he took his leave. As the outer door closed, another opened and Baylin entered the room from a side chamber whence, Ifryn knew, he had been observing the interview through a concealed spy-hole. It was one of many such devices within the court, testimony to the neurotic temperament of emperors.

'He's lying,' Baylin pronounced. 'At least in part.'

'Yes,' Ifryn agreed sadly. 'Poor man. He looked scared out of his wits.'

Captain Ofiah was extremely drunk. It had been four days since he had returned to Xantium, and relinquishing the responsibilities of his latest trip had made him light-headed with relief. However, his military duties had compelled him to stern self-discipline for a time, but now he was on leave for a few days, and should have been able to relax. Yet he could not clear his mind of thoughts about the prisoner and the contents of the mysterious casket. Chancellor Verkho had seemed positively avid to receive it, his extraordinary eyes glittering insanely, but since then nothing significant had happened. Indeed, the Chancellor had seemed almost invisible recently. But the lunatic ramblings of the prisoner could not be forgotten, and Ofiah had taken refuge in drink and the all-pervading passion of the city, gambling.

Martyn had had some difficulty in tracing him, but he had eventually tracked the soldier down to an inn near the Stadium, in the southern part of The Levels. While Sagar kept well out of sight, observing from a dark corner, Martyn joined the Captain's group, and soon inveigled him into a game of emperors. Pretending to be as intoxicated as his opponent, the northerner contrived to lose most of the first few series and, as more ale and stronger spirits flowed, the game grew more animated.

At the start of a new round, Ofiah threw his set of seven red dice and produced four water symbols.

'Bea' tha',' he slurred, looking up smugly.

'No' bad, for'a start,' Martyn conceded. 'All that water – you mus' be traveller.' He rolled his own set of whites and got no more than two weak pairs.

'Trav'llin's part o' job.' Ofiah tapped his captain's badge with an unsteady finger.

'Where y'been lately then?'

'Down sou',' he replied, adding with exaggerated care, 'Bright-hav-en.'

'Though' you sholdier, not shailor,' Martyn deliberately provoked him.

'Ssailors! Pah!' Ofiah added a few choice insults, much to the amusement of his audience.

Martyn asked why he had been in the port, and the Captain laughed, then snarled, taking another drink before answering.

'Playin' nursemaid to a bloody madman!' he declared bitterly. 'From Zalyss, of all places. And,' he went on, full of self-importance, 'bringin' deliv'ry for Verkho himself.'

Ofiah was then prevailed upon to tell all about his recent prisoner and the enigmatic cargo, which he did at length, protesting all the while that it was actually secret, but – much to Sagar's frustration – without actually naming the man from Zalys. Eventually, Martyn had to ask him.

'Hiss name?' Ofiah looked puzzled for a moment before replying. 'Bow-en Fol-e-gan-dros. Th' gods help him. Verkho has him now.'

CHAPTER TWENTY

What resilience is left? Can our world resist the iron blows of savage force, the cruel twists of mechanical devices? Can it withstand the scouring violence of acid or the scorching fury of fire and ice?

I fear none of these so much as mortal words.

Verkho emerged briefly from his self-imposed exile two days after Southan's ineffectual council meeting. He had spent the last five days and six nights in total, sometimes furious concentration. During that time he had eaten only the few morsels that had already been in his study, drunk only stale water and slept hardly at all – and then only when he was jeopardizing his own progress with exhaustion and hallucinations.

When he had first broken the casket seal and gazed upon the talisman within its protective casing, he had expected that it would soon yield to his urgent demands, but the ancient artefact had remained stubbornly, paradoxically remote.

The talisman itself was just visible, a rounded shape, the size of a fist, sheathed in silvery metal. The curious etchings on this housing had been the subject of most of Verkho's research, but as yet he had been unable to decipher any of it. Nor could he recognize the language – if indeed it *was* a language. However, all was encased in a sphere, the size of a man's head, made of some clear material that resembled glass but which was vastly more resilient. The outer surface was dull and opaque, like glass that had been in the sea for many years, but a small piece had been chipped away, revealing the material's true nature.

In the process of his exhaustive examination, the Chancellor had managed to remove a large proportion of the outer layer, flaking away the opaque skin so that the inner treasure could be clearly seen. However, his attempts to dig deeper into the sphere had met with hugely increased resistance. Brute force, a variety of tools, acids and other corrosive substances, as well as intense heat and cold had all been tried, but to no avail. The prize remained tantalizingly out of reach. At this point Verkho set aside his impatience and frustration as best he could, and decided to try more esoteric methods. His vast library contained many books of arcane knowledge, and several tomes held oblique references to the talisman and its supposed powers. However, none – at least none that he had found so far – gave any indication of how to release it from its crystal captivity. The Chancellor was no stranger to what most men called magic, but his own talents were proving ineffective, and he had already vowed not to let any other into his secret until absolutely necessary. So far he had, quite literally, done no more than scratch the surface, but there were other avenues to be explored.

Verkho's sudden reemergence sent shock waves through his staff, all of whom had vast amounts of business waiting for his attention. However, the Chancellor soon made it clear that he was in no mood to even think of clearing such a backlog, and ignored their pleas, simply issuing peremptory instructions about supplies of food, wine and water, as well as more books to be brought from his private quarters. When his servants entered the study, they were shocked by the state it was in, but they had been given instructions not to touch anything, and if anyone wondered what lay under the cloth draped on the large desk, they knew better than to ask.

Within an hour, after giving his final commands, which in effect delegated all decision making to various subordinates, Verkho had retired to his solitary vigil once more, locking the doors again. Those who came later – among them Southan, Clavia and Harios – went away empty-handed – and more bemused and angry than ever.

Ever since his conversation with the Empress, Corton had lived on tenterhooks. To say that his nerves were frayed would have been an understatement; as Grongar remarked, doing nothing to soothe his friend, they had been torn to shreds by something with very big teeth. However, nothing untoward had happened in the last two days, and the wine-master was now beginning to regret agreeing to accompany Grongar on this dangerous and seemingly ill-conceived expedition. Anything outside Corton's own cloistered surroundings was apt to make him feel ill at ease, and he had always especially disliked the rank atmosphere and noisy bustle of The Levels. Yet here he was on his way to a disreputable tavern, to meet perhaps the most dangerous man in all the city!

After the interview with Ifryn, Corton had immediately confided in Grongar, and his friend had greeted the news with unaccustomed solemnity. Grongar had done nothing about his presumed identification of the Swordsman, reckoning after long and arduous thought that it was none of his business. The outlaw's exploits were regarded by many as entertaining and somehow admirable in their daring, and Grongar felt no particular loyalty to Chancellor Verkho, who was the Swordsman's sworn enemy. However, the news that the Empress Ifryn, whom Grongar had always admired from afar, wanted the renegade found – for whatever reason – and the implication that Corton might after all be embroiled in the court plotting had given him second thoughts. He had decided to confront Martyn; if he was right, then his fellow northerner would have to explain where his true loyalties lay or risk being exposed by Grongar. If necessary, Grongar would present him with an ultimatum; either Martyn left Xantium for good, or Grongar would have him arrested.

'Are you sure this is wise?' Corton asked again. 'In so public a place?'

'The more public the better,' the barbarian replied gruffly. 'If it comes to fighting, I want lots of witnesses. And I've got plenty of friends round here.' He actually seemed to be looking forward to the encounter, with a sort of grim excitement, but Corton was not reassured.

'I must be mad!' he muttered.

Grongar laughed.

'"In the darkness of the soul, only madmen see clearly,"' he quoted. 'You've opened your eyes, that's all.'

'One of your northern proverbs, no doubt,' Corton replied caustically. 'In this case I'd rather be blind.'

'*I'd* rather you kept your eyes open just now,' his companion remarked. 'We're here.'

He turned into the lamplit doorway of a dingy tavern called The Silent Woman. Corton noted sourly that the sign above the name was completely blank, a joke he did not find at all funny. It was not a good omen.

Inside, the room was fetid and noisy, with most of the patrons clustered around several games of chance. Grongar had already spotted Martyn at a small table in the far corner, sitting with Folly, his faithful shadow of recent days. Martyn stood as they approached, and grinned.

'Well met, Grongar. And Master Corton, welcome. I fear this establishment has no wine to satisfy your palate.' He eyed the unexpected visitor speculatively, much to Corton's discomfort.

'It'll do him good to have a real drink for a change,' Grongar commented maliciously.

'I got your message,' Martyn went on. 'And I could not resist the thought of free ale and good company. What are we celebrating?'

'Later,' Grongar said. 'Let me fill the tankards first.'

'I'll go,' Sagar volunteered quickly. He was nervous too, and welcomed the chance to get away and observe the newcomers from a distance.

Grongar tossed some coins on the table, and Sagar went to the serving counter while the others sat down. As he waited for the mugs to be filled, he studied the ill-matched pair. Could they possibly know something of Bowen's fate? And if so, how was he to find out? His own investigations had revealed nothing, and the problem gnawed at Sagar's heart. Bowen had simply vanished into the bowels of the court, and Martyn had not been able to find Alasia to ask her advice. Sagar imagined his brother incarcerated, tortured, perhaps even dead – and felt wretched. If there was a chance that Grongar or Corton knew something, then he would be willing to risk much to prise it from them. Then again, why had they asked for this meeting? A simple social call seemed unlikely.

Only one way to find out, he told himself as he paid and picked up the tray. On the way back to the corner he saw a stooped old man, in merchant's clothes and cap, totter into the tavern and sit at a table between theirs and the counter. He banged his fist upon the wood and demanded ale in a querulous, high-pitched voice. One of the barmaids, sensing a customer who might be richer than the usual sort, hurried to supply him, while most of the clientele gave him one incurious glance and then returned to their own concerns.

As Sagar set the tray down, the three men were discussing the tactics of labyrinth. Corton looked at his tankard, foam dribbling down its side, with a mixture of dismay and disbelief.

'I'll help you out if you can't manage it all,' Grongar remarked helpfully, then took his change from Martyn's companion. 'Thank you, Folly . . . or should I say, Sagar?'

All four men became very still. Although the noise

175

around them continued unabated, the room suddenly seemed very quiet. Sagar could hear his own heart thumping, and Martyn gave the impression of a cornered snake, violence coiled within him. Corton was petrified and unable to hide it. Only Grongar remained sanguine – at least on the surface. He picked up his tankard and noisily drained half its contents. Since their last meeting, he had done some investigating of his own, and had discovered the name of the most likely prisoner to have been rescued from Verkho's dungeons. His companions' reactions confirmed his thinking.

'And you,' Grongar went on quietly, turning to Martyn, 'unless I am very much mistaken, sometimes name yourself after your blade.' He waited for a reaction, but got none. The silence grew even deeper. 'No words? The burning sword in The Spires was eloquent enough, I suppose. Though I've never found you short of breath before.'

'What do you want?' Martyn said eventually, denying nothing, still tense and ready for action.

'The answers to some questions.'

'What makes you think I'm the one to answer them?'

'Intuition,' Grongar replied. 'A northerner's intuition.'

Martyn smiled then, but there was little humour in his eyes. They burned.

'You name us rightly,' he said quietly, his voice like steel, and his response provoking gasps from both Corton and Sagar. 'I will answer your questions if I can. In return, you will answer some of mine. Your coming here speaks well of your honour, but be careful what you say. The wrong words and your lives are forfeit.'

'I'll answer your questions,' the barbarian replied, 'but we will answer for our own lives. Bloodshed here would not be a good idea,' he pointed out calmly.

'Little of value is gained without risk,' Martyn stated, and the two northerners held each other's gaze, while Corton and Sagar could only look on, helpless seconds in this duel.

'A trade then,' Grongar offered eventually. 'Truth for truth.' He spat on his palm and held it out. Martyn did the same and they clasped hands briefly.

'Truth for truth,' Martyn confirmed.

'Have you been responsible for any attempt to poison Ifryn and Azari?' Grongar began without delay.

'No.' It was a flat, emphatic denial. 'You know who the expert in venom is in this city.' In turn he asked, 'Have you told anyone else of our identities?'

'No. Nor will I, unless it becomes necessary.' The Swordsman bridled at that, but did not respond. 'Are you truly an enemy of the Empire?' Grongar continued.

'Yes. I cannot deny that. My dearest wish is to see it crumble into dust.'

'Why?'

'For what it did to me, my country, my family. Do not ask me to elaborate. But what are *your* loyalties?'

'I am pledged in service to Southan and Ifryn,' Grongar said easily. 'They have my personal loyalty.'

'And Verkho?'

'He is not worthy of loyalty, only fear.'

'Not even that,' Martyn whispered, his voice filled with loathing.

'So the Chancellor is the focus of your enmity?'

'I will not be satisfied until he is dead at my hand.' Martyn paused and Sagar took advantage, unable to contain himself any longer.

'Do you know anything of Bowen Folegandros, my brother?' he asked urgently. 'He was brought here six days ago.'

Corton and Grongar exchanged a glance.

'We know nothing of him,' the barbarian replied. 'But I will enquire.'

Sagar sank back in his seat, and Martyn returned to his questions.

'What do you intend to do now?'

'We believe that Ifryn is looking for you, for reasons

177

of her own,' Grongar told him evenly. 'Would you be willing to meet her representative?'

'Under certain conditions, yes.'

'We will arrange it.'

'And beyond that?'

'We tell no one.'

'Why should we believe you?' Sagar burst out fearfully.

'In many ways, our interests are the same,' Grongar told him. 'Chancellor Verkho has hidden himself away for several days now.' The gossip in the city streets had said as much. 'His plotting bodes ill for all of us, perhaps even for the Emperor.'

'That's not enough!' Sagar exclaimed.

'My friend is right,' Martyn said more calmly. 'You have a hold over us. What can you give us in return?'

'Me,' Corton said suddenly. 'I will be your hostage until you are satisfied of our trust.' He was shaking as he spoke, but resolute.

'No! I gave my word,' Grongar rasped, clearly shocked. 'This is not necessary.'

'What else will convince them?' the wine-master asked.

Grongar was speechless for the first time, and Martyn saw the real concern on the barbarian's hairy features. Corton obviously meant a great deal to him.

'We accept.'

Eventually, Grongar nodded.

'What conditions do you require for the meeting?' he asked.

The following morning, a written message was delivered to Ifryn's apartment by a disreputable looking man who claimed to be the master of the imperial hounds. Doneta made him wait outside, where guards were in close attendance, while she took the clumsily sealed letter to her mistress. Baylin was with Ifryn, having just told her how his close observation of Corton had finally paid off.

178

'You were close enough to hear all this, but no one recognized you?' the Empress said.

'No one,' Baylin confirmed with a smile. 'I can look much older than my years if needs be, and my hearing is sharp. What should we do now, wait for their embassy? Or take matters into our own hands?'

Doneta came in at this point, handed the note to her mistress, and described the shabby appearance of the messenger.

'They move fast,' Baylin commented.

'Ask him to wait in the outer room, please,' the Empress told her maid, who departed obediently but with a disapproving expression on her face. Ifryn opened the letter and read aloud.

'"My lady, please forgive me if I am intruding on private matters. I confess I was not wholly truthful in our recent conversation and I now wish to set the record straight. However, circumstances prevent me from doing so in person, so I beg you to admit my friend and colleague, Grongar, to your presence. He has information concerning the Swordsman whom, I believe, you may wish to locate. Your humble servant, Corton Magna."'

Ifryn looked at her ally.

'Shall I observe from the other room?' he asked.

'No. Come with me. Let us offer them a little openness in return for theirs.' The Empress led the way into the outer chamber.

Some time later, when Grongar had departed, they talked again.

'You'll go?'

'Yes. This is what we wanted, after all.'

'Even under those conditions?'

'For one in his position,' Baylin said, 'they're reasonable enough. I'll take precautions of my own – and I have the advantage of already knowing who he is.'

'But you'll be careful?' she persisted.

'I'm always careful,' he replied, adding to himself, *after my own fashion.*

179

CHAPTER TWENTY-ONE

A jewelled sword, smaller than the poet's quill, points to a door the colour of another sky. Beyond, the darkness glows. He is like a candle; the brighter he burns, the sooner he will be spent; destroying his own substance by the fire of his life.

In the meantime, we are all moths.

Clavia's anger had gone beyond mere rage and had become something cold and sharp; a steel-hard, shiny instrument of malice. After another fruitless attempt to see Verkho, she was livid, her once beautiful face bloated and crimson. Her half-brother's servants had been condescendingly polite but relentlessly unhelpful – and she had done her cause no good at all by screaming, cursing and threatening. Now, short of finding enough soldiers to risk Verkho's wrath by physically smashing their way into the study, there was no way to see the Chancellor. Clavia had only one other resource to fall back on, and she intended to wield her vengeful fury like a blade.

Southan received her with the casual disregard that made her hate him so violently. But Clavia had the distinct satisfaction of seeing his mood change abruptly when she announced her reason for requesting an audience.

'My lord, I have discovered where General Kerrell is.'

'He is alive?' the Emperor exclaimed, all attention now. 'In Xantium?'

'Yes, but he is held under enchantments by enemies of the Empire.'

'Enchantments?'

'Yes, my lord,' Clavia replied, relishing his sudden astonishment. 'For that reason, we must approach carefully. Summon your men and I will lead you to him.'

Southan reacted quickly, instructing one of the officers in attendance to gather a force of men, and calling together those officials who might have relevant knowledge of the magic arts. All was ready remarkably quickly. Clavia led them in the direction of her own apartments, and thence to a nearby storeroom.

'He is here?' Southan asked. 'So close?'

'That is how I found him,' Clavia lied. 'I heard his cries, but did not have the courage to enter on my own.'

Southan tried the door but found it locked, and signalled his soldiers to break it down. For some time the sturdy reinforced wood refused to yield, but eventually the hinges gave way and the door crashed inwards, echoing hollowly. The room beyond was completely empty, bare whitewashed walls and wooden floorboards illuminated only by a single skylight in the rafters. Clavia stared transfixed, unable to believe what she saw, and the first real doubts disturbed her righteous anger. As the last echoes died away, no one moved.

'Is this a joke?' the Emperor hissed coldly.

'No. He's here!' she cried. 'I swear it.'

'Go in and look,' Southan told one of his men. 'Just to make sure.'

'No!' Clavia thrust them aside and stepped towards the now vacant doorway, leaning forward to peer round the frame.

In that instant, a thunderclap of sound rang out, so loud that it made the stones of the court shake, and for a moment, the room vanished in a sudden white glare. Everyone was temporarily deaf and blind, but they recovered in time to see Clavia topple backwards as if in slow motion. As she fell stiffly to the ground, the onlookers stared in horrified fascination or looked away. The front half of Clavia's head had been sliced clean away, exposing a section of soft grey matter, neatly severed bones and lacerated flesh, now leaking a little blood. Her face was gone.

A face appeared in Kerrell's white infinity, and he groped towards it with clawing fingers and howling thoughts. Time had become non-existent for him – as had everything else – but this was the first variation in his interminable imprisonment, and he clutched at the vision as a drowning man clutches at the mirage of the sun.

It was a face he knew well, one he despised and one he connected – albeit obscurely – with his present predicament. But somehow the face was not real; it was a mask, a dead thing, frozen in a permanent, wide-eyed scowl. And yet it disturbed the fabric of his helplessness, caused a ripple in the all-embracing void, and he fought with all the meagre weapons still at his command to keep it from disappearing.

Help me! he screamed silently as he strove to follow the image's progress. *Help me!*

There was no response. Clavia's expression altered not at all, but the disembodied face settled into a steady orbit around him, always looking towards him, always out of reach.

Kerrell, who had fought valiantly to prevent himself forming a new artificial realm from his own memories – knowing that that would be the final defeat, the last descent into irretrievable insanity – could not bear to follow its path, and yet could not look away.

I am doomed, he thought dismally.

He knew the dead face would be with him even in his dreams.

For the past few days, Bowen had been surrounded by lunatics, men and women who were regularly prey to terrible nightmares, and whose erratic talents were expressed in spasms of anger or violence. He felt quite at home.

The ministry was in chaos. With so many inmates effectively out of control, the jobs of Harios and the other section heads had become impossible. They had done their best, in the absence of any directions from their superior, but the physicians could no longer cope, and even the talented healers had now become a menace to themselves and others. Injuries were commonplace, deaths increasingly frequent. There was no need now to go out in search of ghosts; the spectres came to them, infesting the buildings with a gentle, ominous radiance. Fires blossomed spontaneously; anything breakable was at the mercy of those whose now deranged expertise lay in telekinesis. All was bedlam.

The voice came to Bowen out of thin air – a man's voice, in distress. That was not uncommon in this mad place, but Bowen knew that this was not one of the talents. His plight was what marked him as special – and to be pitied. *Help me!* Bowen tried to shy away, not wanting to be drawn into that grey-white winding sheet of pain, but he could not help himself. There was another face there too, a dead woman, staring. *Help me!* Making a determined effort to break away, Bowen shut out the plea, but another presence came seeking. *Show me,* she commanded urgently. *Where is he?* Bowen reluctantly opened the channels again, let her see, then felt her withdraw with no further word. *I am doomed,* the first voice said.

You're not the only one, Bowen thought. And, as always in times of crisis, his memories returned to Gaye. *You're not the only one.*

Alasia had seen and heard. She had hardly noticed who her guide had been, knowing only that he had opened a door which she had not been able to budge, even when the key was turned by the death of another. *There are*

183

holes in time. But at least now she had been able to see into one of them. Alasia knew where – or rather when – Kerrell was.

It was time to return to The Spires.

Baylin regretted lying to Ifryn, but he knew that if he accepted all the Swordsman's conditions, he had no choice but to put himself at risk. He was relying on the other man's curiosity to keep him alive until he had had the chance to talk. After that, if his words failed to persuade, he would accept whatever fate decreed.

Quite why he had chosen to go along with this elaborate charade was a mystery to him. He could just as easily have waited until Martyn Waysinger was located, and then had him quietly arrested. Perhaps it was concern over Corton's position, perhaps respect for Grongar's trust. Or maybe it was the irrational confidence that he was dealing here with a man who lived by his own code of honour. Whatever the reason, Baylin was willing to gamble with his life. It was not the first time he had done so for a cause he considered worthy.

With a patience born of a life of travel, he sat at an outdoor table, a bowl of herb tea untouched before him, and waited as day turned to dusk. He was unarmed, and in spite of his reassurances to Ifryn, alone. He was not even in disguise.

An hour crawled by, and Baylin began to worry. Had the Swordsman decided against the meeting after all? Then a small boy in ragged clothes sidled up to the table.

'Want to buy a jewel, master?'

'What jewel do you have?' Baylin replied curiously.

'This.' The urchin stretched out his right fist and uncurled grubby fingers. A miniature sword lay on his palm.

The traveller calmly took a few coins from his purse and exchanged them for the tiny metal object.

'Where did you get this?'

'I'll show you. Come.' The child set off immediately,

184

beckoning over his shoulder. Baylin hurried to follow, impressed by the Swordsman's tactics. No doubt his accomplices had been observing him for some time, and would now be careful to see that Baylin made no sign to anyone and that no one else followed him. He was glad that he was working alone.

The boy led him, via a tortuous route, to the entrance to a small, dead end alleyway.

'Go to the green door at the far end,' he said, pointing. 'Knock four times. They'll let you in.'

'They?' But the urchin merely shrugged and skipped away.

Baylin approached cautiously, taking in every detail of his surroundings. The alleyway was shuttered and still. He knocked as instructed, and the door immediately swung inwards. Inside, darkness beckoned.

A voice said, 'Come in. Tread boldly. The floor is dirty but even. Stop after six paces.'

Baylin did as he was told, and the door shut behind him. To the traveller's eyes, the room seemed pitch black, and it smelt of dust and disuse. So much the better. He had seen no faces, and anyone returning here would find only a drab, empty space. That meant the Swordsman was at least considering letting his visitor leave freely once the interview was over.

'I am told you wish to speak to me,' said another voice, which Baylin recognized as Martyn's. 'Why?'

'The Empress and I believe that we share a common enemy.'

'Verkho.'

'Exactly. And avenues are open to you that we cannot take.'

'Such as?'

'Surely you need not have me spell it out,' Baylin said evenly. 'The Empress' position . . .'

'What would you have me do?' Martyn asked.

Calmly, choosing his words with care, Baylin told him. His speech was greeted with silence, and he waited tensely for a response. *It'll come now, or not at all,* he thought, imagining the blade sliding between his ribs.

'I will think about it,' the Swordsman said eventually. 'You may go.'

Behind him the door creaked open, and a faint light filtered into the room. Baylin turned and left without looking into the deeper shadows, his heart lifting with every step.

It was only when he reached Ifryn's chambers to report his progress that he learnt of Clavia's horrific death – and of the renewed speculation about Kerrell's fate.

CHAPTER TWENTY-TWO

*Seven gods, seven dice. Six crowns, one lantern. With
such a throw Gar would have won his last gamble. But
he, like Meyu, had set aside his divine powers for the
contest. When Gar lost, he lost all.*

*Can the single lamp of knowledge shine amid the power
of six? We are all, men and gods alike, waiting for the seal
to be broken.*

Unaware that his half-sister had been dead for nearly
two days, Verkho finally made a breakthrough in his
efforts to reach the talisman. With the help of copies of
ancient manuscripts, he translated a tiny part of the
arcane script etched on to the metal shell. In the long
defunct Aedlerian language, the inscription read, 'Cast
the dice of kings and utter nought'.

'Gar was always the most reckless gambler in the
pantheon,' Verkho said aloud, smiling.

It took him some time to convert the literal translation
into an exact instruction. What precisely were 'the dice
of kings'? The most obvious solution was the set of
dice used for the game of emperors. The symbol representing the highest rank – a crown – could just as well
signify a king, and after all, the game itself was ancient.
However, when Verkho threw a set of seven dice on the
desk next to the obdurate sphere, nothing unusual happened. He tried several times, keeping silent as he did
so, wondering if it was necessary to throw a particular
combination. Then he tested several different dice;
simple numerical cubes, four-sided pyramids, metal

stars, even knucklebones – all to no avail. Then, as his enthusiasm waned, a new idea occurred to him.

'Utter nought,' he murmured. 'Utter nought.'

He went back to his studies, then returned to the sphere with renewed optimism. Picking up the emperors' dice, he held them briefly against the now uneven surface of the sphere. As if sensing his intent, the glass-like substance vibrated, filling the room with a sonorous note like the tolling of a crystal bell. Eager now, Verkho cast the dice. While they were still tumbling he intoned, 'Bera-rucht,' which – as near as he could judge – was the correct pronunciation of the Aedlerian word meaning nothing or nought. As the dice settled the Chancellor was not surprised to see six showing the crown upper-most. The seventh cube, which had no crown, showed the lantern of knowledge, the least significant of all the symbols, but Verkho was not concerned with that. His gaze was fixed upon the sphere.

For a few breathless moments it glowed silvery white, then an outer layer simply melted away into nothing before his eyes, leaving the sphere slightly smaller than before and now perfectly smooth and transparent. It was progress at last – but even so, the talisman was still out of reach. Verkho quickly tried the process again, but nothing happened. The old god was evidently not about to give up all his secrets at once.

It was then that the Chancellor noticed that the inner metal casing had changed. The small part of the inscription that he had translated had vanished, but the rest of it was different now. New symbols, new words, possibly even new languages had appeared. The game must begin again.

Verkho laughed aloud then, out of admiration for his ancient opponent who had devised this trial of skill, but also at his own prowess. He had no doubts about the eventual outcome.

However, it was obviously going to be a longer task than anticipated and, in the wake of this first success,

Verkho's thoughts turned briefly to the outside world. He ventured out to take stock of the Empire. And found himself bombarded with information and requests. He was shocked to learn how much time had passed since the arrival of the talisman, but that was nothing compared to the news of the disruption of the talents, the disorganization of the Empire's affairs and, most of all, Clavia's death. The Chancellor wasted no time mourning, believing that she had earned her gruesome end by her own stupidity, but was furious at her betrayal. What was more, the forces that held Kerrell were clearly out of control, and this did not bode well for the future.

Indeed, the day had been full of omens. It seemed that the whole of Xantium was nervous, after a partial eclipse of the sun had darkened the day in the late morning. Anxious not to be kept from the talisman for too long, the Chancellor worked hard and swiftly to remedy as much as possible of the Empire's maladies. To make matters worse, the first Far-speaker message from his spy on Zalys arrived in mid-afternoon, reporting that the rebellious islanders appeared to be in complete control and that there was no sign of either Farrag or the imperial garrison. There was nothing Verkho could do about that yet, and he returned to his secure study as evening drew in, relieved that he had not been further embroiled in these secondary matters.

The Chancellor had more important work to do.

The eclipse had made the air unseasonably chill, and seemed to Ifryn to be yet another portent of disaster. When Southan had come to her the day before with the news of Clavia's death and her earlier insistence that Kerrell was held under enchantment, Ifryn had been appalled. She had wanted to rush straight to the reputedly spellbound place, but her husband had forbidden her to do any such thing, and told her that the area was now sealed off. After Clavia's appalling end, it was deemed too dangerous to risk a further approach

189

until they could perhaps learn something of whatever evil lurked within. For that the Emperor was relying – much to Ifryn's dismay – on the still absent Verkho, because none of the so-called experts in arcane talents could even begin to explain it.

Clavia's involvement made Ifryn all the more certain that Verkho was behind Kerrell's disappearance, and she cursed the woman for getting herself killed when she might have been able to shed some light on the mystery.

This all came on top of Baylin's encounter with the Swordsman and the uncertainty of whether the outlaw would do as they had asked, and left the Empress even more confused and miserable than ever. She took a small measure of comfort from Baylin's continued well-being and vigilance, but now she could only wait, helpless again. Time and again she took out the tiny sword that Baylin had given her, and wondered what would happen now that the initiative seemed to have been taken away from her.

However, that all changed in the late afternoon. Ifryn was standing at her window, as she often did when she was thinking, when she was startled by a small sound behind her. She spun round. Alasia stood in the centre of the room, her pale face bright in the slanting rays of the sun. She curtseyed solemnly, but Ifryn had no time for any such formality now. She ran across the room, flinging her arms about her friend, filled with a sudden overwhelming elation.

'Oh, Alasia! Where have you been?'

'Flying.'

'I'm so glad you're back. I've been lost without you!'

Ifryn released her friend, and Alasia demurely re-arranged her dress.

'I've seen Kerrell,' she stated baldly.

'What!' This was surely too much to hope for. Could both of her allies have returned? 'Where?'

'Ask rather "when?",' Alasia said.

'What do you mean?'

'He is not in this world.'

'Dead?' Ifryn's hopes sank like a lead weight.

Alasia shook her head.

'Waiting,' she amended.

'Waiting? For what?'

'For the madness to end. For the seal to be broken.'

By this time, Ifryn was ready to tear her hair out, and wanted to rattle her friend's frail bones, to make her talk sense – but knew she would achieve nothing that way.

'Where is he?' she pleaded. 'Is this something to do with the storeroom where Clavia was killed?'

'That is where the seal meets our time,' Alasia replied, as if that answered the question.

'Tell me what to do,' the Empress begged. Privately she was thinking, *What can I hope to do? I have no magic like Alasia or Verkho. I know nothing of such things. How can I fight against such sorcery, such madness?*

'You must wait,' Alasia said simply.

Ifryn almost laughed aloud. Her friend's sudden reappearance had rekindled such hope, but now Alasia was telling her to do the only thing she could do anyway. The irony tasted bitter.

'I can't wait,' she breathed. *I can't bear it.*

'I must go now.'

'No!' Instantly alarmed, Ifryn reached out to restrain Alasia, but her friend evaded her easily.

'The stranger is calling me,' she added by way of explanation. 'Do you want to meet him?'

Does she mean the Swordsman? Ifryn wondered. *What am I supposed to do now?*

'You can only wait,' Alasia told her again. 'As Kerrell waits.'

The Empress felt a sudden urge to cry, and shook her head in an agony of indecision. Nothing was happening the way it should. The movement and her tears blurred her vision momentarily and when it cleared, Alasia – impossibly – was gone. Ifryn stared at the empty room, every fibre of her being crying useless denial. Then, with

191

sudden decisiveness, she turned on her heel and left her apartments. A short while later, she approached the guards at the entrance to the forbidden corridor.

'Let me pass.'

'My lady, the Emperor has forbidden any . . .'

'Let me pass, I say. Do you dare disobey your Empress?'

The soldiers had never seen her in this mood. There was a fierce gleam in her normally gentle eyes, and the taut way she held her slender frame, combined with the ferocity of her words, made their determination wilt.

'Southan has given me permission to view the place,' she lied emphatically. 'Now stand aside.'

As she strode forward, neither man dared balk her physically, and they stepped aside at the last moment. Ifryn walked on, reaching the broken door and staring into the empty room beyond.

That is where the seal meets our time.

There was nothing to mark this as a place of enchantment or of death. Meticulous care had been taken to cleanse the stone floor of the corridor after Clavia's corpse had been taken away.

You can only wait. As Kerrell waits.

So be it, Ifryn decided.

And stepped into the room.

CHAPTER TWENTY-THREE

In darkness, they see. In darkness, they protect. The voices of my friends have found echoes in the world. We have need of such sentinels now.

The screamers' first attack on Nkosa did not last long, and was witnessed by only a small proportion of its inhabitants – but the terror of their coming soon spread as more and more people saw the mutilated victims. And in the days that followed, the attacks became regular events, bringing fear, dismay and stunned disbelief to the island's capital.

The impossible creatures always flew in over the sea, their great triangular wings undulating in grotesque mimicry of their normal motion under water. Long tails lashed above their bulk or whipped from side to side; unnatural teeth were bared in between the characteristic horns at the front of their bodies. They came in groups, sometimes as few as four, sometimes so many that no one could count the number, but as it flew, each one emitted a high-pitched, searing howl, which began on the edge of hearing while the screamer was still far away. All ears soon became attuned to this harbinger of death.

The monsters swooped down into any open spaces in the town; squares, canals, even the narrow alleyways that barely admitted their vast wingspan and where their screaming intensified to a shattering roar. Anyone out in the open was vulnerable, and many were smashed aside by the powerful wings or torn to shreds by the raking teeth and horns. Fen, among many others, was reminded of the horrible injuries inflicted on a diver some days earlier, but nothing could have prepared her for this savagery. She found it all the more distressing because as a child she had often swum with sea-bats, then gentle, inquisitive and friendly creatures whose wide mouths and so-called horns were no threat at all. Now both features had mutated to nightmare levels; the teeth were more reminiscent of those of a large shark and the 'horns', once mere extensions of their fins, were terrible weapons which the screamers wielded with ferocious violence. To make matters worse, their long tails had extended much further than was natural, and could cut like a whip – but also carried a lethal poison in the tip. And as if that were not enough, some of the flying rays had developed long pointed spines, which moved like fins on top and below their frames, and which gave off crackling sparks of blue light. A single touch from one of these spines was enough to throw a grown man several paces, leaving him stunned and helpless.

The monstrous attackers seemed to combine all the feral menace of rabid predators with the pointless malice induced by some loathsome sorcery. They were evil incarnate, and there was no defence against them. Moving at an astounding speed for creatures of such size, they were proof against any weapons the islanders could turn against them. After the initial shock and panic, some of the town's more proficient archers had tried their best, but few could keep a steady aim against such a foe, and even the accurate shots did no real damage. The screamers just ignored the arrows, and several brave men died in vain. Even fire did not seem to daunt the monsters. At first, the flares, torches and flaming bolts made the creatures hesitate momentarily, but then they came on regardless.

All the people of Nkosa could do was hide; their enemies rarely attacked buildings – except for some flimsy wooden structures in the docks and on the outskirts of the town. These were left shattered by the onslaught, but the more solid houses suffered only minor damage. Indeed, the only success – if it could be called that – the islanders had against the monsters was when the creatures killed themselves in insane fury when their prey escaped into such a haven. They battered themselves to death against unforgiving stone or crashed to the ground where they were unable to take off again or slither back to the water. Even like this, crippled and trapped, the beasts took a long time to die, and retained their deadly malevolence to the end. The poison flail at the end of the tail whip ensured that no one with any sense came too close until they were absolutely certain of the creature's demise. At that point, however, the islanders vented their frustrations over the one-sided battle, furiously hacking the carcasses to bits. Even then there were casualties; the venom still killed anyone who was splashed, and the power that sparked from the spines remained active long after the dull eyes clouded over in death.

Dsordas and his colleagues did what they could; watches were doubled and danger signals arranged; shelters and escape routes were set up for all those who had to be outside, especially around the town's most vulnerable area – the lagoon and the docks. Beyond that, all they could do was try to investigate any possible way of combating their terrifying foe. As yet, no one had come up with anything feasible. Even Mouse was stumped – for now.

Many saw the screamers as some sort of punishment, the latest proof of the island's abandonment by the old gods, and they became more and more vociferous in their demands that something be done. Some said that Dsordas ought to press Gaye into service, as she had previously been able to tap some source of vestigial magic, but he rejected this suggestion. He knew how Gaye felt about the screamers, and he would not force her into anything, except as a last resort. He would do it if he had to, but only when it proved absolutely necessary. Nikolas did his best, drawing on his own beliefs in open prayer and the reenactment of ancient rituals. Sacrifices were made, offerings poured into the sea and the pantheon called upon for aid – but all to no avail. On two occasions, Nikolas and a group of believers even braved the Arena. To reach the sacred site involved a dangerously long time in open country, and only the truly dedicated were prepared to take such a risk. Unfortunately, the ancient valley revealed nothing. Once again, its secrets remained hidden. Even so, some were appeased by the efforts of the new Patriarch – but not the majority of those who put their faith in the old beliefs. With the sea still plagued and the new month's high tides due soon, it seemed to them that the old tales were more relevant than ever.

Few boats now ventured out on to the open sea and less went every day. Even the *Frozen Star* and the merchant ship from the far south stayed in port, reckoning they were safer even in a besieged town. Of those fishermen who were bold or foolhardy enough to set sail, some never returned and, although the ocean was still abnormally treacherous, most people assumed that this was the work of the screamers. The possible danger from an imperial fleet was almost forgotten in the face of this new and even more horrendous assault; although a vigilant watch was still kept upon the skyline, almost everyone now believed that the Xantic fleet would not come. The screamers represented a new form of oppression and some, forgetting their supposed destruction of the fleet, began to speculate that they were in fact weapons of the Empire; a new and evil kind of war.

Whatever their source or motivation, the flying rays were the enemy now, and Dsordas and his deputies learnt all they could about them. They seemed invincible – unless they could all somehow be induced into enraged suicide – but no knowledge was spurned. No one knew what small fact might be the vital clue to the island's salvation. But as yet they had little enough to go on. Understandably, fear was not conducive to the accurate collection of information, and few people were keen to observe the monsters too closely.

However, two curious facts did emerge. First, the many and apparently purposeless ghosts who now wandered the island seemed almost as afraid of the screamers as were the living. This seemed absurd; the two alien groups lived in different realms, and so neither would be able to harm the other, and yet the spirits' distress was obvious. The second observation was the more practical fact that no attacks were made at night. That in itself was a small mercy, but no one could offer an explanation. The screamers still flew during the hours of darkness – they had been sighted in the moon-light many times over the sea – but none came close to the shore. The only things that flew in Nkosa at night were large numbers of bats – far more than was usual. And this time Gaye was not responsible for their arrival.

For Gaye this was a particularly harrowing time. Her movements were more restricted than ever, but even in the comparative safety of her home, she could hear the screamers coming well before anyone else. The sound alone was torture enough, but her situation was made even more intolerable by the fact that everyone else seemed to have a part to play in the defence of Nkosa. Even Natali was taking part in Etha's project to save Iceman. It seemed to Gaye that she alone was useless. And to make matters worse, she was still tormented by her unsatisfied yearning to be with Bowen, just to know how he was, *where* he was . . .

And then, of course, there was the mystifying burden of the ghost's advice. His incomprehensible message was obviously important, but no one could make any sense of it. *The circle begins and ends on Zalys. Remember this well.* One of Gaye's first thoughts had been to try and contact her remote friend and guide, Alasia. Perhaps she would be able to explain. At her own wish, the amberine pendant was always kept within Gaye's reach now, and she sensed it all the time, like an invisible beacon, a source of heat and power – but too many unpleasant experiences had made her wary, and she touched it infrequently.

The first time she tried to contact Alasia again was on the day of the eclipse, the day the screamers first came, and her efforts had been disrupted by more immediate concerns. As soon as she touched the stone she felt a new sickness, dreadfully close at hand, and she had withdrawn quickly. Later, when the first attack was made, all thoughts of Alasia had flown from her mind. However, she tried again the next day. The sickness was still there, but it was lying dormant now. It felt like the vile impression she had received from the Far-speakers, but she knew that was impossible. All the Far-speakers on Zalys were dead, except for Iceman, and he was quite different now. Later, Gaye mentioned her feelings to Fen and Dsordas, just in case, but at the time she had ignored the sensation and called out to Alasia.

It took some time for the images to form in her mind, and when they did, the chaotic, infinite tangle appeared even more daunting than ever. There were strands that looked distorted somehow, wrong – though Gaye could not explain why – but there was no sign of Alasia. Gaye persisted, in spite of her increasing uncertainty.

Then, just as she was on the point of giving up, the otherworld realm shifted, the lines and shapes lurching sickeningly, and her inner vision swayed alarmingly. All at once, voices filled her head, but the only face she saw was dead, locked in a fearful grimace. Gaye was surrounded by an absolute whiteness, but the voices cut through the mist with a fine urgency.

Together! Together. It was Alasia, unseen but unmistakable, even in her uncharacteristic intensity. *You can only succeed together!*

There was a pause. The dead face revolved slowly in

Gaye's vision and now two more people appeared, a man and a woman, holding each other's hands and seeming to pull in opposite directions. The man stared at the disembodied face, but the woman's soft brown eyes were locked on him alone, fear and passion mingling in her gaze.

Forget her, Alasia said. *She's gone. Go to him . . . Yes, him! He is the centre of the circle, the breach in the seal. Hurry!*

Trust her, the woman urged. *It's our only hope.* She tugged at her unwilling partner, pulling him towards a swathe of white, searing flame.

We could stay here . . . together . . . the man said, longing and madness in his tone.

No!

No! Alasia echoed. *Get out. Get out. Quickly!* There was panic in her voice now, a mounting terror and fatigue. *I can't hold it much longer . . .*

Gaye was mesmerized by the struggle, but felt as though she were eavesdropping. There was something very private about this encounter, which was suffused with so many emotions, and she wondered whether she should withdraw. But just at that moment there was movement within the harsh glare of the flames, which grew brighter still – and in their midst, Gaye glimpsed another form, another character in this bizarre play.

Bowen! she screamed. His face was contorted with pain, his arms outstretched but his fingers curled upwards, grasping at nothing. The tormenting fire consumed him. *Help him, Alasia!*

Get out! Alasia yelled, her voice filled with anger and desperation.

Gaye flinched involuntarily, shying away from the images but unable to let go completely. She was surrounded by anger, malice and dread, all at once; outside emotions that made her even more of an intruder – yet still she clung to Bowen. But then, in spite of her efforts, he disappeared. His face, his hands, the fire, the man and woman – all vanished in an instant, plunging Gaye into a cold abyss of fear and loss. All that was left was the dead face, still revolving slowly. Gaye dropped the amberine and returned to her own blind world, weeping helplessly.

That had been several days ago, and she had not had the courage to try again. All thoughts of asking for Alasia's advice about the ghost's message, or even about the screamers, were gone. Gaye could not rid herself of the tortured vision of her love within the cruel flames, and despite her desperate need to know what was happening to him, she was too afraid to face such agony again.

CHAPTER TWENTY-FOUR

A child is born from the ashes of the dark fire. Yet other flames still blaze. They persist in their shouting, pointlessly, hurting my ears. Must I always be condemned to listen to the sound of burning, to the crack of sparks and the whispering of smoke? I am lost within the echoes of flame.

'They've stopped talking to me,' Iceman said, sounding both relieved and sad.

'Have they?' Habella smiled. So there would be no more secrets now.

The herbalist was convinced that her treatment and Etha's persistent care were having some effect. Iceman was still tormented by his craving, but it was easing as the days passed and, though his moods varied wildly, in his calmer moments he was revealing more of his own personality. Habella believed that this was due to Etha, who visited as often as she could, bringing food and cheerful company – almost as though the boy was one of her own family. Natali had accompanied his mother on several occasions, and there had been no repetitions of the earlier unhappy scenes. He and Iceman got on well, talking as equals – as if the two were the same age. Habella wondered if, having been robbed of his own childhood, Iceman was now beginning life again. His was a strange tale, but one which Habella believed had now taken a turn for the better.

One day, if the island survived, he might be able to tell them his whole story, but for now he was still struggling with fragmented memories. Although he had recalled little of his earlier life, he had had one vivid flash of a group of snow-covered mountains that made Etha think he might originally have been from the far north, like herself. It was one more subtle link between them.

'They must have found someone else to talk to,' Iceman added unexpectedly.

Habella frowned. Did he mean someone else here? On Zalys?

'Who?' she asked.

But Iceman only shrugged.

'Message relayed and received,' Hunter said.

'Any indication of a reply?' his master asked.

'No. None.'

The spy, who on this mission was calling himself Ranald Onar, swore angrily. It had been like this ever since their arrival on Zalys. Why wasn't Xantium responding? All he had received were simple acknowledgements: no answers to his increasingly impatient demands, nor any queries of their own or request for further information. Given the serious and extraordinary nature of his reports, this was not only perplexing but absurd. What could they be thinking of? Why wasn't Verkho sending him further instructions?

Ranald did not appreciate being left in the dark, especially in this appalling place, made all the more dreadful by the horrifying screamer attacks. He had been in Nkosa ten days now, he realized. Ten days, and not a word! He had done all that had been asked of him, but had received nothing in return. No gratitude, no concern, nothing. Ranald sensed treachery, and knew that he was on his own now, trapped on this godsforsaken island with only a mindless tool as his companion. Unless he heard something very soon, he decided, he would get out as quickly as he could.

*   *   *

'You're going to have to try again, sooner or later,' Fen told Gaye.

'Why?' her sister asked suspiciously. 'Because you and Dsordas want to know what's going on in Xantium?'

'No.' This thought had crossed Fen's mind, but her true motive lay elsewhere. 'Because you're torturing yourself with the memory of it. Until you try again, you'll never understand.'

Gaye was silent for a while, knowing that her sister was speaking the truth. Ever since her attempt to contact Alasia, she had repeatedly gone over the strange and frightening scenes she had witnessed, and had discussed them with Fen and others. The image of her love's fiery agony would not leave her mind, and yet the thought of a second attempt still made her tremble.

'I'm not even sure Alasia knew I was there,' she said eventually.

'I know. We've been over that.'

'It was so confusing. Was she talking to me or to someone else when she said "get out"?'

'I don't know,' Fen replied patiently. 'The only person who can answer that is Alasia herself.' After a moment, she added, 'You and Alasia were able to help Dsordas before. You were all right then. Maybe next time you'll be able to help yourself – and get some answers which might help Zalys at the same time.'

'Don't push me!' Gaye exclaimed accusingly.

'I'm not,' her sister said gently. 'This is eating you up inside. I love you, we all do – and we want what's best for you.'

Gaye burst into tears then, and Fen held her while her sobbing ran its course. Sick at heart at all the misery fate had piled upon her sister, she found herself thinking bitterly that eyes which could no longer see could still weep only too well.

'I'm sorry I keep—' Gaye began.

'Don't apologize,' Fen interrupted fiercely. 'You have

203

nothing to be sorry for. Just do whatever is right for you.
I'll help any way I can.'

'Stay with me.' Gaye dabbed ineffectually at her wet
face.

'Of course.'

'Give me the stone.'

'Now?'

'Yes. If I don't do it soon, I never will.'

Fen picked up the pendant by the chain, and placed it
in Gaye's waiting palm. Her fingers closed about it, her
knuckles turning pale.

'Hold my hand.'

Fen cupped her sister's fist in her own hands, and felt
it quivering with some unimaginable power. Gaye grew
very still, but whatever realm she inhabited now, Fen
knew she could not share it. *There's no magic in me,*
she thought. *I know nothing of such things.* Even so, she
stayed where she was, feeling her sister's hand grow hot,
seeing her blind eyes moving behind closed lids as if she
were dreaming.

Gaye was flying again. Shapes melted and re-formed,
colours flickered in endless rainbow hues; the air – if it
was air – was full of sounds just on the edge of hearing.
Distance had no meaning in this realm, but within its
boundaries nothing was out of reach – however good,
however vile.

Alasia, help me.

There was no response. Gaye flew on, adjusting to her
flight, sensing all around her, recognizing and resolving
mysteries, beyond contentment or fear. For a few
moments she knew only curiosity.

Alasia, help me, please.

This time there was a subtle shift in the infinite com-
plexity, and Gaye instinctively dived towards her goal.
Alasia appeared, bringing with her a sense of peace and
wellbeing, even though she looked tired and drawn. Her
pale face seemed more insubstantial than ever, but her
eyes were smiling. Gaye was certain of her welcome now.

Alasia, is Bowen . . . ? I saw him—

In the flames, her guide completed for her.

Yes. Is he . . . ?

Your beacons still shine, Alasia replied.

Relief poured through Gaye at the words, so much so that Fen saw her relax and felt her own hopes rise.

Can I see him?

You must fly together.

Gaye knew that she was being told that such a meeting was her own responsibility. It was up to her now. Resisting the temptation to try at that very moment, she quickly told Alasia of the message the ghost had given her, and asked what it meant. The other's reply was not straightforward – Alasia's answers never were – but Gaye accepted it gratefully, knowing that it would make sense eventually.

Circles have many beginnings and many ends. Zalys is only one such. Augury is a cursed art. All Xantium will tell you that.

Is that where you are, where Bowen is?

Xantium is the centre of many circles, Alasia replied. *If you would understand them all, you must come here. But beware, this city has its screamers too.*

You know about them? Gaye was taken by surprise.

I must go now.

No, please. I . . .

Fly, Alasia told her, and was gone.

But Gaye was no longer flying alone.

'Bowen,' she whispered aloud, then laughed, her face beautiful with sudden happiness.

Fen heard and saw that radiance, and took her hands away. This was a private reunion and one which, however illusory it appeared to Fen's worldly eyes, was Gaye's alone. Fen watched her sister's rapture, tears now spilling for joy, with mixed emotions. She could not begrudge Gaye a few moments of sweet pleasure, but she knew that when they ended, her return to the real world would be harder still. Even so, she was not prepared for the shocking and doubly cruel way in which the end came.

Gaye's expression changed in an instant from unreal happiness to an ugly, fearsome anger. She hurled her fury forth in an ear-splitting scream which rose beyond the pitch of human speech. When it ended, her rage was not spent.

'Go away!' she yelled, gesticulating wildly. 'Go away!'

The amberine pendant fell from her grasp and she collapsed, and did not respond to Fen's efforts to rouse her. A few moments later, Etha rushed into the room, and other members of the family clustered at the door, their faces pale with concern. Ia was despatched to fetch herb tea and brandy, and their ministrations finally brought Gaye round.

'Did they go?' she asked groggily.

'Who?' Etha asked.

Gaye was caught up in a sudden wave of memory, and swallowed hard.

'They took him away,' she said dolefully. 'I couldn't fly any more.'

Fen and her mother exchanged bemused glances, but before they had a chance to ask what she meant, Dsordas came in, breathing hard. His face was unnaturally pale.

'What happened here?' he asked urgently. 'What did she do?'

'Why? What's happened?' Fen replied.

'There were two screamers heading straight for this house,' he answered. 'I didn't think I was going to make it inside. Then I heard the sounds from in here – and they suddenly veered away and flew back out to sea.'

CHAPTER TWENTY-FIVE

Only mankind marks the rhythm of the years with artificial notes. For the rest, the calendar of the seasons is enough, but men go their own way, as ever. In the march of time, some stride out purposefully, while others dawdle and dream. Most struggle to make headway, but for a few, their birthright is a downhill path; though the way is easy, there is no turning back.

'Happy name-day, Natali!'

Although Gaye's traumatic experience of the day before was still on everyone's mind, they were valiantly trying to put this to one side in order to celebrate Natali's fourth year in the manner he deserved. All the Amari family and several friends, both young and old, had braved the screamers and had gathered for a noonday feast with a somewhat eccentric menu – chosen by Natali himself – which consisted purely of items of his favourite colour.

'All red!' he had exclaimed in answer to his mother's question.

'Like this?' Etha asked, holding up a tomato.

'Yes!' Natali confirmed, clapping his hands.

So it was that the table was filled with plates of mullet, peppers, soup and several varieties of fruit, all of which – in varying degrees – met with Natali's criterion. Etha had consulted Habella about various edible dyes, and thus had been able to produce some suitably coloured cakes and sweets. She had also prepared a few other items, which were discreetly hidden from her son's sight, in case anyone found his diet too restrictive.

The guest of honour was on good form, delighting in his many presents and in being the centre of attention, and yet happily prepared to share his new toys with his friends. It had been on his insistence that one special invitation had been issued. Iceman sat in the corner of the kitchen, Habella and Lesec by his side, and with several others – Dsordas especially – keeping a watchful eye on him. Etha had been delighted at the opportunity to bring her adopted innocent out of his cell and into her world, and she had no qualms about his being in their midst. The former Far-speaker was wide-eyed and evidently bewildered by the commotion, but he ate well and even smiled when Etha was near.

When the meal was over and the adults were finishing their wine – red, of course! – Natali decreed that he and his contemporaries should sit on the floor and play games. The ensuing scramble caused even more chaos in the overcrowded room, and it was only by good luck that some of the smaller ones avoided being trodden on by their elders. Once everyone was in place, Natali looked round, evidently finding something still not to his satisfaction.

'Ice!' he called, beckoning to his friend and pointing at the floor beside him. 'Ice!'

Iceman stood up, then hesitated when he saw the questioning looks on some of the less friendly adult faces. It was obvious that he wanted to join in but was afraid to do so. Etha settled the issue.

'Go on,' she urged. 'You can't disobey the name-day boy.'

Her smile was all the encouragement Iceman needed and he was soon on the floor, incongruously surrounded by children a quarter of his own age, shouting with the rest and laughing at their antics and his own ineptitude at their games. Eventually even Dsordas relaxed.

Some time later, Natali suddenly got up and stood, head cocked to one side, as if listening to something only he could hear. Then he turned to Iceman, who was still sitting cross-legged on the floor and whose face was therefore on a level with his own.

'My papa's coming,' he announced happily. 'Do you want to meet him?'

As Iceman nodded uncertainly, Natali smiled, unaware of the sudden hush in the kitchen. Until that moment they had all forgotten his claim that Antorkas would return on his name-day. Now it cast a sad chill over the festive atmosphere.

'Natali, little one . . .' Etha began, then broke off in a gasp which was echoed by almost everyone there.

Antorkas' ghost shimmered in the doorway. Those nearest drew back instinctively, but no one else moved.

'Papa, this is my friend Ice,' Natali announced, unperturbed.

The ghost's lips moved, but only Gaye heard his words. She had sensed his arrival, and it was all she could do now to keep from fainting at the sound of his familiar voice inside her head.

'Yes,' she replied, as everyone glanced between her and the spectral visitor. 'Yes, I'll tell them,' she added after another silent pause. 'Why—?'

Antorkas spoke again, cutting off any questions, and then turned to look at his family, lingering over each in turn. All except Natali had tears in their eyes now.

'What's he saying?' Etha asked in a choked whisper.

'He says he misses us all, but we are not to feel sorry for him,' Gaye began, her own voice close to breaking. 'And that he . . .' Both the ghost and his translator were now facing Etha. '. . . that he will always love you, and will wait for you as long as the fates decree.'

Etha made a small sound deep in her throat, and Foran, who stood beside her, took her arm in case she should collapse.

'Antorkas . . .' she breathed, but whatever she had meant to say was too late. The ghost flickered briefly on the edge of sight, and then was gone.

'I told you he'd come,' Natali said brightly, then noticed the sad faces for the first time, and frowned, his large eyes becoming solemn.

'Did he say anything else?' Etha asked quietly.

'Yes.' Gaye hesitated, obviously reluctant. 'He said he was able to answer the call of this world because this is the last time all the family will be together.'

That evening, as darkness fell and the threat of screamer attacks receded, Dsordas and Fen left home to meet the deputies. They had reached a decision, but needed the approval of their colleagues before they could take it any further. Skoulli, Mouse and Yeori were already waiting for them in a quiet room on the upper floor of the old garrison headquarters.

'I've decided to go to Xantium,' Dsordas stated without preamble as he and Fen entered the room.

'What!' Yeori exploded.

'Why?' Skoulli asked more calmly.

'Someone has to go, and it's my responsibility,' their leader replied. His expression and tone betrayed the long and arduous process which had led him to this conclusion. 'Some of the reasons you know. Others have only just come to light.'

'The hostage families would welcome it,' Mouse put in. 'They're desperate to find out what's happened to their children – and to help them if possible.'

'That's one reason,' Dsordas agreed. 'The second is that only by going to the mainland will we ever be absolutely certain that they're not sending a fleet against us.'

'But what about the screamers?' Yeori objected. 'Surely they're a worse threat than Xantium now.'

'Yes, they are,' Dsordas said. 'But the idea that the screamers are actually weapons of the Empire is starting to sound more and more plausible.'

'That's rubbish!' Yeori exclaimed. 'How . . . ?'

'Farrag used sorcery,' Fen cut in. 'You saw that yourself. Who knows what evil power Xantium might possess?'

210

'How else can you explain the transformation of the sea-bats?' Dsordas added.

'But they sank the imperial fleet!'

'We don't know that for certain,' Dsordas replied. 'Even if they did, it's still possible that they're the Empire's creatures. What if the screamers were accompanying the fleet as part of the force, but then something went wrong and they turned on their masters?'

'You believe that?' Yeori asked incredulously.

'All I'm saying is that it's a possibility. And whatever the truth, someone in the Empire must know more about the screamers than we do.'

Yeori subsided.

'What could Xantium gain by sending those creatures against us?' Mouse wondered.

'Perhaps it's punishment for the rebellion? Softening us up for their army?' Dsordas shrugged. 'I don't know.'

'So you think Latchi and his lot might be right,' Skoulli added with a slight grin. 'Zalys is still oppressed, and that's why we're still sinking.'

'You know my opinion of the old stories,' their leader replied seriously, 'but the fact remains that we *are* still in danger of flooding, let alone having to face the new hazards in the sea. And we might be able to learn something about that on the mainland.'

'This month's highest tide is due in two days,' Mouse put in.

'And the reasons we don't know about?' Skoulli prompted after a short pause.

Dsordas took a deep breath.

'Gaye's been talking to someone in Xantium,' he said. With Fen's help, he then told them all about Gaye's latest revelation. The men already knew of the earlier message from the ghost, and this seemed to tie in with that.

'"Xantium is the centre of many circles. If you would

211

understand them all, ȳou must come here. But beware, this city has its screamers too,'' Fen quoted.

The deputies listened in respectful silence, remembering Gaye's contribution to the success of the revolt – and the fact that her actions then had been based on advice from the same ghost.

'The result of all this is that Gaye is determined to go to Xantium for reasons both public and personal,' Dsordas concluded. 'She has the right. And I'm going with her – if you agree.'

Yeori glanced at Fen.

'What do you think about all this?' he asked.

'I'm going too,' she replied promptly.

'No! You can't. It's absurd.' Etha was almost choking on her words. 'You're not going!'

'Yes I am,' Gaye responded calmly. 'You can't stop me and nor can anyone else.'

Etha looked from Gaye to Fen and Dsordas.

'So you're all deserting me,' she accused. 'What have I done to deserve this?'

'We have to do this, Mama,' Fen answered.

'But it's insane!'

'Maybe. But what choice do we have? You heard the reasons. It might be our only chance to save Zalys, and Gaye's only chance to be with Bowen again.'

'*You* don't have to go too,' Etha told her eldest daughter, but there was no conviction in her voice. If Dsordas was going, Fen would not be left behind. 'How will you manage?' she asked eventually.

'Yeori's coming with us,' Dsordas said. 'And you know how capable he is.'

'So the four of you are going to take on a whole empire,' Etha commented bitterly.

'We're looking for information, not a fight,' he told her.

'And we've more than enough amberine to pay our way to the mainland,' Fen added.

'I suppose you'll be going on the *Frozen Star*,' Etha said. 'With that pirate.'

'Bark Madden may be many things,' Dsordas said, 'but he'll treat us fairly.'

'And what about the screamers?' Etha demanded, using her last weapon. 'You can't hide from them!'

'We're rather hoping Gaye might be able to help us with that,' Fen told her. 'You know what she did last night. That's another reason she has to come with us.'

Their mother turned away, hiding her face from them.

'Antorkas knew, didn't he,' she said, her voice grim. 'We'll never be together again.'

The next three days passed in a blur of frantic activity. The flood tides took up most of their attention, and the damage to Nkosa was worse than ever, strengthening popular support for Dsordas' attempt among both adherents of the old ways and the more practically minded. At least he was doing something.

But, at last, all was ready for the voyage. Dsordas had appointed Skoulli to take charge in his absence, and it was he who brought them some disquieting news on the morning before their departure.

'Habella says Iceman is almost certain there's another Far-speaker on Zalys, but he doesn't know how to locate him.'

'Gaye had the same idea,' Dsordas said dourly. 'So you think Xantium may be expecting us?'

'Forewarned is forearmed,' Skoulli replied.

'Let's hope so.'

'In any case, we couldn't turn Iceman back into a Far-speaker now, even if we wanted to,' his deputy added.

'What do you mean?'

'All Farrag's toads have disappeared,' Skoulli replied. 'No one knows where they've gone.'

At last, a month after the revolution, the *Frozen Star* set sail. At Dsordas' instructions, few people ventured out into the open to see them go, but the four travellers knew that the thoughts of all Zalys went with them.

There had been some grumbling among the crew about having women on board, but when they learnt of the blind girl's supposed abilities, they grew less antagonistic, and became almost eager to face the open sea. Nkosa's delights were limited for such experienced seamen, and they had been desperate to get away for some days now. Escape, even with the possibility of being attacked by screamers, was now a very desirable prospect, and so Fen and Gaye were accepted.

The islanders were not the only paying passengers, however. A merchant named Ranald Onar and his servant would be sharing the voyage. And there were other companions. To everyone's surprise, the ship was accompanied out to sea by a large swarm of bats, their tiny shadows flickering in and out of the rigging.

CHAPTER TWENTY-SIX

A vigil begins.

One love watches; another hides and, in hiding, declares itself. Above the echoing storm, the silent prayers roll on. Who but the gods know what answers will be returned?

When Southan was told what Ifryn had done, he reacted first with disbelief, then with terror, then rage. He tore through the echoing halls to the fateful corridor, where several officers were now gathered.

'Who was on guard here?' Southan was a big man, and was made even more imposing by his fury.

Two soldiers stepped forward reluctantly and knelt before the Emperor, their heads bowed.

'What happened?' he snapped, his whole body shaking in a fever of anger.

'The Empress insisted on passing, my lord,' the first man replied. 'She said you had granted her permission.'

'Fool!' Southan hissed.

'We dared not lay hands upon her, my lord,' the other sentry pleaded. 'We had no idea—'

Southan struck him, a hard blow with the back of his hand, and sent the man sprawling.

'Did you forget *my* orders?' the Emperor roared. He controlled himself with difficulty, and turned back to the first guard. 'What happened then?'

'She . . . the Empress stood before the door, then stepped inside,' the trembling soldier replied. 'There was a flash of light, and she . . . she vanished completely.'

He kept his head bowed, knowing better than to protest his innocence as his companion had done.

Southan stared at the two men for a few moments, then turned to one of his captains.

'Take them out of my sight,' he ordered. 'Have them flogged, then throw them in the cells.' He looked back at the two miserable guards. 'Pray that the Empress returns safely. If any harm has come to her, you will die.'

As the condemned men were hustled away, Southan turned once more to stare at the doorway. The empty room beyond mocked him.

'Leave me.'

The others melted away, a small number remaining to watch discreetly from the end of the corridor.

Ifryn, why did you do this? Southan wondered desperately. He was distraught and utterly confused. *I should have had it walled up*, he thought, then stopped himself in horror. *And entomb Kerrell?* It seemed impossible that both the General and now Ifryn were really in there. The room looked harmless enough, but he had seen it kill Clavia – and now it had swallowed his beloved wife. Southan stepped up to the threshold several times, but could never bring himself to cross that invisible barrier. Some of his rage turned inwards, and he tortured himself with his own cowardice. He made excuses, citing his responsibilities to the Empire and his children, but they were not really what was stopping him, and he knew it. Southan was afraid – of death, of the unknown sorcery – and could not put himself to the test. Nor would he order anyone else to do so. Deep down, he knew that his harsh treatment of the guards had been unfair.

Ignoring the nervous and watchful group of soldiers nearby, the Emperor finally knelt on the cool, hard stone floor, facing the now darkened room, and began his vigil. As night fell, he prayed to the old gods with real feeling for the first time in his life.

*   *   *

That same night saw renewed chaos among the talents. Bowen found himself able to wander unsupervised among the ministry warren, as officials and their staff tried unsuccessfully to cope with the many emergencies. He watched, without alarm, as any semblance of normality crumbled. He had sensed the talents' growing fear earlier in the day, the intensifying of the grey force which threatened to crush them all, but for himself it was too remote. Later there had been another ripple in the psychic fabric of his new home, but Bowen had deliberately ignored that, not wanting to be involved. He was content just to watch what was happening all about him. Listening was much harder.

That night he saw ghosts attacking live talents, reducing them to hysteria with their frenzied but inevitably ineffectual assaults; he saw telepaths, who had not slept for three or more nights, raving and near to collapse but kept awake by their utter dread of nightmares; he saw a wooden table explode into a million splinters at a single word, blinding one official and shredding the skin of several talents; and, most horrible of all, he saw one of the fire-makers unwittingly turn his arcane ability upon himself, starting a chain reaction in his body which, within a few moments, reduced all his flesh to ash and his bones to smouldering, blackened sticks.

Bowen took all this in his stride. Far more perturbing were the voices in his head; forever calling, pleading, questioning. He had no defence against these attacks, no answers to their pleas. He let the words tumble over themselves so that they made no sense, and tried to ignore the clamour.

Deep in the night, an instinct he did not understand led him to a darkened, inner room. Lamplight from the corridor spilled in as he opened the door, illuminating a macabre scene. The men and women who lay on their backs on raised stone slabs were all young, all vaguely familiar. They had their right arms extended towards the centre of the room, and there was an incision in each wrist from which a slow ooze of blood flowed into shallow bowls and thence, via stone runnels, to a central receptacle cut into another slab of rock. Thin blue flames flickered over the thick bubbling mixture where the blood mingled. Bowen knew, without understanding how, that these were the hostages from Zalys, all in a drug-induced trance, their tainted blood now a source of power. Power that was being drained off to be used elsewhere.

Bowen counted the hostages. There were eleven. *There should be twelve*, he thought absently, then remembered that Sagar was dead. That brought his mind back to excruciatingly painful reality, and with it came memories of Gaye. Bowen fell, matching her fall, and cracked his head on one of the stone tables. He lay there, as still as death, blood trickling slowly from a cut on his forehead.

The same night also saw Martyn and Alasia meet in The Spires, the windswept pinnacles of stone far above the city and its human uproar. After their usual courteous greetings, Martyn came straight to the point; his own concerns first, then those allotted to him by Baylin.

'Sagar's brother, Bowen, the one you call the beacon. Do you know where he is?'

'In the whirlwind below the earth,' she replied. 'The tunnels echo.'

'He's in the ministry? Which section?'

'A beacon shines wherever he is,' Alasia told him, sounding just like a prim schoolteacher. 'All who look will see.'

Martyn's heart sank at the thought of combing the vast labyrinth of the Ministry of Information. It would be like looking for a particular speck of dust in the Deadlands. But he knew he would get no more out of Alasia now. Why couldn't Bowen have been kept somewhere simple, like the dungeons or the hostage enclave? The Swordsman sighed and turned to other matters.

'Where is Chancellor Verkho?' he asked. 'Rumour says he's been out of sight for some time.'

A slight tremor passed over Alasia's pale face.

'He is beyond reach,' she said. 'More than locks protect his lair. Do not think to face him yet.'

Martyn was taken aback by this last comment. That Verkho was ensconced in his study was no surprise – it was what he had expected and hoped for – but did Alasia know of the Swordsman's ultimate objective?

'I do not think to face him yet,' he said carefully, 'but I wish to learn. How can I get into the Chancellor's private quarters?'

Alasia told him the best ways, and Martyn was so pleased that he almost laughed aloud. Could it really be so easy?

'Thank you,' he said. As he prepared to leave, he added hopefully, 'Do you know where Kerrell is?'

'The beacon shone on him,' she answered. 'But I alone do not have the strength to break the seal.'

'Bowen?' Martyn hazarded, confused once more. 'Is Kerrell in the ministry too?'

'He is nowhere,' Alasia replied. 'He has left this world.'

When Ifryn stepped inside the room, the only thing she experienced was a crackling in her ears. The empty room, dimly lit by the lamp in the corridor, looked just as it had from outside. But then the Empress realized, her heart beating even faster, that she cast no shadow. She turned back towards the door, thinking instantly of escape, then hesitated. The corridor seemed out of focus, like an indistinct memory. On impulse she looked up, and saw that the room had no ceiling, only clouds. Her false reality crumbled – and the room vanished.

Ifryn found herself surrounded by translucent whiteness. In the silence, fear squeezed her in its clammy grip. *What have I done?*

And then she saw him, sprawled on nothing, his eyes closed. Her heart lurched in hope and dread.

'Kerrell!' Her cry made no sound; the blank void swallowed his name, but somehow he heard her and looked around. His eyes widened in disbelief and sudden manic joy.

Ifryn! His lips moved but her ears were deaf. She heard his call in her mind.

They struggled towards each other but could get no purchase on the pale haze. There was nothing to push against but, driven by desperate need, they drew closer slowly but inexorably, as if their own yearning propelled this strange flight. At last, their fingertips touched, hands grasped and, with a surge of relief, acceptance and fierce happiness, they held each other tight in a feverish embrace.

You're real, Kerrell breathed in wonder, unconsciously echoing her dream of him in the forest.

What's happening? she asked. *Where are we?*

Kerrell stopped her mouth with a kiss. For a fleeting moment Ifryn was too stunned to react, then she melted in the heat of his ardour. Long before their lips parted, they both knew it would not end there. They could no longer contain their emotions, repressed for so long, and now they had no choice but to release them in a torrent which accepted no barriers, no taboos. Each knew what was in the other's mind without the need of words. It was not a matter of choice any more, but of necessity.

Clothes shifted and parted without hindrance, as if they too were part of love's conspiracy. Flesh met flesh, exploring, caressing, joining, revelling in the textures of skin, the sensations of touch and taste. Between them, in a few tumultuous, timeless moments, they read aloud the whole book of passion, each chapter and paragraph shaped by their unassailable desire.

Only when it was over and they lay, still joined, in each other's arms, did the thought of what they had done cross their conscious minds. Kerrell saw the tremor of fear in Ifryn's lovely face, and kissed it away.

This is all that matters now.

Ifryn shut her eyes, closed her mind and let her body agree.

Much later, their passion temporarily spent, they began a strange, silent conversation.

I have always loved you, Kerrell began. *Ever since I first set eyes on you. It's been agony not being able to tell you, not knowing how you felt.*

Did you doubt my love? she asked.

I hoped, sometimes even believed, but . . .

Now you know better. Ifryn smiled. *You have proof.*

Guilt was impossible in this place; there was only relief, unutterably sweet. They were beyond the concerns of the real world.

I thought you were dead, she said.

So did I.

Have you been here all the time? You've been away over half a month.

Kerrell's astonishment was plain.

Time must be different in here, he surmised hesitantly. *I would be dead otherwise.* He could see the fear returning to her eyes.

How do we get out? she whispered.

I don't know, Kerrell admitted. His tone implied that, for now, he did not care.

Clavia was killed trying . . .

I know. He twisted Ifryn's shoulders round gently and showed her the dead face, still revolving slowly. Ifryn was sickened by the sight, and instinctively drew her clothes about her, covering herself from those dreadful, unseeing eyes.

How horrible.

It was Clavia who lured me here, Kerrell said, remembering.

Then Verkho is responsible, Ifryn concluded. *This is the proof we needed. If we ever get the chance to use it*, she added solemnly.

221

To keep herself from thinking, she told Kerrell as much as she could remember of events while he had been away; of her alliance with Baylin and the Swordsman, of Alasia's fight with Verkho over Coulson, of the Chancellor's self-imposed isolation. Kerrell listened but his thoughts were evidently elsewhere, and eventually she ran out of words. The look in her eyes said, What do we do now?

Kerrell kissed her again.

CHAPTER TWENTY-SEVEN

The raging candle spills a cursed light, and melts the crimson wax. But when he has passed by, what shapes of ill omen are formed? When our realm has cooled again, what moulds will be filled, what seals completed?
I have seen such blood-red signs before.

Unlike his more patient alter-ego Martyn, the Swordsman was a man to act decisively, and he went straight from his meeting with Alasia to Verkho's private quarters in The Domain. The entrance was as easy to find as his guide had said, and soon, having survived only a few uncertain moments, he drew near to what he knew must be the inner sanctuary. The Chancellor's apartments contained a huge number of rooms, designed for every imaginable purpose, but a few were reputedly only accessible to Verkho himself – and perhaps to a few personally chosen guests. It was there that the Swordsman was headed.

Once the outer rings had been penetrated, he met no sentries. Either Verkho felt secure in the belief that no one would dare to intrude so far, or these chambers were guarded in other, more subtle ways. Indeed, the whole place seemed deserted, deathly quiet. Only a few lamps burned, leaving the hallways in semi-darkness; none of the rooms was locked.

The Swordsman moved cautiously nevertheless, treading lightly on the matting and rugs which covered the stone floors, his careful eyes searching for hidden perils. Yet he found none, and came to the conclusion that the

Chancellor's confidence had grown into arrogance.

The rooms were opulently furnished, and at times it was all Martyn could do not to smash the many treasures and works of beauty with which Verkho had adorned his quarters. But he held himself back from such petty revenge, knowing that his reason for being there was far more important. So, feeling like a curiously invincible fly, the Swordsman crept slowly towards the centre of the web. And, at last, he found a room that was not empty. As he opened the door on silent hinges, there was a rustle of movement from within.

'At *last*,' a woman's voice said. 'I thought you'd forgotten me.'

The bedchamber was lit by two lamps, their glow diffused by the deep red colour of the glass, giving the room a sultry air.

'I'm wearing your favourite outfit,' she breathed and stepped gracefully from the bed, her arms outstretched in welcome.

She was naked, except for gold jewellery round her wrists and ankles and dangling from her ears. The Swordsman did not react, but just stood perfectly still, and the woman suddenly knew her danger. As quickly as she moved towards the bell pull on the wall next to the fireplace, he was quicker. Pinning her arm against the wall with one hand, the other now held a knife pressed to her throat. His face was a mask of cold-blooded malevolence, so close to hers that she could not see it properly.

'One sound out of you and you're dead,' he whispered harshly.

She knew she was trapped. Even her legs were pinned by her assailant, and she kept perfectly still. The Swordsman sensed her terror and enjoyed it. Any woman prepared to be Verkho's whore deserved to suffer.

'Where are the Chancellor's private chambers? Where he works, where he sleeps?'

'He sleeps here, when he chooses,' she replied, a flicker of pride in her quivering voice.

'His *private* chambers,' the Swordsman hissed, and the knife pricked her neck.

'You can't go in there. No one can. Anyone who does will be cursed.' She clearly believed what she said, but the intruder was not impressed.

'I'm immune to curses,' he told her. 'Where are his rooms?'

'Through the door back there. The next room and the one beyond are where he keeps his papers.' She added quickly, 'Don't hurt me. I'll do anything.'

The Swordsman gave her a look of the utmost contempt, then drove the knife up under her chin and into her brain, in one savage thrust. She was dead by the time he lowered her to the floor.

He wiped his blade on the bedcover and went into the dark recess she had indicated. The door there was locked, but a key hung from a hook on the wall. It turned easily but he hesitated at each faint click, waiting for a response. None came. The Swordsman turned the handle, pushed the door open with a foot and stood to one side in case of attack. The room beyond remained still and quiet and pitch dark.

After a few moments, he took one of the red lamps and stepped inside. The flame dipped and fluttered as he entered, and he felt an odd tingling run through his body – but his progress was unhindered. On investigation, this outer room proved to be full of books, piled high on shelves, tables, even on the floor. There was nothing here to interest the Swordsman. He went on, cautious still, through the open door to the innermost retreat.

At the centre of this workroom stood a vast wooden table. It was bare, but its surface was scarred and pitted as though it had been attacked on many occasions by blades, claws and fire. There were yet more books on shelves round the walls, and others lay on chairs scattered around the room. None of the papers the woman had mentioned were to be seen, but the Swordsman had not really expected to find anything like that.

Briefly, he studied a few of the tomes. One dealt with old religions, another claimed to contain magical secrets, and a third was open at a section describing a mythical talisman. All of which was just so much nonsense to the Swordsman. Then his eye was caught by a cabinet in a corner of the room. Pulling open the double doors, he leapt back as crackling blue sparks erupted from the wood. There was a sucking sound in the wavering air as the sparks spread into an iridescent screen across the opening. Within the cupboard, he could just make out several jars and other objects, most of which were unidentifiable – but one tray on the bottom shelf held what appeared to be several rows of rings, each with their own insignia. Pieces of sealing wax lay next to them.

The Swordsman carefully closed the cabinet doors, pushing them together with the tip of his knife. The blue screen vanished from sight behind the wood. When his eyes had readjusted to the dim red light, he retraced his steps and made his escape. Martyn emerged, thoughtful but triumphant, into The Levels just as the sun rose.

Daylight brought some relief for Harios; as the dreams receded, some semblance of calm returned to the ministry. He had been awake all night trying, in vain, to cope with the chaos, and desperately needed to sleep, but decided to check on Bowen before retiring. The islander had proved a big disappointment to Harios. He obviously had great talent, but was already insane and rarely coherent – and yet the official was not ready to give up on him so soon. He had noted how Bowen remained calm while others became hysterical – or worse – and had determined to discover his secret. The trouble was that Bowen was less than biddable; nothing seemed to affect him. Kindness and threats left him equally unmoved. It was time, therefore, for more extreme measures. Harios decided that the use of nectar might give them some control over him. It was risky, but worth a try.

The islander had been returned to the cell where he usually rested by two of Harios' hard-pressed assistants. He was still unconscious when the official dribbled a very weak solution of nectar between his lips and stroked his neck to make him swallow.

As soon as the dark liquid went down, Bowen's reaction was immediate – and horrifying. He sat up, his eyes bulging, and clutched at his throat as though he were being strangled. His breath came in tortured gasps. Harios drew back fearfully, knowing that he had probably made a mistake, but observing out of habit nonetheless. Mottled purple-black patches appeared on the dark skin of Bowen's arms and face, undulating as if they were alive. The prisoner stared, wild-eyed, at these obscene, bruise-like markings, and screamed.

Then he burst into flame.

Sunlight, as always, had come early to The Spires. But as Alasia sat in her bright, windswept eyrie, her attention was on another, more intimate blaze. She had sensed the potency of the beacon's white fire, and knew that this was her only chance to guide him, to use him for her own ends. He would be the one to open the door, to break the seal – if only she had the strength to shape the power.

Kerrell and Ifryn drifted within the white silence, clinging to each other for comfort. Even their thoughts were quiet now.

Suddenly, a new artificial brightness in that artificial realm claimed their attention. White flame burned fiercely, cutting a swathe of heat through the neutral haze that surrounded them. Both stared, not under-standing, but mesmerized nonetheless. Then Alasia's voice sounded – familiar yet strained – inside their heads. She had been horrified and astonished to find Ifryn there with Kerrell, but she had recovered quickly.

Move towards the flame. It is your only chance.

Ifryn began to struggle, concentrating the efforts of both body and mind, but Kerrell hesitated, holding her back.

Think yourself there, Alasia insisted. *Use your thoughts.*

Still the two opposed each other. Ifryn gazed at Kerrell, not understanding his reluctance. At the same time she became uncomfortably aware of another observer, of blind eyes watching from afar. It was an eerie and unnerving sensation.

Together! Together, Alasia urged. *You can only succeed together!*

But Kerrell was staring at Clavia's slowly revolving face, and was unable to move.

Forget her, Alasia ordered. *She's gone. Go to him.* In the midst of the white blaze, the tortured face of an unknown man appeared. *Yes, him!* she cried, in answer to Ifryn's unspoken query. *He is the centre of the circle, the breach in the seal. Hurry!*

Trust her, Ifryn pleaded. *It's our only hope.* She pulled at Kerrell physically, while directing all her thoughts towards the flames.

We could stay here . . . together . . .

Ifryn saw the eternal longing in his eyes, heard the madness in his voice.

No! she cried, tugging at him again.

No! Alasia echoed. *Get out. Get out. Quickly! I can't hold it much longer . . .*

Ifryn heard the alarm and growing tiredness in her friend's voice, and doubled her efforts. At last Kerrell gave in, acceding to her will and adding his own. The fire drew closer, but so slowly that she despaired of ever reaching it.

An unknown, faraway voice screamed.

228

Bowen! Help him, Alasia!

Kerrell was jolted by the intrusion, glancing round in vain, but Ifryn had no time for such things.

Get out! Alasia yelled again.

With a sudden determination, Ifryn twisted round, turning to face the man in the flames and appealed to him directly. Such was his agony that at first she thought he would not notice her. Then his spectral hand reached out, caught hers and drew her onwards. With her other hand Ifryn still held Kerrell's tightly, as they passed into the fire and were blinded by the furnace light.

An instant later, they stumbled out on to the stone floor of the corridor. Before them, kneeling, was Southan, looking from one to the other in a mixture of astonishment and delight. His prayers had been answered. The Emperor got stiffly to his feet, gazing at the two dishevelled and bewildered creatures who had emerged from a sudden flash of light.

The real world came crashing down upon Ifryn and Kerrell, and they instinctively released their clasped hands as they faced Southan. The terrifying blaze had not harmed them, but they were speechless now; shame was only one of a cataract of emotions which surged through them. As Ifryn stepped forward obediently into her husband's arms, she was wondering how they could return to normality now. Surely it wasn't possible. Not after all that had happened . . .

She looked over Southan's shoulder as he embraced her tightly, sweeping her round in his delight and murmuring in her unresponsive ear. Kerrell gazed back, saw the pleading and haunted pain in her eyes. But he was mute, held by the centuries-old tradition of honour and obedience. Every fibre of his body was taut but murderously controlled. He bowed his head, unable to witness the imperial reunion. Ifryn knew that their chance was gone – irretrievable now – and for a moment, she wished they had remained in their false haven. She began to cry and sensed, rather than saw, Kerrell step

229

forward, then draw back in defeat and humiliation.

'I thought you were dead,' Southan whispered, releasing his embrace a little to look at her. There were tears in his eyes too, though he tried to hold them back. 'What would I have done without you?'

Ifryn thought dully that, in one sense, she truly *was* dead.

'What happened in there?'

In a faltering voice, Ifryn described her experience as accurately as she could – leaving out only their lovemaking – while the more distant onlookers drew closer so that they too could hear. Southan listened, aghast, then turned to Kerrell. Doneta, who had been waiting at the end of the corridor, ran forward to help her mistress and the Emperor and his General embraced.

'Welcome back,' Southan said.

Kerrell could find no words. Anything he said now was bound to betray him. Others were close now, not knowing when the Emperor would allow them to join the celebration. However, one lieutenant-general on Kerrell's staff stepped forward, at the head of a group of soldiers, and his face was grave.

'Your majesty,' he began, 'I do not wish to spoil this happy reunion, but I fear I must. I have just received orders from Chancellor Verkho to arrest General Kerrell.'

Southan glared at the interloper, incredulous and angry.

'On what charge?' he demanded.

'Treason, my lord,' the other replied.

CHAPTER TWENTY-EIGHT

How can treason be measured? Virtue, honour, loyalty; is there a gauge for such qualities, a scale to mark the boundary line of guilt? Where does the pendulum come to rest in the geometry of gods?

Love is the purest form of treachery.

'This is preposterous!' Southan declared furiously as the mood turned from rejoicing to dismay.

'I thought so too,' Lieutenant-General Penderos replied gravely. 'Indeed, I would have staked my life upon it – until I saw this.' He produced a rolled parchment and showed it to Kerrell. 'General, is this your seal?'

Kerrell, still unable to speak, nodded, and glanced instinctively at the ring on the middle finger of his left hand. It bore the same device. The wax seal had been broken, but its origins were unmistakable.

'What is this?' Southan demanded.

'A letter from General Kerrell to the barbarian leader Haresh-al-Keth, my lord,' Penderos replied. 'In it he states that he and the late Lady Clavia were conspiring to depose you and your son and take over the Empire.'

'This is ludicrous!' Ifryn cried.

Southan glanced at her.

'Give it to me,' he said to Penderos.

'Why are you even considering such deceit?' the Empress demanded.

'Silence!' He unrolled the parchment and scanned its contents, taking in the signature at the bottom of the sheet.

'As you see, my lord,' Penderos went on, 'the letter also offers the lands of Idiron, Tilesia and Agrea to Haresh in return for a promise that his forces come no further west, and for his support against any invaders from the north.'

The Emperor's face was grim now. Ifryn seethed with rage and indignation, and silently implored Kerrell to defend himself, to dismiss the ridiculous slander, but he seemed to have lost the use of his tongue. He looked wretched and alone.

'Well?' Southan faced the General squarely.

At last, Kerrell spoke, the words forcing themselves out.

'I am . . . indeed . . . a traitor.'

'No!' Ifryn screamed.

Penderos drew his sword, as did several other officers, while Southan gaped in disbelief.

'I must ask you to come with me . . .' Penderos began, and stepped forward.

Kerrell moved then, his slack, dishevelled form suddenly whirling into action. Penderos was sent sprawling by a lightning quick turn and throw, his sword clattering to the floor. He skidded towards the fatal doorway, trying to stop but unable to prevent his legs from crossing the threshold. They disappeared in a flash of white as he finally grasped the frame and hauled himself back. The Lieutenant-General screamed, then fainted as both his legs were reduced to neatly severed, bloody stumps. At the same time, Kerrell fled down the corridor in the opposite direction. For an instant no one moved, then the shock was overcome and several soldiers ran after the escaping General. Others bent to attend to Penderos, and one officer drew the stricken Emperor aside.

'Leave it to us, my lord. This corridor is a dead end. The traitor won't escape.'

Southan nodded, speechless himself now. Eventually he turned back to Ifryn, who was curled in Doneta's

232

arms, resting on a stone window seat. She did not notice him look at her. The Empress' world had collapsed utterly. She knew that, in Kerrell's mind, he *was* guilty of treason. But not for the crime of which he was now accused.

Harios stared at his prisoner, unable to believe his eyes. The cleansing fire had gone, leaving him unharmed, his skin unblemished. Bowen smiled, his anguish only a memory now, and stuck out his tongue in a rude gesture, like that of a child. And even that was unstained by nectar.

It was not until that evening that Ifryn's world took a minute turn for the better. She had retired to bed, feeling absolutely exhausted, her whole body still throbbing with memories of the pleasure that had now turned to pain. Doneta had kept the children away, aware of her mistress' acute distress, but she could not bar entry to the Emperor. Southan was deeply troubled but, as always, solicitous and gentle, and Ifryn felt her betrayal acutely. Even so, she could not help but be cheered by his news. Kerrell had not been captured, in spite of the officer's assurances, and he was now being sought throughout the city.

'You can't *really* think he is guilty?' she said.

'It's difficult to believe,' he replied sadly. 'But he admitted it himself . . .'

In the pause that followed, Ifryn wanted to tell her husband the truth, to explain – but in the end she could not.

'And that letter,' Southan went on. 'You saw the seal. There are no two rings like that. It's been in their family for generations.' He shook his head.

'But . . .'

Southan silenced her, placing a finger on her lips.

'These are sad and dangerous times,' he said. 'But you need to rest. Even I can see that.' He kissed her gently

233

and reverently on her forehead, and withdrew. Ifryn could not find the words to call him back.

Corton had just worked out that this was his fifth day in captivity when they came for him. The bare windowless room was comfortable enough, and the food had been adequate, but it had been the longest time in his adult life that he had been without wine. Boredom had been his biggest enemy; none of the masked men who brought his meals were inclined to talk, or to accept his offers of a game of labyrinth. Nor had they been able to bring him any books. Corton had passed the time reciting from memory the vintages – and their special qualities – of the wines in his care, and fretting over whether his assistants were acting properly in his absence. Eventually, however, he had begun to worry about his own situation, and so it was a considerable relief when Martyn and Sagar arrived.

'We have messages for you to take to Baylin.'

'Who?'

'Ask Grongar,' Martyn advised.

Corton realized belatedly that he was being set free.

'I can go now?' he asked.

'Yes. Your friends have proved trustworthy – so far. And I'm willing to take them on their honour.'

From his expression, it was obvious that Sagar did not feel the same way, but he evidently had no say in the matter.

'What messages?' the wine-master asked.

Martyn described his exploration and what he had seen in Verkho's private chambers.

'It doesn't add up to much yet, I know,' he added, 'but it's just a beginning. As for Kerrell, I learnt nothing.' News of the General's reappearance and his treason would not be generally known in the city until later that morning. 'I think he's dead,' Martyn concluded.

'And Bowen?' Corton enquired.

'That's *our* business,' Sagar told him, speaking for the first time. Martyn merely smiled.

Then Corton was blindfolded and led to some stables – he could tell by the sounds and smell – where he was helped into an enclosed wagon. It drove off immediately. Some time later, after many twists and turns on the rough cobbled streets, his blindfold was removed.

'You can get out here,' Martyn said. 'Tell Grongar that I'm relying on him. If he fails me, you will both die.' The Swordsman's tone carried a chill sincerity.

Corton swallowed hard and nodded. He clambered down and watched, blinking in the unaccustomed sunlight, as the wagon lumbered away.

'Well, that's that. Message delivered,' Grongar said as he entered Corton's small apartment and flopped down into a chair. 'Though what good it'll do them, I don't know.'

'We've done our part,' Corton replied, his relief obvious. 'It's up to them now.'

The wine-master had spent the latter part of the day in his cellars, making sure that all was well. Much to his satisfaction, his principal assistant, Leputs, had managed admirably, covering for his master's unexplained absence with the minimum of fuss.

'A game?' Corton suggested hopefully, wanting the reassurance of normality.

Grongar looked doubtful, then grinned.

'All right, but just one,' he said. 'I'm meeting Mariella tonight.'

'Another of your conquests?' Corton smiled, but felt rather hurt. He needed company tonight.

'Not yet,' his friend smirked.

'Why not bring her here – at least for the early part of the evening?' the wine-master suggested.

Grongar looked surprised, then saw the advantages of such an arrangement.

235

'We could get in a game or two that way,' he said. 'Are you sure you don't mind?'

'Not at all,' Corton replied. 'I don't want to drink alone tonight. Does Mariella like wine?'

Grongar's smile widened.

'She likes anything as long as it makes her feet go numb,' he said.

Ifryn had not moved from her bedchamber all day. There seemed to be no point. Each time she had a visitor she expected to hear the dread news of Kerrell's capture, but it was not to be, and she went to bed grateful for that at least. Her whole body ached and she was very tired, but when, just on the edge of sleep, she heard a tiny sound in the room, she was instantly alert.

Alasia's pale face glimmered in the faint starlight that flowed through the open shutters. Ifryn made to sit up, glad of the familiar comfort of her friend's presence, but Alasia pushed her back down and took her hand in her own. The Empress wondered fleetingly if the healer could tell why she was so very tired. Her next thought was even more terrifying – could Alasia tell whether she was newly pregnant? But her visitor said nothing, and just smiled serenely.

'Thank you for saving us,' Ifryn whispered.

Alasia's expression was dismissive. She required no gratitude. For her it had simply been a necessary and instinctive act, a duty which she had to fulfil.

'Do you know where Kerrell is?' the Empress asked hopefully.

'Not waiting.' Alasia laughed at her own enigmatic joke. 'Not waiting any more.'

'What do you mean?' Surely Kerrell had not fled the city?

'He is safe,' her friend replied. 'He will come to you at this time tomorrow.'

Ifryn almost fainted with expectant joy.

'You mean it?' she exclaimed. 'Here?'

Alasia nodded.

'He wishes to talk to you and Baylin alone.'

'Oh.' Helpless loving thoughts fled from Ifryn's mind. Perhaps Kerrell could not trust himself alone with her. Perhaps he wanted to think only of other concerns. But they couldn't go back! They couldn't undo what had happened. Could they?

'Wait for him in the outer chamber,' Alasia went on. 'Do not let Doneta or anyone else in here.'

'All right.' Ifryn was recovering her composure. Just to see him again would be wonderful. And tortuous.

'You should sleep now,' her friend said. 'You need to rest.' She reached out, but the Empress stopped her hand.

'Why wasn't I killed, like Clavia?' she asked.

'The seal only faced one way,' Alasia replied. 'It was not set to prevent entry, only exit. Clavia made that mistake. You went on.'

'Who was the man in the fire?'

'A beacon. He burns brightly.'

And Alasia was prepared to give no more. She touched her fingers to Ifryn's forehead, and this time the Empress did not try to prevent her. A sense of peace spread through her whole being, and she slept.

In her dreams, Alasia flew away.

237

CHAPTER TWENTY-NINE

By definition, we are blind to sorcery.

Whose eyes can look inward? Which minds know their own hidden potential? Power lies dormant in every one of us, in the unknown spaces, the internal abyss. But we lack the resolve to search within the darkness and bring it to the light.

In desperation, some reach for the tainted designs of blood. But truth is thinner than blood, lighter than air. Magic, not mankind, speaks with the tongue of butterflies.

'We must be careful,' Baylin emphasized. 'Now that gossip is connecting Kerrell and Clavia, it's put paid to some of the rumours about you.' Ifryn held his gaze only by the strongest effort of will. 'But the fact that you were with him in that . . .' The traveller paused, lost for words. '. . . that *place*, means that you're still open to suspicion to some. I've been circumspect. Few people have seen me come here but my friendship with Kerrell is well known, so after tonight perhaps we should meet less frequently. We can exchange messages safely enough.'

Ifryn nodded reluctantly. During the last few days, Baylin had been the one sure landmark in her turbulent world and, even though she saw the sense of his caution, realizing that his previously impregnable confidence had been dented came as an unpleasant surprise.

'You could always come in disguise,' she suggested.

'That also has its risks,' he replied.

The two were seated in the Empress' outer chamber. Vrila and Delmege were asleep, and Doneta was fully occupied elsewhere. The day had crawled past – indeed, Ifryn did not know how she had survived it – but now the appointed time was growing near and she was as nervous as a young girl, caught between expectation and doubt. When at last the bedroom door eased open and Kerrell peered round, she jumped to her feet and almost rushed to meet him. But his eyes flicked from Baylin and back to her and the warning in them was clear. Ifryn felt as if her heart was being embalmed in ice as she stopped, waited and watched his formal bow.

'My lady . . . Baylin.' His voice was tightly controlled in greeting, devoid of emotion.

'Well met, Kerrell,' the traveller responded, also standing. He had noted the silent exchange, but kept his thoughts to himself.

All three sat down, while Ifryn wondered how Kerrell had found his way into the bedchamber. Through the window? By the secret ways Alasia used? It did not really matter, and she knew better than to ask.

'How did you manage to get away?' she asked instead.

Kerrell smiled weakly.

'I've been playing hide-and-seek in this place since I was a boy,' he said. 'Very few dead ends in the court are really what they seem. All I needed was a head start.'

'And some agility,' Baylin commented.

'Desperation gives you that,' the General replied, looking surprised. 'You know about the bat tunnels?'

'I was a child here too.' Baylin grinned.

'Where have you been since then?' Ifryn asked Kerrell.

'Best you don't know,' he replied, winding one more layer of ice around her heart. 'But I've been able to move around a bit. That can wait though. What have you discovered? Verkho's been one step ahead of us all the time – the trap must have been set up in case I escaped.'

'Certainly,' Baylin agreed. 'Verkho must have

arranged it when he heard of Clavia's death, because he was safely ensconced in his study when you and the Empress got out.'

'He couldn't have foreseen your involvement,' Kerrell added, turning to Ifryn, 'but having Southan there suited his purpose admirably.' He glanced suspiciously at his ring. 'The letter is a forgery of course, but I can't understand how he got the seal so perfect.'

'We can,' Ifryn said.

Baylin told Kerrell of the Swordsman's findings, including the magically protected cabinet that contained the selection of rings and seals.

'But how could he have copied it?' Kerrell wanted to know. 'This ring never leaves my finger.'

'I don't know,' his friend answered, 'but it's there. Martyn swore it, and he has no reason to lie.'

'You trust him?'

'In this, yes.'

'If we can prove that Verkho faked the seal, then Southan *must* believe you,' Ifryn stated. 'I can't understand how he can think that you're a traitor. He's turning his back on centuries of trust.'

Kerrell said nothing, but just looked at her sadly until she could no longer meet his gaze. She longed to enfold him in her arms again, to kiss away his pain, to tell him that their love would overcome everything, that it was *not* impossible. But she could not. *I am . . . indeed . . . a traitor.* Oh, that those fateful words had never been spoken. Or that, in Kerrell's mind, they were not true. Ifryn carefully studied her hands, folded in her lap, thinking that the earlier rumours about their impropriety had substance now.

'Emperors need to be suspicious,' Baylin said eventually, ending the silence as tactfully as he could. 'What *we* need, as you say, is proof.'

'But with Clavia dead, the only one with proof is Verkho – and he's not likely to oblige,' Kerrell said.

'He can't be reached,' Baylin added. 'He's still locked

240

away. Southan lost patience this afternoon and had some men try to smash the doors down, but they wouldn't budge. Something more than wood and iron is protecting the Chancellor's study – and the Emperor was made to look a fool in front of his men.'

'The ring, then,' Ifryn put in. 'Take Southan to Verkho's chambers and show him the ring.'

'That won't be easy,' Baylin said. 'One of Verkho's mistresses was found murdered, and his servants are scared stiff.'

'Martyn killed her?' Ifryn exclaimed, horrified.

'He must have,' Baylin replied. 'We have a dangerous ally. There are guards everywhere in Verkho's quarters now – and I'll give you one guess as to where their first loyalty lies.'

'Surely Southan can order them to let you in!' Ifryn objected.

'But who will convince him to try?' Kerrell asked. 'And how? We can hardly tell him how you know about the fake seals.' He paused for a moment, then added, 'We'll try our other options first.' He exchanged glances with Baylin.

'I could do it,' Ifryn said quietly. 'Southan would look if I asked him to.'

'No,' Kerrell replied. 'How would you explain your involvement with the Swordsman? He would take that as treason. You can't afford to be implicated.'

'Doesn't the fact that Verkho's locked himself away prove he's up to no good?' Ifryn wondered.

'No doubt he'll emerge with a story making his seclusion essential to the wellbeing of the Empire,' Kerrell replied cynically. 'We can only wait and see.'

'And Verkho has a hold over at least half the senior army officers,' Baylin said.

'Even if he didn't, they won't trust me now,' Kerrell added bitterly. 'My running away will be taken as evidence of my guilt.'

'Why *did* you run away?' Baylin asked quietly.

After a long, uncomfortable pause, the General sighed. 'You can't imagine what it was like to be in that place for such a long time,' he said awkwardly. 'And being arrested for treason the moment I got out of there was not exactly what I was expecting. I just wasn't thinking straight.' He glanced at Ifryn, but her eyes were still lowered, and another unpleasant thought occurred to him. 'How is Penderos?'

'Alive, but barely,' Baylin replied. 'The surgeons say he might still die.'

'He was a good man once,' Kerrell said dourly.

'His command's been taken over by Kaikoura,' the traveller went on. 'All the talk is of war in the east. Troops are already on the move.'

'Idiron?' the Empress asked, instantly anxious for her old homeland.

Baylin nodded.

'The whole eastern border,' he said. 'But your mother must be well away by now. And there's nothing definite yet. Latif has been talking to his fellow kings in Tilesia and Agrea. Raamon and Besistral are nobody's fools.'

'But no match for Verkho,' Kerrell added grimly. 'I'd wager this is his doing, in part at least.'

'The south is boiling up too,' Baylin went on. 'It's a real mess – all sorts of skirmishes, but there doesn't seem to be any pattern to it yet. And with a good part of the Southern Fleet having been lost . . .'

'What!' Kerrell exploded, and his friend gave him the details. 'Gods,' the General breathed. 'I didn't even know Zalys had rebelled. What's going on?'

'We've problems enough in Xantium,' Ifryn reminded them angrily. What did the affairs of a remote island matter?

'True,' Baylin commented.

'We'll do what we can,' Kerrell tried to reassure her.

But what can a man in hiding do? she wondered. *And what am I supposed to do?*

'I'd better go now,' Kerrell said. 'I've already stayed too long.'

'When will I see you again?' she asked quickly.

'Alasia will let you know. I'll keep in touch.' There was reluctance and pain behind his determined words.

'Good hunting,' Baylin said.

Kerrell stood. Ifryn made to follow, but his glance held her in her chair.

'Farewell for now, my lady.'

He went into the bedroom, closing the door carefully, but did not look back. Ifryn stayed frozen in her place.

'I should go too,' Baylin said. 'Try not to worry.'

'That's easy to say,' she responded helplessly.

As soon as the traveller was out of the door, Ifryn ran into her bedchamber, half hoping that Kerrell was waiting there for her. But he had gone.

That night, Harios and the other section heads finally managed to bring the ministry talents under control. It had taken severe, and in some cases even brutal, measures – but the disruption had already gone on for far too long. Before their nightmares had begun, most of the talents had been cooperative – indeed, many had been only too happy to indulge their supernatural skills in return for a comfortable life – and so had been granted a fair degree of freedom within the confines of their quarters. The unwilling few had to be kept under lock and key and *encouraged* in various ways, but the majority were grateful for the chance to live well and to receive praise for abilities which in the outside world often led to persecution.

However, that had all changed now. The talents were being treated as prisoners, kept in cells and physically restrained if necessary. Several of the more demented talents were drugged at night. And, of course, many of those involved in the more advanced experiments – those whom Chancellor Verkho had overseen personally – were already insensible, far beyond the reach of dreams. Bowen, on the other hand, had been very quiet ever since he had been engulfed by the white flames – which in the end had not even scorched his hair or clothes. Following his own eccentric path as always, he had been subdued and cooperative and was now settled in his cell, in what appeared to be a deep, self-induced trance. His guards were content to leave him alone; they had enough to attend to. Harios realized that his problems had not been solved, but at least they were under control now. But for the Swordsman, he would have been right.

Martyn had made the mistake of thinking that there would be fewer guards on duty in the ministry at night, and as a result had decided to take only Sagar with him, despite the vast area of the labyrinth. They were to try and locate – and, if possible, bring out – Bowen, and would be relying on speed and stealth rather than any strength of arms. If necessary, they could return later with more men. In many ways Martyn would have preferred to work alone, but Sagar would not be denied.

'All right,' Martyn had conceded, 'but leave any fighting to me – unless you've no choice.'

The outer and upper levels of the vast ministry complex were easy enough to penetrate, but held nothing of interest. To reach the talents it was necessary to get to the core of Verkho's monolithic creation. The first indication that they were nearing their objective was the sound of unearthly wailing and hysterical laughter echoing in the tunnels – and then they encountered their first pair of sentries. The two men died so silently and so fast at the Swordsman's hands that Sagar was stunned, appalled yet admiring. His own hands were sweaty as they gripped his as yet unused knife, while Martyn hid the bodies as best he could. To the ex-hostage's relief they managed to evade the next two sets of guards and so avoid violence, but the Swordsman was angry now.

'What's going on?' he whispered as they hid in a shadowy recess. 'It's as if they're expecting us.'

'All the prisoners are very restless,' Sagar pointed out. 'Perhaps that's why there are so many guards.' They had passed several occupied cells by now, and had seen many agitated, even insane, faces. There had been no sign of Bowen.

'We won't be able to cover half the place at this rate,' his companion said. 'It's time for a few diversions.'

'What . . . ?' Sagar began, but the Swordsman had already moved on.

The next cell held a prisoner who was pacing restlessly, muttering to himself. Each time he reached the door, he looked through the metal bars with mad red eyes, seeing nothing, then turned away again. The key was in the lock, and before Sagar could stop him, the Swordsman turned it and threw the door open. When the prisoner completed his next circuit, he strode straight out into the corridor, paying no attention to the intruders. A little further along, a low-burning oil lamp hung on the wall. The man stared at it for a brief moment, and the wick flared. The oil spilled and ignited, flames leaping down the wall and across the stone floor.

'That's more like it!' the Swordsman said, his eyes gleaming. 'Come on.'

Leaving the talent to watch the results of his handiwork, the two men ran on, glancing quickly into each cell. The Swordsman opened several more doors as they passed, but, to Sagar's relief, they did not linger to see the results. In the next hallway they almost collided with two officials running towards the light and noise of the fire. Martyn killed one of them in an instant, but Sagar managed to stop the other's death. As the terrified man was slammed to the ground with a knife at his throat, the islander intervened.

'Wait!' he hissed, and knelt down. 'Where's Bowen Folegandros?' Though his lips quivered, the man did not speak.

'Bowen Folegandros,' Martyn rasped. 'Where is he?'

'I . . . I . . . don't know.'

'He's a hostage from Zalys,' Sagar added desperately. 'Arrived a few days ago.'

'Him?' The official's eyes widened further.

'Yes. Where is he?'

'Harios' section . . . second . . . no, third corridor on the right, down the steps on the left, then . . .'

'Come on.'

'One of the cells down there . . . don't know which . . .' the man gibbered before the Swordsman silenced him permanently.

Feeling sick, Sagar ran on behind his ruthless ally, moving further away from the commotion behind them. They found the staircase and reached the bottom without further opposition, but then they heard the sound of many booted feet hurrying along the corridor. Martyn found and unlocked a side door and shoved Sagar in ahead of him.

'Quiet,' he breathed.

They listened in the semi-darkness as the soldiers rushed past. As their heavy footsteps echoed up the stairs, Martyn waited, then glanced around the cell. As his eyes grew accustomed to the dim light, he made out the recumbent figures of two women laid out on a large wooden table, head to toe. The left hands of each had been placed together in the centre and what looked like a huge silver nail had been driven through both, so that their blood mingled in a pool between their fingers. Their faces were quite inert, eyes open but unseeing, and they were barely breathing.

'That's disgusting,' Martyn said.

He reached forward over one of the women and grasped the metal, ignoring Sagar's warning cry. As his fingers closed upon the spike, blue flares shot through the Swordsman's fist and he gasped in pain, but did not let go. Yanking hard, the nail came away and he flung it aside. The two bloody hands had been dragged apart by his actions and now they twitched feebly and lay still, the blood congealing slowly.

'They're dead,' Sagar whispered a few moments later. 'You killed them.'

In the Chancellor's private quarters far above their heads, in a room not even his closest servants were allowed to enter, a wooden cabinet began to smoulder. After a little while, the doors swung open of their own accord. The blue screen had vanished and so had the poisons, the seals and the rings. All that lay inside now was dark ash.

'Better dead than like that,' Martyn said, his revulsion clear. 'Let's go. Bowen must be here somewhere.'

Sagar followed, hoping that his brother had fared better than the two women. During his long sojourn in the hostage enclave, he had read as much as he could about the history and theory of magic, and although he had learnt enough to know that he had no discernible talent of his own, he had found the subject fascinating. He knew that blood was much venerated but that it was a conduit, not a source, of power. The mysterious energies that men called magic lay hidden in their minds, inaccessible to all but a very few. Linking the two women's blood had been a barbaric way of linking their minds – for a purpose – but there was no telling what that had been.

They found Bowen shortly afterwards. He was sitting quietly on a pallet, staring fixedly at his cupped hands, which were held out in front of him like an offering. He did not react, even when Sagar called his name or when Martyn unlocked the door and opened it.

'Leave him to me,' Sagar said, almost pushing his companion aside in his haste. Kneeling beside his brother and looking up into his empty eyes, he said, 'Bowen? It's me, Sagar. Your brother.' The prisoner did not even blink, but just gazed into the empty bowl of his hands.

'Come on. Wake him up. We haven't got all day!' Martyn was by the door, alert for the possibility of more guards.

'He's not asleep.'

'Well, shake him out of it, whatever it is.'

Sagar still hesitated, feeling an enormous, inexplicable reluctance, as if the wrong move might be as fatal as removing the spike from the women's hands. If only he knew what was going on behind those blank eyes. Tentatively he reached out to touch his brother's fingers, but when he was still a short distance away, Bowen spoke in a flat, unemotional tone which was more unnerving than if he had shouted.

'Don't break the circle.'

Sagar froze.

'What circle?'

'Stop dithering!' Martyn snapped. 'We've no time for this.'

'We have to stop it speaking,' Bowen stated.

'What?'

'The grey shroud,' he replied in the same monotone, still unmoving. 'Over the city.'

'I don't understand.'

'The winding sheet,' Bowen said impassively. 'No one can listen if it doesn't speak. My friends . . .'

'Come *on*!' Martyn hissed. 'Soldiers coming.'

Sagar shuddered. He did not know what his brother was talking about but he was sure it was important – and it filled him with dread.

'I . . .' he began, but the Swordsman, furious now, grabbed Bowen's hands and tried to pull him to his feet.

'No!' Sagar tried to stop him, but it was too late. As he was dragged from the bed, Bowen came back to the world, and his face crumpled in fear.

'The circle is broken,' he wailed.

'I'll break more than a *circle* if you don't move,' the Swordsman growled.

But Bowen collapsed, his whole body going limp, and he slumped to the floor as boots tramped into the corridor. The Swordsman muttered an oath.

248

'Leave him,' he commanded. 'We've some fighting to do.'

In a much higher part of Xantium, Verkho sat in his court study, staring at his obdurate opponent. For all his efforts, he had got nowhere, and his brain felt as if it was full of mist. Now, abruptly, the fog cleared. He felt rejuvenated, eager once more, and gazed at the transcriptions he had made of the latest markings on the talisman.

'Of course!' he exclaimed aloud. Why hadn't he seen it before? That symbol was the old form of the letter *keer*, in the ancient monastic language known as 'the tongue of butterflies'. Verkho stood up and went in search of the volume he needed. He was sure now that the second layer would soon be removed from the talisman's protective sphere.

Only much later did he wonder exactly what had brought about his sudden change of fortune.

CHAPTER THIRTY

The cost of sorcery is high, beyond the common rates of gold and silver. There is no defence against such contagion, no immunity.

The red executioner hides beneath a humble cowl – but he will extract his price.

'The tongue of butterflies' proved to be as elusive as the creatures it was named for. It took Verkho well into the following night to translate the small section he had identified, and even then he was left with a riddle. 'Rest in the tears of the virgin . . .' The literal translation was dry-maiden. '. . . who turns her face, but does not turn. Let bones tumble and offer gold in silver.'

After his previous success with the dice, Verkho decided that the tumbling bones probably referred to knucklebones. He had a set on his desk now, and was quite prepared to sacrifice the gold chain and coins which lay beside the talisman. But why was it 'gold *in* silver'? No jeweller would hide the more expensive metal within the other. While part of his mind gnawed at this problem, the Chancellor returned to the first part of the instruction. He had thought of sending for a virgin, but had dismissed that as too simplistic. In any case, even given that it would be easy enough to induce tears, how was he supposed to rest in them?

Eventually, a stray memory from his early life led him to the solution. He had lived for some months in a remote mountain monastery, and some of the monks had evolved peculiar but fascinating theories about the sights in the night sky. Verkho recalled one old madman assuring him that the moon was made up of the souls of all those who had died as children; he had even claimed to be able to identify the spirit of his own niece.

'The virgin who turns her face, but does not turn' was surely the moon, which turned from light to dark and back again each month, but which always showed the same side to the observers below. And therefore her 'tears' were moonlight. *Silver* moonlight.

Verkho threw back the shutters from one of his windows and was rewarded by the sight of the crescent moon, which shed a faint light on to a patch of the study floor. He carefully picked up the talisman and placed it in the centre of the silvered area, then laid the gold beside it. He took a deep breath and threw the knuckle-bones on the floor. His rapt expression changed to an exultant grin as they landed in the highest possible scoring position.

The silvery glow was suddenly much brighter than before, and Verkho was forced to shade his eyes. When he could look again, another layer of the sphere had vanished – and so had the gold. It was a small price, and he was glad to pay it. Feeling elated but suddenly very tired, the Chancellor picked up the talisman and placed it back on his lamplit desk. As he had expected, the lettering on the inner casing had changed again. The game continued.

Verkho surprised himself by sleeping soundly the rest of the night and well into the next morning. Yet when he awoke, far from feeling refreshed, his whole body was weary and stiff, and the thought of the next stage of deduction filled him with dismay. He had enough experience to know that most acts of sorcery were gained only at a cost, and wondered whether the talisman was extracting ever greater sacrifices from both his body and his mind as he drew closer to its ultimate secret. If that was so, he knew he would have to be careful. He was not used to paying his own debts – that was what he used the talents for – and to fail now because of exhaustion would be inexcusable.

Allowing the seal that protected his study to be relaxed for a short time, the Chancellor called in the Focus and senior members of his staff one by one to hear their news and to issue them with instructions. They left knowing better than to discuss their orders with anyone, and went about their business quietly and efficiently. They had all been secretly shocked by the appearance of their master. His glittering eyes seemed duller now, sunk deep in their sockets, and he moved slowly, conducting most of his briefings from his hastily prepared bed. If they did not know better, they might even have thought that Verkho was ill.

Ifryn's mother, who had until recently been Queen Zephia of Idiron, arrived in Xantium the next day. Southan greeted her with condolences and welcome, then left the two women to talk. They spoke at length of Fyles and of the events following his death; they cried and laughed at their memories of him, and Zephia renewed her acquaintance with her two granddaughters, whom she had not seen for several years. And she met Azari for the first time. It was an emotional day and, however much her own concerns preyed on her mind, Ifryn could not bring herself to burden her bereaved mother with her woes and fears. However, Zephia's parting words before she retired to bed left Ifryn with an even stronger feeling of approaching disaster.

'You know, Latif's a good enough boy,' she had said, 'but he'll never be half the man your father was. Idiron's in the middle of a region that's been on a knife edge for years now, and unless it gets some strong leadership from Xantium, I dread to think what's going to happen.'

The following morning, Verkho sent word to Southan

that he wished to have a private conference, and the Emperor arrived quickly, though he knew that he should be the one doing the summoning. When he entered the Chancellor's study, he was shocked to see Verkho wrapped in blankets and propped up in bed.

'Forgive me for not rising, your majesty,' Verkho said. 'As you see, I am unable to do so.'

'Are you ill?'

'I have been poisoned.'

The Chancellor then told the astonished Emperor that his supposed immunity was not total. He had been given enough poison to have killed a dozen men, but had survived – just.

'The poison was most unusual,' he went on. 'That's why I did not detect it until too late and, worst of all, it produced a contagion that could have been passed on to anyone who came into contact with me. So I was forced to shut myself away until I could be sure I would no longer infect others.'

'Is such a thing possible?' Southan asked in amazement. Verkho did indeed look ill, but the existence of such a venom was scarcely credible. And yet it must be so – why else would the Chancellor have retreated in such an inexplicable manner? All of which led to the inevitable question. 'Who did this?'

Verkho shifted slightly, and winced as if in pain.

'Can you not guess?' he said. 'Such treachery is hard to comprehend, let alone stomach.'

'Kerrell?'

'And my cursed sister!' Verkho grimaced. 'They turned on me when I foiled their plot to poison Azari.'

'But you said that was the Swordsman!' Southan cried, plunging to new depths of despair.

'That was but a ruse, my lord. Do you not remember how Kerrell called out at the banquet? I should have known his guilt then, but I could not credit it until I found the proof.' Verkho went on to give Southan details of the conspiracy, producing two more letters which bore Clavia's seal and which confirmed Kerrell's part in the betrayal.

'Now I hear that the General has admitted his guilt and run for his life,' the Chancellor concluded. 'I would not have thought to add cowardice to his list of crimes.'

'It seems I did not know him as well as I thought,' Southan replied sadly, wondering what effect this latest revelation would have on Ifryn.

'Indeed,' Verkho agreed gravely. 'He will be caught and brought to account eventually, but in the meantime, now that I am on the way to recovery, we have much to do.'

The two men then discussed the state of the Empire, and Southan accepted Verkho's suggestions on all aspects of its administration. He left feeling too distraught to even think straight.

For the next few days the Chancellor's routine returned to normal, with his staff and the military commanders much relieved at being able to consult him once more. Generals outlined proposed defences and reported on border skirmishes; Harios and other senior officials presented their reports and were calmed by their master's unruffled acceptance of the setbacks; and the Focus continued to bring reports from all over the Empire – including several from the spy on Zalys, which Verkho read with interest but which told him nothing new or of sufficient importance for him to respond. He found it amusingly ironic that the mysterious creatures that had apparently destroyed Barvick's fleet were now attacking the islanders whom their earlier actions had saved.

Verkho remained in bed for most of these consultations and, at times, found it necessary to shut himself away again in order – or so he claimed – to rest. This was a minor inconvenience, and the running of the Xantic Empire seemed once more on an even keel.

Ifryn had not seen or heard from Kerrell since their meeting with Baylin and, as the days dragged by and no word came, she sank deeper into anxiety and gloom. Her only comfort was that there had been no news of his capture. But set against that, the Swordsman seemed to have vanished from the face of the earth, Alasia had not come to see her, and Baylin did not know how to help. Even Zephia, who had begun to understand a little of the complicated politics of Xantium and of her daughter's concerns, was of little help. Most of the life seemed to have gone out of her, and she was bad-tempered and irritable, summoning little enthusiasm for anything except her memories. Even her grandchildren soon learnt to avoid her when they could. So Ifryn was not surprised when her mother visited her in tears, angrily bewailing the fact that she had lost her locket containing a few strands of Fyle's hair.

'It's gone,' she cried hysterically. 'Just vanished!'

'It can't have gone far,' Ifryn consoled her. 'We'll find it.'

But they did not. The locket was nowhere to be found and, once the search was over, Zephia insisted on questioning the servants, all but accusing them of theft – and achieved nothing except her own increasing unpopularity. Ifryn comforted her as best she could, but her own patience was wearing thin.

When Verkho solved the third puzzle, he felt a surge of confidence and excitement. This was indeed a challenge – but one he was uniquely suited to overcome.

In the geometric script of the desert nomads of Montecrocia, the clue read, 'Choose from the being that has hands but no fingers. My outer for yours. Cleave both or none at all. That done, call forth a silent walker and let him be entombed.' The first part was easy, so easy that Verkho doubted the solution at first, but he eventually decided that it could only mean a pack of cards. Gambling was a common element in the answers he sought. After that came the instruction to cut his own skin in order to 'cleave' another layer of the talisman's

255

protective covering. Presumably blood was needed for the next step, which was to summon a ghost – or silent walker as the nomads called them. The Chancellor did not know how a ghost could 'be entombed', but that did not seem to be his responsibility. All he had to do was provide the spectre – and he knew exactly who it was to be.

The arrangements took some time, but eventually all was ready. Verkho carefully cut the cards and laid his choice face up on the desk. It was, appropriately, The Red Executioner, the most powerful card in the pack. Next he picked up a sharp knife and determinedly sliced open his left palm. Drops of blood fell on to the cards as he clenched his fist, staining the Executioner's axe red. Then Verkho opened the stolen locket, pinched the hair between his right thumb and forefinger and concentrated.

Fyles had no option but to answer the call, but he came unwillingly, fighting all the way. Verkho persevered, and succeeded – even though by the end he was filmed with sweat. The old king wavered before him, his face filled with rage and fear, shouting silent words into the void between worlds.

Now what? the Chancellor wondered. He had done all that had been asked of him. Surely he could not fail.

Verkho was shaking now, the pain and exertion making him giddy. His injured hand went into spasm and drops of blood flew in all directions. A few landed on the sphere, with instant effect. The outer layer of the glass-like substance began to shine, but instead of simply vanishing it began to *flow*, like clear, molten metal. As it moved so did Fyles, his ghost drawn towards it, his shape distorting as though he too were a liquid being forced down a funnel. There was a flash, a small readjustment of reality, and then – with one last silent scream – the ghost disappeared. The molten crystal gathered itself into a globule, slithered across the desktop and enveloped the bloodstained card.

Then the small sphere rolled slowly across the desk. Trapped within its red-flecked substance, like an insect in amberine, was The Red Executioner. But the card's design had changed now, and the man who wielded the bloody axe had the face of a dead king.

Verkho caught the ball, stared at his victim, frozen for ever, and laughed.

The Chancellor let it be known that he was suffering from exhaustion, in danger of a relapse from the long-term effects of the venom. Yet he insisted on continuing to work, heroically managing the affairs of state as only he could.

By now it was generally known throughout the city that Kerrell was a traitor – a story that most people accepted – and to know that Verkho was back in charge was comforting for almost everyone – including Southan.

The Chancellor found his enforced confinement frustrating and yearned to return to his real task, but he knew his limitations. The last effort had left him weak and tired, and it would be some time before he could make his next assault. In the meantime, he contented himself with his other work, and with the thought that the talisman's secrets would soon be known.

CHAPTER THIRTY-ONE

The legends say that the gods first came forth from the sea, and that mankind crawled out in their wake. Unlike the gods, we cannot return. So who is there to chart the ocean's depths, to persuade its relentless tides to turn back, its currents not to flow? We touch only its topmost layer, leaving undisturbed the mysteries below, where only dead men go.

Although none of them had been to sea in so large a vessel before, the travellers from Zalys were all familiar with the ways of boats and, rather to the disappointment of the crew, none of them was even discomfited by the swaying decks. Gaye especially, who was so pale, looked a candidate for sickness. But, while her mobility was necessarily restricted, she remained at ease, and this obviously surprised the sailors. Although they usually spoke in their own harsh language, they sometimes used the universal trading tongue, and the passengers caught references to 'the blind witch', in tones that varied from scorn to wonderment. At first Gaye was hurt by their words, but she soon found them amusing and turned them to her advantage, learning which of the crew regarded her with nervous awe and getting them to run errands for her with threats of dire punishments if she was displeased.

One of the youngest seamen, a cabin boy who brought them their food, made a point of being rude to the two women when Dsordas and Yeori were absent. He was obviously doing this to impress his older shipmates – but was still clearly apprehensive. Eventually, Gaye promised to turn him into a toad unless he was polite, and her voice was so stern that he paled and left in a hurry. Fen and her sister collapsed with laughter as soon as the door shut, and the boy may have heard. However, he was polite after that, and even smiled shyly, until eventually they became friends. He told them that his name was Rekyar, that he had been at sea since he was nine years old, and that the *Frozen Star* was much better now that Bark Madden was captain – but he displayed no curiosity about where the islanders were going or why.

'You're different,' he conceded on one occasion. 'Most girls are useless at sea. They get sick – just like that soft merchant.'

Fen decided that she quite liked being called a girl again.

'Ranald?' she asked idly.

'Yeah. Him and his stupid servant haven't even been out of their cabin yet,' Rekyar replied, his contempt for the landlubbers plain.

'Perhaps his stomach's not as strong as ours,' Gaye suggested.

'He's just soft,' the boy stated adamantly. 'One time I went in and the servant had a bandage on his head. What good's that going to do?'

'What sort of bandage?' Fen asked quickly.

'Just a bandage,' Rekyar said. 'Not a very good one either. It had a lump in it.'

Ranald had been so desperate to leave Zalys that even when he had heard who else would be aboard, he had decided it was worth the risk. He knew of Dsordas, Fen and Yeori and their positions on the island, and of Gaye's reputation. But as they seemed to be the reason for the *Frozen Star*'s leaving Zalys, he reasoned that if anyone subsequently accused him of deserting his mission, he could claim to have been following the island's leaders. However, he did not wish to tempt fate, and the easiest way to avoid direct contact with them was to feign seasickness and stay in his cabin.

There had been no need to send further reports to Xantium – indeed he had not wanted to alert them to his departure – and so he had only had Hunter contact the city infrequently, just in case anyone there had been trying to reach him. But they had not. Now, two days after the bats had escorted them from Nkosa harbour, the confinement of the small space with only the unresponsive Far-speaker for company was becoming oppressive.

'I'm going for a walk on deck,' Ranald decided. 'Don't leave the cabin.'

Hunter nodded dully.

'Give me a pendant,' Gaye said, as soon as Rekyar had left them.

Fen did as she was told, and watched her sister's face contort with revulsion when she touched the stone.

'Is it . . . ?'

'It's dormant, but he's ill,' Gaye replied. 'Horribly ill.' She dropped the pendant in disgust.

'A Far-speaker? I must tell Dsordas.' Fen ran from the cabin, leaving Gaye to worry alone.

Dsordas was standing in the bows of the ship, staring at the eastern horizon, his dark curls rippling in the early morning breeze. He turned at Fen's call and hurried to meet her, sensing her distress.

'What's the matter?'

'Ranald's servant is a Far-speaker,' Fen told him breathlessly. 'Gaye sensed his sickness, the nectar. Do you know where their cabin is?'

'Yes.' Dsordas was already on his way.

'Be careful!' Fen cried, running after him. 'Where's Yeori?'

Dsordas paid her no attention, and disappeared below decks. Fen tried to follow, but he outdistanced her easily. He drew his knife as he reached the merchant's cabin, then threw all his weight at the door. It gave easily, the lock splintering, and crashed inwards. Dsordas crouched, ready to attack, but the only occupant was Hunter. He lay on a bunk, and his only reaction to the sudden intrusion was to blink slowly. Dsordas grabbed his shirt front and pulled him up.

'Show me your tongue!' he shouted.

Hunter's eyes showed signs of alarm now as he recognized his peril, but he hung limply from his assailant's fist.

'Show me!'

As Hunter's mouth gaped open, displaying a purple-black tongue, Dsordas snarled in disgust and rage and stabbed once, driving the blade into the Far-speaker's heart. Then he heard Fen shouting and pulled his knife from the bloodstained chest and let the body fall back as he turned to the door. As he emerged into the corridor he heard Fen scream, and ran towards the sound. Turning a corner he saw his love held from behind by Ranald, a knife at her throat. Dsordas froze, just as Yeori came up behind him.

'What's going . . .' his deputy began but fell silent when he saw Fen.

'Come any closer and she dies,' Ranald said.

Fen dared not struggle. As she looked into Dsordas' brown eyes, she felt terribly afraid. It was as if they had turned to stone.

'Move back,' the merchant ordered. 'Away from my cabin. I think it's time to report your little expedition to Xantium.'

Dsordas and Yeori began to edge backwards, keeping their eyes on Fen. Dsordas was so intent that he might not have noticed the implication of Ranald's words – but he had. If the Far-speaker had not yet sent word to Xantium, there was still a chance of reaching the mainland, and later the city, undetected. But first he had to find a way to rescue Fen. When Ranald found Hunter dead . . .

The spy pushed his hostage forward as the men retreated slowly. Then a shadow moved in the dark corridor beyond Ranald. Dsordas barely saw it, but his hopes lifted and he did his best not to betray their possible ally. Instead he tried to keep Ranald's attention on himself.

'Hurt her and you'll die,' he told him coldly.

'Brave words – but anything you do will only mean she is hurt all the more. She and I will be sharing a cabin until we reach the mainland. Then . . .'

'You have to sleep sometime,' Dsordas pointed out. The shadow moved closer.

'There are ways round that,' Ranald said scornfully. 'Keep moving.'

Dsordas caught a glimpse of an iron rod in the shadows, and prayed that the sailor wielding it would do so with sufficient force. A half-hit would be Fen's death warrant.

The shadow struck. There was a dull crunch as metal met skullbone, and Ranald's knife fell from nerveless fingers. Fen stumbled forward, suddenly released, as her captor collapsed and lay still. Dsordas leapt forward to catch her, discarding his knife and hugging her to him. The iron rod clattered to the floor and their saviour raised trembling fingers in front of his face, as if seeing them for the first time.

'I . . . I killed him,' the newcomer said, his voice shaking.

It was Nason Folegandros.

'Stowing away was an incredibly stupid thing to do,' Yeori said. 'But I'm very glad you did.'

The five islanders were crowded into one cabin. Nason had recovered slightly, and had stopped shivering now. After realizing what he had done – even though he did not regret his actions – he had felt cold and ill. Ranald and Hunter were food for the fishes now. A search of their cabin had revealed the amberine headband but nothing else of interest.

'We all are,' Gaye agreed. 'But why did you do it?'

'My parents would never have let me go,' Nason replied. 'Neither would you if I'd asked.' No one bothered to deny this. 'So I *had* to stow away. They're my brothers,' he added defiantly.

'We could turn back,' Dsordas told him sternly.

'But you won't.' There was just a touch of uncertainty in Nason's voice.

'No. You've made your choice. You'll have to live with the consequences.' Turning to his deputy, Dsordas added, 'Come on, Yeori. We need to see Bark.' He paused at the cabin door, and turned back to Nason. 'Thank you,' he said quietly. 'I am in your debt.'

There was an awkward silence after the two men left.

'Your parents'll be frantic,' Gaye said. 'I hope you know what you're doing.'

'Do *you*?' Nason challenged.

'Good point,' Fen replied. 'This voyage is like . . .'

'The blind leading the blind?' Gaye suggested with a smile.

'I was trying to put it more tactfully,' Fen said, pleased that her sister was able to joke about her situation.

'Don't worry about me,' Gaye went on. 'All the best witches have a sense of humour.'

Nason looked from one sister to the other, wondering if they had both gone quite mad.

'Did Ranald ask where we were headed?'

'Yes,' Bark replied. 'I told him somewhere near Brighthaven.'

'Nothing more specific?' Yeori asked.

'No.'

'But we're not actually going to Brighthaven itself, are we?' Dsordas said.

There was a pause.

'Listen,' Bark replied. 'I'd rather you didn't spread this among the crew, but I'm not sure *where* we'll hit the coast. My navigation was never as good as the old

263

captain's. I get by, but until we sight land I won't know where we are. But then, what's a few dozen leagues between friends, eh?' The sailor laughed.

'Just make sure we don't sail into Brighthaven by mistake,' Yeori said, grinning. 'I don't think we want to meet what's left of the Xantic navy.'

'No problem,' Bark assured him.

'How soon do you think we'll see the coast?' Dsordas asked.

'In about three days,' the Captain replied. 'As long as the wind holds in the west – and we don't have to fight any screamers.'

'Any sightings?'

'Not since the few we saw near Zalys,' Bark said. 'It's my guess they've lost interest in us.'

'Let's hope so,' Yeori added. 'We could do without any more excitement on this trip.'

CHAPTER THIRTY-TWO

It flows in me like an eternal tide, a river of life. Yet there are dangers hidden within. How delicate the balance is, how vulnerable. Who is to say what secret monsters lurk inside our own bodies, what small things might cause foments of the blood? Thoughts cannot choose their sensitivities. Men's bodies, like the world, live with their own aversions.

Bark Madden's prediction proved accurate. The mainland was sighted three days later and, having identified it as the coast a few leagues south of Brighthaven, they set course for the much smaller port of Slope. The harbour there was a natural inlet, well sheltered but shallow, so the *Frozen Star* anchored in the bay and the travellers were rowed ashore. Once on the docks, which smelt of seaweed and rotting fish, the islanders took their leave of Bark and his men and made their way into the town. It felt odd to be on solid ground once more. They had no intention of going far that afternoon and Dsordas decided to find an inn, then spend the rest of the day investigating the purchase of horses. They hoped to set out for Xantium the next morning, going via Brighthaven – which from Slope they could enter unobtrusively – where they would endeavour to learn the real story of the fleet.

They chose one of the less conspicuous taverns. Although the public drinking hall was dark and dingy, the two bedrooms they took were reasonably priced and surprisingly clean.

Once installed, Dsordas and Fen prepared to begin their investigations, leaving Yeori to keep Gaye company and protect their belongings. After a short argument in which Nason pointed out, correctly, that he knew more about horses than any of the others, it was agreed that he should go too. On the advice of their amiable landlord, they went to the northern outskirts of the town where several livestock merchants had brought their animals to market. They took with them a few small pieces of amberine and some money. The mounts they required were found easily enough but a good deal of haggling was needed before all was settled; Dsordas was quite prepared to pay good prices, but did not want to draw attention to themselves by overpaying. Eventually terms were agreed for five animals, and stabling was arranged for the night.

Only Nason was a seasoned rider, but all except Yeori – who admitted his own complete lack of experience – had at least been on a horse before. However, Gaye would probably have difficulty riding on her own, so if necessary, she could double up with Nason on one of the larger mounts, leaving hers as a baggage carrier.

On their way back to the tavern, they were passed by four imperial soldiers in slovenly uniforms who were strolling down the street. Even though the guards took no notice of them, the travellers felt nervous, and had to try hard not to show their feelings.

'We're going to have to get used to this,' Dsordas said when the soldiers had gone. 'Even if Ranald *did* let Xantium know we were coming, they're hardly likely to look for us here.'

'They didn't look as though they could find their own belt-buckles,' Nason remarked with youthful contempt.

'The garrison here obviously isn't the cream of the Xantic army,' Dsordas said wryly.

'Even so,' Fen put in, 'we should change a good part of the amberine into imperials. Some of the horse traders were surprised by the stones, and if we carry on dealing with it, it'll be an easy trail to follow.'

Dsordas nodded.

'There were some jewellers' merchants in the main square,' he said. 'We'll try there now.'

'And we should get ourselves some new clothes,' Fen added. 'Ours obviously aren't from around here.' She wanted very much to contribute to the success of their mission, and so she was pleased when Dsordas nodded again.

As a jeweller by trade, Dsordas had a good idea of the value of their stones and he and Fen made a good bargaining team, but even so they only ended up with about two thirds of the amberine's real worth. It was enough. Plain but good quality clothes – suitable for riding – were then purchased, and they arrived back at the inn, feeling pleased with their efforts, in the early evening. The place was already lively. The drinking hall was half full of people taking their evening meal, with serving maids ferrying trays from the kitchens to the tables. Two musicians played in one corner. The islanders were all hungry now, so they changed their clothes and went down to the hall. The entrance of two beautiful blonde women could not go unnoticed – especially as one was evidently blind – and indeed there was some comment, but this was lost in the general bustle. The travellers chose a side table in the shadows, and once they had begun their meal, no one took much notice of them. The music continued, the drink flowed and the occasional bursts of singing grew more raucous, but the atmosphere remained friendly. However, that changed dramatically later in the evening.

Fen had just suggested that they return to their rooms, knowing that they wanted to make an early start the next morning, when the outer door was thrown open and four soldiers surged in, noisily shouting for ale. One of them was dragging a sorry looking creature who had a rope tied around his wrists. The boy was limping, and his skin was cracked and mottled. He was dressed in rags, and his face wore the dull, lifeless expression of one who had come to expect ill-treatment as his due.

'What's going on?' Gaye whispered.

Fen quietly described the newcomers, feeling sympathy for the captive and revulsion at his treatment. The soldiers pushed the boy into a chair and bound him in place, then lifted the chair and set it on a table. They had obviously been drinking for some time, and laughed uproariously when one of their number overbalanced and fell. By now everyone in the hall was watching them with a mixture of unease and ill-humoured curiosity. Even the musicians fell silent when one of the soldiers yelled at them.

'I bring you a marvel!' the patrol leader proclaimed. 'Th'like 'f which you've never seen b'fore. Who'll wager me tha' I can make this boy's head swell up to th'size of . . . th'size of . . .' His imagination failed him, so he held his hands wide apart. 'This big,' he concluded.

'Rubbish!' someone called.

'How'd you do that then?' another sceptic yelled.

'Magic,' the soldier claimed. 'My own swee' magic!'

'Half an imperial says you can't,' one of the drinkers shouted.

'Half an imperial!' the patrol leader exclaimed derisively. '*Half?* I shan't waste m'time with such paltry sums. There're obviously no gamblers here.'

This was a challenge and an insult which would rarely go unanswered anywhere in the Empire, and the soldier knew it. He and his colleagues were soon busy accepting bets, while the inert boy sat, taking no notice of the commotion he was causing. Eventually the patrol leader was satisfied with the takings and turned to the landlord.

'Bring me a bowl of your bes' shrimp.'

At this the captive showed his first signs of life. His eyes widened in fear, his mouth gaped in a silent scream, revealing several broken teeth, and he struggled futilely against his bonds.

268

'Gods,' Dsordas moaned in a low voice. 'We've got to stop this.'

Fen felt him grow tense and rigid, and sensed his rising anger, but knew that he must restrain himself. The last thing they needed was trouble with imperial soldiers.

'You can't,' she whispered. 'Anyway, he can't mean what he says.'

Dsordas gave her a haunted look.

'Oh yes he can,' he breathed.

By now the food had been brought to the patrol leader, and everyone watched as he stood on a chair.

'Look, Aad,' he said, provoking laughter from the other soldiers. 'Your favourite.'

The boy shut his mouth, shaking his head violently, and almost tipped his chair over. The other soldiers steadied it and one of them pulled the boy's head back by his hair. Though he made every effort to avoid the food, including spitting most of it out, Aad was eventually forced to swallow a few of the small pink fish. The patrol leader smiled and stepped down.

'Behold!' he cried.

Dsordas bent forward, holding his head in his hands, but the others could not take their eyes off the boy. He was rigid now, with only his terrified eyes still moving, his breath hissing in shorter and shorter gasps. Slowly at first, then with appalling rapidity, the colour of the skin on his neck and face grew darker, as if suffused with blood. Then, before the mesmerized eyes of the audience, his neck began to bulge. Cries of revulsion and amazement rang out as the swelling continued and spread upwards to his head and face. Cheeks and lips bulged grotesquely, his forehead distended and his unevenly cropped hair began to stand on end. The horror-struck eyes all but disappeared, sinking into holes in the bloated globe of flesh which was now almost as wide as the boy's shoulders, fully justifying the soldier's earlier claim. Blood trickled from the extended cracks in the boy's hideously distorted skin.

The soldiers laughed and collected their winnings from the awed onlookers, then called for quantities of ale. The boy, Aad, his purpose served, was forgotten by his captors and slumped in his chair, shaking feebly. His oversized head lolled to one side and his breath came fast and shallow. All around him the bustle of the tavern resumed at even greater volume. The show was over.

Fen could not speak. She thought she had never seen anything so vile, so callous and, like Dsordas, she was filled with a sick rage. She could tell from a quick glance at Yeori and Nason that both felt the same way. Gaye, who had been spared the horrific spectacle, was nevertheless also deeply affected, sensing her companions' distress. For some time no one moved, then Dsordas broke the silence, sounding as though he were in pain.

'Let's get out of here.'

No one argued, and they trooped up to their rooms and tried to settle for the night. Sleep came eventually but, deep in the night, Fen woke to see Dsordas quietly leave the room. She listened as he roused Yeori from the chamber he was sharing with Nason, then heard the two of them go downstairs. She was tempted to follow, guessing their intent, but did not want to leave Gaye alone. Instead she lay awake, worrying.

An hour or so later Dsordas returned and slid into bed beside her.

'Is everything all right?' she whispered.

'Yes,' he replied, sounding grim but satisfied. 'Go back to sleep.'

Nason roused them very early the next morning.

'Yeori's gone!' he said breathlessly.

'I know,' Dsordas returned sleepily. 'Don't worry. He's with the horses. We'll meet him there.'

They dressed and packed their few belongings, and went downstairs. The innkeeper and his staff were tidying up the debris from the previous evening.

'You'd best be on your way,' the landlord advised,

gesturing towards a corner where the four soldiers lay in a dishevelled, snoring heap. 'They had too much to drink last night and after they'd passed out, some thieves robbed them of all their winnings. And the boy escaped.' He grinned at Dsordas. 'They'll not be too happy when they come to.'

'A few drinks will set them right,' Dsordas suggested with a smile.

'Maybe so.' The innkeeper did not sound unduly concerned. He had obviously dealt with worse than this in his time. 'Farewell, and good journeying.'

'I don't suppose you had anything to do with that?' Fen asked Dsordas when they were out in the street.

'We might have suggested adding a few extra ingredients to the soldiers' beer,' he admitted. 'They'll have quite a hangover.'

'And did you rob them too?'

Dsordas looked hurt.

'No. We left that to the experts – of which there are obviously quite a few.'

'And Aad?'

'Not now,' he told her. 'We must be on our way.'

At the stables, they found that one of the largest horses had gone. After some hurried experimentation, Gaye decided that she felt more secure riding with someone else, so Nason volunteered to share her mount. Dsordas and Fen chose their own and loaded their packs on to the fourth. Then they set out along the coast road, heading north towards Brighthaven.

They had gone no more than half a league when they came upon Yeori and his mount at the side of the track. It came as no surprise to Fen to see Aad, dressed in Nason's old clothes, sitting next to the solid islander. The boy's head and neck were back to their normal size and his skin seemed less mottled in the morning sunlight. As the riders approached, he looked up and smiled and, as Dsordas vaulted down from the saddle, Fen saw Aad look at him with undisguised adoration. When they had all dismounted, Dsordas went up to the boy and took his hands in his own.

'How are you feeling?'

'Much better. Thanks to you.'

The healer's touch evidently told Dsordas much the same because he let go, nodding. Aad turned to Fen.

'He's a wonderful man,' he said. 'He took my pain away and let me breathe again.'

Dsordas shrugged and smiled sheepishly, glancing at Fen. She did not think she had ever loved him more than she did at that moment.

CHAPTER THIRTY-THREE

He holds a mirror to the beacon's light. He is more blind than she, but doubly blessed; hearing only echoes, he is immune to the screaming of the white fire, and feels only its warmth.

His reflection will be welcome in this darkness, his augury a bright counter to my own.

Over the next few days, Aad proved to be invaluable, informing the islanders about many aspects of the land they were travelling through, and as he showed no sign of wanting to leave and return to his own home, they were only too happy to have him as their guide. He had obviously been in the soldiers' clutches for some time – although that was something he would not talk about – but before that he had roamed over much of the coastal region of Nadal and knew many of the roads, towns and inns. Kindness was the best cure for him, and his health returned quickly, but he still regarded Dsordas with devotion and gratitude.

Brighthaven was their first stop on the way north. While the others stayed on the outskirts of the town, Dsordas, Fen and Aad went in to try and discover the fate of the Southern Fleet. They were able to confirm that it had set out for Zalys very soon after the revolt, but there were conflicting rumours about what had happened to it since. Mass mutiny, a vast storm, battles with unknown enemies and sea monsters were all quoted but, whatever the truth of it, it was clear that something had indeed happened to the ships. So, much to their relief, it seemed that Zalys was out of danger – at least for the time being. No other naval forces had been sent to the island. They returned to the others buoyed up by the news and eager to continue their journey.

When they told Aad of their eventual destination he showed no surprise or concern, simply assuming that he would be going with them.

'Are you going for the Grand Tournament?' he asked.

'What?' Yeori asked, puzzled.

'Surely you've heard of it?' Aad exclaimed. 'Everyone has.' He went on to explain that each year, for several days in the late summer, the city was convulsed with an orgy of gambling, together with a vast carnival that made the rest of the year – even in that remote and fabulous place – seem tame by comparison. Aad had never seen it himself, but the reputation of the Grand Tournament was legendary. It was immediately obvious that the travellers now had the perfect excuse should anyone ask why they were going to Xantium.

'Getting there will take time and money,' Aad warned them, 'and the city itself is horribly expensive. What are you doing for money?'

Dsordas explained about the amberine, and showed him some of the remaining stones. Aad whistled appreciatively.

'Beautiful! Money's no problem then. Did you use this to buy the horses?'

Dsordas told him how much he had paid and how much he had received from the jewellers. Aad looked stricken.

'You *do* need my help!' he exclaimed. 'These are worth far more than that.'

He proceeded to prove his point at the next sizeable town by bargaining a price for a single stone which was as much as Dsordas had got for two in Slope. Handing over the coins, Aad smiled proudly.

'Your trouble is that you're thinking in Zalys prices,' he told them. 'The nearer you get to Xantium the more

274

expensive this stuff becomes. And the merchants can tell you're not from around here. On the coast we're used to all sorts of barbaric accents.'

'Barbaric? Us?' Fen pulled a face and the others laughed, but Aad was momentarily nonplussed. Then he laughed uneasily, not sure whether he had given offence.

'I didn't mean . . .' he began.

'Don't mind her,' Dsordas told him with a grin. 'She's never been able to live down her northern heritage.'

Fen hit him.

They travelled as fast as they could, their horsemanship improving every day at the expense of stiff and sore bodies. Heading northeast whenever they could, they took the most direct route to Xantium, anxious now to reach their goal, and were soon beyond the boundaries of Aad's knowledge. Even so, he continued to deal competently with most situations and the others let him do as much as possible. The roads were dotted with villages and towns, and finding beds and stabling was rarely a problem. The only difficulties were caused by their understandable reluctance to stay in or near any of the fortified imperial way-stations. On the whole, however, their journey was remarkably uneventful – until, several days after leaving Slope, Gaye decided to try and contact Alasia.

Both Nason, who still rode with her, and Aad had begun to feel protective towards the blind girl, and it was Aad who brought her the amberine when she requested it. He liked touching the crystals whenever he could, and waited eagerly when Gaye took it from him. The others, more familiar with the strain Gaye was under, watched with concern, ready to go to her aid if necessary.

They sat in silence for a while, then Gaye's face began to display a rapidly changing mixture of laughter, disgust and incomprehension. But the overriding emotion and the one which remained with her at the end was fear.

'I will. We will,' Gaye burst out urgently, then dropped the stone and returned to their world.

By then both Fen and Nason were at her side, and they held her as she trembled. Aad, in contrast, was staring at his own hands in wonder.

'How did you do that?' he asked with a disbelieving smile. 'You made my hands tingle.'

Dsordas glanced at the young boy, but his main concern was with Gaye.

'What happened?' Fen asked gently. 'What did you see?'

'Terrible things . . .' her sister whispered. 'Things I can't even understand . . . happening in Xantium. And Bowen is in the middle of it all.' Her face was distraught. 'He needs me. Alasia said so. We have to hurry or it'll be too late.'

'Too late for what?' Dsordas asked.

'Everything,' she replied.

After that, they increased their pace whenever they could, travelling with a growing sense of unease. Gaye had been unable to clarify her impressions, knowing only that Bowen was in peril and that they had to reach the city as quickly as possible. No one even thought to contradict her. Her sense of foreboding was too strong.

Augury is a cursed art, Fen quoted in her mind. *All Xantium will tell you that.* And knew that her sister would agree.

Aad had been downcast by Gaye's distress, especially as he had been unable to hide his own delight at the time. While she had been in the otherworld realm, he had felt warmth and gladness radiating from her and the amberine. It had made him happy, and his hands had tingled wonderfully. He had never felt anything like it before, but when he told the others, no one could explain what had happened – except for Yeori's half-joking remark that perhaps shrimp was not the only thing he was sensitive to. That made no sense to Aad;

276

the two reactions had been worlds apart. And in any case, what could he have been reacting to?

For her part, Gaye was now desperate for the journey to end, and felt a weight on her shoulders that grew with every league. Alasia had sounded weary and anxious but had said nothing to contradict her earlier words, which Gaye clung to in feverish hope. *Your beacons still shine.* All that mattered to Gaye now was to reach Xantium – and Bowen.

At last, close to exhaustion and very saddle-sore, the travellers reached the edge of the Deadlands. Here they were forced to rest in a village which contained an imperial way-station, but no one paid them any attention. There were many travellers heading for the city and the Grand Tournament, which was due to begin in two days' time.

Next morning, following the dust trail of the party ahead, Dsordas and his group set out across the red desert, awed by its vast desolation. Although they were carrying plentiful supplies, the Deadlands made them feel vulnerable and insignificant. Dsordas was now suffering with one of his crushing headaches, which seemed to get worse with every step, but they pressed on at the best pace their tired horses could manage.

It was late in the second day when they caught their first glimpse of Xantium, the eccentric outline of The Spires peeking over the horizon. As they drew nearer, hoping to make the gates by nightfall, more of the city became visible. When the walls lay before them, glittering in the last of the sunlight, they paused to stare and consider the daunting prospect.

The sight evoked in Fen a curious and inexplicable mixture of emotions. It brought back many fears and uncertainties about her involvement in this voyage – and a sense of being out of her depth. But at the same time, she felt as though she had never seen anything so beautiful. In the midst of the barren plain, Xantium was like a magical creation, full of wonders and hidden enchantments. She knew, without understanding how, that fate had brought her to the the right place. *But beware*, she quoted to herself, *this city has its screamers too.*

Gaye was also thinking of something Alasia had said. *Xantium is the centre of many circles. If you would understand them all, you must come here.* She sat on her horse, holding on to Nason as the others stared, and knew a part of what they saw.

Well, I've come, she thought as the horses started forward, towards the heart of the Empire. *Now what?*

Into the silence, as if in answer, came the distant sound of a bell ringing.

CHAPTER THIRTY-FOUR

It is said that anger is a short-lived madness. But in madness lies power – for good or ill.

It is said that the colour of anger is red, like blood and fire. But madness holds a double rainbow. What pictures may be painted with such a palette?

'You don't understand *anything!*' Ifryn shouted.

Southan had never seen his wife like this before, and was taken aback by her vehement accusation.

'My love . . .' he began.

'Don't!' she warned. 'If you loved me, you wouldn't try to fob me off with pretty words.'

The Empress had finally lost patience. Her own impotence, the apparent desertion by her allies and Southan's feeble acquiescence to Verkho's will had driven her to this outburst. She had lost count of the days since she had last seen Kerrell; Baylin's messages were vague and required no answers; Alasia had vanished, and all Ifryn was left with was the interminable grumbling of her mother. For a while she seemed to have lost all initiative, her resolve trickling away – but now she was at least determined to try.

'Kerrell is not a traitor,' she stated baldly. 'You were a fool to believe it in the first place, and you're even more of a fool to persist in it now.'

Southan fought down the anger he felt at being spoken to in this way and tried, as ever, to calm her.

'I know it's hard to believe,' he said reasonably. 'I would never . . .'

'You can't even see what's plain in front of your eyes,' she snapped.

'You say that?' The Emperor was furious himself now. '*You* are the one being wilfully blind. Kerrell *admitted* his own guilt. You heard him. And you saw the letter that condemned him in his own hand.'

'Both are false!' Ifryn declared.

'How can they be? You're letting your emotions cloud your judgement.'

'My emotions are more reliable than your *proofs*,' she replied defiantly, stressing the last word with contempt. 'Kerrell loves you. He loves me.' After the slightest hesitation, she added, 'He loves the Empire. Why would he turn on the very thing that has been his whole life, his whole reason for living?'

'Then why admit his guilt, why run away?' Southan asked, thoroughly exasperated.

'He was trapped by that foul sorcery for *such* a long time. I only experienced it for a short while, but that was bad enough. You can have no idea what it was like in there. The shock of release was too great. When Penderos accused him, he didn't know what he was saying.'

'No.' Southan was equally definite. 'The Kerrell I knew would have stayed to defend himself.'

'And be executed for a crime he didn't commit?'

The Emperor was now convinced that there was something more than met the eye to his wife's hysteria.

'There's still the letter,' he said calmly. 'He identified his own seal.'

'It's fake.'

'That's absurd. There's no other ring like his – and he was still wearing it.'

'There *is* another.'

'What do you mean?' Southan demanded.

Ifryn had gone too far now to step back from the brink. In a way, she no longer cared.

'Verkho has a copy,' she claimed. '*He* is the real traitor.'

This silenced Southan for a few moments.

'How do you know this?' he asked eventually, his tone dangerously quiet.

Ifryn was desperate now and frantically grasped at a solution which would not betray her complicity.

'Clavia told me,' she blurted out.

Southan was now seriously worried about his wife's sanity.

'She's dead,' he pointed out calmly.

'Her face is in that room,' the Empress claimed. 'And she can still talk.' Rushing on so that she gave him no time to think, Ifryn added, 'She told me that Verkho was planning to implicate Kerrell in treason, using a duplicate ring formed by sorcery. It's Verkho who was responsible for the magic that swallowed Kerrell. Who else could it have been? That's what he uses all the talents shut up inside the ministry for. Sorcery! In time he'll use it to claim the Empire for himself. *He* is the traitor you should fear, not Kerrell.'

Southan's eyes had gone cold during her outburst, and though his expression betrayed nothing, Ifryn sensed his fury and concern, and was suddenly afraid that she had gone too far.

'Why didn't you tell me this earlier?' he asked quietly.

'It shouldn't have been necessary. It seemed impossible that you'd think Kerrell was a traitor – and I kept expecting him to return and sort everything out. Besides . . .' Ifryn hesitated. 'I didn't think you'd believe me.'

'But you expect me to believe you now?'

'Yes,' she said quietly.

'Where is this magical copy of Kerrell's ring?' he asked grimly, deciding to humour her, to end this nonsense once and for all.

'In Verkho's private chambers in The Domain.'

'Then let us go and see it,' Southan said, turning to the door. 'Come.'

281

While he slowly recovered from his third and most arduous success with the talisman, Verkho had plenty of time to consider recent events. His preoccupation with his new treasure had blinded him to much but now, from his sick-bed, he was able to put it all in perspective. Kerrell's escape from the enchantment had been unexpected, but the Chancellor's foresight had prepared a way to turn even that to his own advantage. The fact that the General had not been recaptured was tiresome, but it did at least mean the avoidance of a direct confrontation. Verkho thought that Kerrell had probably left the city by now.

The murder of the Chancellor's mistress had been another irritating distraction. Although she had been pleasing, she could easily be replaced. What annoyed Verkho more was the fact that someone – Kerrell perhaps – had been able to infiltrate his private chambers. He had taken measures to ensure that such a thing could not happen again, and the guards in charge of security had been suitably reprimanded.

Then, of course, there had been the curious incidents reported by Harios. The fighting in the ministry had resulted in several deaths and the escape of Bowen Folegandros, as well as in the loss of the protective screen for his own private cabinet. This last was not serious; he would have had to destroy such evidence anyway – but it was vexing nonetheless. Verkho wanted to find whoever was responsible. Had it been Kerrell, perhaps? Or possibly the prisoner's brother, Sagar, who had escaped earlier with the presumed aid of the Swordsman? Or even Alasia, using some hitherto unknown aspect of her magical ability? Whatever the truth, the Folegandros family were proving a nuisance, and if either of them were ever recaptured, Verkho swore to make them pay for their insolence. In practice, the result of the attack had been the drafting in of even more soldiers to guard the complex, and instructions to

Harios to keep a special eye upon certain experiments.

In addition, Kerrell, the Swordsman and Alasia were all being sought by the Chancellor's men, but even his resources were limited. All had evaded their hunters so far, leading to the suspicion that they might be working together. That, Verkho decided, would indeed be interesting. Such speculation was meat and drink to the Chancellor and, for a time, he even wished he could return to the intrigues of Xantium full-time – but that was impossible. The talisman demanded his attention. Even though solving the riddles was taking far longer than he had ever envisaged, there was still a little time for other games.

Now that Clavia was out of the way, their plans to claim the imperial throne were no longer quite as urgent, especially as Southan was proving so cooperative. And Verkho knew that such things would be irrelevant once he had obtained the talisman's powers. But, in the meantime, perhaps it would be appropriate to make a few contingency plans. It would still be interesting – from a theoretical point of view – to see whether he could reduce Azari, the imperial heir, to a helpless, mindless *thing* – as he had intended to do before other avenues had opened up. Reports of Ifryn's increasing unease had reached Verkho's ears, and her instability might well assist him. For instance, if Azari met such a hideous fate, would the Empress not blame herself, her depression turning perhaps to thoughts of suicide? All that would be left then would be to see Southan out of the way, leaving Azari as Emperor and Verkho as Regent – and Emperor in all but name. If it became necessary – and in the event of the talisman's shield continuing to resist his advances – such an arrangement would have obvious advantages. The Empire was in a perilous state and it would be so much simpler if the running of it was completely in the Chancellor's hands, without even the pretence of his subservience to Southan. Verkho smiled. Some preparations were needed.

During the last few days, Verkho had rarely left his study and when he *had* done so, it had been in a device of his own invention. This was basically a chair with wheels attached to either side so that an assistant could push him through the corridors of the court. Such a mode of transport was not really necessary – apart from the few times when Verkho was truly weary – but he liked to maintain the illusion that he was actually still suffering from the after-effects of poison, and so save his energy for more rewarding work. In fact, the Chancellor did indeed look exhausted, even haggard, though he himself was unaware of the changes. The lustre of his dark hair had dulled a little, and a few strands were silver now. But although his normally glittering eyes were filmed with tiredness and his bandaged hand still ached and seeped blood on occasion, Verkho's brain was as active as ever.

The servant who accompanied him when he used the chair was one of the talents Harios had discovered. Shinasi was a large young man whose bulging muscles told of strength but whose face held the blank expression of the truly witless. He could obey simple commands, but spoke only in grunts. And yet he had one extraordinary ability, which was unique even among the bizarre collection of talents in the ministry complex. He could, on request, shield anything he touched – in this case Verkho and his chair – with a pulsating dome of blue light that repelled any assailant, any blow, and which could even deflect the flight of an arrow. Much research had already gone into such shields, some of it with usable results, but Shinasi's mobile adaptability was remarkable. The Chancellor's own powers of self-preservation were formidable enough, but with this new protector, he felt truly invincible.

Verkho called for the young man now and climbed into his wheelchair, allowing an attentive steward to cover his legs with a blanket.

'My apartments in The Domain,' he ordered.

*   *   *

It took Southan some time to reach the inner chambers of Verkho's realm. He had only been there before at the Chancellor's invitation, and the Emperor's sudden – and ill-tempered – intrusion caused panic among the domestic staff. Ifryn followed her husband, afraid of his anger, afraid of what she had done, and afraid most of all of not finding the ring.

When they finally managed to reach their destination, Verkho was there to greet them, seated in his mobile chair. He smiled – a sight which made the Empress shudder.

'My lord. This is an unexpected pleasure.'

'I trust it may be so, Chancellor,' Southan responded briskly. 'Please take us to your library.'

'My personal study here holds only books on esoteric subjects,' Verkho replied. 'Might I ask why you are interested?'

'Just take us,' the Emperor commanded.

At a signal from his master, Shinasi led them to the library. From the description that she had been given, Ifryn recognized the room well enough, and she looked immediately to the far corner. To her dismay, all she saw was the blackened shell of the cupboard.

'Please excuse the mess,' Verkho said, noting her glance. 'You will have heard of the murderous intruder who broke in here recently. One of his lesser crimes was to break into that cupboard – where I stored several potent and volatile fluids. He must have broken some of the containers and the mixture produced a fire, as you see. Fortunately it did not spread. Many of these books are irreplaceable.'

'Did you keep any rings in there?' Southan asked dourly.

'Rings? I would not keep jewellery with such unstable solutions,' the Chancellor replied, feigning surprise.

Southan turned to Ifryn, who remained speechless.

285

'Might I ask . . .' Verkho began mildly.

'No, you may not!' the Emperor snapped. He took his wife by the arm and pulled her from the room.

Verkho watched them leave, and smiled again.

CHAPTER THIRTY-FIVE

They inhabit a simpler world, rewarding kindness with unquestioning trust and endless devotion. Yet what is really known of them? Do they understand laughter? Are human colours theirs to see? What sounds are music to canine ears?

The room that had once held Corton prisoner had become a refuge for Martyn, Sagar and Bowen – a small space that had been their whole world now for several days. There were two reasons for this. The first was that both Martyn and Sagar had been injured as they fought to escape from the ministry complex. The wounds were unpleasant but not serious, but it would have been difficult to explain them to anyone.

The second reason for their self-imposed confinement was that, during the fight, several people had seen the intruders' faces and, despite the Swordsman's attentions, some of them had survived. So it seemed advisable to lie low for a while. They had no way of knowing how much importance their enemies attached to Bowen's disappearance, but it was best that he be kept out of sight.

The memory of the conflict was still vivid in Sagar's mind. In the confined spaces, their enemies' superior numbers had counted less than the Swordman's lightning-fast reflexes and ferocious violence. Compared to his ruthless ally, Sagar had been practically worthless, almost a liability, and even the Swordsman would have been overwhelmed eventually if it had not been for an unexpected intervention. At the height of the battle,

Bowen had emerged from his cell and shouted. He did not utter any words, and the noise he made was not even human; it was more of a vibration, a deep, rumbling reverberation that seemed to shake the walls and which completely disorientated the soldiers. After that, the Swordsman quickly won a way through and, with that first great hurdle cleared, he eventually managed to lead the brothers to safety.

After his incredible outburst, Bowen had remained silent, obediently following the two other men. In spite of Sagar's efforts to coax some response from him, he had not uttered a sound in all the days that had passed since then.

By now, Martyn's wounds were almost healed and he was becoming very bored. It would not be long before they ventured out. Then, or so Sagar hoped, they might be able to make plans for Bowen and himself to leave the city and begin the long journey back to Zalys. Before that, however, he must fulfil his oath to the Swordsman. *Brothers in arms*. It was not a comfortable thought.

There was a knock on the door and Martyn got up to open it. One of his colleagues, a wiry character known to everyone as Rat, came in carrying a tray of food.

'Someone's been asking after you in the taverns round here,' he informed Martyn. 'And asking for you by name.'

'Who?'

'Man called Baylin.'

Martyn and Sagar exchanged glances.

'No word out of your brother?' Rat asked.

'No.'

'He's got a healthy enough appetite,' Rat remarked as Bowen began to eat. Food was the last thing on Martyn's mind at that moment, however, and when Rat had gone, the Swordsman came to a decision.

'It seems we've been betrayed,' he said. 'I think it's time to pay Grongar a visit.'

*   *   *

288

The kennel that housed the imperial hounds was a low wooden construction, built in the shape of an L on two sides of an enclosed exercise yard. In the shorter leg of the L were individual stalls for pregnant bitches, mothers with their young and the occasional trouble-maker who needed to be isolated from the pack. The rest of the building consisted of one large hall where the majority of the dogs resided. There was a latrine pit at one end and food troughs at the other; the floor was simply covered with straw. The pack slept here, and the warm air was full of their thick, rank smell.

When agitated, the hounds could create a deafening barrage of sound, their howls shaking the rafters. Ordinarily, however, the creatures were relatively quiet, content with their lot and secure in the fellowship and hierarchy of the pack. Most humans were outsiders who came and went unnoticed, usually betrayed by their natural fear, but – unless they were very foolish – treated to nothing more aggressive than a growl or two. Grongar was different. The hounds, who had all known him since they were puppies, regarded him as one of the pack, on an equal standing with their own leader, a giant whom Grongar had named Shark.

The barbarian was the only man allowed to touch some of the more hostile animals. He boasted of their prowess, claiming that he would rather go into battle with six hounds at his side than any twelve men. When others saw them in the exercise yard during their mock fights and training bouts, it was not hard to understand Grongar's point. The northerner and his pack held each other in mutual respect, but the relationship went even deeper than that. The only human word that came close to describing it was love.

That evening, once all his assistants had finished for the day, Grongar began to feel rather melancholy. He brought a small casket of ale from the converted stall which was his own home, and returned to the pack. He sat down on the fragrant straw, leant back on the wall, broached the casket with a single blow of his gnarled fist and dipped his mug into the dark brew. Even before he drank that first tankard, several hounds had drawn close, sitting or lying around their master. Shark took pride of place at Grongar's shoulder. Sitting on his haunches, the great dog was taller than the barbarian by a head. His body was covered in coarse, bristly hair, his tongue lolled over the fangs which had given him his name, and alert eyes and ears cast about, inspecting his tribe. To all but Grongar, Shark was a terrifying monster; to him, he was a thing of beauty.

After a second mug of ale, Grongar felt the need to confide in his friends.

'You know, some women have no taste,' he muttered. His dalliance with Mariella had been sweet but brief. In retrospect, it had been a mistake to invite her to Corton's chambers, where the hearty, unkempt lass had experienced refinements of living she had not known existed. After that, she was never quite satisfied with Grongar's undoubted generosity. Then, that very morning, she had told him that she no longer wanted to see him.

Grongar sighed, and Shark yawned massively in sympathy.

'The pity of it is, she had plenty of flesh,' Grongar said, remembering. 'And most of it in the right places.'

Shark clacked his teeth as if in agreement. Sensing his master's unhappiness, he nuzzled his neck affectionately – something which would have sent most people into convulsions – and allowed Grongar to ruffle his thick hair.

'Still,' the northerner added, brightening a little. 'Plenty more where she came from.'

His mug was mysteriously empty, so he refilled it and drank again. Some time later, he found that he was having difficulty replenishing his tankard, so had to resort first to tipping the casket and then, in desperation, drinking the last few mouthfuls straight from the keg.

Some spilled into his beard and down his threadbare tunic, but Grongar didn't mind.

'Really scraping the barrel, eh?' he said to the hounds, and laughed at his own wit.

It was quite dark now, but moonlight fell on the yard beyond the open door, and something in that cool radiance touched a nerve in Grongar's heart. The words of an old song came into his head, and he had no choice but to set them free. What the barbarian's voice lacked in pitch and intonation he made up for in volume and gusto, as he related the tale of a legendary northern king and his heroic deeds. The chorus was wordless, an ululating wail which in a competent singer's voice would have been called yodelling – but Grongar's rendition sounded like the death throes of a diseased and angry bull. The hounds, of course, lacked such musical discernment and joined in enthusiastically, howling as if to wake the dead.

Thus it was that none of them heard the approach of the lone figure who now stood, silhouetted by moonlight, in the doorway. It was Shark who saw – or perhaps scented – him first, and Grongar felt the great dog stiffen at his side. Struggling to focus, he peered at the intruder.

'What d'you wan'?'

'Come out here and I'll tell you.' The cold, menacing voice seemed familiar.

Grongar still had enough sense to stay where he was.

'Who *are* you?'

'The man you betrayed. The man who's going to kill you.'

'I betrayed no man!' the barbarian cried, sobering up fast. 'Martyn?'

The figure in the doorway took a step forward. Shark and several other hounds sensed the newcomer's antagonism, and growled. The deep-throated snarling gave even the Swordsman pause for thought, and he stood still.

291

'If you did not betray me, how is it that our friend Baylin is asking for me by name?' he enquired softly.

'That's none of my doing.'

'Who else knew it but you?'

'If I can guess, then so can others. Baylin's no fool, and he's a master of disguise,' Grongar responded. 'Who's t'say you've not given yourself away?'

Martyn snorted, measuring eyes still fixed on the hound-master.

'You think I'll accept that?'

'Do what you like. I don't care.' The pack that surrounded him and the ale that filled his belly re-inforced Grongar's normal belligerent confidence.

'What did he want with me?' Martyn asked.

'Baylin? How would I know? Any friend of Kerrell's must be in a tight spot now. Perhaps he wants your help.'

'Does Baylin know where Kerrell is?' Martyn was intrigued now, his anger abating.

'If he doesn't, no one does,' Grongar replied.

'You swear you did not tell him who I was?'

'I swear,' the barbarian said solemnly. 'As a north-erner and as your friend.'

'I could kill you from here, you know,' the Swordsman told him quietly. 'My knife would be in your heart before you could move.'

'And you'd be dead before you'd gone three steps.' Grongar indicated the hounds, many of whom had got to their feet and were staring at Martyn, ready to pounce.

The two men faced each other in a contest of honour that neither could win.

'Perhaps I'd better see what Baylin has to say before I deal with you,' Martyn said eventually. 'You won't always have the dogs.'

'Hounds,' Grongar muttered. 'They're hounds.' Then as his opponent turned to leave and his charges stirred, he added quietly, 'Easy. Easy. Let him go.'

After a few moments, he picked up the empty, broken

keg and hurled it violently at the wall. It shattered noisily, provoking several barks and a sudden tense watchfulness in the pack.

'Never get mixed up in politics,' he said to Shark. The hound watched him narrowly. 'I know. You told me not to. You've got more sense than me.'

The Empress was fuming. Her dejection had suddenly turned to anger, her emotional tide turning from ebb to flood in an instant. How dare they treat her like an irrational, hysterical girl? How *dare* they? She was the Empress! It was the first time she had ever felt the need or the desire for the title.

A small internal voice answered her own question. *Perhaps they dare because you are* acting *like an irrational, hysterical girl*. She found that she was clenching her fists so hard that her nails were digging into her palms. She forced herself to relax, trying to be calm so that she could think.

In truth, she could not blame Southan. Her absurd story about a dead face talking, together with the fact that she continued to defend a confessed traitor and that her supposed evidence could not be found, would have combined to make even the most reasonable man suspicious. Southan clearly believed that she was distraught and that this had tipped over into a temporary form of madness. He had not said so out loud, but his silence spoke volumes.

Worse still, Ifryn knew that she had brought suspicion on herself from another, far more malevolent source. Verkho would now be aware, if not of her opposition, then at least of her antagonism. She was in danger. So were her family: Southan, the girls. Azari – especially Azari.

None of which altered the simple fact that Verkho was a traitor and Kerrell wasn't – whatever he believed. And something had to be done about it.

Yet the Chancellor had been one step ahead of them

all the time – and without proof it seemed that all they could do was wait for him to make a mistake.

Refusing to admit to hopelessness, Ifryn considered the forces she could marshal in the coming battle. There was her own power as Empress, whatever that amounted to. She had never had cause to test it. She had allies; Kerrell – if he was still alive and in Xantium; Baylin – but where was he? She wondered bitterly if the two friends had decided to exclude her from their plans. Then there was the Swordsman. Could she contact this dangerous ally directly? Or via Corton and Grongar? There *must* be a way of bringing them all together, welding them into a unit capable of opposing Verkho.

Ifryn resolved to take the initiative, to assume a measure of control over her life and – frightening thought – the fate of the Empire. But to do that she would have to take risks. For herself she did not care, but she had to consider her children and their future before she could make any move in the most deadly game she had ever played. And before she could do anything, Ifryn needed to be able to communicate with her elusive friends and make contact with other possible allies. To do that she needed one person above all others. Alasia.

'It is unfortunate, my lord,' Verkho said unctuously, 'but I understand fully. The Empress has been under more than considerable strain recently.'

Southan nodded glumly. The affairs of the Empire were bad enough, but having such disturbances within his own family left him feeling at a complete loss.

'I regret the necessity of asking such a question,' the Chancellor went on, 'but have you considered the position of your son?'

'Azari? What of him?'

'Do you think it is wise that he remains in the Empress' care?'

'Ifryn is his mother!' Southan was horrified. 'Surely you cannot think . . . ?'

294

'You said yourself that she is unstable,' Verkho said evenly. 'I am only thinking of the future of the Empire.'

'No. It is impossible.'

'It need only be for a short time,' the Chancellor went on reasonably. 'Until the Empress has recovered and we are no longer subject to these unpleasant circumstances.'

'But . . .'

'For his own protection,' Verkho persisted, 'I would be willing to place Azari in an easily guarded suite of rooms in my apartments. And a wet nurse could be provided.'

'That will not be necessary,' Southan replied, summoning his last reserves of pride. 'If . . . if Azari is to be separated from his mother, then I will accommodate him in my own quarters.'

'As you wish, my lord.'

The Chancellor resisted the temptation to smile.

CHAPTER THIRTY-SIX

The fountain plays no longer. Once the dolphins rejoiced amid the spark and music of sunlit water. Now they are lifeless above the dark, silent mirror. A place of dual prophecy, the former joyful words now overlaid by fate.

When augury presents opposing wills, which am I to obey?

Having planted the seeds of doubt in Southan's mind, Verkho was content to sit back and wait for them to grow and flower. In the meantime, he was glad to return to the talisman. His last success had been many days ago, and he had recovered much of his strength. This time, however, four days of toil were to pass before his efforts were rewarded.

The language of this clue had seemed particularly obscure, until Verkho realized that it was a code used by the astronomers, mathematicians and horologists of Kyperounda, an ancient desert kingdom which had ceased to exist several centuries ago. That gave him a pointer to the contents, which were in the form of a bizarre mathematical equation, using numbers and signs as well as letters in the conundrum. It read:

'5 live: the longer they stand, the shorter they grow.
+
5 ends: nails but no metal, joints but no wood.
×
5 roll: 1 to 6 (your cast), measured by your beat.
=
The price: One earth-circle turns for each pulse.'

When Verkho was satisfied that he had made a correct translation, the solution seemed more or less obvious – and very unpleasant. He spent some time reconsidering the problem, hoping that he was wrong, but knew the truth all along. The first part was a common riddle indicating five lighted candles. The second could only mean five fingers – or, absurdly, toes. Adding the two together presumably meant putting his fingers into the flames and, if he had interpreted the third part correctly, keeping them there for the number of heartbeats decided by rolling five six-sided dice. That in itself would be painful enough, but the most disquieting aspect of this equation was its product. If Verkho read it aright, it meant that for each pulse he would age one earth circle or year. So if he threw five sixes he would become an old man in an instant – and perhaps even die. This time the sacrifice and the gamble were far more daunting than any that had gone before.

Then again, he had long ago learnt that his modest but very well focused telekinetic abilities were able to guide the supposedly random fall of dice. In theory, therefore, he could lose only five years – a small price to pay when the eventual prize was immortality. However, the Chancellor knew that such an easy course was not feasible; the powers that had designed the talisman's protection would not allow such meddling with the vagaries of fate. And in earlier throws he had not had to influence the cast to achieve the highest possible score. Could he risk doing so again? In the end, though, he knew he had no choice.

Verkho chose to make the attempt in the late evening, so that he would have a night's rest immediately afterwards. Having sealed his study, he made his preparations. Five white candles were set on the desk, placed so that they matched his outstretched fingertips. After lighting the candles, he discarded the bandage on his left hand – the cut palm had stubbornly refused to heal – and held the dice in his right. It was then that inspiration came. The phrase 'your cast' could be construed as a choice, in this case the choice of which of the many dice games was to be played. In the game called Sunstroke, twos were wild, and five twos were therefore the highest combination. Ten years. That would still leave him relatively young.

'My choice is Sunstroke,' Verkho said aloud, looking at the talisman.

He rolled the dice and watched them fearfully, but did not attempt to influence the way they fell. Four settled almost at once. They were all twos. The last spun on one rounded corner. Its motion became both hypnotic and infuriating, but Verkho urged himself to patience. It settled at last and the Chancellor stared, disbelieving. *A six*. Had he done something wrong? Was the ancient riddle-master laughing at him now? Doubts assailed him, but then calm returned. Fourteen heartbeats, fourteen years. *So be it.*

Deliberately he spread the fingers of his left hand. Blood oozed from the lacerated palm and dripped on to the desk as he pushed his fingertips into the flames and held them there. Pain lanced through him, and blood roared in his ears. *Three, four.* He had expected his heart to be racing with excitement but it beat resolutely to its normal, sedate rhythm. *Seven, eight.* His teeth were bared in a soundless snarl as the skin of his fingers burned and split. *Ten, eleven.* Verkho's whole body shook, yet he refused to be beaten. *Fourteen.*

On that instant he withdrew his tortured hand, clenching it in a crippled fist of agony and roaring at the ceiling. The candles spluttered and went out. The globe began to glow and the Chancellor gave a gasp of relief. To have endured such torment for no purpose would have been unbearable. Once again, the talisman's outer skin peeled off and vanished, leaving only a thin veneer of the clear substance – perhaps two more layers – around its newly inscribed centre.

So close, Verkho thought, then wondered for the first

time whether he would have the strength to meet the final challenges. He felt weary beyond his years.

'You're a brave man. I'll give you that,' Martyn said.

It was dawn. Baylin had come to the deserted courtyard alone, as instructed. Here, should the Swordsman wish it, the traveller could be cut down or overwhelmed by hidden foes. The two men faced each other openly.

'I need your help,' Baylin stated simply. 'If I don't trust you, how can I ask you to have faith in me?'

'Your needs must be desperate for you to ask the help of a common outlaw again.'

'The Swordsman is no common outlaw, and I know that you are he.'

Martyn bowed mockingly.

'I have that honour,' he said. 'Who told you?'

'You did yourself,' Baylin answered. 'I was the old merchant in the tavern when you admitted as much to Grongar.'

Martyn smiled, accepting the story and appreciating the other man's skill.

'What do you want me to do?' he asked.

Ifryn woke with a sudden, inexplicable surge of elation. The last few days, since she had made her resolution, had been both exhausting and frustrating. She had been active for most of the time, seeking out help wherever she could, but finding her efforts limited by the common wariness of the court's inhabitants. Kerrell and Baylin still evaded her, as she had expected, but she'd been able to talk to Grongar, Corton and many others – although she hadn't learnt very much. Even Southan was elusive now, not that she had much to say to him – yet. But her main efforts had been directed towards finding Alasia. She had even gone up into The Spires on two occasions, and had enlisted all possible aid in locating her friend – to no avail.

But somehow this morning was different. Something was going to happen! Ifryn leant over to look at Azari, still sleeping peacefully in his cot beside her bed, and smiled.

'Today!' she told him in a whisper.

'Today?' a familiar voice echoed from the other side of the room.

Ifryn spun round, scrambled out of bed and ran to embrace Alasia. She arrived while her friend was still in the middle of her curtsey and so they got in an awkward tangle, but the Empress did not care.

'I'm so glad to see you,' she breathed. 'You can't imagine. Where have you *been*?'

'Flying,' Alasia replied, as enigmatic as ever while she rearranged her crumpled dress. 'I bring danger.'

'Danger? To me?'

'Yes. I did not want to come.'

Ifryn's spirits fell.

'Why *did* you come, then?'

'You called. I must obey.'

It's not supposed to be like this, the Empress thought, then her resolve hardened. She had gone too far now to turn back. Alasia was her friend, but she was also the only link to the other people she needed to see.

'Do you know where Kerrell is? Why hasn't he been to see me?'

'I fly above, he crawls below,' Alasia replied. 'Collecting.'

'Collecting what?' Ifryn was bewildered.

Alasia shrugged.

'Take me to him,' the Empress pleaded.

'It is forbidden.'

'No!' It was a cry of disbelief. 'By whom?'

'By words.'

'Take me to him!' Ifryn was angry now.

Alasia looked startled, and her pale eyes stared at the Empress as if she had never seen her before.

'You order it?' she whispered.

300

'Yes!'

'Then I must,' Alasia sighed. 'Come to the dolphin fountain at dusk tomorrow.'

The fountain, which stood in a little used part of the court, had long since fallen into disrepair, and the water around the base of the statue was stagnant and dark. Ifryn got there early, and sat hidden in a small alcove while the shadows deepened. It was very quiet, and she wondered if Alasia had decided to disobey the unwelcome order after all. Why had she been so reluctant?

The sound of stone grating on stone made her jump, and set her heart racing. A flagstone beside the fountain was rising slowly, like a trapdoor. Alasia's white face appeared from below, glancing around with the jerky movements of a watchful bird. Ifryn went to her quickly, and followed her down the steps into utter darkness, as the stone slid back into place. Alasia took the Empress' hand and led her along a twisting, upward-sloping tunnel which eventually emerged in the centre of The Spires. Then she pointed towards one of the towers and let Ifryn go on alone.

The Empress almost ran up the winding staircase, her footsteps echoing around the confining stone, until she came to a circular room, lit only by the faint glow of the day's end, filtering in through small arched windows. Kerrell was there, leaning dejectedly against the far wall. He looked up when she came in, but said nothing and did not move.

Ifryn went to him, put her arms around him. At first he held himself stiffly, then relented and held her. She could feel his heart beating. For a moment, that was all that mattered.

'Oh, my love,' she whispered.

'This cannot be,' he said, but although he moved back a little, he could not bring himself to let go, to reject her completely.

'How can you say that?' she asked. 'Words can't stop our love from being real.'

'You are the Empress,' he responded, his voice filled with anguish.

'I'll abdicate.'

'You cannot!' The words came out in an angry spurt. 'Do not say such things, even in jest.'

Ifryn wanted to tell him that she had not been joking, but it was too late. The damage was done. She collected her scattered thoughts as best she could.

'Where have you been? What have you been doing all this time?'

'Contacting my old army colleagues,' Kerrell replied dully. 'Sounding them out. Much good it did me, though. Verkho has too strong a hold. We'll never break it.'

Ifryn hated to hear the defeat in his tone.

'Some proved true, surely?'

'A few,' he admitted.

'Then it's a start,' she told him. 'What news of Baylin?'

'He's been doing much the same, among the minor nobles and some of Xantium's more influential citizens – with much the same results,' he answered. There was bitterness in his voice now. 'Some of them bear the Chancellor grudges but unless our fortunes turn, we can count on few allies.'

'When the truth comes out,' she encouraged him, 'we'll have allies in plenty. All we need is proof.'

'The only way to get that is for Verkho to make a mistake,' he said, echoing her own fears.

'But that could take ten years!' she exclaimed. 'He doesn't *make* mistakes.'

'How else can we—?'

'Why haven't you been in touch with me?' she interrupted, no longer able to contain herself. 'Told me what's happening?'

'What we are doing is too dangerous,' he said. 'We didn't want to involve you.'

302

'I was afraid you'd say that,' Ifryn said sadly, then found her anger building again. 'But you're not going to do it any more. I'm not just a silly, feeble woman to be ignored!'

'I never said you were,' he responded, taken aback.

'But you've treated me that way,' she accused. 'Besides, I'm in trouble now too.' She told him about her argument with Southan and their disastrous visit to the Chancellor's quarters. Kerrell was horrified.

'That was very foolish,' he said. 'But Verkho would never dare move against you openly.'

'I wish I could be so sure,' she retorted. 'That's why we must all fight *together*, all of us with reason to want the Empire rid of that man. It's the only way. What about the Swordsman?'

'I don't think so. He's too unreliable – and he's a murderer.'

'Do you think to stop Verkho without any bloodshed?' she demanded incredulously. 'In any case, you're already guilty of treason. What's one more crime to us?'

Kerrell looked at her as if he could not believe his ears. She had meant to shock him – and had succeeded.

'If the only way we can win is to bring Verkho down by force,' she told him, 'then we'll do it. But we've got to bring all our forces *together*.'

He nodded dumbly, wondering how this firebrand could have been hidden beneath the Empress' gentle form for so many years.

'And promise me you'll let me know what's going on,' she added. 'I need to see you.'

'I promise,' he whispered.

Alasia's voice beckoned from below.

'You must go, my lady.'

Ifryn did not want to go, could not bear to leave him, but knew that she must.

'We'll meet again soon, *General*,' she replied, kissing him briefly on the lips. 'That's an order.' Then she forced herself to smile, and left. They were both torn by

303

the parting but had been given new spirit by the sight of each other.

Alasia led the Empress back wordlessly, emerging from a different tunnel, then waving her away.

'Not all prophecies are truth,' she pronounced unexpectedly. 'I have work to do.' And with that she vanished.

Ifryn returned to her apartments, deep in thought, but when she entered the outer chamber, she was shocked out of her absorption. Doneta sat in a chair, with Vrila and Delmege to either side of her. The maid had a large, ugly bruise on one side of her face, her eye was closed and all three were crying.

'Oh, Mama, where were you?' Delmege cried, running to Ifryn.

'It was horrible,' Vrila added tearfully.

'What's happened?'

'I'm so sorry, my lady,' Doneta said painfully. 'I couldn't stop them. Some soldiers forced their way in here.'

Ifryn felt the blood drain from her face. She knew, with terrible certainty, what was coming next.

'Oh, my lady,' Doneta went on, weeping even harder now. 'They've taken little Azari!'

The past is never entirely lost. It is imprinted in stone and wood, in water and air; its chronicles are written upon the very fabric of the world. Few have the need or knowledge to read from this infinite text, and if there are lessons to be learnt from its tales, who am I to say which are instructive and which misleading?

Who decided that my eyes were only to look forward?

'We're making progress,' Sagar commented.

'You think so?' Martyn responded. 'I don't like this kind of work.'

'Then why are we doing it?'

'Any enemy of Verkho's is a friend of mine.' A sudden grin lit up Martyn's face. 'Besides, when the time comes, it'll make it a lot more fun.'

Sagar shook his head, finding it hard to understand his companion's idea of 'fun'. Since the meeting with Baylin a few days ago, they had been enlisting men for unspecified jobs in the still nebulous campaign against Verkho. All these recruits had been told was that there would be an opportunity for mischief and profit which, as most of them were members of Xantium's criminal fraternity, appealed to them greatly. In reality, their task would be to create diversions that would occupy the Chancellor's troops while those who opposed him made their move. The Swordsman's well-known ability to reach supposedly forbidden parts of the city made him the ideal organizer of such an enterprise, but Martyn privately vowed to be no mere diversion. If Verkho was to fall, the Swordsman would be there.

'Let's hope it's soon,' Sagar said with feeling. 'I want to get my brother away from here.'

'The sooner the better,' Martyn agreed.

Bowen had still not uttered a word. In fact he had done nothing at all, apparently immune to boredom, and spent hours just staring into space. He had not responded to questions, shouts or praise, and had meekly accepted physical manhandling. It was obvious that whatever remained of his mind was firmly fixed elsewhere, and Sagar found his company uncomfortable. His only hope was that his brother would recover once they were away from Xantium's malign influence.

They returned to the tavern for their evening meal, and while Martyn placed their order, Sagar went upstairs to check on his brother. A few moments later he returned, out of breath, all thoughts of food forgotten.

'He's gone!' he whispered urgently, not wanting to be overheard. 'Bowen's gone!'

'What do you mean, he is not to be disturbed?' Ifryn exclaimed furiously.

The guard who had answered her blinked nervously, thinking that he had just seen the eyes of a lioness gazing out from the face of a lamb. He stood his ground, nonetheless. His stony-faced colleague said nothing.

'Those are my orders, my lady.'

'I am his *wife*, your Empress!' she screamed. 'Do you deny me the right to see my own husband?'

'Not I, my lady. The Emperor himself . . .' The soldier was remembering the fate of those sentries who had allowed Ifryn to pass when Southan had ordered that no one should do so. He had no wish to suffer in the same way.

'Stand aside,' the Empress demanded, and stepped forward, only to be halted by crossed spears which crashed together in her path. Neither of the guards could

306

look her in the face. 'You will be punished for this!' she declared. 'I . . .'

Beyond the barrier, a door opened and Southan appeared.

'Let her through,' he said wearily.

The spears were withdrawn and Ifryn swept past, following Southan into one of the Emperor's outer chambers. As soon as the door was shut, she exploded.

'Verkho has taken Azari! He . . .'

'No.'

The single word and the grim look on her husband's face stopped Ifryn in her tracks. She stared at him.

'Azari is safe. He is in my care.'

'*Your* care? Why?' She was finding it difficult to breathe.

'You have been under a lot of stress recently,' Southan began, 'and your health has suffered . . .'

'I'm his mother!'

'And I his father.' There was regret in the Emperor's expression, but an angry determination too. Words did not come easily to him, and these were some of the hardest ever. 'To put it bluntly, I believe you to have become unstable. I have to think of the Empire and of the safety of my heir.'

Ifryn was unable to speak. This was betrayal beyond imagining. Azari's *safety*?

'Your recent actions . . .' Southan went on awkwardly. 'This need only be a temporary measure. Until you are recovered. I'm truly sorry, but after this evening I felt I had no choice.'

'This evening?' The Empress was suddenly filled with panic. Had someone seen her with Kerrell? Had her insistence on their meeting been his downfall?

'You were seen with that madwoman . . .'

'Alasia?' Ifryn felt a small measure of relief. Surely no one could have seen where they had gone.

'Yes,' Southan replied. 'I don't know what you were doing, and I don't want to know, but . . .'

307

'She's no madwoman! She's good . . .' Ifryn paused as she suddenly realized the import of his words. 'You had me *followed*?'

'Yes,' he answered, ashamed but defiant. 'You left my son to go on some wild errand . . .'

'I left him in good hands!' she objected. 'We've always trusted Doneta. And your soldiers hurt her.'

'I regret the necessity for that, but they had no choice,' he said.

'Where is my son?'

'It's better that you don't know.'

'Give me my baby back!' Ifryn screamed, rigid with outrage.

'I cannot. For his own protection.'

'You are a self-righteous moron,' she told him venomously. 'Don't you see whose doing this is? Verkho suggested this, didn't he?' She saw Southan flinch minutely, and knew that her words had struck home. 'You'll regret this idiocy,' she promised. 'Give my baby back to me.'

'No. And please do not repeat your accusations against the Chancellor. It does your case no good.' Southan was immovable. 'We will discuss this again when you are more calm.'

'You may never see me again,' Ifryn warned him, then turned and left the room. She hurried back to her own chambers, weeping with grief and anger – and all the time aware of the guards who followed her at a discreet distance.

The following morning, Verkho found the strength to release the seal around his study and call for servants. Three days had passed since his last agonizing success, and he had slept for almost all of that time. Shinasi showed no surprise at the Chancellor's appearance, but the others were shocked by the change in their master. His skin was grey and pale, his face was wrinkled around the eyes and mouth and he seemed thinner than before.

His left hand was swathed in bandages and cradled in an improvised sling, and – strangest of all – much of his lustrous black hair had turned grey. But while his movements and voice appeared weaker than usual, his brain had evidently lost none of its sharpness. He demanded news of all that had happened, and smiled at the report of Southan's most recent actions. Food and wine were brought and Verkho ate ravenously, apparently recovering a little vitality, but he refused the attentions of a physician.

The entire day was spent dealing with matters concerning the Empire, with members of his staff and officers either visiting the study or receiving calls from the wheelchair-bound Chancellor. His steward urged him to return to his quarters in The Domain for a night in a proper bed, but he refused and returned to his study, a strange, dull light in his eyes.

That same day saw sensational happenings at the old temple. The place had been infested with ghosts for some time now, and so had been shunned by the living, but for some reason the spirits were absent that afternoon, and a peculiar hush had settled over the small hill. The people who lived and worked in the surrounding area were aware of the change, but none felt inclined to investigate further until some children braved the silence and climbed up to the ruins. They were astonished by what they saw, and the news soon spread. So many people drew near that the temple grounds were more crowded than they had been in years.

The spectacle which greeted the onlookers was that of a man sitting cross-legged on the central altar, his eyes closed and his head bent over his cupped hands. That in itself was not unusual; the temple regularly attracted eccentric mystics, but this man was surrounded by a sphere of shimmering white light. Every so often, a piece of this shield would break off and skim away like a miniature shooting star, the sparks moving so fast that no one could follow their progress. At the same time, the air was filled with tiny sounds, none of them recognizable but adding up to a strange, uneven buzzing. But that was not all. In the space around the altar was an ever-changing pageant of colourful images. Visions of men, women and beasts as well as more obscure images flickered in and out of existence – so fast that none could be seen or remembered clearly. It was almost as if someone were reviewing the entire history of the place, searching for one particular incident.

It was a mesmerizing display, and inevitably drew comparisons with Verkho's first appearance in Xantium twelve years earlier. But no one knew who this new starets was – until Harios Kedhara arrived with a large band of soldiers. The crowd drew back to let them pass, and watched enthralled, eager to witness the last episode of this fascinating saga. Harios halted in front of the altar, ignoring the ephemera that flashed about him.

'Bowen Folegandros, you are under arrest,' he announced, more for the benefit of the expectant audience than for anyone else. 'Will you come with me?'

Bowen did not react, and the crowd whispered.

'Take him down,' Harios ordered.

The soldiers obeyed but approached nervously, flinching away from the insubstantial images that surrounded them. As soon as they laid hands on the escaped prisoner, however, the colourful show and the white aura vanished and Bowen, his eyes open now, meekly allowed himself to be lifted down and led away.

Alasia felt Gaye's probing, sensed her mixture of emotions as she saw a great welter of images drawn forth by the beacon's fire, the past brought fleetingly to life in all its joy, sadness, horror and mystery. No wonder she was confused.

Alasia herself had no idea what Bowen was doing, although he seemed very set on his purpose, and she knew better than to interfere. She had other tasks to attend to. It had been Bowen who had shown her the way, his mantle she had inherited within the circle, and she had little time for anything else now.

Alasia knew when the beacon's light dimmed, and felt his drawing in, his fear. She knew that Gaye felt it too – but there was something else, something far more sinister. The beacon was back in the hands of his enemies, whose ignorance would spell doom for them all.

The circle began to break up and Alasia struggled to prevent it, not knowing what had caused the disruption. Gaye was still there; though she had lost contact with Bowen, she could still hear Alasia.

He needs you, she told the girl. *We all do. Hurry. We must be in haste or it will all be too late.*

Alasia put all her unformed fears into the words and knew that Gaye understood, but had the strength for no more. It was up to others now.

CHAPTER THIRTY-EIGHT

Silent no longer, the woman steps out in new clothes. Can raiment be enough to lend the glamour of invisibility?

In Xantium there are many disguises, more so now that storm-clouds gather and the shadows deepen. What lightning will reveal the secret faces, the hidden plans? There is no such thing as a harmless thunder-bolt.

After calming her daughters and consoling her maid as best she could, Ifryn spent a sleepless night, her emotions alternating between rage, despair and fitful determination. Azari was still less than two months old; his rightful place was with his mother, and she vowed to do whatever was necessary to get him back. Alasia's forebodings had proved correct, but that would not stop Ifryn from acting now. She had been passive for too long.

But in the early morning, news arrived that drove all else from her mind. After hearing a timid knock on the door, Ifryn opened it herself to find Corton outside. He looked frightened, and was surprised to be faced with the Empress, but came in at her invitation.

'You may be in danger, my lady,' the wine-master began.

Tell me something I didn't know, Ifryn thought. Aloud she asked, 'How so?'

'Two captains came to me a little while ago and demanded some wine,' Corton said. 'They had the proper chit, signed by one of the Emperor's stewards, but they were the Chancellor's men, Information Officers. There were no vintages listed and when I asked what was required, they laughed and said anything with a strong flavour. This wasn't satisfactory,' he went on, relapsing momentarily into his usual pompous attitude, 'and I asked for what occasion it was needed. They told me it was none of my business, so I got a few samples out for them to taste. As they drank one said, "She'll never taste anything in this." I wasn't supposed to hear, but the wine cellars echo in strange ways. The other replied, "It'll look like a broken heart. Not surprising, under the circumstances."'

'Poison.' Ifryn felt cold, knowing exactly what the 'circumstances' were.

'I can only assume so, my lady,' Corton said anxiously. 'Of course, they may not have been referring to you. I hope I did the right thing.'

'Yes,' she confirmed, already deep in thought. 'Thank you.'

'I had better go. Please treat any new delivery of wine with extreme caution.'

'I shan't be here to drink it,' the Empress said quietly.

Corton looked shocked.

'What do you mean? How can you leave?'

Ifryn told him about Azari, and about Southan's attitude.

'Where will you go?' Corton asked, stunned by these developments.

'Does it matter?' All she knew was that she had to get out of this nightmare.

'You'll need help,' he said doubtfully. 'There are guards outside.'

'I know. You've put yourself in danger by coming here.'

Corton paid no attention to this, and a glint of excitement replaced the fear in his eyes.

'I'll help if I can,' he said.

'How?'

'You'll know within the hour if we succeed,' the wine-master replied. 'Farewell, my lady, and good fortune.'

Corton left and Ifryn stirred herself into action, her weariness forgotten out of necessity. She woke Doneta, and explained what had happened. The maid seemed more angry than frightened, and Ifryn was glad of her steadfast company. They roused the girls, told them to be prepared for an adventure, and helped them dress. Then the Empress quickly gathered together a few belongings and valuables and, on Doneta's advice, tried to disguise their appearance a little. She didn't know whether this would help, but it was all that they could do in the time.

The hour was almost up when an unearthly howling echoed in the corridor outside. Ifryn glanced at the worried expressions of her companions. She realized that beneath their brave faces, her daughters were frightened, and forced herself to smile.

'Be ready for anything,' she told them.

Grongar had liked the idea immediately. It was a chance to show the court – and his many detractors within it – just what terror his charges could bring. Of course, the Empress' apartments were some distance from the kennels, so arranging that the hounds should 'escape' in that direction took some doing – but in the end he had succeeded admirably.

He had only taken three dogs, Shark among them, and had released them at his chosen spot. Then he chased after them, yelling in vain for them to come back, while a series of whistles gave them their real instructions. In the face of this gleeful, hairy onslaught, everyone in their path ran for their lives. The hounds were enjoying themselves immensely, barking for pleasure at this unexpected romp, but the onlookers were not to know that. One look at their lathered tongues and terrible fangs was enough.

Even guards on duty took rapid evasive action as the

three animals, then Grongar, ran past in a furore of howls and curses. If the spectacle had not been so terrifying it would have been comical, and indeed many people laughed – once the intruders were safely on their way.

As they neared the Empress' apartments, Grongar took stock of the situation. There were two guards at this end of the corridor, two more by the entrance and presumably another pair at the far end. The nearest sentries were staring in horror at the rampaging hounds. They yelled and waved their spears but, when that had no effect, they looked for a place to hide. Finding high alcoves to either side of the corridor, they leapt into them, fear giving the two men unwonted agility. Grongar whistled, and Shark's two companions halted below the alcoves and looked up, growling deep in their throats but appearing almost to smile. Grongar caught up with them, gasping for breath, and patted each hound on the head.

'Well done,' he said to the guards. 'Look after these two for me, will you? I'll be back soon.'

The soldiers looked at each other over the heads of the dogs. They had no intention of moving.

Shark had bounded on, taking great leaps in his excitement at this new game, and howled happily as the two men by Ifryn's door tensed.

'Don't run!' Grongar yelled as he ran on. 'You'll only make him angry.'

The guards hesitated. Shark howled again.

'He'll never get both of you!' Grongar called helpfully.

That was enough. Their nerve broke and they ran, pelting away as fast as they could, with the hound bounding after his new playmates. Grongar reached the door and knocked. Ifryn opened it immediately.

'Now's your chance,' he gasped. 'Come on.'

The four trooped out, glancing nervously towards the end of the corridor, whence the sounds of barking, screams and oaths were echoing.

'Shark'll have taken them far enough by now,' Grongar said. 'Let's go.'

They followed him at a run. Reaching the point where the corridor branched, Grongar peered round the corner, then listened.

'It's clear that way,' he said, pointing. 'You're on your own now. I have to get my hounds.'

'Thank you,' Ifryn responded.

As the barbarian ran on, they took the other route and hurried along the deserted hallway. It wasn't long until they left the court and entered The Domain. No one paid the group any attention, and the two women walked calmly through one of the western gates into The Circle, each holding a child by the hand. Now at least Ifryn knew where they were going – if only she could find the way. She knew that Baylin's house was somewhere in this quarter, and even though she knew that they would not be able to stay there long, at least it would be a temporary haven. And she had not been able to think of anything beyond reaching her first goal. To have got even this far seemed miraculous.

They wandered irresolutely for a while, growing more agitated all the time. The traveller's description of the place did not seem to match the reality. In the end, it was Delmege who solved the problem by marching up to a street vendor, staring up at him with her huge brown eyes and asking where Master Baylin Parr lived. The man knelt down and gave his charming young visitor directions – and a free pasty. Delmege returned proudly, told her mother where they should go and generously shared the pasty with her sister.

As it happened, they were very close to their destination, and before long Ifryn recognized the street name and they reached the traveller's modest terraced house. The door was opened by a large, middle-aged woman who peered at the visitors with short-sighted eyes and ushered them all inside, clucking delightedly over the children.

'The master's still abed. He was out late last night,' the woman told them indulgently. 'I'll wake him. Whom shall I say is calling?'

Ifryn, who had covered the lower half of her face with a silk scarf while they were in the streets, let it fall and their hostess stared, feeling that the visitor was familiar but unable to place her.

'The Widow Mehtar,' Ifryn replied, using an eastern word for ruler, 'and her children, from Idiron. We met Baylin there some months ago.'

'Welcome, welcome. He'll be down soon.'

The woman bustled off and, as the four fugitives waited in the small lounge, the enormity of what they were doing almost overwhelmed Ifryn. In contrast, her daughters' earlier fear had been replaced now by a sense of adventure.

'Mama, who was that man with the dogs?' Vrila asked.

'He was funny,' Delmege added.

'He's a friend,' Ifryn replied, smiling. She hoped that Grongar would not get into trouble. He and Corton had risked much for her sake, and she wondered what she had done to deserve such loyalty.

They all turned at the sound of footsteps coming down the stairs three at a time. Baylin appeared in the doorway, dressed in a crumpled robe, his hair dishevelled and his eyes full of sleep.

'My lady!' he exclaimed. 'This *is* a surprise.'

An hour later, the party set out again, their number now increased to five. The four ladies of the court were now dressed in different clothes, and their faces were partially concealed as they stepped out into the free world of The Levels. Ifryn, her arm through Baylin's, could not remember the last time she had been outside the city's inner walls.

'Well, there's one good thing about all this,' she remarked quietly. 'At least now you and Kerrell won't be able to keep things from me because they're too dangerous.'

Baylin had the decency to look shamefaced, then smiled.

'Circumstances have changed,' he admitted.

'Where are we going, Mama?' Vrila asked from behind.

'We'll be there soon,' her mother replied. 'Then you'll see.'

'My dress doesn't fit properly,' Delmege complained.

'I'll fix it for you later,' Doneta said.

None of them had any idea how their clothes had been obtained, or what they had been doing in Baylin's house in the first place, and Ifryn had no intention of asking. The traveller continued to lead them on with a confident stride, while they looked about curiously. This was a whole new world to the girls, and they gleefully pointed things out to each other, taking an unhealthy interest in the more squalid aspects of life in Xantium.

'Where *are* we going?' Ifryn asked softly.

'To an inn I know,' he replied. 'It's not very salubrious, I'm afraid, but with the Tournament only a few days away now, most of the better places are already full.'

'And they'll be less likely to look for us there?'

'Exactly. I'll do all I can to make your stay as comfortable and as short as possible.'

Some time later, when the girls had begun to complain about having to walk so far, Baylin told them they were nearly there and pointed to a tavern.

'The Silent Woman,' Ifryn read aloud. 'I hope that's not a hint.'

Later that day, a disreputable-looking group of men met in another hostelry, discussing their plans in conspiratorial tones.

'Tomorrow then, at dawn,' Martyn confirmed. 'You all know what to do?'

There were nods of assent from around the table.

'Until then,' Martyn concluded.

All but one of his companions stood and went their separate ways.

'And this time,' the Swordsman added, under his breath, 'it won't just be Bowen we get out. If we can, we'll make a mess of the whole ministry.'

'You really want a lot of crazy people roaming the streets of Xantium?' Sagar asked.

'Yes. They'll fit right in here,' Martyn replied. 'Especially now. The place is full of lunatics waiting for the Grand Tournament.' He paused. 'And we'll put a stop to Verkho's experiments too, if we can. Whatever their purpose, it's bound to be something vile.'

'Will nine of us be enough for all that?'

'You haven't seen these guys at work,' Martyn said, grinning. 'They make me seem like a tame bunny rabbit.'

CHAPTER THIRTY-NINE

The lightning strikes. What curse guides its path? What malison allows the fire to reverse so that white ash turns to ember, embers to dark wood?
I cannot read the pattern of these flames.

After yet another trying night in the ministry, Harios was glad when dawn came. The feeling did not last long.

At first he thought it must be a false alarm. One of his most recent innovations had been to ring the central complex with a series of elaborate devices designed to alert the guards to intruders. Some of these devices were mechanical, while others depended on the special talents of his inmates. Unfortunately, several had been set off by his own men by mistake before they had become used to the system – but now, without any warning, they were all operating at once. Bells rang, screams echoed, metal barriers crashed down and flares spluttered in a reverberating cacophony that seemed to be coming from everywhere at once.

It soon became clear, amid the ensuing pandemonium, that several intruders had been killed or trapped, while others had been turned back, but that a few had actually got inside – and seemed intent on causing as much havoc as possible. Fires were started, cells opened and many of the talents left to run wild. But in the end, all the invaders were either killed or managed to escape. This was something that Harios regretted. He would have liked to interrogate some of them, because the attack had clearly been planned – but at least it had proved the effectiveness of his own preparations.

Leaving his subordinates to clear up the mess and restore order, Harios hurried to his own rooms to write his report.

'Gods, what a shambles,' Sagar gasped.

He and Martyn had finally met up again back in The Levels. Neither had any idea what had happened to their colleagues, and would have to wait until they were contacted by any survivors.

'What happened?' Sagar wondered aloud.

'They were ready for us,' Martyn said through gritted teeth. He was bleeding from a gash on his arm; his own sword, now concealed beneath his cloak, had also tasted blood before retreat had become necessary. 'Your damned brother's the cause of all this. If he hadn't made such an exhibition of himself and got arrested again . . .'

'He's still a prisoner!' Sagar exploded. 'Isn't that punishment enough?'

Martyn grunted.

'Let's hope so,' he said. 'Some of the talents must've been killed in that mess. After being taken by surprise like that, the guards may not have been too choosy about who they hit.'

Sagar said nothing.

'At least we'll have disrupted their work down there,' Martyn concluded, with some small satisfaction. 'I hate to think of all those people using their powers by working for Verkho.'

The Chancellor stared at the talisman in disbelief. Was this a trick? He had only been studying the new inscription for a day and a night, and had had no real expectation of success for some time yet. But now it seemed to have been handed to him on a plate.

He had sensed the disruption among the talents, and had felt the protective wall around the study fall away for a few moments, then reinstate itself stronger than ever with no prompting from him. But there had been something else, something mysterious, as if some strange power had reversed its effectiveness for an instant before reverting to normal. And in that fleeting moment, the words on the talisman's metal shield had transformed, displaying themselves in the universal trading language for him to read. The markings were incomprehensible again now, but the memory of their inexplicable translation was fixed in Verkho's mind.

'I am your servant.
Ask me for refreshment.
Three goblets. Two wines. One poison.
Leave the poison only, or your life.'

The Chancellor had no idea what it meant, but knew that this would come soon. And he also knew that it was important that he understand just what had happened. Was it possible that the gods were helping him, willing him to succeed? Or could it be that something – or someone – had been working to prevent him solving the puzzles, and that some psychic convulsion had momentarily turned their hindrance into positive help? How could such a thing have happened? Verkho decided that the best person to consult would be Harios, and determined to call on the official for a report as soon as he had solved this latest riddle.

Or *was* it a riddle? Perhaps that too had been translated. On impulse, Verkho turned to face the talisman again.

'Bring me refreshment,' he commanded.

Instantly, a shimmering glow hovered over his desk and, with a sound like sword blades being drawn against each other, three identical silver goblets appeared.

So, the Chancellor thought. *This is the gamble and the sacrifice*. He knew that he would only have one chance in three of surviving the test; there would be no immunity to the gods' poison.

He stretched out a tentative hand, and touched one of the cups. The metal was cold and real. These were no mere illusions. He had to drink from two. Which should he choose? And did he really have the nerve for this? Leaning forward, he sniffed the bouquet of each, but all three gave off the same enticing aroma, and all three were the same deep red. He could sense nothing unusual about any of them – further proof that the venom was beyond his powers. Only chance would decide his fate.

How ironic, he mused. *My own methods used against me.* It occurred to him suddenly that the Empress might already be dead or dying from tainted wine, and he smiled despite his fear.

Suddenly he picked up one of the goblets, threw back his head and drained the contents in one long gulp. He waited. And felt only the warm glow of alcohol, tasted only the legacy of the vine. Breathing deeply, Verkho set the goblet down. *One more.* His eyes shifted from one to the other. *Which shall it be?*

He chose and drank. Again it was only wine. The Chancellor laughed aloud, standing up as the cups disappeared and the talisman shed another skin. Only the thinnest film was left, and beneath that only one inscription remained. He was nearly there!

What was more, he felt absolutely wonderful. This time, his elation was not tempered by pain or fatigue. He was tired – as any man of his newly advanced age would be after such effort – but in spirit he was rejuvenated.

Fate had spoken. And the words of prophecy were to the Chancellor's liking.

By that evening, Verkho had learnt all he needed to know about recent events. Ifryn's escape did not concern him. Azari was still in Southan's care, and those two were the only ones who might still matter. A long talk with Harios had revealed much of interest, including the disruption caused by the raiders, but there was nothing to explain his astonishing change of fortune. Perhaps that had been only the random touch of luck, one that was unlikely to be repeated.

Xantium and the Empire were clearly close to a decisive turning point. Violence could not be far away. But he need only hold the fabric together for a few more days – and then it would not matter any more. The talisman would be in his hands.

That same evening, Baylin came to visit Ifryn and her party. They had stayed in the room all day, and the lack of action was grating on the Empress' nerves. She was very glad to see him.

'Azari?' she asked immediately.

'He's safe enough for the moment in Southan's chambers,' the traveller told her, 'but he's obviously part of Verkho's plans.'

'I have to get him back.'

'I know. We'll do it somehow. The Chancellor's locked himself away again, still recovering his health if the stories are to be believed, but he won't remain quiet for long.'

'Which is why we must move quickly,' Ifryn said urgently. 'All of us who oppose him must work together.'

'I agree, but Kerrell . . .'

'Kerrell will see sense. I need him to,' she told Baylin. He lowered his eyes at the passion in her voice, but the Empress went on adamantly, 'Set up a meeting. Here, if you like. Tomorrow. You, Kerrell, the Swordsman, even Grongar and Corton if you think it's worth it. I'm sure they're friends. And Alasia. She knows more than anyone. If we're to have any chance of working together, we've got to get together and talk first.'

'I'll try,' Baylin promised, but did not sound hopeful.

'How's the recruiting going?' Ifryn asked. 'We're going to need a strong group if we have to take Azari back by force.'

'There are still some people I need to talk to,' he

replied cautiously. 'We're going to be a strange ragbag of an army.'

The traveller left soon afterwards, and Ifryn sighed helplessly.

'If only there was something I could *do*!'

'You are,' Doneta told her.

The Empress looked at her expectantly.

'You're getting men to do your bidding,' the maid explained. 'Always a neat trick, that.'

In the event, Ifryn's meeting took place two days later. It was set for noon, in the basement of a private house a short way from The Silent Woman. Ifryn went with Baylin, leaving the girls in Doneta's care, with the assurance that some of the traveller's friends would be watching out for them.

When the Empress arrived, everyone else was already there, sitting in silence around a rough wooden table, and eyeing each other suspiciously. All but one stood when Ifryn came in, and he joined them reluctantly a moment later.

'My lady, this is Martyn,' Baylin said. 'Otherwise known as the Swordsman. And his companion, Sagar.'

'Well met, gentlemen,' she responded. 'Please be seated.' She glanced at Kerrell, but he would not meet her gaze, and she knew that this was not the time for personal feelings. Ifryn already knew that Baylin had not been able to find Alasia. That was disappointing, but everyone else she had asked for was there, and even this gathering of allies would have been beyond her wildest dreams only a few days ago. *I must be doing something right,* she thought to herself. Aloud, she said, 'We have much to discuss.'

Ifryn returned to the children and Doneta in the late afternoon, tired but reasonably satisfied.

'How did it go?' her maid asked.

'All right. But nothing happens fast enough for my

325

liking.' She gave Doneta a detailed description of the gathering. The group had proved to be a volatile mix, and at times the discussion had been acrimonious. Kerrell and Martyn especially had clashed several times, and it was clear that only their abiding hatred of Verkho was persuading them to even consider working together. The Swordsman's and Sagar's tales of the ministry added to the group's joint knowledge, but this was only one part of a complicated equation. Even their individual aims were diverse. Ifryn's primary concern was to reclaim Azari; Sagar wanted to rescue his brother; Kerrell needed to clear his name and save the Empire from ruin, while Martyn's sole desire was to kill Verkho – and, if possible, see the Empire crumble. Corton and Grongar were not so involved, having no particular axe to grind. However, their knowledge of the court might prove valuable in due course, especially if Grongar's hounds could be usefully employed. Everyone there, in one way or another, was a fugitive in their own city.

Given all the problems, it was a tribute to Baylin's calm good sense and Ifryn's determined passion that any agreement had been reached at all.

Much later, when her daughters were asleep, Ifryn looked over at Doneta's injured face and sighed.

'You know, it's probably a good thing I'm not a man,' the Empress said. 'I'd probably have killed a few people by now.'

'Women have their ways too,' Doneta replied. 'It's just that we don't rely on brute strength. If there's any killing to be done, we'll not shy away from our part.'

That night, in the bleak time before the first hint of dawn, Verkho translated the final riddle. He neither knew nor cared whether his sudden success was due to his own renewed vitality, to the stratagems of fate, or to some outside influence. He had survived the course so far, and was now only one step from victory. Unfortunately, that step was one he might never take.

The last inscription was, appropriately enough, in the old language of the Xantic Empire. Although this was countless centuries old, it had survived until comparatively recent times as the tongue of religious observance. Even now, certain fanatics still had tombstones inscribed with the archaic script, in the hope that the gods would recognize and favour one of their devotees. Even so, it had taken Verkho a long time to recognize it; the letters were tiny and etched in an ornate style which added numerous and unnecessary curlicues and adornments. Once a fair copy had been obtained however, translation was easy. This time it was no riddle at all, but seemed more like a series of instructions, set out like a prayer.

'Meyu bids you discard all undue favour.
As the gods did, so must you.
What you renounce you lose for ever.
Gar bids you don the gambler's cape and the stakes be
    known to all, and entered into willingly.
As the gods did, so must you.
What you win you must kill.
I ask one last libation, poured from her heart's blood.
What you desire shall be yours.'

Whichever way Verkho read this, it meant the same thing. The legend of how Meyu and Gar, two of the old pantheon, had renounced their divine abilities to rely on chance alone for their last match was well known. Verkho would have to do the same, meaning that he would never again be able to use his telekinetic talent. Then he must win a woman in a fair contest, a woman who knew that the stake was her life and yet agreed to it willingly. Then, having won, he would spill her forfeited blood in exchange for access to the talisman.

The Chancellor had no qualms about murder, or even about relinquishing his talent, but where was he to find anyone who would play him for the life of another –

and both of them willing? These were circumstances in which his reputation would work against him. Everyone knew that the Chancellor could not lose; even if he publicly denied himself the use of his talent, who would believe such a claim? It was galling to think that all his effort and sacrifices might go for nothing, not because of any failing on his part, but because of his special skill! It was almost as if the talisman's designer had known who would be undertaking the task of releasing it.

And yet what choice did he have but to try? Verkho took up a pen and began to compose a proclamation. When he was satisfied, he summoned a bleary-eyed steward and instructed him that it was to be posted and read all over the city that very morning.

At least, Verkho thought, *I've chosen my time well. The Grand Tournament begins in two days' time.*

If there was a gambler in all the Empire mad enough to take up this particular challenge, the chances were that he would be in Xantium now.

CHAPTER FORTY

Are all things measured by a pile of coins – or of promises? There is so much that cannot be valued by such a reckoning. Can I bargain with fate, or haggle over the price of augury?

'You need a guide, master?'

Dsordas looked down at the speaker. His loose-fitting robe was dirty, and a gold earring pierced one lobe. His eyes were bright blue, and sparkled as though he enjoyed life. As he spoke, he reached out a hand to take hold of the horse's bridle, his fingers surprisingly long and delicate.

'I think not,' Dsordas said coldly, resenting the man's attitude.

'You'll not find rooms without me,' the man prophesied, not moving his hand. 'The night's drawing in. You wouldn't want such pretty ladies to lack shelter.'

Dsordas hesitated. They had just passed through the massive southwest gate and, after the open vastness of the Deadlands, Xantium appeared chaotic and intimidating. The streets were thronged with people; noise and smells washed over the newcomers.

'Move along!' a voice behind them called irritably. 'You're blocking the way.'

Dsordas dismounted and led his horse to the side of the road. The others followed. Their would-be guide stayed alongside.

'Come,' he cajoled. 'I show you. My name is Acevedo. I have many friends, and I can find rooms for you even during the Grand Tournament. Good rooms, and at fair prices too. Some innkeepers are charging four times the normal rate.' He spat theatrically, as if to demonstrate his outrage at such blatant profiteering.

Despite himself, Dsordas smiled. His instinct was to send the persistent guide packing, but they were all tired and might indeed need help finding accommodation.

'To prove that I am honest,' Acevedo went on tenaciously, 'I will accept no payment until we find rooms you like. You trust me. I trust you, yes? We have a deal?'

Dsordas was thinking that he would not trust him further than he could throw his horse, but realized that although Acevedo was obnoxious, he was probably necessary. Dsordas turned to the others for advice, but only Aad did more than shrug. He nodded slightly.

'Your fee, if you succeed?'

'I shall succeed, master, have no fear. I am the best guide in Xantium – and the cheapest. For you . . .' He had already checked on the party, their clothes and their mounts, and assessed their wealth. 'For you, only five imperials.' He put a comradely hand on Dsordas' shoulder.

The islander laughed derisively, noting Aad raise a single finger as he did so.

'I'll give you a half,' he said, certain that the innkeeper would be paying Acevedo as well – while charging the travellers what would no doubt be grossly inflated prices.

The guide looked mortally offended.

'Please,' he said, 'do not insult me. Four.'

'There are other guides, you know,' Dsordas pointed out.

'Pah. Take them. You will end up paying a fortune for a rat-infested hovel.' Acevedo pretended to turn away, then returned, grasping the bridle again. 'My friend has stables too,' he told them. 'Three and a half.'

After a while, they agreed on one and a half imperials, and once the bargain was struck, the guide's attitude changed. He was no longer so aggressive, but remained eager to talk, lavishing praise on the tavern to which they were headed, pointing out features of interest along the way, and advising them which streets to avoid. He chattered about the great number of people attending the Grand Tournament – which this year was apparently bigger than ever.

He led them down a large thoroughfare to a small square. At its centre, lit by a circle of torches, was a statue carved of glimmering white stone.

'Who's that?' Fen asked.

'The Empress Ifryn,' Acevedo replied, sounding surprised that they did not know this. 'See the inscription there on the base?'

The incised words were in the old imperial language, and Fen could not understand any of it, but she did not like to admit her ignorance.

'She's very beautiful,' she commented.

'Of course. If you were a sculptor, *you'd* make sure the Empress looked beautiful,' their guide answered cynically. 'Make her ugly and you'd get no more commissions – even if you managed to keep your head.'

'I've heard that Ifryn really is a beauty,' Aad said.

Acevedo shrugged indifferently.

'So they say. We don't see much of her down here in The Levels.'

'Where do the hostages from other lands live?' Dsordas asked. He was walking beside their willing tutor while the others still rode.

'Friends of yours there?' Acevedo asked carefully.

'No. Just wondering.'

'You'd never get near them,' the guide declared. 'They're all shut away in an enclave in The Domain, up on the hill. No one ever gets to see them unless they've got friends at court or an awful lot of money.'

'Money?'

'It'll get you anywhere if you've enough,' Acevedo said. 'Xantium is run by many levels of officials – each

331

with their own price. But you'd need a fortune to make any impression – and even then you might be paying for promises that wouldn't be kept.'

'I can think of better ways of spending a fortune,' Dsordas remarked, thinking that this particular conversation had gone far enough.

'Me too,' Acevedo agreed, laughing. 'And if you have the sort of luck to win one in the Dice Halls, ask for me. I can get you anything you want,' he added, winking confidentially.

'Do you know of a lady named Alasia?' Gaye asked unexpectedly.

'Alasia?' Their guide glanced curiously at the blind girl. 'No. Never heard of her.' To Dsordas, he whispered, 'Does she have talent?'

'Not beyond a keen mind and her looks,' the islander replied, trying not to look surprised.

Acevedo nodded thoughtfully.

'There are some,' he explained, 'blind like her, who claim to be able to see the fall of dice before it happens.'

'A useful trick.'

'Indeed it is – if you can do it undetected. The Dice Halls tend to discourage people like that.'

By now they were in a slightly smaller but still wide street which, like all the rest, was thronged with people. Fen was beginning to feel overwhelmed by the city. Xantium was so noisy, so relentless, so *big*. Suddenly, for the first time since leaving Zalys, she was swept by a violent wave of homesickness. Her memories of the island seemed very sweet at that moment: the blue sea, the serenity of the mountains and the peaceful countryside; the homely buildings of Nkosa and, of course, her family and friends. Except, she recalled grimly, it wasn't like that any more. The screamers had seen to that. Fen deliberately pushed her daydream aside and concentrated on the scene around her. A notice, nailed to a post in the centre of crossroads, caught her eye. It was headed, 'A Challenge'.

'What's that?' she asked.

'That?' Acevedo said. 'Old Verkho's finally gone mad, if you ask me.'

'Verkho?' Dsordas stopped in front of the poster.

'Verkho. The Chancellor,' the guide responded, his tone saying *Don't you know* anything?

Fen dismounted and stood beside Dsordas, and they both read in silence.

'Even for the Grand Tournament, this is crazy,' Acevedo declared. 'Caused quite a stir when it was posted yesterday. People are still talking about it,' he added with the air of one who had dismissed the topic as not worthy of consideration.

'To gamble for a woman's life?' Fen whispered. 'That's sick.'

'And what about "only chance being allowed to determine the fall of the dice"?' Dsordas asked.

'Don't you know?' the guide responded. 'Verkho has many talents, and one of them is to make dice fall any way he wants.'

'But not for this wager?' Fen was confused.

'So he says, but no one'll believe that.'

'And you can name your stake in return,' Dsordas went on. '"Anything within the power of the Xantic Empire to allow." He must be desperate.'

'There won't be any takers,' Acevedo predicted confidently. 'Most people are a little mad during the Tournament, but nobody's *that* stupid. It'd be suicide. I don't know why Verkho is bothering.'

The travellers now had another reason to believe that they were in a totally alien place. That anyone, let alone such an obviously important person, wanted to gamble for such a prize purely for the thrill of it – for what other reason could there be? – made them realize just how corrupt and decadent the Xantic Empire was.

Acevedo led them on, and as they turned into the first of several smaller alleys, they began to appreciate the

333

necessity of a guide. They could very easily have become lost in such a maze.

'Is it much further?' Dsordas asked.

'No,' their guide answered cheerfully. 'Almost there.'

The tavern belonging to Acevedo's 'friend' turned out to be a large, ramshackle building called Ingol's Oven. The proprietor, one Ingol Norcas, was a large, red-faced ex-baker who, like Acevedo, took care to assess the travellers' appearance before naming the price of his rooms. After another round of haggling – which, for all the innkeeper's dramatics, was basically good-natured – agreement was reached, and two rooms taken. Acevedo was reluctant to leave, even after he had received his payment, and repeated his promise to get them anything they needed. The guide kept looking at Gaye, and Fen began to wonder if he had formed an attraction for her.

'You like the rooms, yes?' he asked.

'Yes. We've already told you,' Fen replied. 'We can manage on our own now. Thank you.'

'The Dice Hall is only a short walk away,' Acevedo added helpfully.

'Good,' Dsordas said, gently manoeuvring him away. 'We'll call on you if we need you.'

The guide finally got the message, and left with one final piece of advice.

'Remember. Don't be tempted to wager your horses,' he said with a grin.

'Why?'

'Because,' he replied, 'when you've lost everything else, you'll still have the means to get home.'

CHAPTER FORTY-ONE

*I look upon a weather-vane when there is no wind, a
sundial at night. What is there to see? Power creates its
own movements in the air; the stones cast their own
shadows.*

I am preoccupied. And time is short.

The travellers' energies had been directed for so long
towards reaching Xantium that, once installed in their
rooms, a strange lethargy crept over them. It was hard to
believe that they were actually there, in the fabled city at
the heart of the Empire, and even harder to recall their
reason for coming in the first place. They were all
desperately tired but before they went to bed, the six
gathered in one chamber.

'Well, what now?' Yeori asked.

'That's easy,' Dsordas replied. 'We win vast sums in
the tournament, and bribe every official at court so that
we can get the hostages out.'

'This is no time to be flippant,' Gaye snapped.

'Sorry.' He subsided wearily.

'We all need some sleep,' Fen said. 'There'll be time
enough in the morning to make plans.'

'We can do some scouting around,' Nason put in
eagerly. 'Find the enclave and ask about my brothers.'

'And Alasia,' Fen added.

'I'm going to try to contact her,' Gaye said. 'She'll
help us.'

'Get some rest first.' Nason's expression was one of
genuine concern. 'You know how tired it makes you.'

335

'He's right,' Fen agreed, and smiled at the boy who had been able to overcome his natural impetuosity. Gaye would always inspire such protectiveness.

'I wonder what's happening on Zalys,' Yeori said quietly.

They were silent for a time, all except Aad deep in thoughts of their island home.

'If I know Skoulli and Mouse, they'll have found a way to combat the screamers by now,' Dsordas said optimistically. 'I just wish there was something we could do to help.'

'They'd had some unusually high tides in Nadal,' Yeori commented, 'but no one seemed to think there was anything else strange about the sea. And there'd been no sign of screamers along the mainland coast. I don't see how we *can* help. The best thing we can do is to help the hostages however we can, and then get home fast.'

'But Alasia said "this city has its screamers too",' Gaye said. 'What did she mean by that?'

'It's important for us to be here,' Fen put in. 'I feel it.'

Dsordas gave her an odd look.

'All I feel is the oppression of this place,' he said. 'Bearing down on us.'

'Me too,' Gaye added. 'But Fen's right. Alasia also said that "Xantium is the centre of many circles," and that we had to come here to understand.' She was trying to be as matter-of-fact as possible, painfully aware that no one wanted to mention Bowen by name.

'Well, we're here,' Yeori concluded. 'And we'll do what we can. Come on, you two.' Nason and Aad said their goodnights, and followed him out.

Later, as he lay beside Fen, Dsordas glanced over at Gaye who was already asleep on her own pallet, and sighed.

'I dread to think what it'll be like for her if we find that Bowen's dead – or if we have to leave without finding him at all,' he whispered.

336

'He's alive. Gaye's sure of it.'

'Isn't that just wishful thinking?'

'I don't think so,' Fen said. 'And she won't go until she finds him.'

'But she can't stay here on her own!'

'She will if she has to.'

Some time later, Dsordas said, 'The worst thing is that we're so isolated here. We don't know anyone, and there's no one we can trust. What can we do?' There was a note of helplessness in his voice.

'We can only try,' Fen told him. 'We've come too far to give up now.'

'Do you really feel we're meant to be here?'

'Yes. I've felt that way ever since we first saw the city. Do you remember the bell ringing?'

'A welcome, or a warning?'

'Perhaps both,' Fen whispered. 'We'll find out soon enough.'

Gaye was woken in the dead of night by the sounds of revellers in the street outside. For a few moments she was disorientated, not knowing where she was. But when she remembered, a longing came over her, a temptation too strong to resist. She felt rested now. It was time to begin.

She got quietly out of bed, listened to the steady breathing of Fen and Dsordas as they slept, and felt her way to the table on which their baggage was stowed. She found the bag containing the amberine easily, as if she were being drawn towards it and, holding one of the pendants by its chain, she slipped back to her bed. Only then did she clasp the stone and ask for help.

At first she was caught up within spirals of countless images, circles within circles, that moved so fast it was impossible for her to comprehend anything. Was this the otherworld Xantium, the vast, complex focus of what men call magic? Or was it just a hallucination, a screen set up to ensure she could never make sense of the vision? Where was Bowen? Or Alasia? Why didn't they respond to her calls?

Gradually, however, the swirling stopped, fading into the background and then disappearing altogether as the whole realm was smothered by a mountainous grey blanket, deep as oceans, wide as the sky. It threatened to crush Gaye and she loosed her hold on the amberine, returning to her own dark world. She knew now that the grey mass – whatever it was – was the force that weighed so heavily on her shoulders, and upon Dsordas' too.

She went back to sleep, feeling rejected and dispirited – and found herself in someone else's nightmare.

The screamer was coming straight towards her, the undulating wingbeats belying the speed at which the monster was moving. A small voice shouted *Go away!* and the night was filled with thin, cutting sounds. The screamer came on, vast now and getting bigger by the moment, cruel teeth agape and mad eyes staring at nothing. A cry pierced the air and the creature reared up like a startled horse, then shot up into the sky at an incredible speed.

The same person said, *Thank you,* in a sleepy voice, and this time Gaye recognized who it was.

Natali?

I'm flying, he said artlessly. *With my friends. They make the nasty ones go away.*

The screamers?

Yes. There are more of them now. I don't like them.

Is Mama all right? Gaye asked. *And the others?*

They cry a lot, Natali answered, as though he did not understand why. *Everyone's unhappy.*

Gaye felt a lead weight settle in her heart. The situation on Zalys was getting worse. It was what they had expected and feared.

When are you coming home?

I don't know, little one.

Tarin says if you don't come back soon, there'll be nothing left of Zalys, Natali said. *That's not true, is it?*

338

Of course it's not. Gaye sensed her brother's distress. *Tarin is very silly to say such things.* Privately she wondered where Tarin had come across such an idea. It was not something a ten-year-old boy would make up on his own.

The screamer came back then, diving out of the sky like a malevolent thunderbolt. Enmeshed in the dream again, Gaye felt Natali cower, and threw her instinctive, high-pitched defiance at the monster. She just had time to see it veer away when she was wrenched back to reality by Fen shaking her shoulders.

'Wake up, Gaye. It was only a nightmare. You're safe. We're here.' Dsordas stood behind Fen, his face white in the faint, pre-dawn light.

Gaye found her fist clenched round the amberine, and realized that she must have held it in her sleep.

'I'm all right,' she whispered. 'I've been talking to Natali.'

In the next room, undisturbed by the cry which had roused Fen and Dsordas, Aad smiled in his sleep.

As the new day dawned, the islanders discussed Gaye's link with Natali. No one was in any doubt that it had been a genuine communication and not just a dream but, apart from the intriguing possibility that she and her brother might be able to exchange news in this way again, what they had learnt was depressing – and yet told them little. The only slight touch of hope was provided by Natali's flying 'friends' who made the screamers go away. Gaye decided to ask him who his friends were next time – if there *was* a next time. Could he mean the bats, whose world Gaye had also shared, and who had escorted their ship from Nkosa? But how could bats combat such monstrous creatures? It was a mystery.

'I don't understand how I could contact Natali, who's such a long way away, but not Bowen or Alasia who are here in Xantium,' Gaye said, displaying a moment's doubt. 'They *are* here, aren't they?'

'That's what we're going to find out,' Dsordas replied, honesty compelling him to be no more encouraging than that.

'Perhaps there's something in Xantium . . .' Fen began, then stopped as Gaye gasped. 'What's the matter?'

'Where is he?'

'Who?'

'The ghost. I feel him.'

A shimmering figure stepped through the closed door, and stood looking at the group. Dsordas and Fen stared back at the transparent image of a man in military uniform. He had a stern face, marked with a scar on his left cheek.

'He's here,' Fen whispered.

'I don't want any more riddles!' Gaye burst out. 'If you've come to help us, speak plainly, I beg you.'

The spectre's lips moved, but only Gaye heard the silent reply.

Words have their own laws.

'Who *are* you?'

My name was Coulson Adjeman when I lived in your world.

'What do you want?'

There is a power—

'I know,' Gaye cut in impatiently. 'Emerging from an age-long dream. To oppose it—'

You remember well, the ghost interrupted in turn. *I add this. This same power is responsible for the abominations you call the screamers, but its core dwells here in Xantium. That is why you were drawn here.*

'Here?' Gaye asked. 'How can anything in Xantium be responsible for the screamers?'

Fen and Dsordas, already frustrated by hearing only one side of the conversation, grew even more tense at these words.

The power still sleeps, the ghost replied, ignoring her question. *But it is close to waking. We must all do what*

*we can to prevent that. Otherwise there is little hope for
any of us, but especially for those you have come to save.*

'Bowen?' she exclaimed in sudden panic. 'The hostages?'

The screamers are not the only evil.

'But . . .'

Your time is short, the phantom concluded, sounding
utterly weary.

He vanished then, and Gaye knew it, even though she
could not see. She was too exhausted to protest, and
wondered in passing if such communications were as
tiring for the ghost as they were for her. Perhaps that was
why he only stayed for a short time, why he couldn't or
wouldn't answer her questions. At least this time she had
been given a little encouragement along with his enigmatic advice. Their trip to Xantium had obviously been
necessary. But how were they supposed to fight a power
they could not even recognize, and which spread its
malign influence as far as Zalys?

'What did he say?' Dsordas asked urgently.

Somehow Gaye found the strength to tell him.

CHAPTER FORTY-TWO

The dice's odds are equal for all men. But are all men equal to the dice? Let us dance and wager while we can. How long will it be before we are all trapped in the greatest tournament of all?

'What's the meaning of this?' Southan demanded as he stormed into the Chancellor's study, brandishing a copy of the proclamation.

Verkho still looked frail, but the glitter was back in his eyes.

'My lord, I apologize for not consulting you,' he said. 'I did not wish to burden you with what may be a mere trifle in these difficult times.'

Southan was rather taken aback by this apparently sincere apology, and his anger subsided. He was already frantic over the disappearance of Ifryn and the girls, blaming himself for her departure. He was haunted by her last words to him – *You may never see me again.* Perhaps he had acted too hastily over Azari. But then again, didn't Ifryn's running away prove that she really was unstable? Southan did not know how to cope with the situation.

'Difficult times indeed,' he said. 'First Kerrell, now the Empress. And you – when you should be making every effort to find them, you're wasting your time with this!'

'I have every available man searching for your wife, my lord,' Verkho replied calmly. 'We will find her soon,

I am sure. But you realize we must be . . . discreet . . . in such matters.'

'We can hardly put *that* in a proclamation,' the Emperor agreed bitterly. 'We haven't even been able to find the damned hound-master, to ask whether he saw them leave. *Everyone* seems to be vanishing!'

'Your son is safe. That's the main thing.'

'I suppose so,' Southan said dejectedly. 'I can't tell what's important and what isn't any more.' He paused, remembering his reason for visiting the Chancellor in the first place. 'But I know this isn't.' He waved the poster again. 'What *is* it?'

'During my recent studies,' Verkho replied, 'I uncovered an ancient prophecy which indicates that such a gamble would be worth while.'

'Explain!'

'The text states that an empire on the brink of disaster may be saved by the loyal oath of a woman who has willingly gambled her life away. I am merely trying to fulfil such a condition.'

'You believe such nonsense?'

'Ordinarily I would pay it little attention, but it does seem to describe our situation with remarkable accuracy. War on the eastern borders, the treason of a high-ranking officer, discord in the imperial family . . . Shall I go on?'

'No.'

'I could show you the original manuscript if you like,' Verkho offered. 'It is in an old dialect, difficult to translate.'

'But it does not state that the woman must actually die?' Southan asked uncertainly.

'No. All that is required is that her life be forfeit. Then she will have no compunction about swearing her loyalty to you. And that,' the Chancellor concluded, 'according to the prophecy, will ensure that the rule of the Empire remains within your dynasty for countless centuries.'

'And if the condition is not fulfilled?'

'The augury is not specific, my lord.'

'But we may assume the worst?'

Verkho made no reply. Outwardly he remained solemn, but he was laughing inside. *An ancient prophecy!* he thought. *Just the sort of thing to appeal to this weak-brained fool.*

'Let me know if there's any response.' The Emperor left the poster on the desk and turned to go, feeling more confused than ever.

'There has been none so far,' the Chancellor said, with genuine regret, 'but I am hopeful.' *And,* he added privately, *you will be the last to hear of it if I do succeed.*

The Empress' chambers had lain empty for several days now, neglected and forlorn in their abandonment. Southan was not the only one distressed by Ifryn's flight. Her mother was suddenly without her only real friend at court, and her depression deepened greatly. In the absence of anything better to do, Zephia took to drinking alone, hoping to drown her grief. This rarely worked and, as the rest of the court were preoccupied with their own concerns, she was left to her solitary and unhappy existence.

On the morning that the Grand Tournament was due to begin, the area near Zephia's quarters was even quieter than usual, and she found herself wandering the deserted corridors until she reached her daughter's apartments. She went inside and searched the rooms, without knowing what she was looking for. There were signs of a hurried departure, but nothing to indicate where Ifryn might have gone.

Zephia went back to the outer chamber and sat down in a chair, having seen a decanter of rich red wine on the table. It had presumably been there ever since the Empress had left. Either way, Ifryn had no use for it now. Zephia found a goblet, poured, sat back and drank. A few moments later she was dead.

*   *   *

When Southan returned to his own chambers after visiting Verkho's study, he found one of his stewards waiting nervously for him. Several senior army officers stood nearby.

'What's going on?' the Emperor asked hopefully. 'Have you news of the Empress?'

'No, my lord. But this has just been delivered to the court.' The steward handed the Emperor a sealed parchment. The wax bore the imprint of Kerrell's ring.

Southan tore it open and scanned the brief message. One of the generals approached.

'What news, my lord?'

'Er . . . Kerrell's gone . . . he's left Xantium,' Southan replied falteringly, as he folded the paper again.

'Then we may breathe a little easier,' the General said.

Southan nodded and went into his chambers. He wanted to be alone. Once inside, he read the message again.

'My lord, I am not the traitor you believe me to be. If there is any love left in your heart for me, as there is love for you in mine, come to The Spires at midnight. I will accept your judgement. Kerrell.'

Southan stared at the familiar signature, and realized that he had already decided to go alone. Whatever his crimes, Kerrell deserved that.

The opening day of the Grand Tournament was the most colourful day of the year in Xantium. Unlike the celebrations two months earlier, this was not a ceremonial occasion. The people were honouring nothing except the freedom to win a fortune or to lose everything they owned – a freedom which, in theory, was common to every citizen, from the poorest street beggar to the richest nobleman. There were no formal parades, no grand displays or inspections, but the streets of the city were, in effect, one huge parade.

Everyone played their part, according to their means. Many decked themselves out in fantastic costumes, most of which were as flamboyant as possible; some continued the theme of the festivities, dressing as characters from a pack of cards – skeletons, lovers, hermits, mermaids. The boldest came as The Red Executioner, and whenever two such met on the street it was a signal for a battle of wills and extravagant horseplay – much to the amusement of the onlookers. Others disguised themselves as giant dice or gambling counters, or as those animals considered to bring good luck to a player – snakes, bats and fish. Together with musicians, acrobats, jugglers and clowns, they formed an ever-changing tide of entertainment that flowed through the streets of the city – impromptu parades forming and dispersing at the whim of the participants.

In many squares and other open spaces, other, less mobile entertainments took place. Mystics walked with bare feet through flames; actors portrayed ancient heroes and villains, evoking tears, laughter and – for the less competent – abuse and a hail of rotten debris. Large bands of musicians, including the endlessly inventive drummers of the southern Levels, played while their audiences danced and applauded.

Hundreds of vendors wandered among the crowds, offering all kinds of food, including the traditional tournament fare of spiced dumplings and a potent spirit known as 'smoke' – so called because when mixed with water, it turned a cloudy grey colour and became even more violently intoxicating. Wine and ale were also in plentiful supply and, with so many visitors in the city, the eating houses, inns and brothels did a roaring trade. Thieves and pickpockets also profited greatly from the general abandon, in spite of the sporadic vigilance of the city guards. Xantium was not a place for the faint-hearted.

Once the festivities had begun, there was no let up. While individuals might flag and need the temporary respite of sleep, the city's riotous orgy of hedonistic pleasure would continue unabated for several days and nights.

But, of course, the real action took place in the gambling rooms – from discreet private chambers where the stakes were limited only by the players' wealth and imagination, to the tables in the streets where the city's poor could indulge their fancy, wagering a few small coins on any number of varied games of chance and skill.

And the unquestioned heart of all this activity was the Great Dice Hall, the largest and most sumptuous temple of gambling in all the Empire. Its vast central room, with its marble pillars, stained-glass skylights and polished mahogany furniture, was a testament to the lure of risk and money. Normally only the rich or privileged were allowed into this hallowed place. The Hall went to considerable lengths to ensure the impartiality of its games, needing no dishonest help to make huge profits. It even employed talents whose particular sensitivities allowed them to recognize and, if necessary, eject anyone using any form of magical enhancement in their play. Strictly enforced rules also decreed that no weapons were allowed inside the building.

Naturally, it was the Great Dice Hall that hosted the most prestigious competition of the entire Tournament. This was a massive version of the dice game known as emperors, a game which tested every facet of a gambler's skill: the ability to calculate odds – and to ignore them when necessary – nerve, observation of an opponent's traits and, last but not least, luck. The entrance fee was one hundred imperials, a sum large enough to make its loss a daunting prospect for all but the rich and the foolhardy. There were many preliminary rounds, however, called 'tributes', for which entry was only ten imperials for ten hopeful gamblers in a winner-take-all contest. The triumphant victors of these games thus earnt the money to enter the tournament proper and claim a seat in the central Hall. The final round of emperors would be played for truly mind-boggling stakes between ten survivors of many earlier rounds, and would be the climax of the entire Grand Tournament. When the eventual winner was proclaimed, he would become an immediate hero, as well as becoming suddenly and immensely rich.

That event, however, was still some days in the future. The festivities had only just begun when two parties, among the thousands in Xantium, made their initial forays into the fevered streets.

The slow passage of time and her enforced reliance upon disparate allies were beginning to take their toll on Ifryn. She found the lack of action exasperating, and wished fervently that she had an army with which to storm the court and take back her son. Her longing for Azari was not only a mental torture, but physically painful as well. The girls were also suffering, becoming restless and tearful as their seemingly endless confinement went on. The novelty of their situation had long since worn off, and was being made even worse by the noise of the celebrations outside. In the end, Ifryn knew that they could stay cooped up no longer.

'Come on,' she announced. 'We're going out.'

Delmege and Vrila jumped up immediately, and Doneta smiled. The maid had done her best to keep their spirits up, but was suffering too, and approved of the risk they were taking.

'Jugglers!' Delmege exclaimed. 'I want to see the jugglers.'

On the way out, Ifryn told Baylin's colleagues what she was doing, but turned down their offer to accompany her. The Empress covered the lower half of her face as before, but let the others go unmasked. She did not think they would be recognized in such a crowd.

The bright sunlit colours in the street were almost

blinding, and their senses were assaulted by a barrage of noise and smells. They walked slowly, savouring the heady atmosphere and enjoying their freedom and eventually, much to the delight of Delmege, they found a troop of jugglers and stopped to watch.

That same morning, the travellers from Zalys also braved the city streets. After some discussion, Gaye had been persuaded to stay at the inn and Nason eventually agreed to stay with her this first morning. He had been torn, balancing the necessity to protect Gaye and his genuine affection for her against his desire to begin the search for his brothers. The others decided to split up into pairs, Fen with Dsordas, Yeori with Aad, and to make their preliminary explorations on foot. They parted at the tavern entrance, agreeing to meet there again around noon. An hour later, Dsordas was hot, weary and frustrated, and suffering from a foul headache.

'This is hopeless,' he complained. 'How are we supposed to discover anything in *this*?'

Everyone they spoke to had no time for anything but the pleasures of the moment.

'They can't keep it up for ever,' Fen tried to reassure him. 'We just have to keep trying. You can't give up yet!'

'We need to get up the hill,' he said thoughtfully. 'Nearer the centre. If this power really *is* in Xantium, it'll surely be up there.'

'You're right,' she said. 'But I think we need someone like Acevedo to help us get there.'

'Perhaps.'

They had stopped at a street corner where a troop of jugglers were performing, tossing coloured balls and skittles with gay abandon. Fen watched for a while, admiring their fluid skill, and then found her attention drawn to the audience on the far side of the street. Two women, each holding a young girl by the hand, were also watching the show. One of the women had a scarf covering the lower part of her face and, as Fen looked at her, the brown eyes glanced up and returned her stare for a few moments.

As Fen gazed at the woman, she felt an immediate affinity with her, an empathy she could not explain. How could a complete stranger affect her so? Their eyes only met for a few instants, yet somehow it seemed that a great deal passed between them in that short time. The masked woman turned away first, and Fen was about to point her out to Dsordas when a new entertainment began, displacing the jugglers. The extravagantly plumed dancers obscured her view and when Fen could see again, the woman and her companions had gone. But try as she might, she could not dismiss them from her thoughts. In spite of the fact that the stranger had been dark-haired and brown-eyed, contrasting with Fen's own blonde hair and green eyes, she could not escape the feeling that she had somehow been looking into a mirror.

'It's past noon,' Dsordas said, unaware of her preoccupation. 'We'd better be on our way back.'

Midnight came. The continuing revels echoed all around the city, but in The Spires all was still and quiet. The lights of Xantium spread out below the hill like a carpet of stars. It had taken Southan some time to find a secret way in, and now, as he surveyed the stone maze, he wondered how he was supposed to find Kerrell. He was soon completely lost, and began to doubt the General's intentions. Southan was a brave man and was not afraid to face anyone in a fair fight, but this strange place offered ample scope for an ambush. *Do I really believe Kerrell would do such a thing?* the Emperor wondered, a hand on the hilt of his sword. *If he really is a traitor, why has he suggested this meeting? I could have had The Spires surrounded and captured him.*

It was then that Southan saw a faint light in one of the

towers. It was no brighter than one of the stars above, but it was the signal he had been looking for. He found the entrance, and climbed warily. Kerrell was waiting for him in the circular room high above the city, and as the Emperor came in, the General knelt, his arms outstretched.

'My lord, I am unarmed. I ask only the opportunity to speak to you.' Kerrell kept his head bowed.

'Your wish is granted,' Southan replied stiffly. 'Get up.'

Kerrell rose, and the two men faced each other in the dim lamplight. The General was nervous. He had not been sure that Southan would come alone – or even that he would come at all. Nor did he know what the Emperor's feelings were about meeting a supposed traitor. So far everything had gone as Kerrell had hoped, but the most difficult part was still to come.

'My lord, I came to make my peace with you,' he began. 'However it may appear, I have *never* plotted against you or the Empire. My only crime is treason of another kind.'

'But still treason?' Southan asked quietly.

'Yes, my lord, for which my life is forfeit. I would have yielded it gladly but for the fact that you and the Empire face even greater treachery.'

'Verkho?' Southan enquired sceptically.

'Yes, my lord.'

'You and Ifryn are of the same mind, it seems. Do you have any justification for this joint insanity?'

'Only my knowledge of the truth.'

'And your own treason?'

'It concerns the Empress.'

'Ifryn?' Southan was eager now, and he took a pace forward. 'You know where she is?'

'No, my lord,' Kerrell replied truthfully. He had been careful not to let Baylin tell him where Ifryn was lodged. 'I . . .'

But he got no further because, at that moment, the

351

lamp was knocked to the ground and the moonlight coming through the arched windows splintered. The air was full of tiny fluttering wings, and both men were startled, defending themselves as best they could against the dark invasion. Southan drew his sword and flailed wildly at their unseen foes, while at the same time, Kerrell heard the sound of several voices shouting below. He looked out of the window and saw torches moving over The Spires, converging on the tower. So Southan had not come alone after all. He slipped past the Emperor, who was still occupied with the marauding bats, and ran down the spiral staircase. If he could just make the tunnels . . .

Meanwhile, Southan finally overcame his shock and made his own way to the base of the tower, where he was greeted by several soldiers, their swords unsheathed. Two of them held the forlorn figure of a small, pale woman, and all were astonished to see the Emperor.

'My lord, what are you doing here?' their leader gasped.

'I could ask you the same question, Captain.'

The man recovered his composure and replied briskly, 'Orders from the Chancellor, my lord. We've been trying to find her for some time. We knew she came here from time to time, so we left a watch, but she always got away.' He paused before adding proudly, 'Not this time, though.'

Southan looked at the captive, his thoughts lost in a stew of anger and confusion. Alasia did not acknowledge the Emperor's gaze. All the light had gone out of her eyes.

CHAPTER FORTY-THREE

*What do these dice foretell? When death and danger are
equally split, power rules the unknown love of the stars.
Four moons rise in other realms, but they too can be
eclipsed.*

*Can I measure anything within the sweep of time's
scythe?*

Dsordas looked round at the solemn faces of his
companions.

'So, to sum up,' he said. 'All we learnt yesterday was
that no one's paying attention to *anything* while the
Grand Tournament's running. We can't get into The
Circle, let alone The Domain, because all the gates are
guarded.'

Yeori nodded.

'Especially now,' he confirmed. 'With so many outsiders in Xantium, they're being very careful. Of course,
there are ways.'

'Such as?' Fen asked.

'Getting invited in by a high-placed official or someone at court. Or by paying a suitably exorbitant bribe
to one of the gate captains.'

'Even getting anyone to talk to us costs money,' Aad
put in. 'Our funds won't last for ever.'

'"Your time is short",' Gaye quoted softly.

'Money's the only thing that seems to mean anything
in this place,' Yeori concluded.

'All right,' Dsordas said decisively. 'Then let's get
some.'

                    *   *   *

It took Dsordas most of the morning to find a tribute
with a spare seat. He had reckoned – and the others had
agreed – that it was worth risking ten imperials. If he
were to win, the money would give them a little more
leverage. When Fen objected that winning would also
attract attention to them, Dsordas surprised her by
replying that perhaps that was what they needed.

Once the decision had been made, Aad had been very
enthusiastic. He and Yeori had scouted the Great Dice
Hall the day before, and knew both its layout and its
restrictions. They quickly dismissed any thoughts of
trying to use Gaye's talents to help Dsordas win, as there
seemed no way that she could do so undetected. In any
case, Gaye had decided to stay in her room to try to contact Bowen or Alasia again. Yeori volunteered to stay
with her. Fen went with Dsordas, and Nason and Aad
tagged along, hoping that they could get close enough to
watch.

While waiting for his turn, Dsordas had been able to
observe various games in progress in one of the outer
chambers of the Great Dice Hall, and had familiarized
himself with the rules of this particular version of
emperors. The players sat around specially designed
tables, each with forty counters worth a quarter of an
imperial in front of them. Each player, together with the
eleventh person at the table – a Hall official known as
the caster – had a set of seven dice, marked with seven
symbols, a different symbol missing from each die. The
markings were, in order of rank, a crown or emperor, a
skull, a crescent moon, wavy lines representing water,
a star, a scythe and a lantern. Fortune-tellers ascribed
various meanings to these symbols, but no one here was
paying any attention to that.

Before each round, every player put the minimum bet
on the inner table and then cast his dice in a cunningly
devised compartment which concealed his throw from
the other competitors. He then chose four of these and

discarded the others before closing the lid of the compartment. There was then a second round of betting, competitive this time, that measured the strengths of the initial casts. The most usual scores at this stage were two pairs or three of a kind, with the highest available add-on. If anyone was lucky enough to throw four of a kind, he obviously kept those. Some gamblers, if they were foolish or desperate enough, kept four different dice in the hope of completing the highest possible cast, one of each of the seven symbols – the Circle – but the odds were always heavily against that.

It was then the caster's turn to throw. Taking two of his own set, chosen at random, he rolled them in the centre of the table in plain view of all. The scores on these dice were for common use, adding to all the players' hands. After another round of wagering, another die was rolled by the caster; then more betting, a final die and a final round of betting. Once that was complete, the remaining players revealed their hidden scores and the highest set of seven, using any or all of the common dice, won the entire prize. Before long the weaker or unlucky players lost all their money and dropped out, until only the winner remained with the entire stakes of the table.

But for seasoned gamblers, the real beauty of the game was the fact that it was not necessary to have the best score to win. At each round of wagering, every player had the choice of dropping out, abandoning what he had already staked rather than lose more in a showdown. Therefore, if one player could bluff his opponents into believing that he held the strongest dice, he could win just by making the others surrender. To succeed at this version of emperors thus required not only a grasp of strategy and good luck, but also psychological cunning.

Dsordas chose to drop out early in the first few casts, reckoning that with so many players still in, it would take a very good set to win. Nothing he had thrown so far was strong enough, and the time for bluffing would come later – if he survived. He used the time to study his opponents, their mannerisms and reactions, hoping to use this knowledge to his advantage later on. Two gamblers went out in this early phase, leaving their opponents richer and therefore more powerful.

Finally, Dsordas got the throw he was waiting for. He was able to retain three skulls, with the best possible add-on of an emperor. He was betting last on this round, and none of the earlier seven wagered a large amount. Dsordas bet two imperials. That was enough to frighten off most of his opponents, but two matched his bet. The caster rolled a skull and a star, improving the islander's score further. He bet another two and a half. Both adversaries stayed in, and Dsordas tried not to show his nervousness; if he lost now he would probably not recover. The next roll produced a useless scythe. All three players added minimal bets. The final die was an emperor, meaning that Dsordas now held four skulls and two emperors – a powerful set, which could only be beaten if one of his opponents held four of a kind or three emperors, or unless someone had fluked the Circle. None of those was at all likely, especially as the initial wagering had been so half-hearted. It was time to play.

Trying to keep his expression neutral, Dsordas pushed the rest of his counters forward. It was all or nothing now. One of his antagonists thought for a long time, then dropped out. Dsordas' hopes rose. The other player left in was a small, sharp-faced man called Rack. He had more than enough counters to meet Dsordas' challenge, as he had already won two casts. He studied Dsordas carefully before counting out the matching stake, then throwing his lid open. The exposed dice were three skulls and a star. Inwardly Dsordas sighed with relief. He had won, matching Rack's four skulls, but his pair of emperors beat the other man's pair of stars. Dsordas opened his compartment. The audience murmured in appreciation as the caster, his face betraying no emotion, pushed the large pile of counters over to the winner.

Having established his credentials as a player to be reckoned with, Dsordas began to enjoy himself. He also found himself getting better luck, and won one cast with a very weak set by aggressive bluffing. Before long, only three players were left. Then Rack knocked out the other opponent.

'Well, stranger, just the two of us now.' The sharp face twitched in a smile, hoping to gain a psychological advantage, and confident in the knowledge that he held almost twice as many counters as Dsordas. The islander, who had not spoken an unnecessary word since he had sat down, simply nodded.

The next few rounds were played cautiously, with one or the other usually dropping out early, waiting for a better opportunity to attack. Dsordas won more than he lost, evening the piles a little.

The decisive cast, when it came, was dramatic. Dsordas held two pairs, emperors and moons. The common dice produced first an emperor and a moon, then a lantern, and then – much to the interest of the fascinated onlookers – another emperor. By now, the size of this particular stake was already large, both men evidently feeling that they had strong sets. Dsordas' four emperors and three moons was very powerful, but the danger was that Rack's compartment concealed three emperors, giving him five in all. In the end, Dsordas decided that he would never have a better chance, and he bet all his counters. Rack paused, then matched the amount and revealed three moons and an emperor, giving him a very good four-three set, but one marginally weaker than Dsordas'. That was effectively the end, and Rack's last hopes were soon quashed.

'You play well,' he conceded at the end. 'I hope your luck stays with you in the Grand Tournament.'

Dsordas smiled at this double-edged compliment.

'Thank you,' he replied. 'You were a worthy opponent.'

357

'There are other tributes,' Rack said philosophically. 'I hope we meet again.'

The caster asked Dsordas whether he wished the Dice Hall to retain his one hundred imperials as his entry fee for the Grand Tournament, and he found himself agreeing. It had not been what he had intended, but somehow it seemed inevitable now.

Fen was the first to congratulate him when the players stood up, but Nason and Aad were not far behind. And they soon found out that several other people were eager to make the acquaintance of the stranger who was the latest entrant in the Grand Tournament.

CHAPTER FORTY-FOUR

I have prayed to Zidon many times. For guidance, for truth, for release. Has she heard me, has she answered or ignored my pleas? All oracles cultivate ambiguity, and only the immutable laws outlive their makers.

While the others were at the Great Dice Hall, Gaye and Yeori had begun a quest of their own. Gaye was determined to use her special talents effectively – why else had she come all this way? – and she made Yeori promise not to interrupt, no matter what happened. He agreed reluctantly, but Gaye's excursion into the netherworld was quite brief and caused her no outward distress. As soon as she clasped the amberine, Bowen was there – as if he had been waiting for her. Joy surged through her, but he gave her no chance to express it. Although she sensed the yearning in him too, he was being driven by an even greater urgency, and only had time to give her some instructions.

You must go to the old temple, to the stone faces, he began. *I tried, but they wouldn't let me finish. You must do it.*

Do what?

Find out what happened when Meyu defeated Gar.

The gods? Gaye exclaimed in disbelief. *That's just a legend, from before Xantium was even built.*

That doesn't matter, he told her earnestly. *Their story is embedded in all the places where they were worshipped. You must find it.*

I can't.

You can! You did it in the Arena. He was begging now.

Gaye remembered the advice of the island's ghosts. *Choose a story. Make it real.* That seemed to have happened eons ago, in another world. *This is different!* she objected.

All we need is knowledge, he persisted.

What for?

When Gar was defeated, he was exiled. Even gods cannot kill gods. But he is coming back, and the key to his release is here in Xantium.

So this was the power the ghost had warned her of, the power that had spawned the screamers. Gaye found it difficult to comprehend.

We must stop Verkho turning that key! Bowen added, a desperate urgency in his voice.

Verkho?

Unless we stop him, he will be the one to release the evil. I tried but . . . it's not enough. For the first time, his fear betrayed him. *The circles aren't enough.* Bowen's thoughts were becoming confused now as the grey mass rose up to claim him. *The winding sheet. Go to the temple.* He was almost gone now. *I love you.*

All that was left was a dull, blank ache inside Gaye's mind. Bowen's last words rang in her head like a farewell.

'I love you too,' she whispered aloud as she dropped the pendant.

'Are you all right?' Yeori asked quickly. 'What happened?'

'I'll tell you as we go.'

'Go? Go where?'

'To the old temple,' Gaye told him. 'I have to talk to the gods.'

Even on horseback, getting to the temple took longer than expected. But they made it eventually, threading their way through the celebrating crowds and climbing the small hill to the quiet, deserted ruins. Yeori, who

360

had led the horse for the last part of the journey, helped Gaye dismount, and took her hand to guide her over the rough ground to the central paved area.

'Stone faces,' she said quietly. 'I can feel them looking at me.'

Yeori regarded her anxiously.

'Is there somewhere I can sit?' she asked.

He led her to the altar and she sat on the ground, leaning her back against the ancient pitted stone.

'Go back a bit. I need you to watch what happens.' Gaye sensed his hesitation. 'Go on. I'll be fine – and your sight's better than mine!'

'Not in these matters,' he replied, and then reluctantly did as she asked. Yeori had seen much in recent times that had changed his view of the world and he was no longer nearly as sceptical as he had been, but he still could not quell a dreadful nervousness. What Gaye was about to attempt seemed utter madness to him.

'Ready?' she called.

'Yes.' *As ready as I'll ever be*, he added to himself.

Gaye took the pendant from her pocket and touched the cool, smooth surface of the stone. She did not try to contact anyone this time, but relaxed, letting herself become filled with the memories of this place. Images flickered in her mind, moments from history. She saw a time when the temple was a truly wondrous building, its gilded halls full of worshippers; then came the stages of its construction and finally a time before man had ever come to this place. The small hill stood in the midst of a vast forest, the serpentine glint of a great river just visible through the foliage, green hills rolling into the distance. It had been a sacred place even then. Gaye thought of the contrast between this vision and the description the others had given her of the Deadlands. She sensed too that she was not alone, that there were *guides* with her. But all that was forgotten in an instant when the voices came – voices that seemed to fill the sky. Their words shook the whole world – and yet Gaye saw nothing with her mind's eye. The speakers were invisible to her.

The Fates have spoken, Meyu declared.

I submit to your judgement, brother, Gar replied with patently false humility.

For your crimes, you will be sealed for ever beneath the airless sea.

For ever? There was fear in Gar's voice now. *You deny me even the chance of Elcar's fire? This cannot be!*

I decree it, Meyu roared. *You have forefeited the protection of the laws.*

Must this be so? Gar appealed. *What say you, Zidon?*

Augury upholds the laws. Was there a hint of complicity in the female voice? *For all.*

No! Meyu bellowed furiously.

You must leave me in the world of men, Gar stated triumphantly. *Nothing there is immortal, nothing lasts* for ever.

Gar is right, Zidon affirmed.

Thus I leave your fate to men, Meyu said, suddenly calm. *I will grant you Elcar's fire if one man can complete these tasks.* Reality twitched. *But if he fails, your doom is set. Thus are the laws satisfied. What says the world's oracle now?*

It is done, Zidon said.

Treachery! Gar cried, shaking the earth and the sky. *What* man *could do such?*

That is not at issue, his brother answered grimly.

And to submit the laws to a game of chance, all for a paltry human life! Gar went on. *It is barbaric. Unworthy of the pantheon.* He was desperate now.

Your life was mortal when we cast our dice, Meyu pointed out.

Fortunes reverse, brother, Gar snarled with the last surge of defiance. *Time will challenge my end.*

But it is certain now, Meyu said mercilessly. *And so that you do not have to witness your fall, you go to the ocean blind.*

Gar's scream echoed down the endless centuries, a howl of agony composed of the tortured cries of every living creature.

Gaye dropped the crystal, trembling violently as the terrible sound swept through her like an icy wind. Moments later, Yeori was at her side, his arms around her.

'I'm here,' he murmured. 'Are you all right?'

Gaye nodded weakly. She felt dizzy with weariness, and yet exalted at the same time. She had been given the answer Bowen wanted. Only then did it occur to her to think what that answer implied.

'Did you hear them?' she whispered.

'I heard nothing. But I saw.' He sounded awestruck.

'Tell me.'

'First there was a jumble of images, nothing that was clear. Then . . . the ghosts appeared . . . hundreds of them, all around.'

'They were guiding me,' Gaye told him.

'After that,' Yeori went on, 'the crowds disappeared and three figures were there, two men and a woman. At least that's what they looked like,' he added uncertainly. 'One of them shone so bright that it was hard to look at him.'

Meyu, Gaye thought. *The Sun-god.*

'The other man had antlers on his head and hooves instead of feet.'

Gar, the guardian of all living creatures.

'But I could hardly see the woman at all,' Yeori continued. 'Her robes swirled about her – and she kept changing.'

Zidon, the goddess of augury.

'I could see that they were arguing, gesticulating angrily, but I couldn't hear what they said. Then they all disappeared and you dropped the stone.'

'Have the ghosts gone too?'

'All except one,' he admitted unhappily.

Am I so weak that I can no longer sense them? Gaye wondered. Aloud she said, 'Coulson?'

363

I am here.

'Could we do it?' she asked. 'Can we beat him?'

Augury marks the healer to cast the dice for us all.

'But can he win?'

Your purpose may be served. Alasia is among the hostages now. She asks for your help, as do I.

Gaye sat in silence for a while.

'He's gone,' Yeori said eventually.

'Take me back to the tavern,' she said. 'I need to talk to Dsordas.'

'You can't be serious,' Dsordas pleaded, stunned as they all were by Gaye's revelations.

'I can and I am,' she retorted. 'This is our only chance. Don't you see, it solves everything. If you defeat Verkho he'll never be able to release the power, and so Gar will be confined in the ocean again. He'll never be reborn through Elcar's fire. The screamers will be trapped and Zalys saved. And you can wager for the release of *all* the hostages, not just Bowen and the others from Zalys. And that in turn will weaken the Empire so that it will never again be able to oppress all the peoples of the world!'

Gaye's mind was burning with all she had heard at the temple, from the memories of the place itself and from Coulson. She knew that it all fitted. *This* was why they had come to Xantium.

'And if I lose?' Dsordas asked helplessly.

'You can't,' she told him. 'It's been prophesied. You've *got* to do this.'

'Verkho's the one who can't lose,' Dsordas responded. 'You heard what Acevedo said. Playing him would be madness.'

'No. He has to be honest. That's part of the bargain.'

'You believe that?' Yeori asked.

'There are talents at the Dice Hall who can detect magic,' Gaye replied. 'You told me that yourself.'

'Verkho's the Chancellor!' Dsordas exclaimed. 'You think he couldn't buy a few tame talents to say what he wants?'

'He can't buy me,' Aad said unexpectedly.

They all looked at him.

'I can't *do* any magic,' he explained. 'But I'm sensitive to it. You were right, Yeori. My hands tingle whenever I'm near it.'

While the others digested this extraordinary piece of information, Gaye's thoughts were racing ahead.

'I don't think he *can* renege on the bet,' she said, 'but we can make sure the match is as public as possible, just to make certain.'

All of this was moving far too fast for Dsordas.

'But even if he doesn't cheat,' he objected, 'I could still lose.'

'Alasia wouldn't mislead us,' Gaye replied confidently. 'Neither would Bowen. This is *meant* to happen.'

Dsordas felt torn and wretched, no longer in control. It was one thing to test his skill for mere money, yet another to submit to such appalling stakes. To save Zalys and the hostages in one fell swoop was an appealing prospect, but the price of failure was unthinkable. Gaye was relentless in her conviction, though, and would not let him alone.

'If you don't do it,' she told him, 'sooner or later Verkho will find *someone* willing to take the risk. And then he'll win. We *have* to stop him. Don't you see?'

Dsordas felt as though he was being suffocated by the grey mass pushing down upon him, and pain lanced through his head. Could he *really* contemplate being the agent of the greatest disaster the world had ever known? Could he risk unleashing an age-old malice which would make the screamers seem like playful kittens? And could he be a part of the obscenity of wagering for a woman's life?

As if reading his last thought, Gaye spoke again, gently this time.

'I'll gladly be your stake.'

'No.' It was Fen who contradicted her sister. 'If Dsordas is to meet Verkho's challenge, it is my life he will play for, no one else's.'

CHAPTER FORTY-FIVE

*Destiny does not provide a map. We all have to choose
our own routes through the labyrinth, with its pitfalls and
dead ends. Is it my fault that most signposts are ignored?
Or that most clues are illegible, even to those who can see?
Who can step aside from fate's arrow?*

The news that someone – and a *foreigner* at that – had
actually dared to accept Chancellor Verkho's challenge
spread through Xantium like summer wildfire. Extra
fuel was heaped upon the blaze of rumour by the even
more remarkable reports of what the stranger had
chosen to wager for. Most people had expected anyone
insane enough to face Verkho to ask for an unimaginably
vast sum of money, or at least the lordship of several
lands. Yet, when he could have demanded *anything*, this
Dsordas Nyun had chosen to demand the release of all
the hostages in the city – and nothing more. Of course,
nobody expected him to win but, nonetheless, the
general opinion was that he was either mad or hopelessly
ignorant – or, more probably, both. The fact that
Verkho had actually agreed to such terms made people
think it all the more certain that the Chancellor would
win. Even so, the encounter was now eagerly anticipated, overshadowing even the progress of the Grand
Tournament, and entry to the Great Dice Hall – where
the match was to be held – was being fiercely sought.

At the Chancellor's decree, the contest was to begin
one hour before noon on the day after he had received
news of his challenge being taken up. As this would be

the third day of the Grand Tournament, the Great Dice Hall was forced to hurriedly revise its timetable, and its staff were plunged into feverish activity. The central hall was cleared of all except one table, and stands were erected to give as many people as possible a good view of the proceedings. The best caster and detector were assigned to supervise, and other personnel instructed to provide anything required for the comfort of the two participants. It was a tribute to the Hall's management that all was ready well before the appointed hour.

Dsordas had surprised himself by sleeping well and dreamlessly that night. His headache had mysteriously vanished the moment he had made his decision to accept the challenge, but although this had given him some comfort, he could not explain its significance. Was it a sign that he was doing the right thing? Or just that he was doing something positive after the mounting frustration of recent days? Was he, in some unfathomable way, healing himself? Dsordas had no way of answering such questions, and so could only calm his many fears by thinking of Gaye's enthusiastic certainty.

But when he awoke in the early morning, he felt empty, his whole body an aching void, when he remembered that it would be Fen's life, and not his own, that he would be risking. Everything else became irrelevant when he looked at her beside him, still asleep after a night half spent in tender, mutual passion – to which Gaye had turned a sympathetically deaf ear. All the rest, all the horrors and hopes, meant nothing when matched against his love for her.

'I can't do this,' he whispered.

'You have to,' she replied, asleep no longer.

Her smile told him that there was no turning back now.

Verkho, naturally enough, was beside himself with glee. He knew now that this was what his life had been leading to, ever since his revelations as a boy which had transformed his life and set him on the path to ultimate power. Even without his forsaken talent, he was certain that he would win – it was his destiny – and he knew that this contest would have to be worthy of the occasion, an appropriate stage on which to display his prowess before the people of Xantium. Thus he was more than willing to accept Dsordas' conditions about the venue and the game to be played. Emperors would have been his own choice – not least for the aptness of the name – and initial stakes of one hundred imperials each was fair enough. The money meant nothing, of course; it was just a convenient way to keep score. The real stakes were vastly more meaningful. Verkho knew that the challenger had already made a small name for himself by winning a tribute, which was all to the good. The gods would demand a worthy opponent.

He called for Shinasi and settled into his wheeled chair. Then, accompanied by stewards and a squad of soldiers, the Chancellor made his way to the Great Dice Hall. Soon he was at the head of a slow-moving cavalcade as his progress was followed by many court associates and other interested parties. By the time he left The Circle the procession was several hundred strong and, once in the crowded Levels, the parade became even more vast. Most of the followers had no hope of witnessing the fateful confrontation in person, but just to be near such an event was an experience in itself, an extra excitement amid the entertainments of the city's carnival.

The Swordsman waited in a window on the uppermost floor of a building along the Chancellor's route. A powerful crossbow, already loaded, lay ready on his lap. He knew that Verkho would soon pass by, and this was too good an opportunity to miss. Martyn did not know what the Chancellor was up to with his foolish challenge but, by definition, it had to be evil – and therefore killing

369

him before he reached the Dice Hall was an especially gratifying prospect. Martyn had not spoken to his supposed allies, except Sagar, since their recent meeting and so had no idea what – if anything – they were planning. Kerrell and the others had seemed almost afraid to act and, in any case, the Swordsman was happier operating alone.

At last the parade approached, preceded by the clamour of a large number of excited people on the move. At the head of the procession, Shinasi pushed the Chancellor. Martyn was surprised to see his enemy confined like an invalid, but it would make the shot even easier. He opened the shutters a little wider, stood up and raised the crossbow.

The soldiers accompanying Verkho were looking around carefully, not allowing anyone to come too close to their master, but Martyn knew they would not see him until it was too late. As his target drew nearer, the Swordsman took careful aim. Then he hesitated. There seemed to be a slight blue haze around the Chancellor, almost invisible in the bright sunlight but definitely there. Was this more vile sorcery? The Swordsman dismissed the thought. He had been waiting for this moment for too long. He squeezed the trigger, and felt the bow jump as the bolt sped downwards, straight towards Verkho's heart. The Swordsman followed the fleeting moments of its steel flight with jubilation but then, at the last instant, there was a flash of blue light and the arrow veered suddenly, impossibly, and missed the Chancellor altogether. Screams and shouts rang out as the diverted bolt thudded into the chest of one of the soldiers, piercing his breastplate as if it had been made of linen. He stared stupidly at the shaft protruding from his body, then collapsed. The squad captain reacted quickly, and soldiers ran towards the building as civilians scattered.

Martyn cursed, threw down the useless bow and ran, unable to believe what he had seen.

Verkho, unperturbed, glanced up at the now empty window and smiled before ordering the equally unmoved Shinasi to proceed.

'Are you ready to go?' Acevedo asked.

'Yes,' Dsordas replied, though he sounded like a man who had been asked if he was ready for the walk to the gallows.

'I've managed to keep it quiet about you staying here,' the guide added proudly, 'but we'll have to take a roundabout route to avoid the crowds.'

'Whatever you think best,' Dsordas told him indifferently.

It had been Acevedo who had delivered Dsordas' answer to Verkho's challenge, finding ways of cutting through the layers of officialdom that normally surrounded the Chancellor. The guide was revelling in his astonishing good fortune at being the self-appointed mentor of these people, who would soon be famous by sight as well as by reputation.

'Come, then,' he said, putting a solicitous hand on Dsordas' arm. 'You won't forget me when you win, will you, master?'

'When he wins,' Fen reassured him, 'you will have the hundred imperials.'

Acevedo beamed, then turned to lead the way. All six travellers followed him along a tortuous route which took them through several filthy alleys, so narrow that they had to walk in single file, and also through a number of buildings, the inhabitants of which either ignored their passage or waved to Acevedo in disinterested greeting.

When they eventually reached a side entrance of the Great Dice Hall and identified themselves, they were quickly admitted and taken to a private room where they were greeted by the senior manager and offered refreshments. No one, except Acevedo, felt like eating, but Yeori gulped down a large cup of wine.

It was not long before a messenger arrived to inform them that the Chancellor was approaching, and they were taken to the central hall where they were shown their seats, Dsordas at the table, Fen on a single chair behind him. The rest sat on a bench at the front of one of the packed, tiered stands. As they parted, Gaye kissed Dsordas and smiled. Yeori wished him good luck, but Aad and Nason were tongue-tied in full view of so many people. Fen held him last, aware of all the stares directed at them. She smiled determinedly, gazing into his worried eyes.

'You'll win,' she told him quietly. 'I know you will. You didn't save me from Farrag's poison to lose me this way.'

Dsordas made no reply. He had run out of words long ago.

'Pretend your mother's watching,' Fen added with a grin. 'You wouldn't dare do anything but win with her about!' With that she kissed him and took her place. However successful her cheerful front, she couldn't help feeling like a sacrificial virgin waiting at the temple.

Everyone in the hall stood as Verkho entered, and Dsordas stared in horror at the cloaked figure in the wheelchair. This was Farrag reincarnated, the same terrible eyes, the seemingly invincible confidence, the same overwhelming sense of *evil*. Then he heard a small voice in his head say, *You beat him once. You can do so again*.

The Chancellor sat alone at the table opposite Dsordas. He knew he had no need of special protection here in the Great Dice Hall.

A tense silence settled over the assembly as the caster read out the formal challenge and acceptance, listed the stakes being played for and asked the players for confirmation that the details were correct. When he had finished, Verkho looked directly at Fen.

'You willingly forfeit your life if I win?' he asked.

'I do,' she replied, surprised to find her voice steady.

372

'Then let us begin.' The Chancellor picked up a set of dice in his undamaged hand and looked at his opponent. Dsordas took a deep breath, meeting the glittering stare as best he could, and took up his own dice.

To the islander's astonishment – which he concealed as far as possible – his first cast produced four scythes. As a consequence he wagered quite heavily, adding five imperials to the agreed minimum stake of one imperial. Verkho matched him. The first two common dice produced a pair of moons. This time, with Verkho betting first, the roles were reversed. The Chancellor pushed forward another five counters.

That gave Dsordas pause for thought. Was Verkho bluffing, hoping to gain early psychological mastery? Or did he hold the two moons which, with any other pair, would now put him ahead? Then again, there was still a reasonable chance of getting another scythe. Dsordas stayed in. The next dice produced a star and a lantern respectively, neither of which improved his score at all. The Chancellor wagered another five, making the total stake eighteen imperials, including the two bet after the penultimate die.

If I give in now, Dsordas thought, *I'll only lose thirteen – but he'll have my measure. And he could still be bluffing.* Fatalistically, he staked five imperials and opened his compartment.

'Four scythes,' the caster announced, then turned to Verkho, who opened his own lid, revealing two pairs – water and moons. When the caster called this out, there were a few cries and a smattering of applause from the spectators.

Dsordas' heart sank like lead in water. Only one cast, and already he had lost almost a fifth of his total stake. It was not an auspicious start.

The next few casts were not nearly so dramatic, and the betting was much lower. Dsordas boosted his own confidence a little by winning sometimes, proving that he could do it, but overall his pile of counters grew slightly smaller. The audience was held spellbound, gripped by the unfolding drama and the consequences of defeat for either man. The sight of Fen, sitting alone, beautiful and vulnerable, only added to the spectacle's allure.

After they had been playing for just over half an hour, Dsordas lost with another strong set, four emperors and two moons, when the final die gave Verkho his fifth skull. That reduced the islander's pile of counters still more, and a quick calculation told him that he now held less than fifty imperials. His opponent had three times his strength; unless Dsordas did something soon, he was bound to lose. A glance at the Chancellor's feral eyes and the slight smile which twisted his lips told its own story.

On the next cast, Dsordas was appalled to see that he had thrown one of each symbol – the Circle. One of the great ironies of this version of emperors was that these dice – the best set of all – were useless at this initial stage. Once three had been discarded, it was the weakest possible holding. Dsordas dispensed with the three lowest ranked dice, a star, a scythe and a lantern, and prepared to drop out. However, when Verkho bet only one imperial, he decided to stay in. There was always the remote chance of filling up his Circle again.

The caster rolled two dice. To Dsordas' amazement, they came up a scythe and a lantern. The odds had changed dramatically now. They were still against him, but if either of the two remaining dice was a star, then he would have an unbeatable score. And it was his turn to set the level of the wagering. He pushed a stack of ten counters forward.

Verkho looked at him for a long time.

'Your cast got better all of a sudden,' he remarked eventually, 'but I think you've chosen the wrong time to bluff.' He matched Dsordas' bet, and raised it by another ten, pushing the islander into a corner. Did he dare risk another ten? Its loss would leave him almost beaten. He needed a star to come up; a star, which the fortune-tellers interpreted as the sign of love or the un-known. Wasn't that what this was all about? Dsordas matched the bet and the Chancellor raised his eyebrows, smiling nastily.

The caster rolled the next die.

'A star,' he declared.

A star. Dsordas could hardly believe his luck, but struggled with all his might to keep it from showing on his face. He could not now lose this cast, and his first instinct was to bet everything he had straight away – but he had to convince his adversary to wager as much as possible. It was time for a few theatrics.

Verkho bet five imperials. Dsordas waited as long as he dared, then shrugged, matched the five and added five more. When the Chancellor stayed in with five of his own, Dsordas laughed nervously. The audience whis-pered, wondering if the stranger was finally losing his self-control.

The caster spun the final die, producing another scythe. This was irrelevant to Dsordas but he reacted to it, then hurriedly stifled his response, knowing that Verkho would have noted the small movement. Hoping that the scythe improved his opponent's score, thus making him more willing to bet, Dsordas made a great play of being undecided, then turned round in his chair. The look he directed at Fen, as if seeking guidance, was so full of sadness and regret that many in the audience were aghast. The foreigner really had lost his nerve. Fen's heart beat wildly. She was helpless, unable to read his real intentions.

Dsordas turned back to the table and slowly, deliber-ately, pushed all his counters to the middle. The spectators gasped as one, filling the hall with their whispers. Here was the first, and perhaps the last, climax of the show. As the speculation died away to silence, Verkho sat motionless.

Take the bait, Dsordas urged silently. *Please take the bait!*

375

'This cast of yours is a wonder,' his opponent said sarcastically. 'I had better see it for myself.'

Verkho counted out the required number of counters and opened his own compartment, revealing two scythes, a star and an emperor, giving him four scythes and two stars in all. Dsordas immediately revealed his own dice and when the caster called them out, ending the announcement with a dramatic cry of 'The Circle!', the crowd went wild. Behind him, Dsordas could hear his friends shouting and laughing, but he dared not look round at Fen again. His task was far from over – but at least now he was back on almost equal terms. Verkho was the only one in the entire hall who remained apparently unmoved.

For the next few casts the play reverted to the earlier, more conservative game of cat and mouse. But now the atmosphere had changed; Dsordas felt his opponent's uncertainty, and even thought he detected some misjudgement in Verkho's play. The islander won a few small amounts, shifting the balance so that he now had slightly more of the total stake money.

More than an hour had elapsed when the first round of betting announced that the new cast would be an important one. The Chancellor counted out twenty imperials on to the table. Dsordas glanced at his own dice – three moons and a skull – before closing his compartment and responding with twenty counters of his own.

The caster's first throw gave a moon and a skull, improving Dsordas' holding immensely. He bet another twenty, which Verkho matched immediately, almost impatiently, signalling to the caster to roll again. The chosen die spun on the table for what seemed like an age before it settled showing an emperor's crown uppermost.

Verkho had no need to lift the lid of his own compartment to know what was there. Even with one die to go, he had a very powerful set, almost certainly good enough to win. There was utter silence in the hall as the

Chancellor pushed his entire stack into the centre and looked up at Dsordas, hoping that he would match but expecting such a massive bet to scare him off.

However, Dsordas already held four moons and a pair of skulls, itself a very good hand, and one he was loath to abandon. He realized that his next move would be critical. He thought he had detected the first signs of desperation in Verkho's play, and knew that he might never get another chance to break the Chancellor in one swift attack. He matched the bet, leaving himself with only a few counters. The entire audience, which had been holding its breath, now sighed and murmured their appreciation of the moment. They were mesmerized as they waited for the caster to complete the round.

But it was Verkho who moved next. Knowing that no more wagering was possible, he flung open his cabinet, provoking a few shouts of surprise.

'Three skulls and an emperor,' he stated. 'Can you beat that?' The Chancellor smirked at the look of shock on his opponent's face. In his own mind he was already holding the talisman in his hand.

Dsordas felt sick. He had been outmanoeuvred. Verkho's four skulls and two emperors were almost certain to win. Only a final moon, giving him five, could save Fen now. Only one chance in six. It was even possible that the die chosen would not have a moon on it, giving him no chance at all.

The caster picked from the opaque satin bag in which his set of dice were stored between casts, and prepared to throw.

'There is magic here.'

At the detector's words everyone froze, participants and spectators alike. They had all forgotten the presence of the talent, a small dark-skinned woman who sat on a front bench at the side of the table opposite the caster.

'Who wields sorcery here?' he asked.

'No one. It comes from outside.'

At this, the bemused caster looked round for advice,

never having encountered this situation before. The senior manager stepped forward, ready to intervene, but the detector spoke again.

'The players are innocent,' she intoned. 'The influence is reversed, removed. You may complete the cast.'

Dsordas' last hope was gone. If Verkho had been caught cheating, then he could have claimed the win by default. Now all that he had to rely on was luck. This time it was not the star of love he needed, but the crescent moon which stood for other realms.

The caster released the die. It rolled along the smooth surface, watched by a thousand eyes. Dsordas was praying as he stared, and at first he thought what he saw was a self-induced hallucination – but then it grew clearer. A spectral hand, transparent and ephemeral, rose up out of the solid table and flicked at the die as it passed, adding a minute fraction of spin before disappearing again.

Dsordas was hypnotized, helpless. Why was there no outcry from the detector, from Aad, from anyone else? Was he the only one who had seen the ghost's interference? Then, in the same instant, he wondered how a ghost *could* influence a die in the living world. It was not possible. *Other realms?*

The die slowed, tipped over once more and came to rest. Dsordas found himself staring at the longed-for moon, hardly daring to breathe. He waited for the objections, the protests at the phantom intervention – but none came. Everyone was looking at him.

'Your dice, sir?' the caster prompted. 'May we see them?'

In a dream, Dsordas pushed back the lid.

'Five moons!' the caster declared. 'The game is over.'

CHAPTER FORTY-SIX

They have no fire, and that is both their weakness and their strength. Together they might outshine any beacon.

Parallel paths can cross. It is only a matter of perspective.

The hall erupted. No one could quite believe that Verkho had lost, but as the reality sank in the noise level rose even higher. Fen had run forward and she and Dsordas were entwined in a dance of joy. Their friends were all clustered round them and some of the audience mobbed them too, despite the best efforts of the overwhelmed staff. Others were scrambling for the exits, eager to spread the astounding news to the rest of Xantium. Verkho remained at the table, transfixed and unable to speak. Eventually he signalled for Shinasi and left, his soldiers forcing a way through the crowds.

At last Dsordas and his fellow travellers were ushered into the privacy of the reception room. Acevedo followed them. The mood of jubilation was overpowering, with everyone hugging everyone else in turn.

'We did it! We did it! We did it!' Fen chanted.

'Bowen,' Gaye breathed. 'I'm going to see him soon,' she added with unconscious irony.

'I'm rich. I'm rich!' Acevedo cried. He had taken the precaution of collecting Dsordas' nominal winnings.

The others were not even able to form coherent words, and just whooped and yelled like madmen. But Dsordas, for all his happiness, was still bemused. Eventually, he was able to corner Aad.

379

'Did you feel anything at the end?'

'Yes,' the boy replied. 'I wasn't sure at first because it was very faint, but there was something, remote and weak. The detector must be very good to have picked it up so quickly.'

'And afterwards, when she said it had gone?'

'Nothing. Why?'

'It doesn't matter,' Dsordas told him.

'When are the hostages going to be released?' Gaye asked.

'This afternoon,' Nason replied. 'Verkho told the manager to announce it as he left. They'll be coming out of the south gate of The Circle.' His voice was full of anticipation at the thought of seeing his brothers again.

'Do you think he'll honour the wager?' Yeori asked, introducing the first element of doubt into their celebration.

'He has to!' Gaye stated. 'And we'll be there to greet them.'

'We have to get out of here first,' Dsordas said. 'And that's not going to be easy.' He turned to Acevedo.

'Leave it to me, Master Dsordas,' the guide said, grinning happily.

Baylin left the Great Dice Hall as astonished as anyone who had witnessed Dsordas' victory. His gaudy costume and false beard served as a disguise but passed unnoticed in a city already full of outlandish sights. He went straight to Ifryn, and gave her a full report of what had happened.

'It'll be all over the city in an hour or so,' Baylin concluded, 'but I still don't think anyone understands what's going on. Why did they do it?'

'Anyone opposed to Verkho ought to be a potential ally for us,' the Empress replied.

'But if he really *does* release the hostages, it'll weaken Xantium no end.'

'I don't care about that now,' she told him. 'The

380

Empire was bound to fall sooner or later. All I want is my son back, and an end to Verkho's machinations. I want to meet these people.'

'I'll see if I can arrange it.'

'Have you told Kerrell about this yet?'

'No. I've not had a chance. He didn't turn up at our arranged meeting place yesterday.'

'Do you think something's happened to him?' Ifryn asked, immediately anxious.

'I don't know,' Baylin replied honestly. 'But he's missed meetings before. I don't think we need to worry yet.'

The door of the dungeon cell was thrown open violently and Verkho strode in, lamp in hand. Alasia shied away from his anger and from the sudden bright light.

'Something happened, didn't it?' he demanded. 'Did you have anything to do with that last throw?'

'I cannot walk in other realms,' she replied, her voice quavering.

'But you can see into them, can't you? Tell me what you saw, or I'll have you cut into a thousand pieces.'

Alasia had got over her initial shock and was not affected by his threat.

'I'll fly away,' she told him mildly.

The Chancellor made a gurgling noise deep in his throat, as if he were strangling on his own bile. After the detector had declared that the magic had gone, he would have looked ridiculous if he had protested at his loss. But *something* had interfered, he was sure of it. The bargain had not been kept, and so he must be due another chance. But for that to happen, he would have to make at least a show of releasing the hostages. If he were to renege now, there would be no hope of anyone else coming forward. Verkho swore in disgust and went out, slamming the cell door violently behind him.

Acevedo had somehow procured a room in a tavern

overlooking The Circle's south gate. Dsordas, Fen and Gaye waited there while Yeori, Nason and Aad mingled with the crowd outside as the hostages began to emerge. They came in small groups or pairs, looking around nervously, evidently bemused by their sudden change of fortune. There was little rejoicing at their newfound freedom – it was all too strange. Fen watched the procession, her heart filled with pity as well as expectation. Xantium had been responsible for the abuse of so many people's lives, so many children: Sagar and the other hostages taken from their homes when most were too young to understand; Iceman and the other maltreated Far-speakers; even Natali and the other children on Zalys who had been part of Farrag's experiments.

As time passed and the numbers emerging reduced to the occasional wary group, the islanders grew increasingly worried. There had been no sign of Bowen or Sagar – or any of the other Zalysians. Nor of anyone who fitted Gaye's description of Alasia.

'He's got to come. He's got to come,' Gaye kept repeating, angry at not being able to keep watch herself.

And then, after a long agonizing gap when no one came out, a man they recognized as the senior manager of the Great Dice Hall strode up to the gateway.

'Thus the wager is met!' he cried to the assembled crowd. 'I have inspected the hostage enclave myself, and it is now empty. All the hostages have been released.'

'No!' Gaye screamed. 'No!'

Fen went to hold her sister, and looked up at Dsordas as Gaye sobbed helplessly. He could only shrug miserably at Verkho's deceitfulness. *We should have expected no less,* he thought. *But what do we do now?* Gazing in sorrow at the two sisters, Dsordas suddenly turned on his heel and left the room. Moments later, the others saw him approach the manager, who still stood in the south gate talking to the captain. Dsordas was obviously protesting, but the other man only shook his head and turned away, refusing to take any further action.

Dsordas looked up at Fen, who was waiting in the window. She could not bear to see the despair and defeat written on his face.

Southan was fuming. He had discovered that he was unable to see Verkho, but on this occasion it was not because the Chancellor had shut himself away in his protected study. No one, not even his chief steward, knew where he was.

There were three things the Emperor wanted to discuss urgently. First, and by far the most important, was the release of the hostages. Southan fervently hoped that this was a ruse, that arrangements had been made to recapture the prisoners, because – if not – it was madness, a madness which could undermine one of the cornerstones of Xantium's power. Secondly, there was Zephia's death – from poison. Southan did not understand that at all. Who would want to murder the old woman? And why? And how had it come to happen in Ifryn's apartments? Thirdly, there was something he had found by accident in the Chancellor's study. It looked like a glass paperweight with a playing card embedded within, but the curious thing was that the illustration on the card looked like a remarkably realistic picture of Fyles, Ifryn's late father. It might just be a meaningless trifle – but Southan had his doubts.

In fact the Emperor's mind was suddenly full of doubts about Verkho. He longed for someone he could trust, someone he could turn to. But they had all deserted him.

Baylin returned to The Silent Woman with a heavy heart. The news he bore was not what Ifryn was hoping for. The evening was drawing in, and Delmege and Vrila were already asleep when he entered the room.

'What is it?' Ifryn asked quickly, seeing his grave expression.

'My lady, I'm so sorry . . . your mother is dead.'

'Oh.' For a moment she felt only relief, for which she

was quickly ashamed. She had feared for Azari, and for Kerrell.

'She was poisoned by wine – in your apartments.'

'So Corton was right,' Ifryn said quietly. 'Poor Mama.' Strangely, she did not feel like crying. Zephia would be happier reunited with Fyles, and Ifryn had too much else on her mind. There would be time for mourning later. After a long pause, she asked, 'Did you find Dsordas Nyun?'

'I did,' Baylin replied. 'More by luck than judgement. We can go there now if you wish.'

Leaving the girls in Doneta's care, they walked through the still lively streets to the tavern near the south gate. Baylin had made himself known first to Acevedo, and then to Yeori, who had decided he was a man worth listening to. Thus when they arrived there was no problem getting past the inconspicuous civilian guards arranged by the guide to protect his clients.

The door of their room was opened by Yeori, and all six travellers were waiting inside. Fen and Ifryn recognized each other immediately.

'You!' they cried simultaneously.

'This is the Lady Mehtar . . .' Baylin began.

'No,' Ifryn said softly. 'She knows who I am.'

'Ifryn?' Fen whispered. 'The *Empress* Ifryn?'

The other woman bowed her head in acknowledgement.

When their initial astonishment had passed, the two parties exchanged their stories. Fen and Ifryn did most of the talking, each instinctively liking and trusting the other. The travellers were all amazed and appalled by a side of Xantium they could never have imagined, and the Empress was equally moved by their tales of dangers and separation, of magic and prophecy. Before long there was an unspoken agreement between them to work together for the release of Azari and Bowen especially – but also against their common foe. They had just begun to discuss what their next steps should be when they were interrupted by a newcomer who rose up through the floor, silencing them all in shock.

'Mama,' Ifryn breathed.

Zephia's ghost scowled at her daughter, and her lips moved.

'What?' Gaye said.

The spectre turned to the blind girl and spoke silently again.

'I don't understand,' Gaye responded.

'You can hear her?' Ifryn was astonished, but was silenced by signs from the others.

The phantom vanished in the next instant, with not so much as a glance at her daughter.

'What did she say?' Ifryn asked.

'She was complaining that she couldn't find her husband,' Gaye reported. 'She said he should be there somewhere, but that he'd disappeared. She sounded as if he'd done it on purpose, to escape from her.'

'My father died some time ago,' Ifryn said. 'He *should* be there.'

'How can a ghost disappear?' Fen wondered, but no one answered her. The next moment there was a knock on the door, and everyone tensed, but relaxed when they heard Acevedo's voice.

'It's only me,' he called.

Yeori opened the door and the guide came in.

'I've just heard a bit of news,' he informed them. 'I thought you ought to know. Verkho's challenge has been taken up by someone else. There's going to be another match.'

CHAPTER FORTY-SEVEN

Forgive me. I, of all people, should have known the ways of augury. I should have prayed to Meyu, not to Zidon.

I can no longer fly. Is that punishment enough? What else will be reversed before my end?

'No!' Gaye cried. 'This can't happen!' Surely all their efforts could not have been entirely in vain. 'What went wrong?'

Dsordas thought he knew, and told the others what he had seen.

Aad was confused.

'But if there was more magical interference, why didn't I feel it? Why didn't the detector say anything?'

'And why didn't anyone else see the hand?' Fen wondered.

'I'm still not even sure *I* saw it,' Dsordas said.

'Perhaps you were the only one *meant* to see it,' Gaye put in. There was silence as everyone considered this. Eventually they decided that they could make no sense of the phantom hand or its purpose, and returned to more pressing matters.

'Do you know who the challenger is?' Baylin asked.

'Someone called Martyn Waysinger,' Acevedo replied.

'Gods!'

'The Swordsman?' Ifryn exclaimed. *Truly, a dangerous ally.*

'We've got to stop him,' Baylin said, echoing the thoughts of everyone in the room.

'It's too late now,' Acevedo told him. 'The match is set

for midnight tonight, less than an hour away. The Hall'll
be full already.'

'I've got to try,' Baylin decided, then turned to Ifryn.
'You'll stay here?'

The Empress nodded, and Baylin left hurriedly. No
one expected him to succeed. All they could do now was
hope that Martyn would win.

'What is he playing for?' Ifryn asked.

'Verkho's life,' the guide answered.

Martyn had easily escaped from the soldiers earlier that
day, and had later heard of Dsordas' victory from
someone who claimed to have witnessed it in person.
The Swordsman rejoiced in the blow struck against the
Empire, but regretted that more concession had not
been forced from Verkho. Then Martyn began to
speculate. If Dsordas had won, why shouldn't *he*? The
more he thought about it, the more the idea appealed to
the gambler in him. After the failed assassination
attempt, he was willing to try anything.

He went to see a woman of his acquaintance, whose
hatred for the Chancellor was as virulent as his own. She
was also in bad health and living in abject poverty, her
only income her pitiful earnings as a whore. It took some
time to get her to agree to wager her life on his skill,
but the doubly pleasurable prospect of Verkho's death
and the large sum of money Martyn would also demand
on her behalf finally persuaded her. After that it had
been easy to get a message to the Chancellor – who
had jumped at the opportunity of another chance.

Now, as he sat at the table in the Great Dice Hall,
surrounded by a crowd who could not believe their luck
at witnessing such an exciting double spectacle, Martyn
was feeling confident. His one regret was that he had not
been able to bring his sword inside with him. He would
have taken immense pleasure in butchering Verkho
before an audience such as this, but the Hall's regu-
lations meant that he would have to wait.

There was a stir as Verkho arrived in his chair, but as soon as he entered the hall, he rose and strode to the table where a new set of counters had been set out. Once more the conditions of the match were announced.

'If I win,' Martyn restated, 'your life is forfeit. I may kill you without fear of any penalty of law. You agree to this?'

'I do,' Verkho replied evenly. 'If I win, the woman's life is similarly mine to do with as I choose.'

'It is.'

'Does she agree?'

The woman rose from her seat, and pushed back the hood which had covered her face.

'I do,' she said. 'Remember me, Chancellor?'

For a long moment Verkho did not speak. Then he sounded surprised.

'Maissa?'

Maissa Uldara had been seduced by Verkho eleven years earlier and then exiled with her falsely disgraced father. Her seducer had subsequently taken her father's position in the Imperial Treasury – one of his first steps on the road to power.

'I had not realized that you had returned from your travels,' the Chancellor said pleasantly.

The audience buzzed with speculation at this latest intrigue as Maissa sat down without another word and the game began. Both men played cautiously at the start but, for all his outward calm, it was clear that the Chancellor had been disconcerted by the visitor from his past. Martyn's pile grew steadily and his confidence rose even higher – and then, as the Swordsman's thoughts took over, a series of rash bets and unwise bluffs suddenly changed the course of the match. But the Swordsman was unable to return to Martyn's more sensible way of playing and the more knowledgeable gamblers in the audience were already certain of the outcome.

When at last Martyn was forced into wagering all his

remaining counters on a holding of five stars, he was
certain that he was back in with a chance. But it came as
little surprise to others that Verkho held five stars *and* a
pair of emperors. The game was over.

Verkho stood and beckoned to his escort. As the
soldiers dragged Maissa away, she screamed and
struggled, but their strength was more than equal to the
task. The Chancellor gave Martyn one last, venomous
look which said, as clearly as if the words had been
spoken aloud, *I will not forget you.* Then he stalked from
the hall, leaving the Swordsman stunned and unable to
move.

Under Shinasi's dome of protection, Verkho made his
way back to The Domain. Now that he was assured of
success, he put some long-laid plans into operation.
Coded messages were sent to all of 'his' men within the
army and other parts of the administration. The Empire
would soon be his to command. And his alone.

Southan was roused from his lonely bed and put under
arrest. Azari remained in the Emperor's quarters, and a
guard was posted on the door. Anyone who remained
stubbornly loyal to Southan was either killed in the
sporadic fighting which spread throughout the court
and The Domain, imprisoned, or forced to flee to the
outer regions of the city. The senior commanders of
the coup were delighted by the success of their strategy
and were soon able to go to the Chancellor's study to
report their triumph. However, they were unable to do
so; Verkho had sealed the room with only him and
Maissa inside.

'I got there too late,' Baylin explained. 'There was
nothing I could do.'

It was a strange group gathered now in the islanders'
room. Their faces were grim, and the air was full of
dread. On his way back from the Great Dice Hall,
Baylin had been able to contact Kerrell, who had joined

the others. The General was filthy and unkempt, having spent the last two days in some of the deeper tunnels under Xantium's main hill. He and Ifryn had greeted each other warmly, and Fen had not been the only one to see the look in their eyes as they embraced.

Nothing of what was happening in the court had so far reached their ears but even Kerrell, who had only just been told what Gaye had discovered, was aware that they would have to move fast or not at all.

'So it must begin,' he decided soberly. 'I had hoped to avoid this, but we have no choice now. If only Southan had seen sense.'

'We didn't make it easy for him,' Ifryn said. Then she added prophetically, 'He'll soon learn the price of his folly.'

'There's nothing for it now,' Baylin agreed. 'If we're to have any chance of stopping Verkho, we have to fight.'

'What about Martyn?' Ifryn asked. 'Surely we can't rely on him now.'

'We'll contact his deputy,' Baylin said. 'Get him to organize the Swordsman's allies.'

'Where is he?' Kerrell asked.

'Sagar? I can reach him at Myla's place . . .'

'Did you say Sagar?' Nason burst out. 'Sagar Folegandros?'

Baylin looked at the astonished faces of the islanders.

'Yes,' he replied. 'Do you know him?'

'He's my brother,' Nason said.

'And Bowen's brother too,' Gaye added.

'We thought he was with the hostages,' Dsordas explained.

'He may have been once,' Baylin said. 'But not any more.'

'I'll come with you when you go to see him,' Nason said. No one even thought to argue with the boy.

'Let's go then,' Kerrell said with solemn finality.

'What can we do to help?' Dsordas asked quickly.

'This is going to get ugly,' the General told him. 'Are you sure you want to be involved?'

'Yes.' Dsordas spoke with certainty for all of them.

'So be it. And welcome.' Kerrell had already come to like and respect the islanders, even though he did not understand all they had told him. 'I hope when this is over – one way or another – that we are all able to meet again, in happier circumstances.'

A brief discussion followed and then they went their separate ways.

The civil war began.

The talisman lay on the Chancellor's desk, waiting.

One last libation, he thought. *What you desire shall be yours.*

He looked at the pathetic creature who would provide the means to this end, and felt no pity for her, only disgust. He could not imagine how he had ever found her attractive. Maissa was cowering now, trembling and weeping, but when he told her to come to him, she looked up with naked hatred in her red-rimmed eyes.

'I am no longer willing,' she hissed.

'That is irrelevant,' he told her. 'You were when the bargain was made. You have no choice now but to keep it.'

'Murderer!' she screamed. 'I curse you. I have hated you every waking hour of my life. I will not aid you now.'

Verkho smiled.

'You never could resist these eyes.' As he spoke, Maissa could not help but be trapped once more by his glittering stare. All will drained out of her and she stepped forward to her fate, knowing that she would die unavenged.

The heavy, razor-sharp blade did its work, and Verkho filled a silver chalice with bright red blood as the last moments of Maissa's life ebbed away. The Chancellor turned, his victim forgotten, and poured the warm liquid over the talisman. It burned away to nothing as it touched the sphere in an incandescent blaze. When the chalice was empty, Verkho gazed mesmerized. The last of the glass-like covering was gone and now, as he watched, the metal shield on which the riddles had been written slewed off like a snake's skin, revealing a milk-white orb within.

In the next instant, the room was full of the most appalling noise Verkho had ever heard, a mixture of wild anger, sudden fierce joy and a thousand howls of feral agony. In amongst the cacophony an ancient voice said, 'You go to the ocean blind.' An ages-old curse was being redeemed, reversed.

The talisman *blinked*. Gar's single eye opened and looked at the world anew.

CHAPTER FORTY-EIGHT

It takes shape now: the formless grey has a name, and an identity. War brings a false dawn, carried on a warm breeze. In this light not even a beacon may shine.

On a foul midden heap near the Stadium, something stirred.

Nearby, the caged animals which were kept for contests in the slaughter-pit, shifted restlessly in the pre-dawn gloom, sniffing the air as if there were a new scent in the world. The pit-master had been gathering wild and ferocious creatures for the gladiatorial battles against the slaughtermen, one of the most eagerly awaited public events of the Grand Tournament. And it would indeed be quite a show but, as even the pit-master would admit, there would be nothing to match the fight held two months before. Then the spectacle had climaxed with the appearance of a 'sea-dragon', a monstrous lizard of prodigious strength and poisonous fangs. It had provided the crowds with splendid, bloodthirsty entertainment, killing several of the city's best slaughtermen before succumbing to archers and a heavy sword.

After the sea-dragon had been killed, the pit-master had discovered that the creature had been female. Inside the mutilated carcass there had been half a dozen eggs with soft, leathery but impenetrable skins. He had kept them warm for a time, hoping they would hatch and provide future sport, but nothing had happened, and in the end he had given up and thrown them away.

Now the malleable shells that had proved impervious to any blade were cut through easily from within by black talons. Six miniature copies of the dead mother emerged from the mucus, burrowed up from the rotting debris and looked about them with small red eyes, their fangs bared in square snouts.

The newly hatched monsters were ready to explore the world. They were inquisitive, fearless and possessed of unnatural strength and speed. They were also very hungry.

An eerie silence had fallen in the ministry complex, and guards and officials looked at one another, anticipating the worst. But nothing happened. All the talents had become quiet; there was no screaming any more, no hysterical laughter, no insane, one-sided conversations. But they were not asleep. All those not already part of an experiment seemed to have entered a catatonic state, and just stared into space, hardly even breathing, their bodies rigid. Indeed, some were not breathing; they simply died where they sat, destroyed by a force no one could understand.

Harios was frantic. What was going on? From cell to cell it was the same story, as though the final nightmare had arrived. Whatever they had been afraid of had arrived at last.

All was silent. But Harios, who only a short time ago would have wished devoutly for such a situation, now felt the stillness to be a deception and could not escape the feeling that an explosion was coming. The air was full of waiting.

One talent was still awake. Contrary as always, Bowen was suddenly alert – helplessly aware that his sanity had returned to him in a single moment. He knew where he was, but the past two months were nothing more than a blur. Magic had been part of it, he knew – but that was alien to him now. The only thing that was clear was that he had to get out of this place, to escape, and get back to Gaye. *Gaye!* He whispered her name aloud, once more feeling all the agonies of their separation, raging at the injustice done to them. He longed to hold her again, to tell her how much he loved her. Bowen felt cold, and very afraid.

What am I supposed to do now?

At that moment, he was startled to see a ghost appear through the wall of his cell, bringing back memories of Zalys, of unwanted feelings and half-heard conversations. The man, who was dressed in military uniform, beckoned to the prisoner and Bowen sensed, rather than heard, his instruction to follow. The spectre slipped through the closed door.

Easier for you than for me.

Follow.

Bowen tried the handle and found, to his amazement, that the door was unlocked. He opened it and followed the ghost down the corridor. Everywhere was quiet, and his footsteps echoed down the hallways of stone.

Their route twisted and turned, took them up and down stairways and finally led to a dank tunnel, which seemed even less hospitable than the rest. It was of older construction, and the bars in the cell doors were of thick iron. The phantom guide pointed into one room, then vanished.

When Bowen looked through the bars, he was startled to see the face of a woman on the other side, only a handspan away from his own. She smiled.

'A true beacon still.'

'What?'

'You are a beacon,' she explained patiently, making no sense. 'You must learn to use your light wisely.'

'Who are you?' he breathed. Something about her was familiar, but he could not remember why.

'My name is Alasia. You are the builder of circles.'

'Circles?' A few details were slowly falling into place in Bowen's newly awakened mind. He had been linking with others, trying to prevent . . . what? The cold realization of failure washed over him.

'Magic exacts its own price,' Alasia told him. 'A circle only has one side, but you can travel round it in two ways. And when it is broken, there is a distortion in the fabric of the world which normality corrects – but so quickly and so violently that just for a moment it achieves the opposite of its original purpose.'

'A backlash?' Bowen asked. 'You mean when I was trying . . . but then I was stopped . . . I actually *helped*?' He felt revulsion at the very idea. His own efforts had been turned against him.

'Verkho used those backlashes,' Alasia said, liking the word. 'Now we must too.'

'No! I can't.' Bowen's entire being was rebelling. He didn't want to act, didn't want to get involved. He wanted to be safe. 'I can't!'

He ran away blindly. Alasia looked after him, and her eyes were sad.

'Baylin! Thank the gods you're here,' Sagar burst out. 'What's going on? I . . .' He stopped abruptly, and stared at his other visitor.

Baylin had thought he might need to introduce them, but saw the recognition in their eyes and knew this would not be necessary. They had been seven and thirteen years old respectively when they had last met, but there was no doubting that they were brothers.

'You've grown,' Sagar said.

'So have you,' Nason replied.

The awkward moment ended with two young men in each other's arms, speechless through having too much to say.

At least one small piece of good has come out of this mess, Baylin thought, watching.

'You'll have time to talk later,' he told them firmly. 'Right now we have pressing business. Including trying to get your other brother out!'

*   *   *

The men had all gone. Gaye sat, slumped in misery, while Fen stared out of the window, trying to see a little of what was going on. She felt aggrieved at having been left behind like this – but someone had to stay with Gaye, and it was true that the others would be of more use in a sword fight. Even so . . .

There was a sudden knock on the door, followed by Acevedo's voice. He sounded breathless.

'There's a visitor for you.'

Fen opened the door to find Ifryn standing there, her face flushed with resentment.

'So they left you here too!' the Empress exclaimed. 'Men!'

'A battle is no place for ladies,' Acevedo tried to placate them.

Fen looked at him thoughtfully.

'You think so?' she asked, exchanging glances with Ifryn. 'Acevedo, stay here with Gaye. You're to look after her, you understand?'

Gaye said nothing, but reached instinctively for her pendant.

'Wait!' the guide called. 'Where are you going?'

'To get my baby back,' Ifryn said.

At the old temple, reality shifted.

No one was there to witness it, but Gaye – who now clutched her amberine pendant – heard their voices, and was terrified.

You have broken the eternal laws, Zidon declared. *Now your folly is turned against you and you must pay the price.*

I upheld the laws, Meyu objected. *If the dice had not fallen so . . .*

That was the bargain, the goddess countered. *You cannot cheat Elcar's fire. Your hand is tainted now. Gar will return. Your meddling has been to no avail, and soon you will have to face him once more.*

397

Gaye discovered then that it was possible for even a god to feel afraid.

News of Southan's arrest spread quickly because Verkho had commanded that it should. This was a miscalculation. The Chancellor held a firm grip on the army, especially those units based in The Domain, but Kerrell gained more recruits because of the direct challenge to imperial sovereignty. Few unbiased citizens looked forward to being ruled by Verkho, and so the renegade General's rallying cry was more effective than it would otherwise have been.

Even so, Kerrell knew that he would only be able to muster a fraction of the forces ranged against him – and his enemies would have the advantage of defending the higher ground from the inner walls. His only hope was a concentrated assault aimed at Verkho himself. Kill the Chancellor, and there was every chance that the tide would turn.

However, once the first fateful steps had been taken, the General found that he could not control the progress of the battle. His 'army' consisted not of well-disciplined soldiers, but of a ragbag of loyal officers, assorted malcontents and a few nobles with more ambition than imagination, plus a large number of citizens who were just along for the ride. Because of this, as the fighting spread across the rich district of The Circle, the skirmishes often degenerated into a struggle to protect vested interests from those who were more concerned with possible looting, rather than with who sat on the imperial throne.

The situation was made even more confusing by the outlying city garrisons, those based near the Great Gates and around the outer walls. Initially most of these had sided with Verkho, but some units mutinied when they sensed popular opinion, disposed of the Chancellor's lackeys, and chose their own allegiances.

In The Levels, where little fighting took place but

rumour nonetheless ran riot, most citizens hid behind closed doors and shutters. They did not understand the reasons for the conflict – nor did they know who was on what side. Even those engaged in the battle could rarely be certain who was friend and who was foe. In a single night, Xantium had gone from carnival gaiety to the fearful uncertainty of war.

After leaving the inn, Fen let Ifryn take the lead. This was her city, after all. Quite why the two women trusted and felt so much for each other was not clear to either of them – but it was undoubtedly the reason they were together now. Fen was as determined to get Azari out as Ifryn was – and the Empress would do all she could to further the islanders' cause.

'Where are we going?' Fen asked.

'To find Grongar. He has three of his dogs with him.'

'Dogs? How can they help us?'

A little while later, Fen regarded Shark and the other two hounds as their master held their leashes.

'Oh,' she said. 'I see.'

'The Circle's easy enough, even now – if we pick the right route,' Grongar told them. 'Then if we can get into The Domain, pick up the rest of the pack . . .'

'The wine-cellars!' Corton was there too, looking pale and frightened. 'I can show you a route into The Domain. The doors are locked, but I still have the keys.'

Grongar looked at his friend, and smiled.

'We'll make a warrior of you yet,' he said. 'Come on.'

And so the wine-master led them underground into the cold stone tunnels, onward to the vast echoing cellars – deserted now – and then up towards the court. Above ground once more, Grongar took a careful look around.

'Where are we?'

'Outside the southeast quadrant of the court,' Ifryn replied. 'The hostage enclave is that way. The entrance to the court is down there.'

'Which is it to be?' the barbarian asked.

399

'Who stays here?' Fen put in quickly. 'We need someone to make sure we can still get out later.'

'I will,' Corton volunteered. 'I can keep the doors locked against anyone else, and keep a look out for you.'

'Good. We're too far from the kennels here,' Grongar went on. 'We'll have to make do with these three.' The hounds growled and whined, straining at their leashes. For some reason, he was having trouble controlling them.

'The hostage enclave is empty now, isn't it?' Fen said. 'Can we get into the court from there?'

'We can try,' Ifryn replied, and led the way.

There was a six-man sentry detail at the southern entrance to the enclave, even though it was supposedly empty. Grongar released the hounds and, at his command, they attacked in a frenzy. One man was thrown down, his throat ripped out, and the others fled in panic with the dogs in furious pursuit. Grongar ran after them, trying to call the hounds back, but they would not obey, and easily outdistanced their master.

Fen and Ifryn were left alone, the way into the enclave open to them. They glanced resignedly at the torn and bleeding body and at the barbarian's retreating figure, and made up their minds. The Empress relieved the dead man of his short sword – Fen already had her own knife – and they went through the gate into an alien world, which had obviously been hastily abandoned. The enclave covered a large area, and it took the two women some time to find the other exits, but eventually they surprised themselves by being able to walk into the court without hindrance. The gateway through its outer wall was unguarded.

'Where will Azari be?' Fen asked.

'In my husband's apartments,' Ifryn replied. 'At least that's where he *was*. This way.'

Kerrell and two of his officers stood atop one of the battlements of The Domain's outer wall, looking

400

inwards across the ring to the court and The Spires beyond. Nearby, already confused by the first run of fighting, Dsordas, Yeori and Aad stood together, waiting to be told what to do next. Kerrell was planning the routes, both over and underground, by which his main forces would travel through The Domain and then on to assault the court defences. But before he had finished the hurried consultation, Aad cried out, glanced at his hands, then stared up at the hill. All eyes turned to follow the boy's gaze.

'Too late,' Dsordas breathed.

A vast, transparent dome had flickered into existence, covering the whole of the court to its outer wall, and also enclosing The Spires. It flashed and flickered like liquid fire, and cast a ruddy glow over the whole city. A warm breeze blew down the hill towards them.

CHAPTER FORTY-NINE

Memories awaken, like a melting glacier, and flow in icy torrents. What chance have ants before such a flood?

Verkho reverently picked up the newly living talisman. He touched it gingerly, almost expecting it to be soft and wet, but the eye was cold, dry and as hard as stone. Gar and the Chancellor looked at each other.

'You are mine,' Verkho exulted. 'Your power is mine!'

The eye blinked again. The god had been blind and asleep for so long that he had forgotten his predicament. He would need to humour his mortal saviour for a while – until he was able to create a new body for himself. Then this human would learn all about the *real* nature of power.

Gar was already beginning to remember the world, to feel his effect upon it. But he could afford to wait. It would amuse him to do so. After the sightless realm of the dark ocean, the place of his awakening was interesting. It was like an anthill, crawling with insignificant mortals who scurried to and fro on pathetic errands of their own. He would soon show them their place. When he was ready.

Verkho was distracted by the noise of fighting. He put down the talisman – Gar had allowed the manhandling, knowing that *this* human could be useful for a time – and went to the window. The signs of battle put the Chancellor into a fury. Who dared to oppose him? They would pay dearly!

He took up the eye again, feeling the almost infinite potency that lay at his fingertips. Taking but a fraction of that power, he shaped it, via a well-practised art. The group of comatose talents, their minds blood-linked, directed the energy, as they had done previously to protect the Chancellor's study and other small spaces. This time, however, there was no need of such restrictions. Verkho gave the instructions and felt a rush of triumph as the circles moved to obey, taking all the power they needed, and creating a massive sphere which spread over all the court and The Spires like a dome, and which also reached underground to entrap some of the tunnels of the ministry complex. Its red fire would protect him from any foe beyond its borders, while he dealt with any left within. It was also sending a signal of his invincibility to all who cared to look.

Verkho laughed. *I have the power of a god!*

But even as the thought passed through his mind, one tiny corner, which he did his best to ignore, wondered if such power was only being lent to him on sufferance.

Pushing aside these petty doubts, the Chancellor prepared to demonstrate the inadvisability of opposing his will.

As dawn reached the outside world, Fen and Ifryn emerged cautiously into an open courtyard to find that the sky had turned red. They stared up in horror at the membrane of liquid, crimson fire – but that concern was immediately replaced by a more pressing problem. Two soldiers had entered the courtyard from the opposite side and were also looking up at the dome, but it could only be a matter of time before they saw the women.

'Come on,' Ifryn said determinedly.

'But . . .'

'Just follow my lead.' She strode out into the open, with Fen at her shoulder. The guards saw them, and stared in amazement at the approach of their Empress.

'I have returned, as you see,' Ifryn announced. 'No one shall escape the vengeance of my red fire.' She turned to Fen as the men continued to gaze at them like witless idiots. 'Wizardess, bring down the fire. Burn these two,' she commanded.

As Fen raised her arms to the crimson sky, light flashed like blood on the blade of her knife. She began to intone nonsense syllables, but the men did not wait to hear. They ran off, dropping their spears.

'Let's go,' Ifryn said, leading the way.

'That was taking a chance,' Fen told her as she hurried to keep up. 'I can't imagine anyone with less magic in them than me. What would we have done if they'd taken no notice?'

'I'd have killed them,' Ifryn replied simply.

They went on. Their goal was close now, and they managed to escape attention, but in order to reach Southan's quarters they had to pass a crowded guard-room. The men inside, still unaware of the latest events outside, were happy in the knowledge that Verkho's takeover had gone smoothly, and were looking forward to the benefits of having backed the right side.

'My turn,' Fen decided. Taking two full oil-lamps from their wall brackets, she crept up to the open door. Then, in one fluid, violent motion, she smashed both down in the threshold. Flames leapt up in a fierce barrier as the men swore and shouted in surprise.

'Wizard's fire!' Fen yelled above the noise. 'Its touch is death!'

The two women ran on, down another corridor. The entrance to the Emperor's chambers was only a short distance away now. A surreptitious look showed Fen that there were two guards on the door, but there was no way to approach unnoticed.

'I think it's time the Empress really *did* return,' Ifryn said.

With that she walked out into the open and marched boldly towards the men, with Fen close behind her. The soldiers tensed, their spears held ready, not sure what to make of this invasion.

'I wish to see my husband and my son,' Ifryn commanded with all the authority she could muster.

The sentries were at a loss. None of their orders had concerned the reappearance of the Empress.

'No one may enter,' one replied uncertainly. 'Southan and Azari are under arrest.'

'Then arrest me too,' Ifryn said impatiently. 'But let me pass.'

'There are new rulers here now, my . . . lady,' the other man said. 'You no longer have authority over us.'

'I *will* see my son,' she assured him. 'Do you dare hinder me?' She was only a few paces away now. The men had lowered their spears threateningly, but hesitated. Ifryn went on. In an instant, the sword which had hung limply from her hand was wielded in a sharp downward stroke and a spear shattered, falling from the soldier's grasp. The Empress turned to the other man, furious determination blazing from her eyes.

'Get out of my way!'

Years of ingrained obedience made him falter, but the other guard was now attempting to draw his sword. Fen flew at him, her blonde hair whirling as her knife slashed at his arm, and the impetus of her attack toppled them both to the ground. At the same time Ifryn stepped aside from a feeble spear thrust and lashed out, putting all her strength into the blow. The disconcerted sentry tried to parry her blade, but only succeeded in deflecting it upwards. The sword bit deep into his neck and he collapsed, blood gushing from his wound.

'I *will* see my child,' Ifryn reaffirmed, pulling free and turning to find that Fen had also won her duel, her knife stained from a fatal stab to the man's heart. The Empress took her friend's hand and pulled her up, remembering Doneta's words. *Women have their ways too. If there's any killing to be done, we'll not shy away from our part.*

The key was in the lock and Ifryn turned it immediately, throwing the doors open.

Alerted by the noise of their struggle, Southan was just inside, holding a broken chair leg like a club, ready to defend himself and his heir with any available weapon. He almost struck out reflexively, but then saw who it was.

'Ifryn!' he cried, then threw down the wood and embraced her as the bloody sword fell from her hand.

'Azari,' she said urgently. 'Where is he?'

Southan pointed and she ran to her son, while the Emperor stared at the unknown Fen, who was now at the door, watching to see whether any more guards were coming. Inside the adjoining chamber, Azari lay in his cot, while the wet nurse cowered in a corner. Ifryn paid the woman no attention, scooped up her baby, and returned. Southan was still stunned and unable to speak. He had so much to apologize for, to explain, that he did not know where to begin. His wife saw the familiar confusion in his eyes.

'First things first,' she said. 'Let's get out of here.'

Acevedo had described the lurid red dome to Gaye, but she had not really needed his awed words. She was still holding the amberine crystal and was lost in the netherworld, and there the sphere of power was clear to her, like a vile stain upon the world. She knew also that Bowen was inside – and her only concern was to get him out. Ignoring everything else, she focused on him, imploring him to hear.

Bowen was back in the ministry complex, which was the nearest thing he had to familiar territory. It was still very quiet, and in several rooms groups of unconscious talents lay in unnatural slumber, their blood mingling. Bowen ignored them. A faraway voice in his head was telling him what to do, and she was the only one he was prepared to listen to now. He found the room where the toads were kept. There was no one about, so he slipped inside and picked up one of the vials which the keepers stored on a wooden bench. Removing the stopper with great care, he sniffed cautiously. Then he sealed the vial again, and set out once more.

The appearance of the red dome had slowed the progress of the battle outside. When it had come into being, matching the circle of the court's outer wall almost exactly, many of Verkho's men had been caught on one side or the other. Some had even been thrown from the parapets by the force of its creation. This self-evident disregard for his own men, plus the ever-growing doubts about Verkho's real intentions and his unearthly sorcery, made many decide that this was a conflict not worth fighting. Although the situation remained very confused, many local truces were agreed, and the violence lessened as more and more people began to realize where their best interests lay. And this process was accelerated when a few pieces of red fire broke away from the dome, flying out like shooting stars and landing at random on various parts of the city. The fires thus started were small but fierce, and some spread rapidly, increasing the general dread and turmoil.

Kerrell was still at his vantage point on the Domain wall when the fireballs began. Messengers were coming and going, keeping him informed of the progress of the diminishing battle.

'Gods! What now?' the General exclaimed as a red thunderbolt flew overhead.

'How can you fight that?' Yeori asked quietly.

'We have to somehow,' Dsordas said.

They were interrupted then by Grongar, who toiled up the steps, quite out of breath. Between gasps, he told them how he had helped Fen and Ifryn, but how, after they reached the hostage enclave, the hounds had become uncontrollable.

'They're running wild now,' the barbarian said. 'I can't

do anything with them.' He sounded bewildered by the dogs' inexplicable betrayal.

His audience had listened, aghast, but now returned to their primary concern.

'So did Fen and Ifryn come back with you?' Kerrell asked.

'Where are they now?' Dsordas demanded.

Reluctantly, Grongar pointed up the hill.

'In there,' he said.

CHAPTER FIFTY

*The stone eye watches my friends. I am free as long as
they still fly, but how much longer can I protect them now
that the strange winds blow?*

Gaye knew now that they could never beat Verkho. The
power he controlled was unimaginably vast, and when he
learnt to wield it effectively . . .

To oppose it will take a circle of all the world. Gaye
recalled the ghost's words, and dismissed them as asking
the impossible. She had her own set of priorities now,
which could no longer be ignored.

Clutching the amberine tightly, she concentrated
fiercely on Bowen, knowing that he heard her – but only
faintly. There were other voices in the void, pleading,
begging for her help, but they were no longer her
concern. Even if the world was to end, the only thing
that mattered now was that she and Bowen saw it end
together.

Choose a story. Make it real.

This time the story was from her own memory; she
had no need of ghostly advice. This story would be for
her.

Bowen had reached the point of no return. In his
wanderings through the Ministry corridors, he had seen
only a few nervous officials – who had completely
ignored him – and had caught a glimpse of a man he
thought he recognized from his recent experience. The
one called Martyn. But now he was alone. The tunnel

ahead of him was blocked by a pulsating shield of red, flowing like the blood of mountains. He felt its power rejecting his approach, felt the pressure, pain and malice directed towards him. Pushing on until he could bear it no more, Bowen halted some six paces away.

Now, the voice in his head urged. *You need the fire now*.

He took out the vial, unstoppered it and gulped down the disgusting grey nectar before he had time to think. His hands twisted as he felt it burning through his veins, filling him with agony.

Gaye's distant voice began the tale of how the white fire had breached the seal between realms so that others could escape. But this time the story twisted. This time it was the bearer of the white fire himself who escaped, using his pain to force a path through.

Bowen sensed the flames begin, saw the light that he was creating reflected off walls, floor, ceiling. Even the red barrier was tinged with pink. Through his anguish he strained to hear the story and to believe in it. A sudden vision of a multitude of ghosts – both in the old temple in Xantium and the Arena on Zalys – gave him strength. He took a pace forward, staggered, and almost fell. Another pace; the pain doubled. He wanted to turn and find a place to hide, but the remorseless voice drew him on. Two more steps. He was almost there now. White fire and red were almost touching.

Another pace. The torment was unbearable now, every nerve end screaming. Bowen saw only a haze of burning blood. He could only move his feet by edging them forward, sliding them agonizingly over the stone floor.

Fire met fire, exploding in shards of light, heat and pain. Bowen cried out and hurled himself forward, collapsing in a trembling, exhausted heap. *Outside* the shield. The white flames burned away to nothing, leaving him drained. He crawled on, moving away from the red glare. When he was out of the range of its immediate malice, he stopped, wanting to sleep. But the voice was still there, and he knew he could not rest until he was with her. That was all that mattered now. Slowly, his every movement marked by searing stabs of torment, Bowen got to his feet and began walking.

The talisman watched Verkho with cruel but indulgent amusement. Gar's rescuer saw so little, even though he now had access to so much. How limited his ambitions were! Why had he gone through all that pain and trouble if he was incapable of enjoying his success? The only things Verkho had asked for, except power for the shield, were those few things that could not be granted; his lost fourteen years of life, his telekinetic talent, even the simple healing of his damaged hand – all these were forfeit to the ancient bargain and could not be restored.

For his part, the Chancellor knew that he must be careful what he asked for. Each wish demanded that he be able to control the power released, and each might bring unforeseen consequences. He could not simply say, for example, 'Make me immortal,' if by doing so he condemned himself to live for ever in a decaying body, racked by endless pain and infirmity. In fact the more he thought about it, the more pitfalls he saw, pitfalls he had chosen not to recognize during his pursuit of the talisman's secrets. But secure inside his burning globe, he was content to wait and learn slowly.

And all the while, Gar learnt with him. The god was particularly intrigued by the bats; they should have been his creatures – like all the rest – but somehow they eluded his influence. He amused himself by producing strange winds, that blew them off course. And waited.

At first, the crimson dome had been a fascinating spectacle for the beleaguered citizens of Xantium. To many, it seemed to resemble the curved roof of a particularly impressive temple, with the half-seen outlines of The Spires within making it appear all the more mysterious. For a time it provided fodder for gossip and speculation, wonder as well as fear. But as the day drew on, the onlookers began to regard it differently. The first few fireballs caused limited damage, but demonstrated hostile intent – or at least primeval indifference – towards Xantium's population.

However, even that began to seem less significant when the rumours of the dragons began to spread. Everyone had either seen or heard about the sea-dragon which had fought so viciously in the slaughter-pit two months ago. Now, it was whispered, there were others loose in the city, eating any living thing they could catch and growing at an incredible rate. It was said that their fangs held a venom so deadly that even a small scratch was fatal.

Most people dismissed such stories as fantastic, weak-minded nonsense, until they realized that there were other changes too. Huge rats and other vermin were becoming more adventurous, marauding even in daylight. Some animals, destined for the slaughter-pit, had escaped, spreading more wild tales in their wake, and the pit-master was nowhere to be found. Swarms of hornets and other stinging insects added to the terrors of the open spaces, and even the most domesticated animals seemed restless, disobedient and prone to sudden violence.

When, later in the morning, the occasional fiery thunderbolt from the dome had become first a steady stream and then a positive hail of incendiary magic, panic filled the city. There was not enough water – always a precious commodity in Xantium – to control all the fires, and soon some districts, where the buildings were primarily made of wood, were ablaze. Flames leapt across the narrow alleyways as people fled to safer neighbourhoods, carrying what few belongings they could.

A warm wind blew from the direction of the red-crested hill, and brought madness with it. All Xantium was being infested with a malice that was more than human.

Even inside the court, where the inhabitants were safe from such predations, people were afraid. They had supported Verkho because of their own lust for power or wealth, but no one had expected *this*. The barrier that trapped them inspired all kinds of terrors, and as a consequence very few people were prepared to go anywhere near it.

Thus it was that when, by a combination of stealth and the occasional determined violence from Fen and the newly valiant Southan, the fugitives reached the southern gate to The Domain, there was nobody about to bar their flight. What *did* bar their way was the red fire. It spread across the open gateway like a film of living blood, malignant, implacable and apparently immovable.

The Emperor got closest, forcing his way towards it by sheer physical effort – but to no avail. When he was still four or five paces away, he had to retreat. But he refused to give up. He ran at the barrier, wielding his sword before him as if he would cut his way through the burning air, only to be thrown back violently, his blade cast aside like a windblown twig. Fen and Ifryn helped him up, glad to see that he had suffered no worse than cuts and bruises. They retreated to the temporary shelter of a deserted guardhouse to watch and hope.

'What do we do now? We can't just sit here until Verkho finds us.' Fen paused, wishing someone else would speak. 'Can we?'

CHAPTER FIFTY-ONE

The lungs of the world breathe in . . .

*The storm breaks, thunder echoing in the labyrinth.
But there is more to be heard than the sounds of fury. Can
I hear the music of the wind, the singing of the rain? They
must be there. All I have to do is listen.*

Breathe in . . . and breathe out fire.

Except for isolated incidents, all the fighting had
stopped. The battle was irrelevant now, having been
overtaken by events. For the citizens of Xantium,
survival was their only concern.

Baylin, with Sagar and Nason close behind, found
Kerrell's vantage point with some relief.

'All tunnels leading to the court are blocked,' he
reported. 'The dome reaches underground as well.'

'And no one can get near it,' Kerrell confirmed
grimly. Messengers from all around The Domain had
been telling him the same thing.

Dsordas groaned inwardly. The tunnels had been their
last hope. When Grongar had told them that Fen was
inside the court, he had immediately wanted to try and
get to her, but the General – who was just as concerned
about Ifryn – had counselled patience, awaiting further
information about the red screen. Now they had that information – and all it had done was make them all the
more certain that their task was impossible. The fire-
spitting shield was impenetrable. Dsordas' anguish, shot
through with rage against fate, was a white-hot pain
which he did his best to hold inside. Even the reunion

with Sagar did nothing to ease his distress or the pounding ache in his head.

Then, just as he thought he could contain it no longer, the world about him became silent, as if he had been struck deaf in an instant. His legs gave way beneath him and he knelt on the stones. Others started to his aid, but hesitated as a spectre appeared on the battlements before him. Even stranger was the fact that – even though it was broad daylight – the air about them was suddenly full of swirling bats.

'Mother!' Dsordas gasped. 'Help me.'

It is Fen who needs help. His mother's ghostly eyes were full of patience and love, as well as a deep concern.

'Is she hurt?' he asked quickly. 'How can I help?'

Listen to the bats.

'What?' He was now utterly confused, as were all the onlookers, who could only hear his side of the conversation.

Into the silence came a complex filigree of sound, a spider's web of echoes that filled his head first with pictures, then with words. To Dsordas, the reverberations of the bats' cries became a new language, a new voice.

They speak for me, inside and out. This time it was not his mother who spoke.

'Who are you?'

I am Alasia, the voice replied impatiently. *You have work to do, healer. You must break the circle. The white one should have done it, but she is gone from me. So is the beacon.*

'I don't understand. What circle?' Dsordas wondered briefly whether 'the white one' meant Gaye.

When Alasia showed him the circle, he recoiled from its sickness. It was vast, corrupt and nauseating. Within it lay the hostages from Zalys, their blood mingling, blue fire now mixed with crimson.

Heal them.

'I can't. Wait!'

415

But Alasia and the voices of the bats had gone, and Dsordas found himself looking into the expectant face of his long-dead mother.

You are a healer, she told him. *Get on with it.*

He felt like a child again, but one with responsibilities no child should have to bear. How *could* he heal them? They were far away, and their illness was all-consuming.

He glanced up at the dome. How could he even contemplate breaching that vile shield? And yet Fen was inside . . .

Dsordas shut his eyes, reached into another world, unaware that Aad was warning the others to leave him alone. *Help me.* He found the hostages again, but did not know where to start. *It's too much,* he wailed silently, then felt the force of his mother's disapproval. She had been a healer too, and she expected her son to do what he could. *Eleven hostages,* he said to himself. *Start with one.*

Letting his awareness expand, Dsordas directed it towards one of the victims, and felt a horrendous jolt of sickness. How could they bear it? He let the tendrils slowly ease within the comatose body, sensed it tremble at his alien presence, and felt it respond to his prompting. The poison lost its potency by degrees, and the incision on the hostage's wrist closed by minute movements until the blood no longer flowed. The fire dimmed a fraction. *One down. Ten to go.* Dsordas moved on. He was already weary.

'Don't touch him!' Aad cried. 'Don't stop what he's doing! It's important.'

The others were all transfixed by the kneeling figure, the calm ghost and the whirling bats that surrounded him. Suddenly, Aad turned on his heels and ran, giving no explanation. No one else moved until Yeori, after a moment's indecision, tore himself away and ran after the boy.

*　　*　　*

The Swordsman held his breath while a pair of guards passed by, then slipped out of his hiding place and headed in the opposite direction. He swore silently, repetitively. Ever since he had killed Verkho's whore, he seemed to have been haunted by bad luck. Everything he had done had turned against him; even his few successes had turned sour. What was it she had said? *You can't go in there. Anyone who does will be cursed.*

And now, having got into the ministry complex earlier in the night, he found himself trapped, all the exits blocked by unnatural fire. The only way left for him to go was up, towards the court, but those passages were heavily guarded. Even so, the Swordsman intended to go that way eventually, in one last desperate attempt to reach Verkho. But before he did, he intended to create a little havoc of his own.

All the talents he had found so far had been unconscious and he had been unable to rouse them, but then he remembered Harios' section, where 'experiments' were taking place. If he could disrupt them, surely that would cause the diversion he needed, and possibly damage the Chancellor's plans too. He was nearly there now, treading softly through the silent corridors, his sword held ready. At the bottom of the final staircase, he paused, listening. All was quiet.

The first room he looked into was empty, but the next held a macabre scene. Eleven men and women, some little more than children, each with one arm extended, lay with blood oozing slowly from cuts in their wrists. The sluggish liquid ran towards a bowl in the centre of the chamber, where it burned with sorcerous fire. The Swordsman felt his gorge rise.

As good a place to start as any, he thought, then noticed that some of the cuts had healed over and were no longer bleeding. As he watched, another laceration closed and the fire dimmed a little.

Let's speed up the process a bit, he decided, and grabbed one of the prone figures, tossing him aside.

Five, Dsordas thought, fighting exhaustion. *Six more.* He was not sure it would be possible. Doggedly, he moved on again – and then gasped, feeling another presence, an elemental force, disrupting the circle – but violently, furiously, without healing. The hostages were being wrenched physically from their stone beds and thrown aside, awakening to agony and a slow, inevitable death. Those Dsordas had healed might have a chance of survival – but the others were beyond help now. The healer collapsed, his whole being crying out in horror, not knowing whether he had succeeded in breaking the circle.

The Swordsman went berserk. The revulsion he felt doubled each time he touched one of the sleeping victims. Those he moved shrieked and groaned, but he ignored them and carried on, seeing the vile flame sink lower and lower. As the last hostage was thrown down, the fire went out.

Outside, the corridor was suddenly full of noise. The talents were all waking up, and an explosion of diverse powers was released in an instant, with a sound that threatened to crush the world.

The Swordsman ran from the room, only to find soldiers crashing towards him from both directions. Even in his fighting fury, one blade was not enough against them all. In a welter of blood, Martyn's luck ran out. Permanently.

Aad ran, tracing the need through his hands. It led him to the focus of the magic, guided by the woman who spoke with the voice of bats. Halting breathlessly in front of the court's southern gate, he stared in awe at the red barrier. This was the closest he had been to the ever-shifting blur of power, and its ferocity scared him. His hands throbbed painfully.

Footsteps thudded up behind him but Aad did not bother to turn round.

'What're you doing?' Yeori gasped. 'What's going on?'

'I don't know. I just have to be here.'

At that moment, seen through the red veil, three figures emerged from a side building – a man and two women, one of them carrying a baby.

'That's Fen!' Yeori exclaimed.

'And Ifryn.'

'Now what do we do?'

The circle broke. Between them, Dsordas and Martyn had done enough. Aad felt the reversal in his hands, saw the fluttering of the backlash in the crimson pattern. The air was full of strange noises.

'Come on!' he yelled, beckoning wildly. 'Come through now! Fen!'

The three on the far side evidently heard him, but hesitated still. To them, the barrier looked no different.

'Quickly!' Aad screamed desperately, moving closer. 'It's *helping* you. This is your only chance!'

Yeori put a hand on the boy's arm, thinking he had gone mad.

But Fen reacted, throwing herself at the screen and finding herself sucked in and spat out so that she stumbled and fell in the dirt – outside. Yeori stooped to pick her up as Southan and Ifryn came forward. They moved more carefully, but still emerged faster than they went in, staggering as an unknown force shoved them forward.

And then it was over. Aad's hand felt the return of the cruel power. The red dome reestablished itself – stronger than ever – as others moved to complete the circle again and extra energy was poured in from a remote source.

At that stage none of them understood exactly what had happened, but they were not about to question their good fortune. They were free. In a city that was burning.

CHAPTER FIFTY-TWO

The spokes begin to form. Soon they will extend to all the waking realm, marked out by the new wind. Who knows when or where the dust will settle? My powers of augury cannot see that far. But I can still hear the echoes of flame.

A wheel is a circle, is it not?

Of the several reunions which took place on the Domain battlements, the most joyful by far was that of Fen and Dsordas. Neither of them had any time for recriminations, even for questions. Their only concern was that they were together again, and they held each other so tight that Yeori joked that they would have to be prised apart with iron bars.

The most solemn reunion was that between Southan and Kerrell. Neither man knew quite what to say, but in the end it was the Emperor who spoke first.

'I owe you more apologies than I have words for,' he said. 'Whatever crimes you believe you committed, I absolve you. You are no traitor.'

Kerrell knelt, unable to meet the gaze of either Southan or Ifryn.

'Thank you, my lord.' The truth was buried with those words, and the Empress felt a small twist of pain in her heart. She held Azari tight, and tried not to remember.

'Would that I had not been so vain and so stupid,' Southan lamented. 'You both warned me, but I would not listen. Now look what my folly has brought us to.'

Kerrell rose and looked out over the ravaged city.

Smoke filled the air with an acrid haze, and crimson flares still flew overhead.

'Some people have already fled the city,' the General said, 'but if the evacuation is not organized properly, the Deadlands will kill more people than all the fires.'

'Then I must entrust the withdrawal to you,' Southan responded. 'It's clear we cannot remain in this place.'

Kerrell nodded.

'I have to find my daughters,' the Emperor went on. 'We will meet again at the Great South Gate.' He and Ifryn left.

'And we have to get back to Gaye!' Fen said.

'What about Bowen?' Nason cried.

'If anyone knows where he is,' Fen replied, 'Gaye will.'

When they found the room at the tavern empty, the islanders were beside themselves with worry. Had they reclaimed Fen only to lose her sister? No one at the inn knew anything of Gaye's whereabouts – most people had already fled lower down the hill – but as the travellers gathered at the doorway again, Yeori spotted a familiar figure in the street, running towards them.

'That's Acevedo.'

'I left him with Gaye!' Fen exclaimed.

They hurried to meet the guide. His hair was singed, and his robe was stained with soot and sweat. He had clearly been running for some time.

'I looked after her, as I promised!' he gasped defensively, in answer to Fen's abrupt question. 'But she *made* me take her.'

'Take her where?' Dsordas demanded.

'To the west,' he replied, pointing. 'A small park near the Circle wall.'

'Why there?'

'She said she was meeting someone, but she sent me away before they came.'

'You left her alone? In *this*?' Fen asked angrily.

'She ordered me to come back here and tell you that she was all right and that her horse could carry them both.'

'Yeori, Nason, get the horses,' Dsordas commanded. 'Acevedo, you'll lead us to this park.' It was an order, not a question.

A short while later, Dsordas, Fen, Acevedo, and Sagar – with Nason clinging to his back – set off on their understandably skittish mounts. They rode as fast as they could through the war-torn streets, but were forced to make several detours because of fire, or to avoid occasional bands of armed and frightened citizens. When they reached the park, Gaye and her horse were nowhere to be seen. Dsordas had been expecting as much.

'She's gone, and so has Bowen.'

'Gone where?' Fen asked.

Dsordas shrugged, and told them of Alasia's words. *The white one should have done it, but she is gone from me. So is the beacon.*

'The beacon is what Alasia called Bowen,' Sagar confirmed.

'They'll be making for the southwest Gate, surely,' Fen said. 'That's the way home. We'll find them there. Or on the trail. But why didn't they wait for us?'

'At least Bowen got out,' Nason said, hoping that this was indeed true.

'Let's rejoin the others and make our way to the Gate,' Dsordas said. 'We can always ask Kerrell and Southan for help. And the sooner we're out of Xantium, the better.'

'This way?' Southan asked, pointing down the utterly deserted street.

'Yes.' Ifryn was even more anxious now. 'Where *is* everyone?'

'Let's get the girls,' her husband said. 'Come on.'

The door of The Silent Woman stood open, but there

was still no sign of life – until a mottled snout peered out over the threshold. The sea-dragon's mad red eyes cast about for its next victim and settled on Southan. The Emperor knew now why the street was empty.

With Ifryn's scream still echoing in his ears, he shouted at her to get away, and his sword hissed from its sheath. The monster, now fully two paces long, lashed its thick tail but made no other move. It was not like the dragons of legend. This creature had no wings, no scales, no fiery breath – but it was terrible enough for all that. Yawning cavernously, it displayed rows of venomous fangs, then waddled out of the door. Southan tensed, aware of the enemy he faced, his concentration fierce.

The creature shot forward, moving at incredible speed for an animal of such bulk, its jaws snapping at Southan's ankle. He skipped aside nimbly, and dealt it a glancing blow – which bounced off a powerful foreleg without even piercing the leathery skin. This served only to enrage the monster; it swivelled round with the agility of a snake and attacked again. This time the Emperor only escaped by a whisker, and did not even have the chance to get in a strike of his own.

Ifryn, watching in horror as she and Azari backed away, could only pray for deliverance.

The duel went on, with the dragon attacking relentlessly and Southan doing little more than evading its deadly teeth and claws – until a bright flash of light broke their concentration. The fireball crashed into the building opposite the tavern, and plaster and timber rained down from the explosion, starting several small but fierce blazes on the cobblestones. Southan was too surprised himself to take advantage of his enemy's distraction, but then he saw a possible chance and began enticing the dragon towards one of the nearest fires. Choosing his moment carefully, he lunged sideways with his sword, skewering a piece of wood which was still burning with sorcerous intensity, before turning back to face the monster.

Small red eyes regarded this new development for a moment, then disregarded the warning signs. The creature leapt forward again – but this time, instead of avoiding the attack, Southan threw himself forward to meet it. Burning wood and blade disappeared into the monster's gaping jaws, and Southan let go of the hilt and threw himself back just before his hand would have been caught on the poisonous teeth. The dragon screamed, unable to dislodge the scorching flames or murderous fumes from its jaws. It thrashed about in agony but eventually succumbed, the light fading from its dead eyes. The air was full of the smell of burnt meat.

Ifryn came forward slowly, and held her husband with her free arm, her heart beating fast. For all his faults, Southan was no coward, and there was no doubting his love for his family if he would protect them even against evil such as this.

Giving the carcass a wide berth, they hurried into the tavern. The lower rooms were full of the stench of blood, and there were torn bodies everywhere. With dread in her heart, Ifryn led the way upstairs. Her hopes arose when she found the door intact and locked. She knocked loudly and called out to Doneta. The door opened, and the maid breathed an almost unbearable sigh of relief, while the two girls leapt up to embrace both their parents in turn. At the end of the reunion, Southan's face was as tear-stained as all the rest. And for once, he did not care.

The horse moved steadily under its double load. Gaye clung tightly to Bowen, who rode in front of her, the reins in his capable hands. She had not been able to see him when he came to her – but she did not have to. She knew every particle of him, his face, his body, his voice, his smile. Her misfortunes had shocked him – but this was a time of terrors, and many had suffered worse. Their first kiss had lasted a lifetime and then, by unspoken mutual agreement, they had left the city by the nearest gate, crossing the Brown River by the western bridge.

Riding now across the Deadlands, they were headed northwest, but the direction did not matter to either of them. Their love would blossom anywhere, in the desert if needs be.

Bowen knew that part of the madness had returned to his mind, but it felt almost natural now. He and Gaye were a strange pair.

He felt her breath, warm on the back of his neck, and shut his eyes in a moment of bliss. After all the horrors, all the pain, all the confusion, here was the one sure thing in his life – a blind, white-haired girl who talked to ghosts and flew with bats. He loved her so much that it hurt – but it was a good hurt, one he would happily live with for the rest of his life. Even more amazing to him was the fact that he knew she felt the same way. Their world was complete as long as they were together.

Bowen brought the horse to a halt for a moment and twisted round in the saddle. She smiled, knowing that he was looking at her. They both understood all that they needed of the future.

No matter what happened, they would fly together now in body, as well as in spirit.

CHAPTER FIFTY-THREE

I would have been content in this cell. What use is freedom of the body when the mind is trapped? But the door is unlocked, an act of kindness from a frightened man. Perhaps he thinks I can help him escape. But I am still trapped by my duty to the bells. There are worse gaolers.

To his frightened, exhausted and bewildered staff, it seemed that Verkho had finally lost his grip on sanity. Although his study was no longer protected, anyone who entered was soon made to leave again. For most, one glance from the Chancellor's incredibly glittering eyes was enough, but to the more persistent, Verkho demonstrated a new intolerance. A single finger would stab out, unleashing a blast of crimson lightning that detonated either at the intruder's feet – if he was lucky – or threw him bodily across the room if he was not. Very soon they all learnt to leave their master well alone.

The Chancellor now spent all of his time pacing around the study, muttering and arguing with himself, gesticulating wildly and glancing every so often at the talisman, which sat on his desk, calmly alert. Verkho knew that events were now beyond his control, and he was fighting an internal battle to try and regain his mastery of the situation. But the pitfalls seemed increasingly dangerous and although he would not admit it, even to himself, a part of Verkho's mind knew, with a dull, sinking certainty, that he had overextended himself. The talisman should have been his slave but very soon now, it might become his overlord. It was only a matter of time.

The evacuation of so vast a city was a fearfully daunting task, and inevitably not all went according to plan. Even so, Kerrell threw himself into the work with almost manic energy and found many willing helpers, now that his self-evident authority had been officially restored. If matters did not proceed as fast as he would have liked, if there were too many casualties and internal disagreements, it was still a minor miracle that all went as well as it did. The army, newly reunited in the face of an inescapable common enemy, played a large part in mustering supplies, water, carts and wagons, as well as helping to organize the refugees and averting panic. Horses were the biggest problem, as even the best trained were behaving badly, and the other animals in the city presented a constant threat. But somehow progress was made.

And all the while, the ghosts of the city watched the living. They were not affected by the torments which plagued flesh and blood and no one knew why they were there, or even paid them much attention.

Many people, some better prepared than others, had already fled into the Deadlands, but most left in a series of giant convoys moving out of the Great Gates and travelling directly away from the city like the spokes of an ever-expanding wheel. But whichever way they went, the warm wind followed them, blowing away from the fiery hub. Some citizens chose to stay, however, willing to brave the many perils of the city rather than face the unknown beyond the walls. Everyone chose their own fate, for better or worse.

Southan and Ifryn decided to travel southwest towards Nadal, a decision influenced by the fact that Fen and the other islanders were to go that way. Naturally enough, Kerrell accompanied them, knowing that he had done all he could in Xantium, even if satisfaction was denied to him by the thought of all those he had not been able to help. The General's work had become known to almost everyone, and he was being called a hero. In Kerrell's mind such talk was arrant nonsense – he was just a soldier doing his duty – but he, like almost all the other refugees, left with a heavy heart, grieving the loss of so many lives, of the city, his home, and grieving for all those left behind, both inside and outside the red dome.

A seemingly endless line of horses – calmer now as they drew further away from the city – stretched along the southwest trail. Ifryn rode with Azari in a sling on her chest, his tiny face peaceful in repose as the gentle motion lulled him to sleep. To either side rode Southan, with his left arm around Delmege, and Doneta, with Vrila clinging to the maid's back. Whatever awaited the imperial family, they would face the future together.

Kerrell was just behind them, his eyes rarely leaving Ifryn's back. Now that he had time to think, his mind refused to function clearly; it became a jumble of memories, regrets and longing that finally resolved itself into a strange kind of peace. Even in such extraordinary circumstances, he felt his life returning to some sort of normality. Their story was not over yet but, even if he never recaptured the intense joy he had found so briefly, the reality of the past could not be taken away from him. It was enough. Or so he told himself.

Ifryn felt the warmth of his gaze as she went through similar turmoil. She also felt guilty at having escaped with Kerrell and all her children – and Southan – while so many others were suffering. But who was to know what the future would bring? Their story was not over.

Grongar and Corton had been lucky enough to find space among the supplies on one of the wagons, so they travelled in relative comfort, out of the swirling dust. The wine-master was bereft. He had never before been out of Xantium, and the enforced abandonment of his

428

life's work distressed him enormously. The barbarian, on the other hand, was taking the whole thing in his stride.

'Of course, I'm going the wrong way,' he remarked. 'I should be headed north.'

'Why aren't you?' Corton asked listlessly.

'Couldn't let you get away,' Grongar replied cheerfully. 'We have a game to finish. There must be a decent labyrinth set somewhere in Nadal.'

Corton looked at his friend in disbelief.

'How can you even think . . . ?' he began.

'And,' Grongar went on, 'I hear there are some decent vineyards down there.'

'Inferior grapes for the most part. Too much acid in the soil,' the wine-master responded automatically.

'You'll have to teach me some of this stuff. I think it's time I refined my palate.'

This idea was so ridiculous that Corton actually laughed – and found that he enjoyed the unfamiliar sensation.

'There are forests too,' he remarked. 'For hunting. Your talents won't be wasted.'

Grongar nodded, thinking sadly about his lost hounds.

'There'll never be another like Shark, though,' he complained.

'Thank the gods for that!' Corton said.

The islanders began their long journey full of regret at not having accomplished all they'd set out to do, but knowing they could have done no more. There was nothing they could do to help the hostages now, and the power that Verkho had unleashed seemed to be in the process of destroying itself along with the city. They were saddened by Gaye's disappearance – and still hoped to catch up with her somewhere along the way – but, as Fen pointed out, she was with Bowen, and that was all she had ever wanted. Now all the travellers needed was to return to Zalys as quickly as possible, to find out what was happening there. Southan had promised to help them in any way he could, but the Emperor obviously had problems enough of his own. The whole Empire would be in chaos for some considerable time to come.

Because of the scarcity of horses, Nason shared with Sagar, Aad with Yeori and Fen with Dsordas. At one point, an hour or so into their journey, Fen asked Dsordas to turn the horse round so that they could look back at the city. It was a sobering sight. Smoke hung in the sky like a pall, with the dull red glow of the dome looking like the setting sun. A strong, hot wind blew in their faces, whipping the dusty sand plains into a slithering, weaving river that rose and fell, making the horses' hooves invisible. The wind roared in their ears and occasionally stung their faces, making it hard to see properly.

There was magic in that sinuous movement but also a warning, telling them to go on, not to look back.

As they turned away from their last glimpse of the distant city, the faraway ringing of a bell reached their ears. It should have been Xantium's death knell, but Fen heard it as an echo of hope. A new beginning.

'The circle begins and ends on Zalys,' she said quietly in Dsordas' ear. 'Let's go home.'

EPILOGUE

Few fishing boats sailed from Zalys now. Life was perilous enough on land without risking the ocean's wrath. But Latchi Irini had been a fisherman all his life, and would not be denied. The old ways were set deep in his mind and heart, and there was a new certainty about the old man that his fellow villagers marvelled at.

The morning was less than two hours old, but already Latchi and the two younger crewmen had lowered and raised the nets several times. They had caught little – that was the way of it these days – but the old man was not concerned. He was waiting for something else, and his eyes scanned the horizon.

It was no more than a speck in the distance when he first saw it – but that soon changed, and he and the other two sailors stared in awe as a great grey triangle rose from the sea. Within moments it was larger than an ocean-going vessel – and still it grew. Before long, the two younger men were kneeling in the boat, hiding their heads in their hands and praying for their lives, while Latchi gazed on, an enraptured smile upon his weather-beaten face.

He reckoned it was almost half a league away from his boat, but it filled his field of vision, blotting out the whole of the eastern sky. It must have measured a league from side to side, and was almost as high at its central point. It was, quite literally, as big as a mountain, and yet it moved – its shiny grey surface undulating massively, like a slow, loose sail in a gentle wind.

As gradually as it had arisen, so the mountain began to side back into the sea. The petrified sailors looked up d knew that the swell this would create would surely

431

swamp them, but Latchi was unperturbed. He was confident they would survive. Why else had he been given this sign? And the old man was proved right. The awe-inspiring surge of water carried the boat all the way back to the island on a tidal race of silver foam, but then, instead of dashing them upon the rocks, it swept them unharmed into their harbour, where they were able to bring the boat under control.

Many on the island had also seen the impossible mountain rise and fall, and they were terrified. But Latchi called them all together.

'It is a sign!' he proclaimed. 'The old ways are returning. If we obey the old laws, we will be blessed and have nothing to fear.'

'But what *was* that thing?' a voice cried.

Latchi smiled broadly, displaying stained teeth and a tongue streaked with purple and black.

'A wing tip,' he said.